MEETING THE MINOTAUR

ALSO BY CAROL DAWSON

The Waking Spell
Body of Knowledge

MEETING THE MINOTAUR

A NOVEL BY CAROL DAWSON

Algonquin Books of Chapel Hill   1997

Published by
ALGONQUIN BOOKS OF CHAPEL HILL
Post Office Box 2225
Chapel Hill, North Carolina 27515-2225

a division of
WORKMAN PUBLISHING
708 Broadway
New York, New York 10003

This is a work of fiction. Names, characters, places, and incidents are either the product of the author's imagination or are used fictitiously. Any resemblance to actual events or locales or persons, living or dead, is entirely coincidental.

LIBRARY OF CONGRESS CATALOGING-IN-PUBLICATION DATA
Dawson, Carol, 1951–
    Meeting the Minotaur : a novel / by Carol Dawson.
      p. cm.
    ISBN 1-56512-126-0 (hardcover)
    I. Title.
  PS3554.A947M43   1997
  813'.54—dc21   97-4032
                                                             CIP

10 9 8 7 6 5 4 3 2 1
First Edition

For Matt, my father, who likes the action

and for Mother, Justin, Michelle, Nikos,
and Jessica

ACKNOWLEDGMENTS

I would like to acknowledge with deepest gratitude the following people whose writings, knowledge, opinions, support, or example contributed to the consummation of this book: Mark Adams, John Davidson, Robert Draper, Audrey Duff, Moyra Elliot, Dr. Robert Fisher, Zannie Flanagan, Robert Graves, Joel Hagen, William Keith Hardy, Bruce Holthouse, Carl Jung, Mary Martha Cheavens Kvols, Kim McWilliams of the Auckland, New Zealand, Consulate of Japan, Annette Mason, Maria Massie, Kim Prisk, Plutarch, Mary Renault, Tim Rowsell, Tetsuko Sameshima, Marsha Skinner, Marcel Cesar Souza, Carin Wilson, Kim Witherspoon, my mother and father, and my maternal grandmother, Emma Princess Finch Markham, who gave me the birthday money with which to buy my first book of myths. In Japan the following people provided reflection, information, and most generous hospitality: Allison Dew; Kevin English (from the Gaelic); Kiyoshi Asano; Tetsuro Takino; his parents, Mr. and Mrs. Takino; and the Buddhist monks of Gesshin-in—especially Nitta Ryoei and Yoichi Hasegawa. And the *on* I wear to Haruhiko Sameshima is now perpetual.

Most particularly I thank my editor, Robert A. Rubin, whose good advice helped strip Taylor down to reveal his most heroic form, and my friend Linda Holloway, whose observations were indispensable.

For their inspiration—both witting and unwitting—I thank my sons, Justin Hurzeler and Nikos Rossiter. To them Taylor owes his life. To my daughter, Jessica Rossiter, he owes his true name.

And always with love, I thank Peter Black, Cynthia Helene Baur, Bettye Dew, Joyce Fennell, and Marilyn Sainty.

In the absence of an effective mythology, each of us has his private, unrecognized, rudimentary, yet secretly potent pantheon of dream. The latest incarnation of Oedipus, the continued romance of Beauty and the Beast, stand this afternoon on the corner of Forty-second Street and Fifth Avenue, waiting for the light to change.

. . . Today many sciences are contributing to the analysis of the riddle [of mythology]. Archeologists are probing the ruins of Iraq, Honan, Crete, and Yucatan.

—Joseph Campbell, *The Hero with a Thousand Faces*

PENINSULA

When Æthra was delivered of a son, some say that he was immediately named Theseus, from the tokens which his father had left for him under the stone. . . . He was then brought up under his grandfather King Pittheus of Troezen.

Æthra for some time concealed the true parentage of Theseus, and instead a report was given out by King Pittheus that he had been begotten by Neptune [Poseidon, god of the sea].

—Plutarch, *The Lives of the Noble Grecians and Romans*

1

Granddaddy hunkered under the palapa in the sun, drumming his fingers on the table. Beyond his bald head I could see the blue Caribbean, the waves slipping up the sand, the lightpoints dancing across water. "Boy, I think it's time we talk business," he said.

"Business."

"No point in letting the grass grow under our feet. There's no time like the present."

"You mean, discuss some stocks or something?" Granddaddy liked to predict the market. Occasionally he'd enjoy airing an opinion about a private tip he'd received from a client, or some dark horse he'd spotted on Wall Street, or world trends after a Middle East political crash. He only did this with me—a recreational vice, harmless, he contended, in my company.

"*No* I do not. I mean about what you're going to do with the rest of your life."

"Oh," I said. "Ah." I straightened up, alert and businesslike. I'd been waiting for this conversation.

"As you know, I have never poked around overmuch in your intentions."

"No, sir."

"I've always figured that you would find your way. After equipping you with the tools you needed and guiding you as best I could, that was all there was left to do for a time."

"Yes sir, I know it."

"This University thing last month, this whatever it was you did down there in Austin—"

"Dropping out, you mean?"

"Yes, well." He grimaced and wiped his lips on his napkin. "If that is what you must insist on calling it."

"Withdrawing, Granddaddy. Before they expelled me for flunking, is what it was." On the Taylor Troys *Nil Studere Curriculum* aka the Grand Class-cut and Coasting Slalom.

He sighed. "Anyhow, this whatever notion seems to have left you at a loose end. Wouldn't you agree that's the case?"

"I guess so. Yes, sir."

"Yes." He paused, took a sip of iced tea, set the glass down. Then he squinted mistrustfully at the bowl of ceviche, pushed it aside, chewed off a corner of club sandwich, mumbled it between his dentures, and swallowed, his eyes flaring slightly. "So. We must arrive at a thing for you to do. And I have concluded that the wisest thing, since you don't seem scholastically inclined—not that I'm blaming you, son, I know you can't help it— would be to set you up in business."

"Business," I said. The word this time had a different heft in my mouth, an altered slant, an amended blaze. "Like a store, or an office, something like that?"

"Something like that," he agreed.

"Like—what?"

"Well, sir." He paused, eyes gleaming. "Pick an enterprise." His freckled hand uncupped toward me as if offering aces. "You come up with any sensible, realistic-type project, an ongoing concern that would guarantee you an occupation in the years ahead. And I will be pleased to bankroll it."

He closed his mouth to let the full weight of this last sink in: a monumental moment.

"Why," I said, "I don't know what to say."

"Of course you don't." He nodded, pleased, and leaned forward confidentially. "You weren't expecting this. But just attend me carefully. I'm talking about whatever you'd like. Although not necessarily an endeavor requiring you to, you know, gab with people a great deal. Or of course handle mechanical equipment."

"Of course," I said, my curiosity awakening. How long had he been turning this over? "Is there something particular you've already thought of, Granddaddy?" Although it seemed only the latest in a long history of attempts to ground me in the world—Montessori kindergarten, the Handicapped Olympics, summer camp, a military boarding school for physically challenged students, to name a few—I was touched.

"Well, let's see. Nothing too arduous. I had figured, maybe"—he folded his hands ceremonially on the table, so I did, too—"something you might tend to. Like a breeding or growing setup. Preferably, you know, in a rural location. That way you could sort of be out of the way of city pressures—more peaceful, like."

"Gosh." My surprise expanded exponentially. "A country place. Hm." The town of Bernice's "city pressures" consist of five traffic lights, a fruit-cake bakery, three car dealerships, the county courthouse, and a Saturday-night country western dance hall, plus the hyperactive gossip network at the country club.

"Yes! Where you'd be raising something. Some suitable thing. Wouldn't that be nice? There's a real satisfaction in raising things, son. Animals. Plants. So long as it's not Cain, heh heh!"

Or perhaps children. Which meant, in his terms, something with certain prerequisite qualities. Such as: an imperviousness to easy damage. With a robust constitution if it was alive and kicking. A quick healer. And nimble—fleet-footed at dodging falling objects. Or else something totally passive, like carrots or beans. But most of all easy-tempered, docile, forgiving rather than grudge-bearing, and likely to hang around even if the opportunity for escape arose, as we both knew it was bound to sooner or later.

Mentally I reviewed the qualifications just for fun. Let's see, I thought:

that rules out racehorses. Which was too bad, because I would have liked horses. I've always been attracted to them even though I wasn't allowed to ride when younger. It also ruled out most exotica, such as cockatoos, ostriches, emus, or the more popular forms of African game found on Texas ranches of late.

"Listen!" I said. "Llamas. How about llamas?" I raised my brows to show him I was entering the spirit. "I hear they're real friendly and easy to feed."

"Llamas?" He peered over his tea glass. "Good Lord, Taylor. What are you dreaming of? Those creatures cost many thousands of dollars apiece. Besides, what purpose do llamas serve, other than their hair?"

"Some golf resort I read about in South Carolina uses them as caddies. They charge one hundred dollars an hour rental."

"What harebrained foolishness." He frowned. "Dogs, now, at least the species worth raising for money, are a possibility. You could breed pedigreed hunting hounds, for instance. Good blooded pointers. Sell them to sportsmen. Of course, let them train them themselves, you wouldn't want to fuss with that."

I smiled. Granddaddy's diplomacy was often fumbled out like an afterthought.

"Or fish!" he cried suddenly. "Yes. There you go! Catfish. Or rainbow trout! Those are farmed all over the country nowadays. Mississippi, Idaho." He eyed me, willing his optimism into my body. "Dig a couple of tanks. Or better yet, find a little property somewhere that already has a few. Institute turtle control. Buy some fingerlings—"

"Or koi."

"Beg your pardon?"

"Koi. You know, those colorful fish you see in rock gardens and museum pools?"

"Ah—*goldfish,* you mean?" He blinked.

"Well, kind of. They're Japanese carp. Specially bred, long bloodlines going back through to ancient emperors. It's an art form over in Japan. They're real valuable, people name them like pets."

"Is that right?" The canniness had slid from his gaze, replaced by absence. He folded his napkin into finicky squares, tucked it under his plate, and shook his head again. "Sometimes, Taylor, I declare I wonder where in the world you scrounge up these screwy items."

There was a silence.

"Actually, Granddaddy, I think a problem might arise with farming fish."

"What's that?"

"The harvesting might get a little, uh, tricky." I glanced modestly into my lap.

"Why, you know what? You're probably right." He brightened, consenting to look at me once more, his thoughts transparently obvious. "That would be a real slippery job, I should imagine. For *anybody*," he said, and reassuringly patted my hand. I remembered the days he'd come to Fredericksburg to visit me at school and see the paraplegic boys rolling the wheelchairs down the ramps outside class, their faces rigid with gallantry, and how he would stand to one side with me, solemnly beaming in admiration as they passed. "We'll come up with something else."

It made an interesting problem. I reflected, looking out at Mexico. The beach shimmered. Unease nagged at me like a whisper. What would fit, I wondered? Sheep? Organic salad greens?

"I talked to a fellow a while back who'd thought up a scheme of growing blood oranges. Turns out Texas soil is ideal for them, to hear him tell it," he proffered.

"Blood oranges. Why do they call them that?"

"He claimed it's the color of the juice. Or the flesh, one."

"Spooky kind of fruit."

"They fetch inflated prices at the Safeway, let me tell you. How does three ninety-eight a pound sound?"

"For an orange? That bleeds?"

Granddaddy cocked his chin upward, ruminating. "Well. Okay, then, how about bulbs? For fancy nurseries, like Neil Sperry talks about on the radio. Irises. Rare tulips."

For a moment the tulips caught my fancy. "They're nice," I agreed. "I remember them blooming in Grandmother's front beds in the spring."

"She sure had a green thumb," said Granddaddy.

I conjured Grandmother, digging around in her garden long after the day when her memory had finally turned into a flat, shining sea stretching without detail past any horizon. "I think they would make me miss her too much."

"Really?" He looked disconcerted. "Hm. Then orchids, maybe. Or, how about snakes for their venom, for antido—no, never mind." He grimaced hastily. "Well, anyhow. This should be giving you some ideas to mull upon. Churn around through the afternoon. Don't wait, though. We need to push on ahead."

"I will."

"See you in a little while." He shoved his chair back.

But the malaise of the conversation was clapping down upon me like a dark shingle. Then, suddenly, I hit the nail. "Granddaddy?" He stopped. "If you're the one who's going to bankroll this business—"

"That's right."

"Does that mean my trust no longer works?"

His expression froze.

"Has he killed it?"

"Why, Taylor," he said slowly. "I haven't said that."

A little shock went through my heart. *You don't have to,* I thought.

The snubbed old face filled with a mixture of emotions. "It's got nothing to do with trusts. I just want to do this for you. Myself."

Having done every other.

"Tell me one thing." I paused, swallowing my hatred. "Is he still in Dallas?"

He turned his hands palm up, palm down, flexing the fingers, frowning at liver spots. "I don't have his home address, Taylor, if that's what you mean. His lawyers', well, that's—" His lips seamed tight.

"But he's alive," I said. "Whoever he is."

"Son—I really think it's best if you don't fret about it. Just try to leave it be. It's over, over and done with."

RIP.

"You're all right as things are, aren't you?" He dropped a hand awkwardly to my shoulder, where it thumped like a pot roast. "I tell you what. You just figure you out a line of work. It'll all turn out fine, I guarantee."

When I still didn't speak, he gathered himself together. "Whew! It's sure hot, isn't it?"

"Yessir."

"Believe I'll just go check on that other thing I mentioned."

"Okay."

But he was already wandering across the terrace toward the tour office. The audience was over.

SHE WOULDN'T LOOK up.

A drop of water ricocheted off the fountain's edge and hit my nose. I dabbed it off and stole another peek over the red plastic flowers lining the marble lip. *Chic chic* went the keys, naming and sorting through reservations, Visas, MasterCards. A bell jangled on the desk beside her and she reached over, pressed a button, and returned to the keyboard. Just then Ramón hurried through the lobby, waving a bottle of green goo with a gold foil label in one hand. I watched his white shirt bob and glimmer past wicker furniture into the shadowy dining room and vanish behind the bar.

"So, vamonos su llamas," I said.

Now she glanced up, her gaze settling briefly on me.

"If not llamas, what?" I frisked the back of my head, as if to start some dendritic action, get the old brain humming. "I'm damned if I know."

Assessing me, her eyes narrowed. The manager, lounging beside her, murmured a few words behind his angled hand and chuckled, all the while staring straight at her perfect breasts. Scorn and lust had pulled his expression askew; he was usually a somber man. She didn't answer but switched back to the screen. Oh, Jesus.

Five or six people sat at the palapa bar on the pool terrace outside, whiling away siesta hour drinking piña coladas. Farther out in the surf several buoylike butts marked the spots where their owners snorkeled above the dead reef and empty sand. This hotel with its urns, wood, and terracotta stucco could be anywhere in the world nowadays, a replica of the unicultural luxury found from Bangkok to Bel Air to Maui to Johannesburg. There was no local coda to remind me that I was in the Yucatán, surrounded by Mexicans.

Except perhaps for the staff.

"All right. Let's just skip animals—dogs, goats, ermine." I leaned forward, elbows propped on knees, and punched a fist into my open palm. *"No fur!"*

The girl at the computer pushed her chair back and stood up.

I didn't dare look, but lounged back to thoughtfully stroke my jaw as she rustled round the desk's end, stalking through the lobby. Her heels struck tile. Unable to help myself I pictured the V collar of her orange blouse unbuttoning onto a constellation of small moles just above her bra. She had one that actually showed: a genuine certifying beauty mark embossing her upper lip. I closed my eyes and imagined her dark winged brows, the lathed turnings of her shapely legs, thighs brushing, bearing her off on her errand, the bounce and swell, tuck, the crease. . . . When the heels stopped I opened my eyes. She was standing squarely above me.

"Are you comfortable, señor?"

"Ah . . . comfortable!" The cold smoothness of the question made hairs rise on the back of my neck. Her voice had no texture at all. "Yes, gracias. I'm, uh, very comfortable. Thank you."

"May I get you anything?" The deadpan changed to a smile, set, uninflected. "A taxi to town, perhaps? A dive schedule? Our boat goes out again in the late afternoon."

"Oh—no. Thanks! No diving."

"Then perhaps you would like to order something from the bar? A fruit juice? A cerveza?"

She didn't really care what I wanted. Her boss lounged back behind the big main desk, observing her with mineral detachment while she stood there proving she was career rather than his.

"Well now. I wouldn't say no to a lemonade. I'm just sitting here sorting through a few business decisions." I smiled suavely, but it was like having to report to the principal. "Thank you kindly. Un limón, por favor."

She nodded, wheeled, and strode to the threshold of the dining room. Murmuring to someone inside, she unconsciously sleeked the tight skirt over one hip. *Oh, dear Christ Almighty.* I caught the word *veintidós.* So she knew that much. I glanced at the manager behind the desk, who stared at me impassively. I smiled. Then she returned to the desk and sat back down before the monitor, her skin glowing in the aqueous light, her hair dressed high in its loops and coils and braids on her crown. How old? Nineteen? Twenty? Thirty-six? After nearly a week I still couldn't tell. The pulse inside my wrist jumped. Chicken, I thought.

Then—Well: why not chickens?

Suddenly it seemed a perfect answer. I could start a restaurant farm. Free-range pullets, fed naturally. No antibiotics, no additives, only the most select varieties raised to the highest standards. They could eat the bugs in the yard. They could live on fire ants! I pictured the yard: bare dirt, hydrangeas, cannas in the borders edged with bricks set on their corners. Then the house, my very own house, an old cottage with gingerbread trim, shards of peeling paint, a big front porch and a breezeway. I sat on the breezeway with my boots propped up, watching an orb spider suture her web against the screen, frittering myself away exactly the way I'd been doing for the last three years, while beyond the evening light dipped the front gate in copper and the mesquite leaves cooled from yellow to deeper green. What could be simpler? Unease stirred again. I shoved it back down. Then came a vision: Me, striding down the concourse at the state fair, my prize guinea bantam under one arm, the blue ribbons clutched aloft for the newspaper cameras. The piles of order faxes from top brasseries all over the world. The newspapers would publish my name. Certainly *The Dallas Morning News* would—maybe even *The Wall Street Journal*. My full name appearing in black and white, easily available to snag the attention of a man who just might notice, might stop, squint, and frown, his eye snagging upon the old, familiar surname: "Rising whiz kid. Bright new business star. Resourceful young entrepreneur Taylor Thaddeus Troys, twenty years old, of Bernice, Texas, uses America's nastiest pests to produce the superb. A go-getter prodigy at a phenomenally early age."

Perhaps, I thought, this was what Granddaddy secretly had in mind.

But then a voice whispered inside my head: Wrong. *The son of a bitch.*

"Señor Troys." Ramón reappeared. He bent over my chair, a model of formality balancing a tray. Upon it stood the lemonade.

"Hi." I took it, set it down, signed the tab with his gold ballpoint: Room Twenty-two.

"Gracias."

"What are you doing tonight after you get off? Want another game?"

"Posible." He clicked the ballpoint, dropped it into his chest pocket. His eye drifted around the room, noting the manager's siesta disappearance. Tucking the tray under his left elbow, he flapped the receipt book against his palm. "You beat last night."

"Shoot. Last night isn't tonight."

"I don't got no more money." The grin lingered. Ramón would never admit it if this were really true. He knew that I knew it.

"We can play for other things."

He shrugged and looked off. "What other?"

"Well—how soon are you heading back to Dallas?" I asked casually, as if snatching at a stray thought.

"In another month. Two months. It depends on openings."

"Openings?"

His eyelids flicked. "In the company."

"So where do you live when you're up there? Maybe we could meet up sometime."

The surprise flashed out before he could stop it. A wheel of speculation ratcheted behind his eyes: first doubt, then suspicion, possibilities, a weighing, more questions. "Maybe. I don't know. Sure, you want to." His heavy head canted to one side. "Maybe."

"Keep the game going."

He nodded, meditating.

"We can always settle up there. Or run a tab on what we're owing each other."

"Is not professional."

"It doesn't have to be for money, anyhow. Shoot, since when are we cardsharks? I've played many a time for shots of beer even. Or matches."

"Matches?" He looked amused.

"Did that all the time in school."

Smiling, he shook his head and scanned the room.

"And we've got imagination between us. There are always more intriguing stakes possible."

"What kind?"

"I don't know. Other bases of trade. This and that." I shrugged. It was almost an exact copy of his. He recognized it.

"Like what?"

"We'd figure something out. Maybe, I don't know, favors."

"Favors!" Smirking, he tossed his hair off his forehead.

"Sure. You never know who might come in handy."

The brown gaze clamped suddenly back on me.

"You interested?"

His head jerked down, one short snap.

"So how about tonight? Around eleven? Same spot."

"La playa."

"Right."

"Pero, mi hermano . . . my brother wants me to go to a certain place with him."

"Heck, bring your brother. He can play too. Make it more fun."

Ramón studied me warily. "Acaso." His eyes cut over to the girl, a hooded glance.

"She going to tell you off for loitering?"

His contemptuous look made me grin. "Y también . . . by the way. In Dallas I stay at my uncle's in Oak Cliff," he added suddenly.

"Oh yeah?"

"Hasta la vista."

"Yeah, great. See you later, buddy."

The lemonade trickled down my throat. Ramón strolled back into the dining room, whistling between his teeth.

"Taytay!"

I turned. The voice came simultaneous to the sneeze of the elevator doors. Emerging from the fluorescent cell, Mother waved like a maniac. "I've been wondering where you were. What are you doing? Just sitting?"

"Yes ma'am."

"Just sitting in the lobby! On your Easter vacation."

"Thinking," I explained.

"*Thinking.* Ah." Automatically she drew a sharp breath, fanning herself with a scarf end to fume the embarrassment. "Well, um! I hope you've been having a good time this *morning,* at least. Did you even eat lunch?"

"Yessum, I sure did."

"You know to just charge it to the room, don't you." She told me this freshly minted thing at least once a day.

"Yessum, I surely do."

"Don't talk like that, you sound like the yard man. I'm looking for your sister. By the way, how do you like my new suit?" Posing in her one-piece she tipped up on her toes and revolved 360 degrees. She must have decided that this year was one too many down the line for another bikini. I had already seen the bathing suit she'd brought with her, still in its Lou Lattimore bag. She'd worn it our first morning here on Cozumel, a black maillot sewn all over with tiny glass champagne bottles—dangerous if she hit a reef, not that she ever would, since she didn't enter water. On this new one the neckline plunged only as far as her cleavage. She touched the shallow hemisphere of her belly self-consciously and then gave another playful twirl to make the short skirt fly up.

"I like the color."

"Aren't you sweet! Pink is always a safe bet, don't you agree?" she asked. Vagueness was her usual form of tact, but instinct also prompted her to defer to whatever male might be present. "I found it yesterday in a little boutique by the plaza. Dodie went with me. We got her one in chartreuse."

"Oh. That's nice." I pictured Mother and Dodie, brachiating their way through the ready-to-wear racks of Cozumel. It's good when you have a sport you can practice anywhere.

"Do you know where she is? I simply cannot find her on this earth."

"No ma'am." Dodie had jumped into a cab half an hour before in front of the hotel. I'd watched her do it. She hadn't spoken to me, of course. Presumably she had been headed for town. She was not alone.

"Well then, have you at *least* seen your granddaddy?"

"I had lunch with him a while ago."

"Where is he then?"

"He mentioned that he might go over to the tour office. To see about one of the trips to the mainland tomorrow."

"To those ruins at Tulum? Cross the ocean on some tippity old boat for *that*? Oh my Lord." She shook her head. "Don't you worry, anyhow. You won't have to go high up. Just Dodie and me will. Climbing all over those smelly pyramids and rocks in the boiling sun. Rock rooms smelling like somebody's gone tee-tee in the corner. Just like at Chichén Itzá." Testily she shook a fly off her arm, bracelets clinking.

I thought of the carpet of jungle we had passed over in the plane on the way here. The crewelwork of treetops that lay unbroken by line or road or thread, while the plane's shadow skittered across it like a blue moth. In the hot humid darkness of its labyrinth a person would lose all boundaries. The ancient Mayan roads were gone. The temples lay swallowed by bush and decay. There would be no path. There would be no trail through the tumuli of leaves, no stones to follow anchored like footsteps in the layers and mats of old growth, no civilized procedure to shape a life. The only limitations would be those imposed by the jungle itself: the striped roof, the latticework of vines, the caws of birds and the rustle as a coatimundi leaped from a branch. One could walk on and on, slashing the way. When one came to a clearing it would be no evidence of the hand of man. There, in the clearing, under the dense, caloric light, a cenote would lie bowled between the fallen sides of earth. It would lie black and still, its edges bridged by long sinuous roots. Creatures would avoid the rim, no matter how thirsty, knowing the endless vacancy that awaited them. Its shaft would gore down through silt, past the limestone plate, past the strata of rock and clay and primal debris, until it plunged straight to the heart of the world itself. Not even fish would swim just beneath the surface. Water, lapless, like a tube of night, would fill its depths, and it would suck up the light into its dark eye, absorb it so that the light vanished with no reflection.

"Buggy old ruins crawling with guides telling us all about human sacrifice. Ugh!" Mother muttered.

"I think it'll be interesting," I said.

But she had already swung around, distracted. "Maybe Dodie's out on the beach. Or at the hairdresser. She mentioned she might get streaked." She tightened the belt of her cover-up. "If you see her, tell her don't budge, don't *move a muscle*, I'm hunting all over for her." She started down the hall toward the beauty shop in the next wing.

I raised my drink. Something caught my eye. The girl behind the desk was watching. She'd listened to all this exchange. Now she bent down once more, the clicking recommencing.

Since Dodie was not in the beauty shop Mother would be back any second. Carefully I stepped down off the fountain base and maneuvered across the tile floor through the lobby furniture, making it out the French doors without an unwonted incident. The sunlight was dazzling. On the far end of the pool I skirted turquoise water and armchairs. Then I passed beyond the shade of palapas to the beach.

The role of outsider is an old one for me. If my vestibular handicap throws me out of balance with the rest of the world, then the facts of my birth have always pinned me there. For this reason, during childhood I took control of whatever I could, cultivating affability, learning patience, moseying through homework, reading a lot. That way the outsiderhood became my own choice, not the inevitable consequence of my condition. My legs might tump me over, the schoolroom judder like a cement mixer, my consciousness rise and fall at the click of a light switch, but I could always chat my way through anything. Clumsiness plus a quick mouth, a blend assuring doom. Geekhood felt as familiar as an old bathrobe. But now Granddaddy was telling me I had to drop it and get naked.

The sand swept down the coast, clean of litter. Upon its sheet lay a crisscross of tourists arranged on towels. Their bodies in the bathing suits seemed amateur somehow: a group of people more at home in working clothes, ties and low-heeled pumps, trying out the feel of bare skin. The women's flesh looked sweet and homely, peeping through mesh, below and above strings tied taut, like fresh trussed bread loaves. I wandered along the surf's edge, watching the breakers, wishing I could just slope straight out on a boogie board, or snorkle, or even go diving as the girl had suggested. I'd practiced swimming for a few months under the watchful eyes of the boarding school instructors, but ever since toddlerhood at the country club Mother had been too scared to let me so much as dog-paddle alone. The riskiest activity for someone with my condition is to enter the

ocean. The danger lies in getting disoriented while submerged, running
out of air, and striving downward, convinced that you're climbing to the
surface. Granddaddy's zest for these sight-seeing trips was as much to give
me something to do as to enjoy himself.

The beach lay completely deserted behind the next hotel, the Emperador del Mar. Only one wing of the Emperador was in operation yet; the
rest stood in a jumble of rebar and concrete half walls, plastic sheets whipping in the wind. Even the beachward end of the working wing still fes-
tered under construction. In my opinion the whole resort looked to be a
sloppy job, haphazard, patched together by people who must not have the
first clue about building a real structure. How could the finished product
invite credibility? Ramón had explained to me that here in Mexico buildings still in progress couldn't be taxed; it wasn't until they were completed
that they became a source of income for the government, which was the
reason you saw so many cement chunks blocking the path beside open
hotels and cafés. And here was a whole heap of rubble already housing
guests. Expensive, too, probably. I stood behind the sand hill, marveling at
how little you could get by with and still call yourself a professional in this
world.

Well, fine.

Beyond the slabs of masonry a movement flickered on the building
face. A door swung slowly out over the near side of the big patio, a room
door with a number gilded on it. It opened just widely enough to release a
man who slipped through the dark slot as if excreted: a short figure in a
cotton shirt, burdened down with paraphernalia. He wore two cameras
slung around his neck; a third he carried in his left hand. From his right
wrist dangled a yellow, canvas ladies' overnight bag. A large backpack
weighed down his scrawny shoulders. Once through the door he turned to
pull it to, but his hands were overfull, his photographic urge too consum-
ing. Glancing up and down the vacant patio, he started briskly down the
line of wall. Plainly he didn't realize the door had not latched. As he
crossed the patio's length I stepped from behind the sand hill in order to

offer him my help. Just at that moment an entire tourist family came onto the patio through the unfinished lobby entrance: a father, a mother, and two young children—Texans, to judge from their accents. They were all arguing about naps. Despite their shrillness the children looked happy, their whining only halfhearted and routine. All four halted before the door the man had just left. The father glanced at it, stopped his lecture. Spreading his fingertips, he pushed it inward. He turned to his wife and frowned. A sudden silence fell. His lips pursed, opened. His face flushed deep red.

Then I realized what it was I'd just seen.

"Hey!"

The man with the cameras broke into a scuttle.

"Stop! Stop right there!"

The husband wheeled, squinting toward me.

"He's the one!" I yelled. I gestured at the retreating man who was about to reach the far corner of the building. "Hurry! Watch out—," and then I charged from behind the sand hill and scrambled over the loose stones and rusty nails. The family stared, openmouthed. I began running. As the man disappeared around the corner, he put on a new burst of speed. Then he faltered a little, hampered by his baggage. So far I was doing fine. Clearing the last rubble with a bound, I raced across the patio and reached the corner a split second after he did, the breath surging through my lungs, the exhilaration pounding. Thus I didn't hesitate at the turn, and after such temporary success, this proved my undoing.

The quick pivot threw me off center. I stopped, feeling the solid ground shift underfoot, one side rising, the other falling in the old, old pattern, the old inner earthquake, as the gyroscope inside my head spun out of control. Then the gravity that I had fought all day long began its tug. In that instant the man ahead of me paused before rounding the building to the road. He turned. Right before my resistance failed, I saw his eye, a black, oily surface trembling in its socket like a puddle of mercury, rolling without light or personality, steadying, and fixing on me.

My field of vision collapsed to that pinpoint of night.

What came next I do not know. The earth reared up. Still I managed to cry out before radiance overwhelmed me and my cheek slammed onto the paving stone.

For a minute there was no sound.

I lay, dense and numb, under the sky whirling in convexities of blue. A weightlessness buoyed my body upward. I concentrated on lying very still. Overhead the gulls screamed, wheeling, and I heard the people approach.

"Hell," I mumbled. Trying to bend my leg, which was knocked straight out behind me, I felt the kneecap strain.

"Hell's right," said a girl's voice in disgust.

"Hey—where's he gone?" came the anguished wail of the husband.

"Out to the road, I presume," said the female. "He's probably got a car waiting."

"He took our stuff! That son of a bitch, he's cleaned us out!"

I craned my head and looked sideways. The father was now sprinting as fast as his love handles would permit, his face distorted with fury, his breath huffing. He looked like a different person from a few moments before. In the distance I could hear the wife starting to cry as she shushed the kids, who were asking questions in thrilled rapture.

"Too bad you sent a spastic after him, then," said the female.

"Don't be so hard on the poor guy. He was only trying to help," a new voice said, another male this time. "Just because he tripped on something and fell, it could happen to—"

"He always does."

There was a pause, the sound of footsteps crunching on gravel. "Hey. Are you okay?" Kneeling down, the man who had just defended me slid into my range of vision. He looked young, about twenty-four. From this close I noticed things that I had failed to register with my first glimpse of him earlier that day: his wide, flat features, the way the black hair swept back and curled a little too long under his ears, the monogram on his silk shirt pocket. In the hand draped casually over his knee a room key swung, jingling.

"Yes, thank you. I'm okay."

"Hey, that was hard, man. A hard smashup. You better not move. You might have broke something."

"No. I'm okay. Really." Only the usual humiliation.

"He's used to it," said the female voice. "Believe me."

"Just a graze or two." My temple throbbed where it had smacked the paving stone, but other than that my bones felt intact. I could tell from experience I wasn't concussed.

"Taytay hardly ever gets more than a graze or two. Do you, Taytay? He's real brave for a total klutz. Old Rubberboy."

I winched my head around until I could see the speaker clearly, and grinned like a death's-head. "Thanks, Dodie."

She stared at me, spat, and looked away.

"By the way, Mom was hunting for you earlier."

"How wonderful." Her eyes rolled upward.

"I saw you both leaving the Plaza Royale but I somehow forgot to mention it."

"Yeah? You're a real prince." She paused. "As if I care."

The young man kneeling beside me glanced up at her. Her hair, I saw, was tousled, pulled half out of her ponytail. Red lipstick smeared around her lips, its edges blurred on her chin. The lips looked puffy; her eyes winced in the light. She stood before a darkness that at first I could not identify, but, when I focused, resolved into a threshold opening onto a hotel bedroom.

"This is your brother?" asked the young man tentatively.

"Yeah."

"Oh. How do you do?" He offered me his hand. A track of lipstick circled his neck, ending in a rosette. I stared at this crimson torque.

"Hi." I shook his hand with my left. My right was still pinned under my side.

"This is great. Just great. Here, let me introduce you. Eduardo, please meet my brother Taylor. Taylor, this is Eduardo."

Eduardo nodded. Either Dodie's scorn didn't puzzle him or he was too well mannered to acknowledge it. My own mortification he seemed to delicately ignore. His eye, regarding me, said, We are both men here, no problem.

My mouth filled with a bitter ashy taste.

"Now, isn't that nice and proper? So Taylor, would you please do me a favor?" Dodie paced to the door.

"What's that?" Stupid, *stupid* question.

"Get up and fuck off."

I recognized the tic of her hand, the insecurity in her frown.

"I'd be delighted." Painfully I levered myself off the pinned elbow. "Ecstatic." Once in a sideways position I was able to bend my legs without busting the kneecap, and from there to hoist over and shift crouching to hands and knees. Eduardo reached out and grabbed my upper arm to help me up. He must not have realized what would come next because he flinched back, startled, as I kept on rising, and snatched his hand away, staring upward at the eye-level bicep he'd just been holding.

"Many thanks," I said.

Eduardo cleared his throat, glanced discreetly elsewhere. "My pleasure."

"Don't pay any attention. Just ignore him," urged Dodie.

"So," I faced her, "any little messages you want relayed to Mother if she inquires what your plans are for the rest of the day?"

She made a sound. Eduardo shrugged. "That I cannot say," he said. His gaze skipped noncommittal from her face.

"Bug *off*, Taylor!"

"At your service. See you at dinner."

"*Grr.*"

"Good-bye." Eduardo nodded courteously. But Dodie had already turned and stomped back into the room, glaring from a spot beside the bed.

"By the way," I paused beside his ear to murmur, "you might want to watch it. She's only thirteen. Jailbait. Our grandfather's a judge." Then before he could recover I smiled, waved to Dodie, and loped on back up the beach in the gold marine sunlight. I felt, as I so often feel against all logic, like singing.

2

That first day I'd met Ramón he was sitting on the outside steps behind the hotel kitchen, a comic book cover propped on his knees with a black-and-white photo of a shrieking woman in a slip fending off a jealous slasher, hand-drawn speech balloons tethered to their dental work. I spotted the wedge of white pages jacketed inside and asked him what the real book was. With eyes rendered blank and stony he'd let the comic fall to reveal the paperback's esoteric title, translated from German. "Oh," I'd said.

"You have read it?"

"I had to for a college course."

Ramón's face transformed. "For college? No shit?" He glanced down at the book almost shyly. "I think he's good in philosophy, but too much words."

"I'd sure second that opinion." We talked about translations for a minute, then we moved on to other subjects. He worked a daily shift from 7:00 A.M. until 10:30 at night, with holes in the late mornings and afternoons, and this was one of them. He told me what kind of book he preferred: "Novels is better," he said. "Jim Harrison, Dashiell Hammett, Márquez." His eyes kindled. "You read them?" His own personal history struck me as just as novelistic—downright Dickensian, in fact. Born in

Monterrey, he'd moved north to Saltillo as a child and joined a street gang during his early teens, stealing cars, shoplifting, and picking pockets, then getting coached by older thieves in more sophisticated larceny—pastimes that he now refused to discuss, dismissing them as distasteful and far beneath him. His mother had sent him north to challenge his sense of opportunity. For the past two years, before this spring, he'd been living in Texas.

But not until he'd served my lemonade this afternoon had he revealed to me any detail whatsoever of his time there.

Going downstairs to the restaurant for dinner, I pondered what he'd said about staying with his uncle in Oak Cliff. I knew I could consider it an overture to ongoing friendship. Friends were something I could stand having a few more of; my old ones from military school had scattered to their destinies, and weren't exactly masters at keeping in touch. How handy, I thought, that Bernice lies so close to Dallas, Oak Cliff being a quick off-ramp on the interstate. I looked forward to the evening poker game.

In the dining room candle flames flickered on the tables, tugged by the breeze from the open French doors. Mother, Granddaddy, and Dodie glanced up from their chairs. Dodie's face, sultry with blue eyeshadow, scowled pointedly in my direction and then turned back down to her Caesar salad. She was wearing a strapless dress printed with red hibiscus flowers, wild blue plumage, and rain forest leaves, complementing the tropical hickeys that tattooed her neck. I'd seldom seen her look so unhappy or so bruised.

"Taylor, we waited as long as we could, but we've ordered now." Mother tucked her chin: the pigeon reproach, her dead husband had called it.

"Sorry. I fell asleep in my room."

"I'll bet you're mighty hungry," said Granddaddy. "It's been a busy day."

"Yeah. His little walk probably wore him all out. *Thirteen*," hissed Dodie, and fork-stabbed a romaine stalk.

"Thirteen what?" asked Mother.

"Well, now. Do you want a drink, Taylor? Hors d'oeuvres? Waiter! Muchacho, por favor!" Granddaddy waved airily.

"Sí, Señor Troys." Ramón glided to the table.

"Get this boy here a drink, would you please?"

I met Ramón's gaze in apology. "Dos Equis, por favor."

"Certainly." He slid away.

"I think he likes you, Taylor," said Dodie. "Maybe he thinks *you're* only thirteen."

"Maybe." Indulgently I smiled; she went bug-eyed with hatred.

"Now I'll tell you what," said Granddaddy. "I've made the arrangements for this trip to Tulum, and I reckon we're going to love it. You two girls better get plenty of shut-eye tonight so you'll be raring to go at 8:00 A.M. when the boat leaves."

"Ohh!" groaned Dodie, rolling her eyes.

"Daddy, you really shouldn't have," said Mother. "You're just spoiling us this trip. We're getting overeducated."

"Well, I don't want to be accused of stinting anything," he beamed.

"Su cerveza, Señor Troys," said Ramón in my ear, handing a bottle to me from the tray and vanishing. I raised it to drink. Under my palm the label slipped on the wet, cold glass. Then I realized it wasn't a label, but a fragment of brown paper that came away in my hand.

"Pour it into the goblet, *please,* Taylor," said Mother. "We're at the dinner table."

"So uncouth," mocked Dodie. I put the bottle down and dropped the hand into my lap.

No good tonight. Meet tomorrow night. Plaza Cozumel, eleven-thirty, said the note. *Don't bring no money.*

THE IRON SMACK of blood filled my nose. I stood at the top of a pyramid stair, in a room that faced the blue and pearlized sky and the dark green jungle, its back to the sea. There the priest had poised. There the captive had bent, crouched and bound. Up the flight surged the procession: the heads of the nobles, with plumes nodding; the sheen of gold; the jade plates clanking. The people following in a religious trance, their skull pans flattened and coned, a bloodlust beating through their hearts, watching, waiting for the instrument to rise and plunge. Make it right, make it right, make the jungle and earth and sun and all things right.

In the Mérida museum I had seen the knives, pretzeled and serrated, which suggested disembowelment, sawing off of heads, thrusting into the sacrifice; and the overriding thing was that although these knives had been carved so complicatedly all from one piece of flint or obsidian—the god-heads plumed and slant-faced, the notches and looped curves and doubled grips extended as long as a bowie or even sometimes a saber—they were designed not for cutting and slicing but for sticking and pulling, wrenching only, the viscera tumbling out in all its steamy blue yardage. You looked at these knives and that was all you could think of. Never mind the miracle of art.

Far off in the jungle rose the mounds, covering pyramids yet un-birthed. I stood looking over the treetops, knowing they were there, feeling their hum through the limestone and soil. Across the hammered blue a spoonbill flew in a straight line toward the water, its pink wings flapping, outstretched, their undersides the color of girls.

I felt my throat open.

"It's so hot I'll turn to butter!" A line of sight-seers crossed the holy terrace below, straggling in a broken snake, with only the haziest notion as to what they were doing there. The old lady who'd cried out stopped to snap a picture of the broken courtyard.

"This place gives me the creeps even more than Chichén Itzá," said Mother, coming out of the room behind me, still panting from the climb. "At least there you could go into the lunchroom and sit in air-conditioning. Those big buildings on the far side with all those rooms full of ledges remind me of I don't know what."

"The cat house."

"Taylor, don't talk ugly to me, I'm your mother."

"Cages at the zoo. You know. Like those concrete benches the leopard sleeps on."

"Well, whatever it is, I don't like it. I thought Mayans were supposed to be so short. Looks like giants lived in there." She smoothed the raspberry silk shirt over her bosom and then daintily wiped each corner of her mouth with a ring finger. "Are you getting dizzy, Taytay, up this high?"

"No ma'am. I'm fine."

"This place is so close to the ocean. It gives it a much creepier feeling than the ruins in the forest. The waves crashing. All this sky and water."

"I know what you mean."

"The other one, you could almost be at Disney World."

I stared down at an archipelago of old brown stains mapped on the threshold step.

"Who's that boy Dodie's with, do you know?" Mother visored her eyes, gazing out toward the edge of the compound. "I don't recognize him. He's not from the hotel, is he? He looks—he almost looks foreign." She paused. "See, Taylor? Do you see them over there?" she asked in an altering voice.

"Yes."

Dodie and Eduardo were walking away from the outlying buildings. They'd been holding hands, but now as we watched Dodie pulled hers away and wrapped her arm around Eduardo's neck, her elbow jutting like a shepherd's crook, and pulled his head close to her mouth. She seemed to be murmuring in his ear. His arm slipped all the way around her waist so that he caressed her rib cage on the far side. His hand strummed up and down. "His name is Eduardo," I said.

"Oh my Lord."

"I don't know his last name."

"What is she *doing*?" Mother sat down suddenly.

"Having a good time, I think she thinks."

"She can't—can't be actually—"

Dodie and Eduardo disappeared behind the farthest stack of stone, their palms running over each other's butts as they sank into the clinch, tongues darting and wetly visible even from here.

"Oh, God," said Mother. Her face went blank. "Oh, my God."

I remained silent.

"God. What am I going to—"

Carefully I patted her shoulder.

"Taylor, that's your sister," she whispered. "That's my baby. She's only fourteen."

"I know."

"I didn't even know about those things until I was in col—what is she *doing?*"

"Well, I think it's obvious."

"But she's—she looks like it's—so familiar!"

"Dodie's always been precocious."

"She's your *sister*." She stared at me, her blue eyes filling with tears.

"She sure is."

"Can't you do something?"

"Who—*me?*"

"Yes!"

"Like—like what?"

"Can't you just . . . ? You're a man. Go stop them! Stop that boy."

I sat down, astonished. Was Mother truly only comprehending for the first time the nature of Dodie's recreational activities over the past few months? Did she really expect me to take such a role? "You mean, go warn him off or something? Like the head of the household? Defending Dodie's honor?"

"Yes!" Then she seemed to realize what she was saying. She shook her head helplessly, moaning a little as the tears spilled. "I'm sorry. Oh, Taylor, what am I going to do?"

"Forget it."

"If only her daddy was still alive! If Ben was just—" She wrenched at her rings, gazing toward the cairn beyond which, presumably, Dodie was doing more precocious things with Eduardo.

"I said don't worry. I'll take care of it."

"What?" She turned and blinked. Her eyes said: Impossible. Not you.

"No time like the present."

"But, Taylor—I—oh," she gulped, staring up at me.

"Be careful—don't say something silly—"

"Okay."

Picking my way down the steps I aimed straight ahead, like the spoonbill winging out to sea, and didn't stumble or lose my balance once. I never looked back at Mother. I preferred not to see her surprise, weigh her doubt; it was not the time to turn to a pillar of salt. The stones behind which Dodie had vanished stood a few feet beyond the last path of the compound. Apparently she hadn't minded that they would be in full view of tourists taking the long shot through their camera lenses. She lay in the thrall of something more arresting than shame. This I understood as soon as I stood over them both.

"Dodie."

Eduardo had her wrapped around his torso like a cat claw stuck to an instep. She licked his neck, intently. He was stroking her uncovered midriff where her T-shirt rucked up, his other hand cupped on her breast beneath the lace bra; her thighs encircled him as tightly as her arms did.

"Dodie."

Eduardo pulled away, narrowing his drunk-looking eyes. Dodie's head rolled back. Together they squinted against the sun.

"Time to knock it off," I said.

"Taylor? What do you want?" Carnal delirium slowed her voice.

"Come with me."

"What?"

"You heard. Come on, now. Time to join the family."

"You've got to be kidding." Dodie barked out an amazed laugh.

"Get up."

"Hello, Taylor," said Eduardo politely. "Como está?"

"Muy bien, gracias, Eduardo. Now good-bye." A weird strength had started to vibrate in my muscles. The late-morning shadow of the cairn scarcely grazed their heaped bodies. This time I was the one to stand above, to contemplate the vulnerable absurdities of human flesh.

"Taylor, would you just please go away?" groaned Dodie.

I reached out my hand in a gesture of formal courtesy, not made to her.

Eduardo stared for a minute. His handsome face seemed caught in thought. Then the pent-up breath expelled through his nostrils. He shook his head a little, pursed his lips, half smiled. Gently he scooted his hands underneath Dodie's thighs, untwined them from his own, clasped her sides, lifted her out of his embrace, and set her down on the grass.

"Hey!" she said.

He raised his hand, grasping mine. I helped him to his feet. "Thank you."

"Not at all."

"Taylor!" cried Dodie.

"It's nice to see you again." He brushed off his pants. Under the taut black knit of the polo, his chest buckled and stretched. He was very brown, very strong, seemingly sweatless.

"I'm sorry if I seemed too flippant yesterday," I said gravely, gentleman to gentleman. "But I feel I've misled you unfairly."

"How?" He squared his shoulders. His arms hung loosely down, relaxed, his flat features exotic and good natured. His nostrils flared.

"This is my sister, you understand?"

"Qué?"

"I didn't make that clear."

"No, I didn't understand."

"But you do now." I was six foot four inches tall. I could wrestle in ways that no one ever suspected, I reminded myself, honed during long afternoons spent with a titan-armed cripple on the mats of Fredericksburg Military's gym. Eduardo, on the other hand, was charged with deflected arousal. I stared down at the glossy crown of his head, waiting.

He looked at me a long, assessing moment. Then he nodded. "Yes. I do."

A tang of salt touched my tongue. "Good."

"*What* is going on?" snapped Dodie from her position in the weeds, ominously defiant. Eduardo and I glanced down at her.

"By the way, she's not really thirteen," I said, and Eduardo smiled confidently at our little joke. "She's fourteen." His smile dropped away.

"Taylor, you are such a dork. What do you think you're doing?"

"Get up, Dodie."

"Eduardo? Let's just go somewhere else, all right?"

I held out my hand to her. She ignored it, looking up at him; when his hand began to reach, he jerked it back to his side.

It dawned on Dodie that she had somehow suddenly become untouchable.

"Eduardo?" she murmured.

He looked at her, grinned foolishly, and shrugged. His wide, browned hands swung outward, then fumbled to his shirt placket, then fell down to scrabble and hook thumbs into his belt. I felt for him. The awkward response almost unnerved me as well as Dodie, but I knew that this, like everything from now on, was a test.

Pain shot over Dodie's face. "Don't you want to still hang out?" she whispered.

"Lo siento," he said, not looking at her anymore but scrutinizing the fringe of bush across the road. "Well, I have to go. See you later." He smiled again vaguely toward the both of us and strolled away, lithe on the balls of his feet.

It took a second for her to start screaming.

"You bastard!" Jumping up, she threw herself against me, ramming my solar plexus with her skull, fists whaling. "Taylor! You fucking bastard!"

Nails drove first into my belly, then into my ribs as she reached higher; in her eyes blazed the red rage she had been stoking for months. Pearls of sweat collapsed, smearing her upper lip and temples.

"Hey, cut it out." I grabbed the fists and squeezed them tightly. When she lurched again my head snapped back and I had to blink a moment to clear it and support her without tumbling over.

"Why did you, why did you, why—did—you—" She started to pant. Her body flailed at my waist like a trout on a line.

"Because."

"Bastard!" A white froth spat between her teeth. "You—damn—*bastard!*"

"That's hardly the point."

"It's none of your business!"

"Yes, it is." I clamped her fists hard to still her.

"I hate your guts, you retard. All my life. Embarrassing me! Everywhere! The whole town laughing, even my friends in kindergarten calling you—"

"I know."

She yanked her hands and I let go, fearful of hurting her. "At least I had a father," she sneered, "at least he gave me a last name and stuck around before he died. He wasn't a fucking figment of my imagination. I didn't just *hatch!*" When I failed to answer she tilted backward and stared up at me, rubbing her knuckles. Her shorts were rumpled on her skinny shanks, one sandal half off and slapping her heel. "You think you can just barge in. Why did you just barge in?"

"I'm your brother."

People had stopped to watch; the group of old ladies faltered on the path, unwilling either to draw nearer or skirt such a scene. One of them whispered something to another. Their guide folded his arms, patient and interested.

"Big fucking deal. When did that mean anything?"

"You're worth more than this."

She didn't answer.

"TAYLOR?" MOTHER STOOD in the doorway of my room.

"Yes?"

"I appreciate what you did today."

I sat back. "Well. Dodie doesn't appreciate it much."

"Maybe not, but she should. Why, I can't imagine—if I had had brothers, I certainly would have wanted them to look after me and save me and help me behave." She reached up, teased a copper curl back into its appointed place, and stepped inside, shutting the door behind her. "I think maybe she will, after a while."

"It doesn't matter."

"Of course it does. I'm just glad your granddaddy didn't see it, all caught up inside that old tomb. Although he would be very proud of you." Her eyes drifted, fixed on the scratches across my throat. She winced. Then she slid the purse strap off her arm, clicking the catch open. "Anyway, I didn't come in just to tell you that."

"Oh."

"Here." She fished around in the purse's depths, brought out an object, and held it toward me. In the reddened sunset I couldn't discern what it was.

"I was going to give it to you a long time ago, but I forgot. To tell you the truth, it just hadn't struck me as important, or rather appropriate is more like it. Plus I'd stuck it away in a hard-to-reach place—you know how that is? I mean, let me tell you. It had more *stuff* on top of it!" She shook her head fondly at her own madcap fecklessness. "But the other day while I was packing my jewelry up for the deposit box and sorting through a bunch of old costume junk I came across it and realized you should really have it."

"What is it?"

"A gift from your father."

I stared at her pale, extended hand. The knobs of her knuckles enclosed whatever it was.

"A few years too late, I know, but hey, what the heck," she said.

The shock lay in the fact that she'd used his title. Not once in my life had I ever heard her pair those two words, *your* and the other.

"Take it. Aren't you going to?"

On her face hovered an expression both shamefaced and defiant. "It's not wrapped or anything. I've never known why he chose this silly old thing to give me. But he never was one to stand on ceremony. At least, not the kind that involves dressing up."

Reaching out, I took the object from her hand.

It felt heavier than I had expected. A small tin globe, the kind you used to see in a display bin at the dime store, rolled lopsidedly over my fingers. Attached to it was a chrome key chain pitted with rust, the circle clasp sprung. Blue, green, yellow, pink, the continents splayed over the surface, crisscrossed with latitudes. I scraped a thumbnail on the seamed equator.

"I think he had it when he was a little boy or something."

"Ah."

"Kind of gimcrack."

I stared at it.

"You see why I didn't really count it—or rather, I'd always kind of hoped he'd send something else—"

"That's all there is?"

"Yes. I'm sorry." Her eyes dropped.

I didn't speak. I raised my palm closer to my eye and studied it, the earth balanced between the forking longitudes of creases, life line and love line. Rolling it around, I tipped it toward my fingers. Its chain dragged it back. One side seemed more weighted than the other, the bulk repeatedly coming to rest on Africa. Pincering it between thumb and forefinger I lifted it up to the light: a planet poised in its solar orbit, the ring catch dangling like a comet's tail.

"Well, this is some joke."

"I don't think that's what he meant." Her voice creaked.

"Yes, sir! He sure gave you a neat present."

"Taylor."

"I got the whole world in my hand." Even as I spoke, Granddaddy's implication of the day before shocked through again. Now he'd finished with me even in the least obligatory sense.

"Please don't talk that way."

"Why are you giving it to me?" I looked at her.

"I just—thought you might like to have it."

"And why now?"

"Well, it's such a silly toy, really, just a cheap little trinket, and when you were younger—well, you might have felt hurt. But after this morning with Dodie, I thought—"

"Right. Yes. I see."

The weight sank into my cupped palm like a golf ball settling into the hole. Its metal smoothness felt cool, the mountains eroded to nothing, the crust satin. All landmasses lay even and equal. Still I could not bring myself to close fingers over it, the treasure coveted for so long. The fact she had just betrayed—her new, altered perception of me—seemed both the truer gift and the more bitter.

"He have a sharp sense of humor?" I asked after a minute.

"No." She shook her head. The curl shivered back down onto her temple. "He always took himself very seriously."

The anger trembled like a small live thing burrowed just below my mind's level plain. "So this here's his one joke."

"Taylor, I've never told you how it was. I realize that. But I guess it's about time I did."

"You mean reveal the true history, the lineage of the bastard? Shoot. What's there to say?"

"You're not a bastard. Not like that."

"Did you marry him?"

"No, but—"

"Did he marry you?"

"No."

"Ipso facto."

"I don't know what that means," she murmured.

"Don't worry. These days nobody thinks anything about it." Except in Bernice, of course. In kindergarten, as Dodie had said, in elementary school, junior high, Cub Scouts, church. The geek with the staggers, the poor little goofball who can't walk straight, whose mama and real daddy did it without . . .

"I had no idea you were so mad," she whispered.

My hand closed then. The thing inside it popped a little as the tin indented. "Well, I sure do appreciate this touching souvenir of his childhood. Thanks, Mom. At least it didn't cost him much to spare. Unless for the sentimental value."

"Do you want to listen? If you can just hear me through that hateful mood a minute—"

"I'm listening." I sat down and tightened my fingers; the sprung catch crushed into skin. "I'm all ears."

"All right." She sat on the bed's edge beside me, smoothing her dress on her knees. "This is what happened.

"Long ago I went off to college." She took a deep breath.

"You *what?*" I said.

"I know I've told you I never really went to college. But I did. To St. Mary Grove. That's a girls' school in Virginia. I just never graduated. And during my freshman year I only came home for Christmas. See—I was having the best old time, going to dances, deb parties, meeting new friends, spending weekends in North Carolina, Georgia. For Thanksgiving I was invited to a big house party on Cape Cod. Easter we spent on Pine Island in my roommate's family beach house. Before too long I hardly even thought of Texas, although Mama and Daddy phoned me regularly urging me to come home.

"Now, this was when a whole lot was changing. People smoking pot, rock bands—you know." She looked down. "Sex."

"Ah," I said.

"What do you mean, 'ah'?" She pivoted on the bed to gaze at me.

"Nothing."

"Well, you didn't come from some fling, if that's what you're thinking. Some drugged-out one-night stand. Don't sit there looking so superior over matters you know nothing about."

"I'm sorry."

"All right, then. Listen." But I wasn't sorry. She'd spoken to me as if I were normal.

"By the end of my freshman year I hardly knew a virgin anyplace, except myself, of course. My roommate asked me, 'Are you frigid?' But I'd been taught to consider some things priceless. I just kept going to the parties, flirting, dating around. At the end of spring semester Mama and Daddy were begging me to come home for the summer. They were worried. Finally Daddy said, 'If you'll come on down here and commute to SMU summer school to make up your flunked subjects, I'll send you back up to Virginia for the fall. Otherwise I won't.' So when I climbed aboard the Dallas plane I was very dejected. Texas didn't look so great from that distance. Flying into Love Field, I thought, Well, shoot, at least here's a decent-sized city, but it was flat as far as the eye could see, and the heat rippled on the runway, and the fields looked scorched yellow. Mama and Daddy were ecstatic. We drove home to Bernice with them talking ninety to nothing about how nice my hairdo was, and how tastefully I dressed, and how proud they were. I think they felt so relieved they forgot to mention they had a houseguest. I didn't know until I walked into the front hall.

"He stepped through the den doorway. 'Hello, there,' he said. 'You must be the famous Miss Troys I've been hearing so much about.'

"Boots with his jeans, was the first thing I noticed. Old boots so scuffed on the toes you couldn't see the original color. I'd gotten used to East Coast boys in their Brooks Brothers navy blazers. He wore a blue plaid shirt, cowboy material, worn all thin and frayed around the collar, with mother-of-pearl snaps and a Western silver belt buckle. He was handsome as sin. And an utter stranger.

"I don't know if I can explain to you, Taylor. What it felt like seeing him that first time. Here I'd been so sorry to leave the East Coast, dreading Bernice, and I step onto that cool brick floor of the foyer, and there stands Texas. I would have surrendered my virginity to him on the spot." She went quiet a moment. I gaped, astounded. She didn't seem to notice.

"'I've sure heard a truckload in your favor,' he said, and took my hand. 'But it looks to me like you've been underpraised.'

"It was just a normal-toned compliment, you understand, like men say in front of a girl's folks. I blushed red as a stove, wondering what Mama and Daddy must have been telling him. But his eyes looked into mine as he said it. Then they grew real bright, and they didn't look away.

"'Alicia, this is A.J.,' said Daddy. 'He's staying with us for a while.'

"'Hi,' I said and laid my hand in his like a wet fish. His eyes were like nothing I'd ever seen—not in Bernice, Virginia, or the whole Ivy League. And his hair—oh, his hair was so beautiful, I just wanted to reach up and stroke it."

"What color was it?" I asked slowly.

"It was gold. Dark gold, just like yours. You've got his hair and his eyes."

I didn't reply.

"Your curl comes from me, though. His lay straight as embroidery floss over the top of his forehead. And you're taller."

His name, I thought. Now I've heard his name.

"Daddy explained why he was there. 'A.J. has old family business here in town. I've been helping him with some legal work.' His tone let me know he thought highly of him. 'He'll be here at least a couple more weeks, we hope.'

"A.J. said, 'Oh, no, I wouldn't want to put you out that long.' But he kept his eyes straight on me.

"'I'd just as soon it was a couple of months. Heck! Let's not stand out here pawing the ground, let's go on in,' said Daddy.

"'Here, let me take those,' A.J. said and took my bags. He reached up for my train case. Our hands touched." She closed her eyes, swallowed, her throat shifting.

"Over the next three days we spent a lot of time together," she said. "I showed him all over town. He was from Corpus Christi. His daddy had been a wildcatter, and his father and uncles before him. They'd built up a nice little empire. Wildcatting's that way, you know, a gamble: five million in the bank one day, eight million in the red the next, twenty-five million fat and happy the day after, when the new hole starts spouting. But A.J.'s father had died on the wrong day.

"That's why he was in Bernice, to tidy up what was left of his dead grandmother's property before it got turned over to the creditors. A.J. was the last one alive. The family had lost everything: their baseball team, the Acapulco hotel. But the thing that hurt A.J. most was losing the ranch.

"Isn't that the old story?" she said, glancing at me and smiling sadly. The room was darker now. The sea's roar increased. "Now, A.J. had some half brothers," she went on. "A whole slew of them, by some woman he hadn't even known about when he was growing up, and they all lived down near Beeville. Some of them weren't even his daddy's. It meant a nasty will contest, costing tons more money, which got A.J. in deeper. Palantido, was their name." She paused again. "Palantido. Funny I should remember that.

"So there was a lot he wanted to forget. I couldn't sit on the car seat beside him without losing breath. To feel like that about somebody is the sweetest thing you'll ever know," she said, and fell silent.

I stared at her, at the auburn lock trembling above her eyebrow, seeing this side to her hidden until now, utterly unsuspected.

"Where is he?" I whispered. "Where is he now? Is he dead? Is that why my trust . . ."

"Hush. I'll tell you the rest. But you must promise to be patient until I'm finished."

I folded my hands and looked down. After a few seconds, I nodded.

"Mornings he spent working in Daddy's office. Afternoons we'd drive out in my Le Mans convertible through the live oaks and creek bottoms to his grandmother's old homeplace near Tyrone, so we could list what was left in the house and turn it over to the auditors. Once he stopped the car on that little wooden bridge over Crybaby Creek. We could hear frogs peeping and mosquitoes whining and the water rushing below. He reached over and took my face in his hands—" She paused.

"On the third evening, after supper, we left Mama clearing the table and went out to the Dairy Queen for milk shakes, and then Petroleum Park to see the first oil derrick, and we drove past the Ransom estate drive and wondered about Miss Ransom living in her big stone house all by herself, and he said he wished he could visit her and wake her up, and then I took him to the cemetery. By that time it was about nine o'clock. We'd heard the doves and owls calling through the twilight in the Ransoms' woods. Clear darkness lay all around, fireflies sparked under the crape myrtles, the grass felt sharp under my hands as we sat down next to a Confederate marker.

"'Look there,' I said, and my voice shook a little. 'That's the Deloache family plot. See the wooden box by the marble lamb?'

"'Yes,' he said. 'What is it?'

"'Go look,' I told him. I watched him walk past Governor Deloache's obelisk to the box in the corner and stoop down to hunt for an inscription. He scrubbed at the dirt on the glass. 'It's some kind of display case,' he called as he wiped. Then suddenly he stopped."

"He'd seen inside," I said.

"Yes."

"What did he say?"

"He asked me if it was real."

"And what did you tell him?" I stared at her, remembering all too well what the box contained, the rebuke to God or terrible chance that grief had placed there, the dumb, agonized cry against circumstance. I wondered why she, a nineteen-year-old girl in love on a balmy summer night, had chosen that moment to point it out to her lover. Because it was a distraction from the tug of their bodies? Because it was there?

"I got up and went over to him. 'Is it a joke?' he whispered when I reached his side. 'Some kind of a macabre joke?' 'No. It's an old-timey tricycle, perfectly real,' I said. 'It was put there by the family. See that huge front wheel? And that rusty-looking old wreath of artificial flowers on the handlebars? It's nearly a hundred years old.' Then I told him how it got there. 'They had a little boy who loved this tricycle for his special toy. He wouldn't even be parted from it at night. One day when he was four years old he was riding across the high gallery of their house and he went off the edge and broke his neck. He's buried here beside it.'"

"You told me the same story when I was little," I said.

"Yes, of course. That is the story."

"What did he say then?"

She sighed pensively. "Nothing, for a long time. He just squatted beside the box, staring into it. The moonlight shone strong on his face filling with sadness like a glass filling up. Finally he said, 'His parents must have felt just about crazed, to leave this here. So that they could never forget.' He stood up. 'They loved him so much they made sure the whole town would live with his death forever.'"

The words so precisely framed my own thoughts that I jerked.

"He held my arms then and pulled me close," she said. "'How come you to show me this?' he asked me.

"'Oh, I don't know,' I said. 'Truly, I don't.' Then he took my face between his hands, like he'd done on the bridge.

"We went over to the big granite slabs covering the Colletts' graves inside their wrought-iron chaining. We lay down on one." She paused. "Six days later he went away."

"What?" I sat up.

"He had to go."

"He left you? Just like that?"

"He had to do something to rebuild his family fortunes."

"I thought you said he was the last member left alive."

"Yes. He was." She frowned. "But that kind of man has a need to do things we don't always comprehend, Taylor. Even if he's the last one, he's still keeping the family name. Then he *is* his family. And men like that are often very ambitious."

I leaned back, the impulse she was describing stirring within me.

"Well, he went off to Houston, and from there to work on a North Sea oil rig. One of his father's old friends had gotten him the job two years before. On the last night before he left, he took me back to the cemetery. 'As soon as I can make enough money for my plans, we'll get married,' he said. 'Until that time, take this and keep it. Then, if we ever have a baby, he or she can inherit the earth.' He grinned and put that little globe in my hand.

"A month afterward he got sent from Aberdeen to the Middle East. I received one letter from Saudi Arabia with no return address except the oil company's London one. Then nothing."

She stared through the darkness. Her eyes glinted. "He didn't know about you," she said.

For a minute the quiet stretched between us while I started rearranging the conclusions of a lifetime. "You never wrote and told him?"

"I couldn't write it to an oil company." She frowned, and sniffed. "They weren't even American."

"Why didn't he write to you again?"

"I don't know."

"But when you found out you were going to have me, didn't you at least try and contact him?"

"I tried telephoning the head office in London once and asking where I might locate him. They said he didn't work for them anymore. They said they didn't know where he was. He'd disappeared."

"Oh." I clenched my fists.

"Something happened. I know that." She sighed again and adjusted the chiffon panel of her dress. "Of course, Mama had a fit. She considered us ruined. She wanted to send me off to a home for unwed mothers. I wouldn't go. Then I started showing and it was too late. When Daddy started scouring the backwoods for A.J., setting the foreign consulates on his tail, phoning other drilling firms, I told him to quit it. There wasn't any point. I was so confident he'd come back. Our connection couldn't be but uppermost in his mind, I thought. I just trusted him. Hour after hour I used to hold that little globe in my palm, sitting on my bed, and trace it over with my fingertip, and imagine what country he might be in now, pursuing success so that we could get married."

"But he didn't come back."

"No." She pressed her lips together and closed her eyes. "Not then."

"He did later on?" I blinked.

"No. No, he didn't later on either. Not exactly." Her eyes opened, their inky blue bottomless in the small bedside lamplight.

"Not *exactly*? What the hell does—"

"I had to forget about it, Taylor. That time spent in each other's company, the promises we made. I had to just forget it. You were on your way. I had to become someone else."

All at once, I understood the magnitude of what his desertion had done to her. I perceived the caricature she'd resorted to without thought, once her transfiguration had ended in the bloodbath of my birth. The personality I'd watched her demonstrate throughout my life, an erasable cartoon of a shallow Texas belle, was flatter, more trivial than any one she could have consciously made up for herself. Instead she'd simply taken and adapted what was handy, like an insect fashioning its camouflage cloak among dead leaves, and made it reflex: it was now her second nature. She must have run out of energy, I thought. His leaving, her one burst of defiance, my arrival, must have sapped her motivation to bother, to reach toward something better. Whatever graces the East Coast year had nurtured, she'd shed to assume the flimsy mannerisms and highly lacquered shells of the women around her: parroting their slicked-up country sayings, shifting her attention to bridge games and new car upholstery—more Bernice than Bernice itself, but without the inner substance. It could be argued that she'd been raised to it, imprinted, and that was surely what I'd spent my teenage years arguing to myself. But who knew what she might have grown into had I not been conceived? By the time I was ten years old she'd become a hollow satire. Or so I'd thought. She'd become her mother.

I wouldn't forgive him that. Oh, no.

Now, suddenly, I turned to her.

"If he never came back *exactly*, then where did my trust fund come from?" I asked. "Granddaddy once accidently let drop that he'd lived for a while in Dallas. Is that still true? Or is it just where the trust fund gets paid out?"

She stood up. Shoving back her curl, she began to pace the room, walking toward the curtains winged out by the breeze, then swiveling back to face the bureau mirror. "He did come back eventually, in a way," she admitted. She licked her forefinger and touched it to an eyelid, smoothing off a mascara speck.

"*What?*" I whispered.

"But by then I'd married Dodie's daddy. Ben didn't want me to talk with A.J. Not at all. And besides, you'd been sick already and then the problem had developed, and I guess I just felt so guilty I couldn't face him. Not to confess what had happened to his son."

"But Mother!" He had come, I thought, wanting to grind my teeth. He had been here. "But—that wasn't your fault!"

"Oh, I know." She let out a deep breath. "Oh, you just don't know the way women's minds work."

"So where had he hidden out all that time?"

"I've never been informed." She said it shortly; whether her anger was directed toward him or Ben Sikes, my dead stepfather, I couldn't tell.

"But he obviously found out I existed?"

"Daddy wrote to him and explained. Then, to our surprise, he wrote back saying he was now settling down in Dallas and reclaiming his family's old stomping ground, and he would establish a trust for your care and education. 'Tell the boy,' he said, 'that I'm sorry I never saw him. And please remind Alicia of that present I once gave her.'"

"But you forgot." The emotions surging made my head feel hot.

"Yes, I did. Well, sort of."

She stood, emptily inspecting her face in the mirror, dabbing her cheeks, checking a wrinkle beside her nose, prising up an eyelid, as if this ritual could fill the hanging vacuum and anesthetize the pain that swarmed through it around us. How many times since my illness, I wondered, had she stood thus, taking the posture of self-absorption because therein lay oblivion? How many times since the fever seared through my limbs—the meningitis devouring my infant central nervous system while she wracked herself over whether I would live or die, and then, after the antibiotic answered her question, watching while I grew, and staggered and fell and reeled through a room, clutching out for support, and clamped my head to still the swinging universe inside it, and lumbered around the backyard, crashing into azalea bushes while the other boys my age made home runs and won Little League games at Cougar Field—how many moments of panic and fatigue had she smothered by unscrewing the lip pencil, counting the crow's-feet? The doctors told her that the hairs of my inner ear had been killed forever by the streptomycin, in the same way it had murdered the meningitis, my enemy. "But he's alive," they'd told her. "He'll live and grow up strong." *V* for virus. Vestibulum. Victory. She'd paid the stake, taken all responsibility.

She hadn't forgotten, I thought. She'd forgotten nothing. As far as she was concerned, I was hers.

"Why did you give me this tonight, Mother?" I dangled the globe by its key ring, swinging it back and forth. She stared.

"It was time, I guess. You're grown now," she said. Her face collapsed inward, folding into her mouth and the slim flange of her nose, not just with exhaustion from all the long years, but with relief.

AFTER SHE LEFT I sat cradling the globe in my palm. The outrage had subsided, leaving in its wake only the slow contemplation of history.

To be a bastard is an ambiguous thing in this, the late twentieth century. So many other possibilities abound that I've always regarded myself lucky to merely be alive. Having survived Grandmama's social conscience and Granddaddy's endless apologies, Bernice's contempt and Mother's doubts, having emerged fully formed rather than sucked from her womb and dropped down the oubliette, I actually felt grateful for contracting a potentially lethal illness at the age of one year and surviving double. Old Taylor, every time a winner. Like her I'd learned to make do with what lay to hand. There remained the one gnawing thing. So many Saturday afternoons I'd spent at the Bernice Public Library, searching through Dallas telephone directories for my name, the pages ripe with a harvest of Taylors, tracking down the masquerading Thaddeus: T. Taylor, Harry T. Taylor, T. Ronald Tailor, perhaps, because where *else* could she have conjured it? How many hidden objects can you find in this picture? Now here it was. A.J.

A for what?

The globe felt warm and clammy in my hand. I forced my fingers to uncramp. Across the bleached carpal segments was a ridged line, scored by the equator. To leave this token of childhood on deposit with your girlfriend, I thought, you must have felt either that she was the turnstile pushing you into your future, your man's fate, or that it was a talisman worthy of your love. Which had you had in mind? Your secret rite of passage? Or her humiliating gag gift?

What did you respect?

I picked it up between my fingers, dropped it; once again it rolled onto the regions of the Lower Nile. A tiny clink came from inside.

I held it up to my ear and shook.

Calipering it, I inserted my nails in the equator and worked my way around the hemispheres, prying it like a cannister lid. With a snap the two halves suddenly burst open. Something lay wedged inside the Southern Hemisphere. The yellow circlet caught the lamplight. With my forefinger I hooked the shank, pulling until it unjammed from its tin prison, slid down the fingertip to my knuckle, and stopped. I turned it under the lamp. An old-style signet ring, the kind found in safety deposit boxes or on elderly men's hands. The broad table glowed with the depth of high-karat gold. Letters in a block script marched around the bezel. The space inside reserved for a crest was blank. A name? A motto? I squinted to read the single word engraved. DEEDS, it said.

3

The night was cooler than the day had been. Easter throngs jammed the shops and open spaces around the plaza across from the docks. Inside the cafés and restaurants music plinked with tinny syncopation, encouraging tourists to rub up against each other in the dances of their choice. I climbed out of my taxi, looking around. Nobody at the hotel had seen me leave, not even the night clerk. Mother and Granddaddy were presumably in bed. A group of drunken fraternity boys teetered on the pedestal of the plaza monument high above the crowd, hoisting beer cans and yelling out country-and-western songs; their whoops interwove with the odors of fried meat, seaweed, fish both dead and alive, and ominous musks, in a drift net for the senses. The fruity spice of garbage prevailed. Out on the water a cruise liner loomed beside a wharf, white, black, and candescent gold against the hollow blue darkness. The Portuguese flag flapped limply on a halyard. The sky was rinsed in stars.

I strolled toward the plaza carefully. People fenced it round three or four bodies thick, moving or loitering, cramming closer to the middle and pulling away. Below the frat boys clinging to the monument I spotted three blond girls I'd noticed late that afternoon in our hotel bar. One of them was industriously trying to push the tallest boy into the plaza pool while her two friends laughed like witches. Along the shopping grottos the tide of sunburns eddied. Cartier, Chanel, Hermés: the French seemed to have cornered the cheap-imitations market. I stalked past restaurants that looked like sibling franchise chains, painted with giant sunflowers and furnished in sturdy hand-sawn wood. The menus posted outside read identically: grilled camarones, enchiladas de camarones, coctel de camarones, hamburguesas. It was eleven forty-eight and I still hadn't caught sight of Ramón; he hadn't shown up in the hotel dining room once since we'd come back from Tulum. All I could hope was that his note of the night before still applied.

Her timing had been impeccable, I thought. Granddaddy unwittingly delivering the death chop one day, she presenting her memento mori the next. She might not even know about Granddaddy's career counseling session. It didn't matter; fate had taken care of it. Fate and time disposed of everything, it seemed, including the fact that he'd never given a damn. A.bandon and J.ettison. A.bsentee J.erk.

By the lamplight of the hotel room, and again in the neon and lanterned plaza, the burglar's eye rolled to a stopped fix in my mind. I registered once more that pupil; all the inchoate, dispiriting mess of my years so far drew together, reflected sharply against its lens.

To get away from the endless fiesta I stepped beyond the market. The area behind the plaza seemed like another world. Unlit alleys trailed through the blocks. Most of the thresholds lay dark. Occasionally the screen door to a café with a one-bulb interior emitted a patron swabbing his lips and hitching his waistband, the interior behind him sparser and more truly Mexican, its menu featuring carne asada or mole instead of seafood. The other customers hunched over the tables or stood around in grimy T-shirts, chewing and swigging in silence. As I moved back toward the lights I realized Ramón had had his reasons for naming the gringo-ridden plaza as our rendezvous point. It would have been interesting to roam farther into these civil backwaters, to canvass the streets of houses and shacks, the patio yards behind the fences.

Under an archway in front of a display window gleaming with cultured pearls two men sidled up to me and seized my arms.

I glanced quickly left, then right, whipping around—always a mistake. The vertigo whirled like foam in a rock pool. Acid fear burned through it. Instinctively I gripped for the archway's edge, and as I did so the gold ring caught the corner of my eye: the one commodity I had worth stealing.

"Where you been?" asked Ramón.

The voice penetrated the rush of adrenaline. My vertigo steadied. "Looking for you," I said.

"We been here awhile already," complained his companion.

He spoke fast English in a nasally drone. I tried to look at him, but I was still too dizzy to note much. "The crowd's too big. We must have missed each other."

"Don't matter. No problem. This is Juan." Ramón released my elbow from his friendly clasp and gestured to the other man, who was hanging on to my forearm like somebody who'd won a prize turkey. "I wasn't sure if you read what I wrote on that letter, man."

They seemed oddly paired. Juan's eyes bulged up at me, his narrow face ending in a weasel's chin. His bright yellow shirt lay open to the lumpy sternum; gold chains crowded his neck, spiked with crucifixes and wads of saints' medals. A nuggety gold watch dragged down one wrist. It looked newly dug from the mine. Any pimp would have been proud to hock it.

"How you doing?" I stuck out my hand, conscious of the ring I had no right to wear weighting the knuckle. Juan nodded, glanced at it, not shaking.

"So, you still want to play?" said Ramón easily.

"That's what I'm here for."

"Let's go." He motioned us out from under the arch, into the alley. We crossed it, climbed a step, and entered a gateway set in a building's stucco wall.

Instantly the air muted like a cloth had been dropped over our heads.

A smell of old things, mildewed and moldy, surrounded us, a gardeny scent accompanied by coolness. It was too dark to see more than pale clumps—bushes and some low furniture silhouettes scattered around the open space.

"Where are we?"

"Don't you worry about it, chico," said Juan.

Ramón shut the wooden gates behind us, drew a bar, and walked ahead. The courtyard seemed long, an opening under the stars flanked by thick growth and huge leaves thrusting from the ground, barely visible even as my eyes adjusted. Our footfalls stirred a crunching and a slither that resonated even when we halted; small animals disturbed by our presence scurried away into holes or up the walls. All at once it came to me that we'd now truly left the resort world of money-slick Cozumel behind. I was entering another Mexico, the secret country every Texan grows up knowing in his imagination: the legendary place where posses can't follow, where good old boys on a good-time weekend can vanish into a bordertown jail without a trace, where banditos ambush tourists on mountain highways, strip their cars, dump the bodies down arroyos for the buzzards, and make sandals out of the tire rubber. My former fear returned like a stinging drug. After a few steps a patter like rain began behind my back. I paused. Abruptly it stopped.

"What's that?" I whispered.

Ramón and Juan both listened. "Dog," said Ramón.

The patter recommenced, nails clicking on gravel, following much too close behind me as we walked single file across the central space to the far end. My ankle skin grew ultrasensitive, preparing for the first bite. Just as we reached the opposite wall and a hot breath touched my calf, Ramón opened a door.

A frail glimmer showed through the gap. I watched as Ramón, then Juan, shouldered past it, immersing in a new element. To race ahead of them panic-stricken would have been unseemly. I hated to think that I could be cowed that fast. But then I realized while I waited my turn—

tensed, reviewing all the diseases that Mexican canine saliva could incubate—that something had changed; the old instinct to run was gone. I felt an impulse to reach out and thump the dog on his vicious little head. I turned around to gauge my menace. "Piss off," I said. He growled once. Then the patter started up again, retreated, and faded away into the corners by the entry gates. A disc of green phosphorous flickered and snuffed on the darkness.

"You coming?" called Ramón.

I stepped inside.

Beyond the threshold lay a large room. A table stood in the middle. Brackets of hammered iron clamped onto the walls held paper candles with gray bulbs. The weak light was sifting in from another source; the room next to this one, a kitchen from what little I could tell through the doorway, bloomed with the rose of an oil lamp. As Ramón pointed to the chairs around the table and we went to sit down, I heard a scraping. Someone was moving around in there.

Juan glanced up. "Quién?"

Ramón shook his head, flicking the question away with one hand.

Juan frowned. "Ella?" he demanded.

Ramón didn't reply.

"Tiene razón para quedar?"

"No es importante."

"Acaso." Juan's frown deepened.

"Es nada. Lo olvida." Ramón turned to me. "So. You want a beer or something?"

"Sure."

He pushed his chair back and went through the doorway. Between the sounds of footsteps and glass clinking, a murmur floated outward. The answering voice, a woman's, fell too low for me to catch any more. When he returned, alone, he carried two bottles and a mug.

"You got the cards? I could be shuffling," I said.

"They're around here somewhere." He set the bottles down on the table and groped his jeans pockets. Juan, looking bored, picked up his beer. After a moment Ramón paused his search, sipping from the steaming mug. "Maybe I leave them at the hotel."

"How will we play?"

"You didn't bring any?"

"Nah."

"We can't play nothing, then," said Juan. He leaned back in his chair, almost smirking in his unsurprise.

"No, I don't guess we can." I smirked back and rested my arms across my stomach.

"See? He's easy, man," said Ramón. He drank from his mug. "Real relaxed guy." Juan grunted.

From the kitchen came scratching and then a whisper, like legs in nylons brushing together. I wondered if whoever she was was barefoot. Probably Ramón's mother.

"Hey, buddy. Dónde está su pueblo?" Juan shoved his palm against my shoulder, all at once aggressively chummy.

"Huh?"

"He wants to know where you live," Ramón said.

"Texas."

"Yeah. Where in Texas?" Juan demanded. "Hey, I know Texas. I live in Dallas a long time."

"He played soccer for St. Edward's in Austin," explained Ramón.

"Oh. I'm from Bernice."

Juan squinted. "Ber*niccce*," he hissed through his teeth, drawing it out.

"Small town. About thirty-five miles southeast of—"

"Yeah, yeah. Sure, I know where it is."

"That's good. A lot of people don't."

"Stupid."

"Well, not necessarily." I sipped my beer. "It's not exactly a hopping place."

Juan scowled. "Old, right?"

"Pretty old."

"Huh!" He tossed his head.

"I think somebody founded it right after we beat Mexico."

The scowl sharpened. Then suddenly he relaxed and sprawled, tilting his chair backward, his face smoothing with cunning. "Yeah, I heard of Bernice. Bunch of rich people live there."

"A few."

Ramón set down his mug. "Is that so?"

I shrugged. "They found oil there real early on."

Juan slitted his eyes. "I played soccer with this guy at St. Edward's from Bernice."

"Oh, really? What's his name?"

He raised his brows and shrugged. "You know. Named Joe. John, Joel—what was it? Man. Good soccer player."

"What position?"

Frowning, he scratched his head. "Shit. I don't remember."

"Too bad. I probably know him. Was it Joe Hightower, maybe?"

"Nah. That don't ring no bell."

"John Stuyvesant? Johnny Sylvester *Sturgeon* Stuyvesant?"

Juan shook his head regretfully.

"Julian Rigor Mortis the Third?"

"Maybe—no. Sorry." He held up both palms. "No recuerdo, man. He was a good guy."

"Oh, well."

Ramón looked away, grinning.

"You know people in Dallas?" Juan pursued casually.

"Uh, yeah. I guess."

"Many?"

"Not too many. A few."

He tapped his tiny chin. "Like, people from your school or what?"

"Friends of the family. Friends from college. Like that."

Expectantly he waited.

"Distant relative or so." Quite distant, I thought. In a manner of speaking. Maybe even a half sibling or two, who could say?

"Hm. That's cool, man. Like, where in town they live? What neighborhoods? Highland Park? University Park?" He steepled his fingers, his face a calculating, congenial mask. "North Dallas? I mean, you know? Maybe I met them before. Hey, I been to a lot of parties around those neighborhoods."

"They're not partiers as a rule," I said. "More reclusive." Which might be perfectly true, for all I knew. "So, did you get a degree from St. Edward's?" I parried.

"Qué?"

"I said, did you—"

"Yes, sure! In Spanish Literature, qué no?" Suddenly he reared his head back, unnecessarily fierce.

"Oh." Minute pause.

"Juan was in marketing. He got kicked out for dealing," Ramón said.

"Yeah? Dealing what?"

"Coke, man."

"That's too bad," I sympathized. "Did they put you in jail?"

"No problem. First a little prison. Then he got parole. Deported," said Ramón.

"Can you ever go back?"

"Hey. Any fucking time I want to, hijo." Juan could without doubt compete with Dodie in Intramural Glowering and Mood Swing.

"The back way," added Ramón, taking out a knife and a small wooden peg from his pocket.

"What happens if you get caught?"

"What happens if . . . ," Juan mimicked in a snitty tone. "Shit. Get caught? What the fuck you talking about? It's not dangerous when you know who to know, comprende, gringo face?"

But the magic was spoiled, I could see, despite this intimate confidence. I glanced toward Ramón. He studied his pocketknife blades, chose one, and opened it with his thumbnail. "The border is no a big deal," he murmured.

"For you, too?"

"I'm legal."

"Because of your uncle in Oak Cliff?"

"Madre de Dios! Qué dijiste?" cried Juan.

"Que deseo. Cerradas su boca." Ramón lit a cigarette, spat out a tobacco shred, and turned to me. "Is not my uncle helping it. In fact, Juan is my uncle's muchacho. Mi primo. Cousin."

"Hablamos mucho, Ramón. *Bleh, bleh, bleh,*" Juan growled.

"I'm legal porque my job give me green card in United States. Juan got deported when they bust him. It ain't nothing to do with his father or with me." He looked coolly at Juan, to make sure this was crystal clear. "His father my uncle is a very honest man. Not a criminal."

"A little coke don't make me no fucking criminal," snarled Juan.

"Muy bien. Tell that to the United States Immigration," said a voice.

I recognized it instantly, a voice without grain. My nape tingled.

"So what the fuck is a little coke these days? Everybody's doing it!"

"Sometimes you are unbelievably stupid."

Juan said nothing but made a grumbling sound toward the floor. Ramón balanced his cigarette on the table's edge, picked up the open knife and the peg, and started whittling.

"It's La Junta that makes you a criminal," the voice surged.

Juan hissed like a snake. "Shut up!"

"You and your big amigos. Oh so dangerous. La Junta. La Familia! La Mafia Mexicana! Why don't you try working? That's what everybody else is doing."

"That's all you know."

"Unless they're idiots." She poked her head around the door frame, stared at him a moment, and then stepped out of the kitchen.

Her skin still glowed, as if the oil lamp's rays pushed through its golden nacre. Her hair, now unpinned, swung down her shoulders in black ripples. A spiral lay curled against one breast.

"You want to get locked up for your whole life, you can do that coke business. You want to die, stay with your little buddies. You don't want to work, don't work. But don't give Papa any more trouble. I'm warning you, chico. I'm tired of you making him old, comprendes?"

"Buzz, buzz, like a mosquito."

"You understand." She turned imperiously and glanced first at Ramón, then at me. But then something changed; her look was not as incurious as it had been in the lobby. She turned back to Ramón. "And you better watch out too, primo. Since you're so smart."

He shrugged. "Hey, I'm working. No problem."

"I'm not talking about that."

"That's all you better talk about in my life, chica."

She gave him an icy stare.

"By the way, this is Taylor."

"Hi," I said.

"Hello," she bit off. Her eyes met mine, darted elsewhere.

"Nice to meet you."

Her face sealed up.

"Taylor, this is my cousin Teresa-Maria," said Ramón, shaving a curl from his peg. "Maria to the tourists. Eh, Teresita?"

"I know you already." I propped both legs out in front, trying to look like a man arranging himself at his ease.

"Yes. You're Troys, from the hotel."

"Room Twenty-two." She nodded, licked her lips. "I appreciated your thoughtfulness yesterday afternoon. That lemonade sure was good."

"It's my job to make sure our guests are comfortable."

"It worked. I'm comfortable."

"Muy bien."

"You have a beautiful name."

She turned and, for one instant, stared. Then she wheeled back toward the kitchen, determined to keep firmly apart in the midst of these questionable surroundings.

"And you're right."

"What?"

"There are more rewarding ways to make life interesting than to deal cocaine."

She paused.

"Ooh," said Juan. "Man, I knew it. Shit, I knew there was something. Now we have it."

"Have what?" asked Ramón idly to no one. His knife flicked and flicked. Bright pale chips flew down.

"His little plan. The reason he's messing with *us*, man. Buddying around, getting tight with you, playing poker, playing big dumb stupid gringo. What did you *think*? Can't you tell nothing?"

"Have what?" Ramón repeated, looking up from the knife's flash. He tilted his head, first at the air, then to Juan. The look implied, There is no question who is stupid here. His voice fell deceptively bland. "What is it we have?"

"Yeah. What is it we have?" sneered Juan.

"Uh . . . fun?" I said, and shrugged.

"Shit. You got some plan. Don't try telling me you ain't."

"Well, not just yet," I said, and clenched the muscles in my fingers, feeling the gold shank tighten.

Slowly Teresa-Maria stepped to the table. She pulled out a chair and sat down. Her eyes shone with velvet darkness as she cocked her head, inspecting me.

AT BREAKFAST ON the terrace next morning Dodie gave me secret, cryptic looks but still wouldn't speak. I wolfed two plates of huevos con chorizo and pappas fritas, three mangoes, plus a basket of sweet bread. Eventually Granddaddy placed his hand on my forearm. "Watch out, son, you'll do yourself an injury."

"Goodness, Taylor. It's like you've sprung a leak," Mother said.

"Please pass the orange juice."

Dodie gazed down at her bare thigh, scraped some dead skin off her sunburn, and said nothing.

"So, what are you two going to do with yourselves this final morning?" asked Granddaddy. "We need to board the plane by four forty-five."

"I'm shopping with Mom," Dodie said.

"Taylor?"

"I thought I might go to the mainland again. Explore a little deeper in."

Mother asked no questions but smiled wanly, perhaps still wrung out after the throes of confession. Bashfully she reached out to pat my hand. Dodie wrinkled her nose at this. Then her eyes widened and shuttered down.

"You been beach-combing, or did you steal it?" she asked, pointing to the hand under Mother's.

Granddaddy glanced up over his reading glasses to her target. Then he leaned forward, peering. "Why, what a handsome ring, Taylor. Where did you come across it?"

"It was a gift."

"That right?" He paused delicately. "Is it new?"

"I think it's probably very old."

"You mean an antique?"

"Yes, sir. See?" I held out my hand without slipping the ring off. He pushed the glasses up his nose bridge to look. I watched as his lips moved, silently forming the name. At his flinch my eyes met his.

"I'll be damned," he said.

I didn't reply.

He continued to fix me with his gaze. At last he turned to Mother. She was staring at the ring, her mouth open.

"But where—oh! Was it *inside?*" she whispered.

"Yes."

"Inside what?" said Granddaddy.

"The globe," I said.

He frowned, groping, trying to place. "The globe! You know, Daddy," said Mother. "The thing—he—mentioned in the letter all that time ago. That he'd given to me. I showed you it back then."

"What?" Granddaddy asked in slow disbelief. "You mean that *key chain?*" I nodded.

He slumped back, his arms resting on the chair arms. "That dinky little playtoy?" He shook his head.

"He meant it to—he meant me to know—" Mother was beginning to stumble.

"Not a key on it," Granddaddy marveled.

"Who are you talking about?" We glanced up. Dodie was glaring at us in bewilderment.

"Oh, my Lord." Tears sprang in Mother's eyes. "My God."

"Now, Alicia—" Granddaddy lowered a hand onto her shoulder, kneading, and then turned, stunned. "You see, Taylor, this gives a whole new slant on the picture we've always assumed. It seems like—but of course, you're wearing the proof this minute. I'm sorry, I'm just so taken aback here that I—"

"Hey!"

We turned. Dodie rammed both feet onto the floor. "Can't I know what's going on?"

"Now, Dodie. It's just—it's Taylor's business. Taylor's and your mother's. Now just give us a minute here, Dodie. Sit quiet."

To my shock her aggrievement slid away. She redraped her spine down into the chaise and waited.

"Where was he, then?" murmured Mother. It was a question echoing down the recesses of old memory.

"Maybe I should have gone ahead and asked him." Granddaddy sighed.

"I don't know. It just seems like he would have told us without us having to."

"Pride," she whispered.

"Yes, he had plenty of that, I'll grant you."

"Ours, too."

"What?"

"Yours and Mama's." She sniffed and swiped her knuckles on her wet cheeks. A drench of powder slid down the furrows near her lips. "And mine."

"Well, now, honey, he should have been the one to volunteer. Explanations come in mighty handy from the right party at the right time, as any criminal lawyer'll tell you."

"Ben stopped him."

"What?"

"Once he understood my predica—my position, that I'd married Ben and all, he must have seen that it was best not to intrude." She grimaced. "I suspect Ben made that clear somehow."

And he, I thought, had been only too willing to agree.

Dodie reached over without warning and picked up my hand. I felt her warm skin, soft and smooth, tenderized by adolescence and Lancôme body lotion. It was an alien sensation, as if a forest creature had suddenly crept up to investigate a new species. I didn't take my hand away but looked at her down-tilted head shining in the morning sun as she twisted the finger sideways to read the ring's inscription.

"Well. It's a pity he had to interfere. But I expect he felt it was his due as your husband. Although he did prefer not to legally adopt Taylor."

"He thought he'd adopted *me*."

"Hmph."

"But where could he have *been*?" The years behind the wail stretched out and out, from the frontier when her life had ended and begun again.

"I don't know. We'll probably never discover it. Let it go. It's just spilt milk. All water under the bridge. He provided for Taylor's upbringing, at

least. We'll just have to let sleeping dogs lie." The clichés sounded starch-
less, old.

"Deeds," muttered Dodie. She had kept my hand gripped in hers,
bending over it as though to avoid meeting any eye directly. "Is that like
some law thing, Granddaddy? Like for houses or something? What does it
mean?"

But it was Mother who answered. "It's a last name. And it means this.
Even though it's all long gone now, there was once upon a time when he
would've recognized Taylor as his son."

Dodie raised her head, staring.

IN THE TOWN of Tulum I hired a taxi, explaining to the driver how far I
wanted to go. He grinned and pumped his heavy head up and down. "Boca
Calle, sí," he repeated, relishing the distance implied by the words that
Ramón had taught me the night before. He scratched behind an ear with
a stubby finger thick as a banana. "Doce kilometers."

"Yes. Sí."

"Para el campo de pescar?"

"No. Solamente la playa. Yo deseo, uh, nado." I mimed a swimming
motion, and hoisted the speargun, fins, and snorkel mask that I'd rented
that morning from the hotel. "Comprende?"

"Sí, sí."

"Para tres o quatro horas. Y también, por favor, I want you to, um,
esperas para mí. Wait for me."

He digested this. For a couple of moments I waited. We stood outside
a small adobe shop open on the front. Under an awning stood long plank
tables spread with colored blankets, displaying split crates and mounds of
fruits: limes, watermelons, peppers, posol, and bread. From inside the grocery store a radio blatted out a harsh love song. A tiny, compact woman in
an embroidered white dress adjusted some stock on the shelves by the
refrigerator, looked out to me, and nodded hello. A dog stood in the door-

way drooling while flies danced above his head. Two roosters pecked around in the dirt beneath the tables. Across the rutted road scooped with pools of rainwater was a palapa roof supported by plank walls and a stamped metal sign nailed over the door: COMER—RESTAURANTE—CORONA. Even in the midmorning center of town, the encroaching trees fretted the road and houses in a crochet of dark shade.

"Un momento," said the cab driver. He held up one finger, strode quickly away up the cross street, opened a door in a house painted turquoise, and went inside.

The fumes from roasting pork fanned across the road. In spite of the huge breakfast, my mouth watered. A bus trundled down the main Cancún artery, slowed, turned the corner, and wheezed toward the sea.

Shortly the driver came back, leading a woman and a little girl behind him. The woman carried a fishing pole. She held the little girl's hand but walked more slowly than the other two; the child skipped along in a pair of pink plastic sandals much too large for her, trapping her feet like brown slivers inside candy. Her black hair had been brushed up into two handles that stuck out from the sides of her head. She chattered excitedly to the driver, who smiled, reached down, and tugged her ear. "Shht!" scolded the woman. "Bastante."

"Vamanos," the driver said, opening the rear door of the Ford for me. The woman and little girl crammed into the front, arranging the fishing pole so it lanced out through the window.

"It's all right? Todo correcto? Por esperas?" I asked.

"Sí, sí." He slid in behind the wheel, leaned across the woman, and shut her door. His brawny arm bunched under a flower tattoo.

"Bueno. Gracias."

From the bank of the front seat the little girl rose like a miniature Venus and stood, hands anchored, staring at me. The engine coughed and revved. After one shy glance the woman hooded her eyes straight toward the road ahead. We moved off through arching shadows and passed out of the village into the jungle territory.

ONLY A FEW yards down the road the trees closed us in. The humidity made sweat drip down my arms and soak my shirt. I sat thinking about the pyramids set on their grassy lawns deep in the jungle at Chichén Itzá, the big cenote dredged of its gold and bones. The test I had set for myself today would either tear me at last from childhood, the harness of care that had reined me back thus far, or finish with my drowning. Always I'd respected the limits defined by Mother's and Granddaddy's more ghoulish predictions. Always I'd toed the line.

Suddenly in my mind's eye I saw again that dark pupil rolling, stopping, locking on me.

"Excuse me. Está un cenote around aquí anywhere?" I asked.

"Cenote?" bellowed the driver.

"Sí."

"En trece, catorce kilómetros aproximadamente." He shrugged and swerved us around a spray of roots.

"I'd sure like to see it. Yo deseo el cenote, por favor."

"Cenote, cenote, trece, catorce," trilled the little girl in a whisper. Then, as if my question had caused her dam to burst, she began rattling out spurt after spurt of incomprehensible sentences. Her mother made no attempt this time to restrain her. After a couple of minutes the phrases transmuted into a sort of hypnotic litany, like the cries of birds, accompanying us as we bounced alongside the viny interior. "El tigre, el tigre en la cenote," hissed the little girl, weaving it into her chant like a sibyl.

"Sí, no problemo." The driver nudged the car through a scrawny bush and then hurtled it ahead. A couple of miles farther on, he suddenly darted down a side road no bigger than a path and wheeled around some buried stones and another root web. Thus we entered the landscape of my imaginings.

The filtered sunlight looked like gauze wrapping the tree trunks. Spinal leaves and fish-bone leaves and leaves of gold leather thrust through underbrush, the driver plowing past them as if steering a tank. We bumped over packed earth that seemed now to rise up to meet us and then to fall away from the Ford's low-slung undercarriage. Abruptly the little girl stopped talking. Her Delphic eyes never left my face.

"Cenote," the driver said after a little, and braked the car.

We sat looking out at the pool. Its surface was set flush with the forest floor in a mercurial interruption. A spatter of leaves trailed across it like a planned design, listing on the faint wind. Light shot through the upper layers to show live things swimming, an insect reeling over the tense skin of water, a mossy hank wavering against the ribbed limestone. Pebbles flocked with moss lined the pool's lip. More roots hung down into the depths.

I got out. I walked around the pool's circumference, ten paces. There was nothing there. No ghosts of old sacrifices, no tremors under the soil. No brooding, humanless jungle. The air felt empty, denatured by the chrome Ford, the two grape soda cans at the path's edge, the little girl smiling over the front seat.

"Es cenote," the driver said.

"No. No es cenote correcto." The eye seen from a distance—that oily black socket containing destiny and enigma—trembled on the edge of my mind.

"No es correcto?" he asked, puzzled.

"Swimming hole," I said. He chuckled with a rucked-up brow and shook his head.

"Piscina!" cried the little girl.

"No, no. Un cenote para pescar," the father amended, gesturing to the fishing pole stuck out the window. But his wife turned my way, solemnly met my eyes, and nodded.

This was not the place. I would have to go deeper in.

EVENTUALLY WE ARRIVED on a bridge hooked over the wide throat of water. To our left lay a trench of white sand spiked with coconut palms, a long spit, the tumbled ocean. To the right the lagoon system lapped the jungle's skirt. Ahead I could see trees fringing the beaches, but here in thick clumps, massed along the lagoon, grew only the dark green mangroves.

The driver stopped on the bridgehead. "Boca Calle," he said and pointed to the bite where the lagoon poured its stream between sand jaws. "Y también el campo de pescar. Bonefish!"

"Well, I guess I'll see you all in about four hours," I said and opened the car door. "Gracias. Quatro horas, aquí, sí? Okay?"

"Sí, sí," nodded the driver, opening his own door and starting to maneuver the fishing pole out through the window. He held up the watch on his fat wrist, and then dug in his shirt pocket and pulled out a cigarette pack. "Sí," said the woman, smiling openly now. "Sí sí sí sí!" squawked the little girl, trampling on the seat bed in her pink boats.

"Adiós." I grabbed my fins and mask, clambered down the corrugated bridge—steadying myself with one hand against its creosote logs at the foot—and waded across the swamp and marram grass to the boca.

A STINGRAY CIRCLED, poised before my face. It winged off.

The reef lay about one mile out, Ramón had said when I asked where I could go to try my luck. You carry your speargun in your hand, your game bag tied around your neck. You swim in a straight line past the breakers until you reach the first brain corals and then follow them to the fire coral and the branch formations. There at a depth of about ten feet you would find the glittering colors of the Caribbean: parrot fish, clown fish, barracudas with teeth like greyhounds, relays of lobster. A shrimp would creep about within an anemone's embrace and you could watch it struggle, the legs dancing like a racehorse's, until the anemone collapsed. The water was murkier than in the showcase reefs off Cozumel Island. Some real effort would be involved, more *ventura*.

Well, hey.

I turned toward the stingray, now vanishing into cloudy distance. The vault of water expanded outward, swarming with the galaxies of tiny fish and protein matter. Bits of seaweed floated by, and unidentified fragments that touched my arm or leg and then waggled away on the current. The tug pushed backward, forward where I hung suspended over a brain village. All the compensatory tricks failed here. Already the tides were destroying my balance; rings of nausea spun through my belly. I needed to be very careful not to lose my bearing in such big water and surrender to the flip-side effect. Dizzily I looked at the sand below. It reminded me of some giant species whose skulls had split like eggshells and dropped their pickled contents on the floor. Sea fans plumed up from the fissures. I aimed the gun at a lobster, shot. He scuttled under a shelf, sending debris jetting against my mask. The spear drifted downward. I ran out of air.

When I broke surface the bubbles fizzed against the maskplate like geysered diamonds, and I clamped my head rigid to still the whirl. Who cares? I thought in triumph. Then, turning toward land, I discovered the shoreline had disappeared. Nothing but waves, peaking, slipping, as far as I could see. But when I circled, panicking, the beach rose before me, ridged with coconut spires.

I took a wide lungful and dove.

The ocean is full of sound. Ticks and buzzings as steady as high-voltage wires, the liquid spurl of music against the eardrum. I kept the snorkel's tip half an inch above water and struck out between the brain colonies. A whining surrounded me, the joined energies of the lives here conducted through bands of water. The empty game bag floated bladder-like on my chest.

For an untold gap there was only movement as the muscles pulled— stroke, kick—and the seascape glided backward underneath. The current abolished time. Fish schools burst like meteor showers and curuscated from sight. The sun baked the backs of my thighs while the water chill penetrated into muscle. Soon I grew very aware of my body, its sinuosities and strengths, its stuffings, the joints hooking lengths together, glowing palely green. I shivered and the shivering became part of the water's movement. I couldn't gauge how far I'd traveled without looking up. I did not dare look up.

At some point my balance returned, but it had now been forged through water and fire to another sense altogether. I was accepted into the thickened world where green-brown blocks refracted into panels of shimmering light.

Once, twice, I paused to watch a fish eat another fish. With majesty a John Dory approached behind a silver flute and opened its jaws, then sailed out of view. A breed I didn't know, a blue slice banded with red and yellow, stared at me above its pout. I raised the speargun. It waited frozen by curiosity as I aimed, and I watched it watch as the unfamiliar instrument of its own death snicked into place. Suddenly I knew I could not effectuate that irony. At the instant I pulled the trigger the gun lowered. The spear shot out. The fish darted away from a more recognizable pursuer. The spear settled on a clump of coral. When I reached down to retrieve it, a pain stung through my hand and up my arm, scalding me into mindlessness. For a moment I couldn't move. Then, gulping air that was not air but water, I climbed to the glass ceiling, shattered it with my burning fist, and pulled the air inside.

The fire coral grew in scattered seams of rock. To stifle the pain I swam, hoping to hit the reef proper before too much longer, for the brain villages had broken up far behind me, behind the flocks of other swimmers I intersected and passed, and I thought, Well, of course this mile under the air and sky will be different from any I've known on land.

Then abruptly it changed.

At one moment I was hanging as a hawk hangs, looking down on the sloping plateau, and at the next the escarpment dropped sharply off fifty feet and I was soaring over the upper zones of water. I scanned the ledges deep below for a shape, any familiar shape. The quality of systole and diastole had changed; it was no longer insistent, but sucked meltingly through skin and marrow. I could no longer discern colors, or pick out the variances on the ocean floor. Sections of it vanished into blackness.

I was a mote in the endless void.

It was at this moment that I found the familiar shape.

He came from the invisible reaches, appearing through dark into the shifty light as a shadow takes on form and solidity. We were linked by mutual recognition. The fish earlier had not known Man with Leveled Speargun. But the dorsal fin and long slit smile I knew as the matador knows the bull. And he knew me as he knows, universally, all food.

For a few seconds he trailed idle, many feet below. The arc he described with his body lay wide yet fixed me inside its line, like a slowly drifting lasso. I saw the blank pebble of his eye. He cut around. The circle began to tighten.

He rose.

Taylor, you are no mote, I thought. *You are bait.*

Thrashing my hands before me, I paddled upward. A glint bounced off one knuckle. No upward existed; the snorkel's tip rode above the surface already, and I couldn't fly into the air. I was neither here nor there.

He was here.

Silence swallowed the world. Neither crying out nor fast talk were possible. There is no language underwater.

So I hung and watched my death draw in.

Just as he curled back out for the final charge, I looked at my hands. They seemed like things unattached, strange white creatures piloting alongside my coal of consciousness. The speargun was clenched in one, with its promise of nicks, grazes, and fruitlessly spilled blood. How many miles away can another shark smell blood? The right hand stiffened, a starfish pushing back the wave, and again the glint caught and sharpened the downpouring light. Now to wind up entombed in a coil of sharkshit on the bottom of the ocean, back into the earth from whence my father had buried and I'd mined it: his little nugget, the one thing besides money he'd ever bothered to give—which meant it must not have really mattered.

I had no armor, no defense.

I raised my eyes back to the spectacle of end. With regret I waited passively: with regret. They come like a freight train, I've heard. He reached his outer perimeter and wheeled. Then another shadow appeared through the dim curtains, racing toward his side. It swam too fast to distinguish its shape; from how many miles away? I wondered again. But before the shark could launch himself, the shadow rammed him like a torpedo.

For a second I didn't understand. The shadow pulled back and sheered off. Quadrants of light shifted against the murk into which it vanished. The shark juddered on the water. It lay motionless, rolling onto one side, its ghostly belly winking and flattening for a long time. Then slowly the tail moved, and it sank away toward the bottom.

My heart raced. The ache of fear left. The solitude stayed. I looked down to where the shark's body drifted. I couldn't believe it. What had the shadow been?

The ring shimmered, catching vision's edge. I steadied, turned, and began the long swim back to the shallows.

STOPPING MY STROKE, I tried to clear the blur; either the mask was fogged or I was going blind. The shore lay ahead in a pale smear, but it seemed to slip back and forward. I was fighting the outgoing tide. I had no more energy. Whatever the distance, I couldn't cross it. Each flounder weakened me. Groggily I wiped the maskplate clear.

Then I saw Ramón waiting cross-legged on the beach.

He was smoking a cigarette as I stumbled out of the surf.

"Buenos días."

I nodded, too tired to speak, and dropped onto the sand. It felt wet and warm and excellently hard, scraping against my face.

"How far you go out there?"

I didn't answer.

"I watched you from long way out for the last two hours, man. I been here longer. Look like you was miles."

I grunted.

"You came in from twice farther after the tide breaks."

"Deep," I agreed. "It got deep."

"Yeah?" He frowned and ground out the cigarette.

The lead of my limbs and body kept me nailed to the firm sand. I trembled all over.

"You went way past the reef then."

"There wasn't a reef."

"What? Hey—sure there's a reef."

I rolled onto my back and closed my eyes.

"See, look. Hola—Oiga!" He yelled it loudly over the crash of water.

"Sí?" a voice called.

I opened my eyes. Across the roiling boca on the sand apron stood two men grooming a fishing skiff. I hadn't even seen them when I stumbled out of the water. They stared. "Qué?" called the shorter of them.

"Donde esta el arrecife?"

They glanced at one another as if measuring Ramón's good sense. The spokesman pointed straight out to the horizon. "En el mar."

"Qué tan lejos es?"

"Es un milo."

"Gracias!" Ramón turned to me, smiled, lit another cigarette, and flicked the match away toward the palm-tree barrier. "You missed it."

"How? I did what you said. I found the brain. And fire coral." I held up my hand and showed him the red streaks.

"Maybe there's a gap."

I lay back and closed my eyes. The ring felt like it was cutting into flesh, my fingers swollen with saltwater like a drowned man's.

"You must got a lot of stamina, man. Look at your feet." His tone sounded respectful. I glanced down. The fins had rubbed blisters on my heels and insteps that rose like clear vinyl bubbles half an inch high. One instep had already popped, and the skin lay gashed, the inner meat exposed. "Bad news, chico. You need some medicine."

"Nah, it's all right."

"It's going to infect."

"It'll heal."

He peered curiously at my smile. "Okay. It's your feet, your scars. Was that taxicab up on the bridge when I come down here the one that brung you?"

"Yep. I guess."

"I think he's ready to split. Been waiting a long time, looking out here, you know?"

I raised up. "What time is it?"

Ramón shrugged. "I come mediodía. Twelve noon."

"Oh, man!"

"Hey, calm down."

Seizing my abandoned pants I scrabbled through the pocket for my watch. Three o'clock. "Christ. I got to go."

"You should rest, man."

"The last ferry leaves in forty minutes. I was out there five hours."

"Yeah?" His eyebrows rose. "No shit?"

"You coming?" I stood up and flung the pants around my wet-suit shoulders.

"Sure."

I squeezed the ring against my fingers while he clambered to his feet, feeling the letters form their word like braille on nerve endings. All right, I thought. Okay. A great peace descends when you suddenly, finally, understand exactly what you're going to do.

"Ramón. Before we leave—you know that poker game I beat you in the other night?"

"Sí."

"I don't want your money."

"Por qué?"

"I want a favor."

"Favor? What favor?"

"There are some skills I want you to teach me."

"Yeah? Like what, man?"

I smiled.

ISTHMUS

Theseus displaying not only great strength of body, but equal bravery, and a quickness alike and force of understanding, his mother Æthra, conducting him to the stone, and informing him who was his true father, commanded him to take from thence the tokens that King Ægeus had left for him, and sail to Athens. He without any difficulty set himself to the stone and lifted it up, [discovering the royal sword and sandals hidden beneath. But he] refused to take his journey by sea, though it was much the safer way, and though his mother and grandfather begged him to do so. For it was at that time very dangerous to go by land on the road to Athens, no part of it being free from robbers and murderers.

—Plutarch

4

The Bernice streets looked sparse and overly simple with their houses set just right on the lawns and the elms and post oaks bordering clean brick. My eyes were still full of Mexico. I walked down Ficklin, unfolding and refolding the paper in my pocket that Ramón had given me with the number on it. This was the end of April.

"I've arranged for a job in Dallas," I'd explained to Granddaddy when he asked for the final word. "About two weeks from now I'll start commuting up there for specialized training."

"What?" The news dispelled his plans for rural ingenuity. "I beg your pardon? Where is this?"

"It's in high-tech security. I got it through a friend. He'll train me free of charge."

"Doing what?"

"After I learn the ropes I can pretty much start on the ground floor, so to speak, and work my way up."

"Well, how come you to keep so quiet about it all this time?"

"It's an opportunity that's only just recently developed. But you know. Don't let the grass grow underfoot." I smiled.

"Hmph." He sat brooding a moment. "That's fine, son. Just fine. But tell me. Have you now gotten over that little upset?"

"Upset?" I blinked. "What upset?"

"I know it's a touchy subject." He paused. "About your daddy."

"Oh. That. Of course. No problem. Not at all."

"I just thought you might be hoping to, you know, someday catch his eye. Try to contact him somehow. But you weren't thinking of that, were you?"

"Definitely not trying to catch his eye, no, sir."

"I see." He cleared his throat. "Well, it's for the best. Mind you, I'm real proud of your initiative."

"My friends don't even know he exists."

"Finally jump-starting your motivation that way. You've come a right smart piece." He plucked on his lower lip and glanced toward my ring finger.

"I'm glad you think so, Granddaddy," I said.

The brick ended and gave way to asphalt. In the yards the morning sprinklers whirled, the roses bloomed white and red. I passed the Ledbetters' house with its ornamental bridge over the creek and then the six-car garage of the Hicks, all the doors open to array four-wheel-drive selections, plus their two Cadillacs and the classic Porsche. Next door stood the Clays' house, a plain three-bedroom ranch with peeling window frames. After that the neighborhood kind of went downhill. I reset my shoulders to adjust for the slope and headed for the elementary school yard where I had endured my first crucifixions.

Be very careful what you wish for, they used to say. You might get it.

I thought about my goals, arranged like beads on a string. The image of Teresa-Maria rose as I sat down in the grass. Teresa. Teresita. The girls I had been with before huddled bland and pallid beside her. Teresa's mouth would taste luscious. Teresa's eyes enlarged in my memory like black stars. I remembered that voice, a slippery cord. Her high breasts, her firm shoulders, her slender throat, the flowing black hair. I could hardly stand it.

The first woman I ever slept with was a bordertown whore. I was sixteen. I'd gone down to Matamoros with a couple of the ambulatory guys from the military academy. Of course we cruised straight into boys' town after an hour spent sauntering around the plaza and slugging down tequila shots to build courage. The whorehouse stood wide open to the street, with moth-eaten serapes blowing in the upstairs windows. Atmosphere. The whores looking out had seen us before; you could see in their faces that they figured they'd seen us all a million billion times, walking in through that early afternoon threshold with the cocky testosterone gringo-kid walk and pants full of hope plus a hundred in twenties and fives. Matamoros isn't Mexico; it's the gringo's most debased idea of Mexico, Mexico at the sewer line, the gutter that runs between the two countries and catches all the effluvia. My two friends were already a little drunk. Rick collapsed into a wooden chair and stared at his loafers, too shy to leer around at the workers or their clientele. Chelmsford III stomped up to the bar and smacked his withered fists down on it as loudly as he could. It wasn't very loud. He asked for a tequila, sealing his lips and shoving the words out between them like paper through an envelope: Clint Eastwood. The barman poured him one. I'll grant this: even in a sleazy bare-bones dive like that one the Mexican people have grace enough not to laugh. Chelmsford III clamped the glass between his webby permanent fists and hoisted it to his mouth in a motion like one of those mechanical birds dipping toward a water glass. By now the girls were watching. Two of them, about our age but already stale and crumpled-looking at the edges, came up and fastened onto him and Rick. Rick's sat down in his lap. They both started murmuring and suggesting things in Spanglish. "Te gusto cunt?" that kind of stuff. Rick turned red as a fire engine, but Chelmsford III grinned evilly and said, You bet. So far nobody had paid any attention to me; most of the whores seemed to be upstairs for siesta or maybe out shopping. But one woman leaned against the far wall opposite the bar, her eyes agate-surfaced and her purple mouth wicked down at the corners. She twisted the end of a tress around her forefinger, not in boredom but with the inevitability of the hour. She was older than the first two. My head went a little dizzy as I closed my eyes: please keep me upright, don't let me fall, I prayed. Carefully I walked up to her.

"Excuse me. May I offer you a drink?"

She shook her head.

"Are you, um, free right now?"

She didn't budge. "Tal vez."

I thought that it might be in poor taste to ask her how much. Hell, I didn't care how much if it was under a hundred.

"You want to screw?" she asked with her harsh eyes tacked to mine.

"Yes." I had to whisper; my voice was creaking.

"Come up this." She walked toward the stairs and I followed.

In her room I watched her shuck off the tight skirt, ignoring me. She unbuttoned her blouse and dropped it like a husk on the floor, but the skirt she folded carefully. Underneath she wore a slip. She kept her shoes on, battered flat blue sandals setting off the yellow creases on her heels.

"You want naked?"

"Yes, please." I was shaking a little by this time. Her sweat scent climbed up the air, mixed with strong cologne. My hard-on almost burst my zipper. Pulling at the straps, she tugged the slip below her waist. Her large-nippled breasts spilled and swung out over the black nylon as she bent down; her bare arms were still firm and sleek. Her belly emerged, a pale billowing cumulus that held the weather of her life. She wore black underwear. I could see where she'd been, how she'd survived throughout all the years so far, the lusters and scars and erosion, the silvery stretch marks radiant from her navel suggesting children—and also that her life was an absolute mystery, ageless. I had never beheld anyone or anything so beautiful.

"Should I—would you prefer it if—"

"Shh," she said.

Urgency took over. I didn't know where to put my hands. They seemed driven by an uncontrollable force, burning both to scoop up, cover every inch, and to seize and grip the heart of the matter, while the rest of me wanted to press against, ram, slip and slide, everything. Right before I sank into her I started to ask her name. She must have seen it in my eyes through long practice. She said, "Ninguno. Inutil. Is no matter."

Even in vertigo I could see that she was correct. "Yeah, okay."

Teresa would be the first of my life's rewards. Everything so far, I knew, even the place where I'd lost my virginity, had led up to her.

Across the school yard lay a curve in the street lined with house lots. Three of the houses were for sale and had been for some time, ever since this part of the neighborhood started to decline. I looked at the one to the far right. Like the others, it was built of brick and frame, with a steepled front porch. Once it had been occupied by Ronnie Dean Jordan, a spectacled second-grade intellectual who had possessed a brilliance of malice astonishing in a child so young, especially one whose mother made him wear Buster Brown Sunday wing tips to school. His subtle and elaborate art had taken me by surprise during many a milk break; early on he'd comprehended the principle of my weakness and how to manipulate it without detection, and he would sponsor hisses designed to prompt the quick flinch or engender the menacing flutter in the peripheral vision that rolled the room or the sky upside down. He was a master. Sometimes I wondered if I represented for him merely a scientific experiment with a bonus, that of comedic buffoon. Once he organized a group of kids to creep up without my notice and stand at different spots around and behind me and then in all friendliness to call out my name and point somewhere and say, "Look!" (He knew the instinctive impulse upon hearing one's own name.) The name-calling was carefully orchestrated to have a chain effect, so that I would twist right and up, then far left down, then whip to the right almost in a circle. Some unerring intuition told him to use mostly girls. It worked at first. By the time I caught on the playground was careening in all directions, the faces of the girls had become blurred and unrecognizable. I must have looked like a human windmill. They'd already started giggling. For an instant, even as Emily Bristow was softly coaxing, "Taylor—Taylor," I managed to focus by locking onto a post in the far distance. Then I realized that the post was Ronnie Dean Jordan. He had his new Official Frog-man's wristwatch turned to the sun, and as he glanced to me, to it, back to me, his gaze scrupulous and intent, the full import of the scene hit me. He was timing to see how long before I keeled over.

I made for him, veering right and left like a ship correcting course. At the last second I lunged and skidded toward his ankles, planning to throw him halfway across the yard and rip his throat out. But the disorientation had been too great. I lay where I landed, staring up through the maelstrom of light and air into his spinning eyes inside their thick glass jars.

The stupider people of course went wild with delight. "Nine seconds," he said, tilting the green-and-black watch face to the girls, and smiled.

Now Ronnie Dean was forever out of reach. He'd been killed two years before when a pickup full of drunk rodeo bull-riders hit his Mazda. I'd attended the funeral, seen his mother double up wailing, his father's icy grimace, seen the way they'd laid him out in his band uniform in the coffin with his glasses still on and raspberry lipstick tinting his lips. His old house with the Realtor sign stood forlorn: no computer monitors glowed through his bedroom window. That was why, suddenly, I knew what I had to do—the next step toward my new career. It was, in fact, irresistable.

The trick lay in going around to the back without being seen. As far as I understood, Ronnie Dean's parents still lived there, although the flower beds looked neglected and dandelions bristled by the front walk. Mrs. Jordan worked at Ciskill's Florist downtown. Mr. Jordan was manager of the Lone Star Gas Company office. I doubted I would encounter a maid. On the other hand, it was eleven thirty-five and they might be coming home for lunch.

I waited for a couple of cars to rush by before I crossed the street. A pyracantha hedge walled the backyard beyond the carport. I had to ease through it, feeling the thorns comb my bare arms and legs. The yard was a scrub wilderness. Treeless and overgrown, its plain stretched gray with dead bitterweed to the fence line. A redwood picnic table knelt on the patio, two of its legs splintered in half. Beneath it a green plastic clothespin

poked out of a gap between flagstones. Off in one far corner the old trac-
tor-tire sandpile lay studded with the feces of neighborhood cats. A rusted
Duck Tales–enameled beach pail sat neatly beside the patio doors, planted
with a leggy begonia. This relic of Ronnie Dean I found disquieting; I had
had one just like it, bought by my mother at Miss Francie's Toyland down
the block from the Palace Theater. Mine was long gone, but Ronnie Dean's
suddenly connected us in a way our age and classrooms had never done.
Shovel the sand into the pail, then find a doodlebug crawling along the tire
edge and bam! dump the avalanche. Then finger tunnel-holes to see if he
could escape. You too, Ronnie Dean?

I glanced to left and right, checking the houses over the fence, and
turned my attention to the patio sliders.

Drapes of nubby brown material hid the view inside. The lock was a
simple aluminum/steel latch, the third least challenging possible according to my manual. Nonetheless, I studied it for a minute before trying to
pop it. It could be connected to a hidden security system, or have a drop
bolt on the inside that would defeat me.

But it didn't.

Taking the slip of plastic from my wallet pocket I inserted it between
the frame and door edge. So far I'd only practiced on rooms in our house,
and even then the pantry had wound up sealed away for two days until I
could figure out how to pick it with a bobby pin. Fortunately no one had
thought to cook a meal during that time. I jiggled the plastic down into
the lock area, feeling it balk and flex around the metal hook.

Then hey, presto: my first break-and-enter.

Once the door opened I eased past the drapes into a den. Shadows
occluded it, the sunshine cut off clean as a knife against the windowpanes.
Blinking, I saw the room was a long sideways rectangle painted in browns.
I rolled the slider closed. Cold sweat ran down my neck, my heart pounded.
Silence from the outside swelled against taut eardrums, emptied, and then
got replaced by a soft burble. A Barcalounger sloped opposite the television
console, its footrest stacked with frayed magazines. Underfoot, the indoor/

outdoor carpeting bore rake marks from recent vacuuming. Against the wall stood a jewel box of light. Its interior burned with shifting color: green, crimson, gold, electric blue. It was from this the gurgling came, filling every corner and niche as unceasingly as the bloodstream swooshing through the veins in my own head. Fish lolled and darted behind seaweed fronds. Above the glass, half vivid in the refracting light, photographs filed across the wall: Ronnie Dean at one. Ronnie Dean at three, perched on a rocking horse. Ronnie Dean's second-grade glasses branded with high-lights; the twelve-year-old chubcheeks; the junior high math whiz accept-ing a trophy; the spiffed-up dude at the junior prom, his face greenish white under the flash. Ronnie Dean in band uniform, the same he was buried in. It was as if a fissure had opened exposing this motherlode of crystallized images. He stared out amid every stage of his seventeen years through eyes as dead and remote and inaccessible to his parents as he was to me. A frigid chill hung on the air like a substance. My skin bloomed with goose bumps. The room felt spiritually inflamed.

For a moment, scanning from one picture to another, I lost equilib-rium. The room shimmied with a cathedral darkness. I transfixed my head until it stopped, turned to go, and then paused. This seemed too easy. Was repulsion the end booty, the thing I'd performed my inaugural cat burglary to gain? Was this the prize of the test? So far I'd only penetrated a moon-scape of private grief. Now it seemed the photographs rose like a disguise, a barrier excluding me from what I had really come for.

I had to break through their charmed guardianship to get to the real place.

Two chasms stood on either side of the bright aquarium. One held dis-tant, slanting sunshine. The other plunged dark as the mouth of a cave. I stepped past Ronnie Dean's simulacra into the darkness. A hallway scented with floral Airwick led past a folded shutter door and on to the bedroom wing. The first door stood wide, disclosing pink satin bedspreads with lace pillows. The second was the bathroom. The third looked shallower somehow, less recessed in its frame, and I took it as probably a closet. The fourth, on the opposite wall, was shut tight.

I pressed my palms against the wood. After a few seconds I thought I felt a faint vibration. Perhaps it was traffic from the street, perhaps not. The hammered-copper doorknob glinted in its varnished ugliness, prompting me to wonder if it could lock. Are you in there, Ronnie Dean?

I twisted the knob.

The door swung open.

Now the symptoms of panic engulfed me, the sweat stinging out of pores, short breath, cotton tongue. Hastily I shut the door behind me and thumbed down the lock button on the inside knob. Success is a true disrupter of the central nervous system. Before, even at the patio sliders, everything had lacked this final reality.

Ronnie Dean's bed was unmade.

I stood staring at the jumbled spread, the mashed-in pillows. The green cotton blanket lay where he'd kicked it off last. The headboard was strewn with pajama bottoms and a pair of underwear. Above them on a red rope dangled the golden cornet he'd played in the Marching Cougars Band, obviously recently polished. Down along one wall stood a built-in desk surface with an open calculus textbook. In a corner a single brown wing tip shoe listed on its side.

I swallowed hard. You knew, I said to myself, you knew good and well this room would be the shrine, you knew when you saw his mother fold and sink down to the floor by that casket how she'd keep it. The real estate sign had made me wonder, that was all.

I turned and traced a line in the dust. One of the two closet doors was missing altogether, and the clothes hung half in half out like shadowed presences. I remembered how small he'd been for his age in grade school, the narrow wrists. No one had polished anything else, only the instrument. That his mouth had touched. And his hands, and fingers.

A queasiness rode up. It had no part of vertigo and it drove me to the curtained window to clutch for level sunlight. How could they bear to sell the place where he'd lived? How could anybody tour through it, look at it speculatively, after seeing what lay in here? How could they sell this room?

I stared at everywhere Ronnie had been and still was. I thought of his mother's emptiness where he was no longer.

They just could.

I thought of my father and gritted my teeth.

A crunch sounded in the graveled driveway.

Wheeling, I stared at the closed door. Outside a car door slammed. Then a second. Another crunch of tires in the drive braking to a stop, another pause and slam, and then I heard the bell-like tones of women's voices.

Before I could even think, I'd charged over to the door, checked that it was locked, and stood hard against it. From the porch came a clop and scuffing of shoes on cement. I turned, wildly. My balance was churning now, the room rotating like a clothes dryer. Where? Where where where where—then suddenly the image came to me, of the man creeping from the hotel room into the sunlight, overslung with cameras and handbags. His eye as he turned.

Moving straight across the floor I dove into the closet. Scrabbling through the tangle of old dirty socks, I reached a haven behind the hanging clothes. There I panted, trying to huddle, my head and shoulders crunched like Quasimodo's, too much arm, leg, too much body. The awning of shadows blotted out my hair, the broad white shield of forehead, down to below my eyes where the rack commenced, and to trust that camouflage was all I could do. My chief worry was that they'd heard the thumps through the floor. Nothing in the room had been touched or disarranged. This was a comforting thought until I caught sight of the closed door. Then I remembered the lock.

The front door moaned. "Oh, blue," said a voice. "I hadn't expected blue. It's nice."

"Charming. Charming," cooed another voice.

"Is there a hall coat closet?"

"See, you have this cute foyer and then off to the right this pretty lit-tle country dining room. No, there's not a coat closet, but I think standing hat racks are really charming, don't you? Old-fashioned. A nice antique one would be." The footsteps sounded clearly audible, the clip of their heels on hardwood. The house was built with the acoustics of a cigar box.

"We never really needed a coat closet," said a third voice in apology.

"It was colder this winter, that's what all I'm thinking of."

"You could maybe put up some hooks in the den, I guess. My good-ness, it's so lucky I happened to come home for lunch right as you all drove up so I can answer any questions," said the third voice.

"Um-hm. Real coincidence," said the hat-rack favorer, dryly.

"I can show you around."

"Thanks, but that's all right. I'll show Mrs. Harper through," she said, deadly sweet. "Or we can come back in a few minutes after you've gone. We don't want to keep you from your lunch hour."

"You're not! Truly! My goodness! I'm just so glad to help."

The Realtor coughed.

"Oh, look how you've done the window treatments in here. Isn't it cute!" The one who'd wanted a coat closet pushed onward. "And you just go through this swing door to the kitchen, don't you? Oh, my, that inter-esting plaid paper."

"It's kind of old. It was here when we bought it," said the apologist.

"It could come up, couldn't it? I mean, if we ever decided to change."

"I'm sure it would be no problem whatsoever. And beyond here is the den. See what a big room it is. Playroom, TV room, solarium when those glass doors are exposed—" They had entered the burbling ambience.

"What pretty fish!" said the tourist.

Behind Ronnie Dean's final garments I rationed out a deep breath while I considered. There was no way out. The too-small window faced the street. The bed frame stood impossibly short and low, its covers looped and tossed at different altitudes. A pocket of nocturnal dark enveloped the far corner of the closet. I eased over and crouched above a batch of cardigans, breathing in their scent; there was the first outer blossom, a metallic musk that had struck me when I'd entered the room, but now I was noticing strata underneath it, subtler petals composed of mildew and stale acne lotion. All the notes had a vintage quality, seasoned for two long years in the close vacuum of this tomb. It was as if Ronnie Dean was seeping nearer, as if against my will I was being sucked into an intimacy far beyond my original intentions, beyond the surprise ambush I'd hoped for, beyond the satisfaction of a secret, triumphal violation, and he would filiment into my arteries and slip through my bones to the marrow. I was getting to know Ronnie Dean too well. The violation, once more, was turning into mine.

You've got me, boy. This time in your full embrace.

"The bedrooms are of course down the hall. Only two, but then that's all you need, isn't it, just you and your husband? I don't know that a second bathroom would be any use to you, but I've always thought someone could add one in this big storage closet here if they wanted to." The agent was back, presiding over the house's possibilities. Her tones scarcely hid her exasperation. "There's plumbing connections right through the wall on the other side."

"From what?"

"Why, the first bathroom. It's in here, did you not see it?"

"Oh, how nice. Plenty of tilework."

"Murray regrouted it last fall," murmured Mrs. Jordan. They moved down the hall.

"The bedrooms are quite large for this size of house, as you can see."

"Is the other one this big?"

"Yes, I think it nearly is. Let's take a look."

I waited for Mrs. Jordan to protest.

"Because it's tucked back at the end of the corridor it gets a lot of privacy, I suspect. Mrs. Jordan, will you—"

"I'm afraid we better not," she replied timidly.

"Oh, really?"

"Ronnie Dean's always fighting to keep people out of his room. He's been a little put out that we're selling, since he grew up here. He doesn't like us to show it. Teenagers, you know."

For a moment there was a silence.

"I see, well, I think we need to, you know." The Realtor must have reached swiftly down to the knob. I held my breath. Nothing happened.

"It's locked," said the Realtor.

"Oh! How—Is it?" Mrs. Jordan sounded all at once breathless.

"Yes," said the Realtor evenly. "It is." I was just about to heave a huge shudder of relief when she added, "But never mind, I've got my Swiss Army knife in my purse. I'll just—" She scrabbled around for a moment. I heard a steel rattle, then a click. "There!"

"Oh, a screwdriver. How smart!" cried Mrs. Harper, the prospective buyer. Mrs. Jordan let out a whimper of distress. The door swung silently open.

Framed beyond it like a cameo stood three women: a tall, lacquered blonde in heavy gold earrings and green silk suit; a smaller woman beside her in striped cotton knits, with short curly brown hair, a round face, and some of the biggest breasts I'd ever seen. A little behind them both, a tired Mrs. Jordan waited with a spray of violets pinned to the belt of her dress.

"Oh," said the buyer.

The Realtor cleared her throat.

"My, well. It is large, isn't it." Mrs. Harper exchanged a flashing glance with the Realtor that revealed she was in on the tragedy. Her face appeared as a study of restrained pity, caution, and dismay.

"Yes, it is," said the Realtor.

"Oh, dear."

"What?" The Realtor half turned to Mrs. Jordan.

"No wonder he locked us out. He hasn't cleaned his room again, I'm afraid." Mrs. Jordan peered over their shoulders.

The Realtor opened her mouth.

"I asked him, too. I told him to especially."

Silence fell.

"'Take some out time from your trumpet practice,' I told him. But they just don't listen when you want them to. Ronnie Dean's so messy. Just look at this." She sighed a proud, helpless sigh. "Isn't he awful?"

"Ah—ahem," said Mrs. Harper, smiling brightly, blindly at the walls. The Realtor rocked from heel to heel.

"But what can I do? He's always so busy. Wrapped up in his projects. I just don't know."

There was a long pause. I inhaled the emanations of Ronnie Dean from his sports jacket. They seemed fresher somehow.

"With a different carpet, some strong, colorful drapes—," murmured the Realtor.

"Wait until I talk to him tonight. He was so neat when he was little, too. The neatest thing! Then he got caught up in that computer, you know how they do lately"—Mrs. Jordan pointed to the Macintosh on the end of the built-in desk—"and that's the last you see of them. They hardly come out except at suppertime. Murray and I've just shaken our heads over the situation. 'That thing is worse than the TV,' Murray used to say. Now he doesn't even bother commenting anymore. Not that Ronnie Dean has ever been that big a television fan. No, he likes his studies. Math. That and his music." Her voice dwindled on its faint whine.

"Ah," said the Realtor.

For a moment no one spoke.

"But Murray says we need to get our money out of it. The house, I mean."

"I, uh—tell me. I just wonder just what kind of closet space there is in there. It looks as if it might be quite deep, actually." The second woman stepped forward. "Unless it's deceptive." She started across the room at a brisk pace, her breasts shivering with each impact. The Realtor stood back, looking grim and relieved. "I'll just bet anything that if you put the doors back on—"

I watched, fascinated, as she navigated around the bed foot, sidestepping Ronnie Dean's briefcase and sneakers, coming closer in split-second increments. The breasts bobbed under the knit like live things. As she ducked sideways to avoid the trailing blanket one wandered almost into her armpit, and then scooted back when she straightened. I couldn't stop staring. I couldn't help it. Her face was a mask of determination. Any second now.

"He doesn't like it when we mess with his things," said Mrs. Jordan nervously.

"Oh, well, I'm such a demon for closet space. I'm sure he wouldn't mind if I just peeked a tiny bit into the corners, now would he?" Her voice had developed a patronizing edge. For some reason, even in the midst of imminent discovery, this irritated me.

"I just don't know." The reply hung plaintively.

"Just let me twitch these things aside—" She'd reached the closet. Her hands shot out, grasped the hangers. My chest was ready to burst. Then out of desperation, I expelled a long, thin breath.

The hands stopped. "What was that?"

No one answered.

"Did you hear that?"

"Hear what?" asked the Realtor.

"There must be a draft in here."

"What do you mean?"

I filled my lungs slowly. Slowly I let the air back out in a wind-filled sigh.

"That! That." The second woman turned.

"A draft," said the Realtor uncertainly. The room lay still, patently airless.

I breathed in, out again, loudly, sending the stream from the deepest corner of the closet. My mind had become a blank. I didn't know now why I'd done it the first time.

"Ronnie Dean," said Mrs. Jordan.

"It sounds so close," whispered the second woman.

"You mean like a breeze-type draft?" The Realtor paled. She'd heard it now.

"Yes." The second woman began backing carefully away from the closet opening.

"Maybe the window's open. Just a crack, maybe. Or some crack in the walls, between the bricks—"

"Oh, no. This room has always been airtight. The whole house is. Murray takes pride in how tightly it's put together," said Mrs. Jordan. "He checks the mortar every spring, and fills in any tiny little problems the winter might have brought on."

"That's—wonderful," gasped the second woman. She headed straight for the doorway.

"Good that he keeps it up so well," said the Realtor, hurrying after her as she ran down the hall.

Mrs. Jordan stood where she was. She cocked her head for a moment, listening. Their footfalls sounded toward the foyer, and then came the squeak of the front door's hinges, the wheeze as it closed. Slowly Mrs. Jordan walked all the way into the room. She glanced around at the relics, and then put her hands on her hips and peered directly beyond the clothes at the closet mouth.

"Ronnie Dean?" she said softly.

I caught my breath.

"Now, you know better. You can't keep scaring people off this way. It hurts your daddy." She paused, surveying the clutter, and shook her head. She smiled a little chiding smile. "You need to be good."

Then she turned and left, closing the door gently behind her. After a moment the front door wheezed again distantly, and the sound of a car door followed, the motor droning away.

5

The day I started for Dallas I was driving a brand-new Ford Escort, Granddaddy's end contribution to my business endeavor.

It suited me fine. When I considered how many options he might have tried to please with—sporty two-doors, red convertibles, racy Jeeps, all manner of speed-trap candy—I was gratified at the inevitability of his good sense and thrift. Conservative, American, gray and discreet as a June rain cloud: the perfect car to park down the block of a residential street or outside an office building and then rest easy in the knowledge of its invisibility.

Adjusting the air-conditioning to arctic strength, I zoomed up Interstate 35 toward the flatlands, keeping my vision field calibrated from windshield to rearview to sideview mirrors without any sudden moves. Four-lane highways are merciful to the balance-impaired; it's when you get in city traffic that life turns tricky. Texas spread out right and left, green under the infinite sky. I had gotten Ramón's call the night before. He'd just finished dinner after having flown in from Cancún airport. His flight had been paid for by the company. He was ready to roll.

"So what were you eating?" I asked him. Mother and Dodie sat in the living room beyond the phone table, watching TV.

"Qué?"

"What was for dinner?"

"Oh." He considered, sounding puzzled. "Menudo. Enchilados."

"I wouldn't mind some of that. I only had a bad burger."

The credits began for *Melrose Place*. Dodie got up, swilled down her glass of iced tea, and left the room. Mother switched to some footage of a house burning, with blackened bodies carried out on stretchers. "Bomb Site in South Dallas," said a caption.

"Are you doing anything tonight?"

"No sé. Talk with my uncle, maybe."

"Oh. How about work? Have they assigned you a hotel? Do you know where you'll be?"

"Hotel?" he scoffed. "You ask a lot of strange questions."

I watched as Mother turned from the screen. Her only official interest in the broadcast lay in the anchorwoman's yellow suit and faultless mani-cure, which would get critiqued by rote after the weather report. "I don't intend to."

"Forget it."

"Well, welcome back to Texas, anyhow. Hey—by the way. Did anybody come with you?"

Another brief pause; this time I could tell he was grinning. "Tal vez."

"What do you mean? Don't you know?"

"She's on the patio with her madre."

My breath hitched. I pictured this: the homey scene, a few geraniums, a potted cactus or two, the mother bending her head to listen to a work anecdote. The daughter, facing her, lustrous as a lantern in the sunset dusk.

"Well then, guess what?" I said.

"What?"

"See you first thing tomorrow morning."

AFTER WAXAHACHIE COMES the wide sweeping scour of sorghum, cotton, and grazing cattle. Then the interstate veers northwest and Dallas appears in the distance on its skillet of prairie. A lucid happiness welled inside me when I caught sight of it: the buildings pale with aerial space, blocked like shirt boxes and fence posts that some determined child had clustered against the vast emptiness and the robin's-egg sky. As I got closer I could make out belted and cinched concrete loops of interchange, tollway, expressway, overpass, highway, all of it wrapping the Metroplex like a Christmas package dropped on the plain. Unlike Houston, Austin, the other cities I know, Dallas still regards itself as an outpost on the frontier. This view sustains its historic snobbery. And although we were living at the end of the twentieth century, make no mistake, the frontier was still out there: Neiman Marcus exuberance, brassy new money turned old, the joint habits of luxury and outspokenness, these merely reinforced an ironclad will to hold that wild west at bay. Beyond the city limits lay dry tracts and feral lands; to the east, pine woods still shaded Southern front porches. But here among these deep, lush gardens, the trimmed hedges and bulb beds and caladiums and oaks under which housewives pushed their perambulators to the Range Rover to load the baby for Brain Gym, here in the midst of the millionaire gossip and the best private schools, a canny defiance inhabited the soul. This was my mother's territory: Big D—Highland Park, Turtle Creek, Christofle flatware and Baccarat iced tea pitchers by the pool, fifty-thousand-dollar Christmas lights, Guatemalan maids climbing down from the farting city bus for a long day's ironing. Matisses in the guest bathroom. The optimism of brash country folk.

Oak Cliff was something else.

At 8:00 A.M. I parked outside the pink house on Lee Street next to a dirt driveway. In front stood two rusty old cars with primer coats still unfinished. Chrome objects glittered under the sun. A plastic tricycle lay upended by the sidewalk, its rear wheels gone. The houses up the street looked old, the window frames painted dead black, the warped porches bowed in the middle like hammocks. Ramón's uncle's house was more recent—late fifties, maybe, built from cement blocks in a rectangle, with cheap metal window hasps. As I locked the car door I could smell melting creosote and the promise, not to be kept, of rain.

The mimosas along the chain-link yard fence already hung shaggy and bleached with heat. The earth lay cracked like a highway map. A broken glass jar half buried in the dirt nearly tripped me as I walked toward the front door; I had to swing sharply and trim my balance by force. Sidling up the two concrete steps, I knocked on a screen with aluminum cutouts of flamingos. It rattled in the frame. The odor of fried onions and chorizo drifted through it. Mariachi music blared: *Yahh ni-ni-ni-ni-ni-ni-nahh!* My heart bumped.

After a minute a woman appeared.

"Hi. My name is Taylor Troys. I'm here to see Ramón."

"Qué? Ramón?"

"Yes. He's expecting me."

She searched me doubtfully. Her face tensed. Black eyes chill with wariness gauged my height, traveling down, up, then up. Her body looked dumpy as an oat bag tied in the middle with a cloth belt; she wore barrettes in her hair. She resembled nothing like my earlier phone fantasies, but it was evident from the mouth whose mother she was.

"I know Teresa-Maria, too," I said.

Surprise stopped her face. The eyes switched back to mine.

"I met them both on Cozumel."

"Ahh!"

"Don't worry, ma'am. I'm not from the Department of Immigration or anything like that."

"No, no." She shook her head, frowning, and flapped a hand up and down as if the idea couldn't even possibly have occurred to her. "You come in, please," she said, holding the door open.

"Thank you."

A little boy about ten years old with feathery black hair popped up behind her. He stared round-eyed for a second, then scurried away. I was struck by how ragged everything looked: the wallpaper edges torn and deckled, raked with crayon scrawls. Underfoot the old beige linoleum had buckled like gopher tunnels on a lawn, silted with deltas of grime. My hostess gestured for me to follow her to the living room. There, on a plastic couch under a bleak, chain-hung mirror, sprawled Ramón.

His arms were flung wide, one up against the wall, the other trailing to the floor. The old undershirt he wore was mooned with sweat stains and tucked into tight blue gym shorts.

"He's sleeping," observed his aunt.

"Yep. I sure see that."

"There was shooting in the night."

"Shooting?"

"Sí. Next door, they come in a car."

"You mean—like *drive-by* shooting?"

She nodded, studying Ramón for a moment. His mouth caved wide open, we could hear breathing in the back of his throat, like some hibernatory animal. "At one o'clock they come to the Hidalgo house. They got the little baby in the arm."

"They shot a baby's *arm?*"

"No. She was in the arm of her mother. Sleeping. The bullet hit her here." She pointed to her temple.

I didn't know what to say.

"The ambulance man say it's a miracle the baby she's not dead."

"But my God—what are the police doing?"

"Nada."

"But—why?"

"It's just gangs." She shrugged listlessly. "How they catch them?" Then abruptly she turned her back, dabbing her eyes, and scuffed off down the hall.

I stood for a second. Ramón's nose twitched; he drew a rattling snore. A black sombrero rashed with sequins hung beside the mirror. Toy parts lay scattered across the floor, a cereal bowl of mushy Froot Loops sat perched dangerously on the TV's edge.

This was new territory.

Somewhere in this house, I thought, she was crossing a floor, standing beside a sink, drowsing under a single sheet. The danger she'd been exposed to would be haunting her, she wouldn't know where to turn. My nerves sharpened; I prowled to the door and stopped, training my ears beyond the music's thump for some atom of disclosing sound. I could sense her heat. I felt the animal-like power surge, the omniscience granted to few mere mortal men. I knew absolutely that she was only a few feet away.

Ramón gagged out a sigh. A faint laugh floated on the distance. It might have been a child's. The image of her breasts rose, round and pointed under the orange blouse, and quivered like a flame.

"Hey, hombre." Ramón stirred on the couch.

His gravelly voice cut my thrall like a rasp across butter. "Hey!" I said. "You awake now?"

"Sí."

"How you doing?"

"Malo."

"Your aunt said you-all had a rough night. Sorry to hear it." I crossed over and held out my hand.

He shook it. "You see Teresa-Maria?"

"Not yet."

"Hm." Coughing, he rubbed his red eyes with splayed fingertips. "She been thinking about you, man."

"How do you know?"

"She asked if I talk to you."

I walked to the TV and shoved the cereal bowl a few inches back. A milk smear was drying on the plastic. "She did? So, uh—where is she?"

"She stay last night at her friend's house. She'll be back later. Mediodía, probable."

"Ah." I came back and sat down, deflated. Then I thought: She missed the shooting.

He nudged himself up higher onto the couch arm. Smacking dry lips, he made a guttural sound. "I need some water."

"You want me to go ask your aunt?"

"Nah. Last night went bad, man. My uncle, he's worried about the kids around here."

"Yeah. I can see why."

Yawning, he scrubbed his neck and frowned. "It scared mi little primo, man. My little cousin. He's ten years old, little guy. He talked big. 'I join a gang, light up the other gangs' houses. Those hijos de putas.' That bullshit. Already he don't listen to mi tío y tía no more."

"Why not?"

He shrugged. "Kids talk tough when they're freaked out, you know?"

"What's your uncle doing?"

"He wants Juan to come back, talk to mi little primo."

"Juan?" I blinked. My favorite bandito. "Will Juan do that?"

"He's coming from Mexico. My little cousin Ricardo, he honors Juan— you know, respeto."

"Wouldn't Ricardo listen to you? Or Teresa-Maria? She's his older sister, isn't she?" I tried to imagine what eloquence Juan could offer to discourage a young juvenile from neighborhood crime.

He shook his head. "Juan es mejor."

"I thought he can't enter the country."

"More than one way to travel, hijo."

"So when is he due?"

"When he gets here. Dos semanas. Juan don't like Mexico, he prefer the action."

"Don't we all."

"Not me, ese. I want to go to college."

His arms were propped behind his head, the characteristic look of gravity fixed on his face. I remembered how we'd met, our discussions, all that insatiable reading he'd done through the years. How was it I had not seen this most basic truth about him?

"Well, hell. You can do that. No sweat," I said.

He shook his head again. "I need American high school."

"So what? Take the GED, you'll sail through."

He said nothing, brooding toward the far wall.

"What's the hitch? Money?"

"The company pays okay. Not because they know what I plan. They pay if I work first. Juan's connections. I work a little, it can happen." He paused. His eyes narrowed. "I ain't told nobody. This is my private thinking, Taylor."

"Well, naturally."

He nodded. I perceived the trust that had just been offered, and it made me wonder suddenly if I would be as willing to reveal my counterpart: the revenge driving my plans, the reasons for his tutelage. Friendship is a skill one masters as it unfolds, I thought, like burglary.

"Does the hotel company pay the kind of money that will send you through school these days? They got some program?"

"Hotel?" Then he snorted. "It ain't no hotel. Ain't you got it?"

And on some level, of course, I had.

RAMÓN HAD GOT up, shaved, dressed, and was pouring condensed milk into our coffee cups when Ricardo came pounding into the kitchen. "Mama! Mama! Teresa-Maria!"

"Tía Bianca went to the supermarket," Ramón said.

"The baby's dead!"

Ramón set the can down. Ricardo goggled. "They're screaming real loud. At the Hidalgos'. Bobby Hidalgo's going to go shoot the guys."

"They *know* who did it?" I asked.

"Of course!"

But Ramón's eyes had turned to dark stone. Beyond him the light flared and contracted on the wall as the wind tossed leaves outside the window. "Show me where Bobby goes," he said to Ricardo.

"He don't go nowhere yet. He's still home."

Ramón stood up. "Hasta luego," he said, heading for the back door. But by the time he'd reached it I was right beside him.

We hurried across the yard without speaking. When we got to the Hidalgos' front door, Ramón drummed on it very softly with his fingertips. Broken glass crackled underfoot on the porch boards. A spray of bullet holes splintered the wood grain. The old woman who answered his knock looked winded, as if someone had punched her in the solar plexus a few minutes before and she was still trying to recuperate. "Hola," she whispered. Tears streamed unheeded down her cheeks, along the cracks and creases. Her face shone white as candle wax. "Entrada."

He stepped up and squeezed her arm. "Lo siento," he murmured. Her head bowed, her eyes shut tight. After a moment he said, "Dónde está Bobby?"

"En la sala."

Carefully he walked past her into the hall. I followed, ducking in respect. She didn't open her eyes or look up.

The corridor had pine floors and high old ceilings. Bedrooms opened off to either side; behind one closed door I could hear a person sobbing. The whole house smelled of grief, of death, of the ozone before lightning.

At a closed door in the hall's end Ramón stopped, thrusting against it flat-handed. As it swung open the room inside erupted.

"*Who's that?*"

"Bobby," he said.

Two teenage boys stood poised. One of them was aiming a gun straight at my heart.

"*Ssst!*" The hiss seemed to come from low in the boy's body when he looked up and saw me. His eyes widened. His features froze.

"Put it down." Ramón stepped in, staring.

"Ramón! Shit! What do you want?"

"Not to get shot, for first."

"The fuck you doing here, man?"

"Talking to you, ese."

"You better knock, you don't want to get shot by mistake."

He was about fifteen. A black down veiled his upper lip and chin; the cheeks were sunken, stressing the cusp of his jaw. He looked underfed. His eyes darted nervously toward me, jaw clenching fast as a clock tick. "Who's this?"

Ramón glanced briefly to me. "A friend."

"You bust in here, bring some pendejo."

"He's with me, man. He's cool."

"He's Anglo, man!" Bobby licked his lips. The gun wavered. His friend gripped a beer bottle like a club. They both wore white T-shirts, sleeveless, flawlessly ironed, each hem tucked into dark blue pants, but spattered across Bobby's left shoulder were flecks of rusty brown. A sharp stink of sweat distilled on the tepid air from an old fan unit throbbing in the window.

"Es mi amigo, I said. Chill out."

"Chenga te. Those bastards killed my little sister. Ain't nobody chilling out, man." His mouth twisted into a rictus. He swung the gun down to his side, holding it there. The muzzle twitched convulsively against his thigh.

"You're too quick-tempered."

"Mira!" Bobby cried, and slapped his stained shoulder with his other hand.

For a second no one spoke.

"Comprendo. But don't go crazy," said Ramón at last.

"You come in here give me shit. What you expect?"

"Sit down. Talk."

"I'm going to kill those mothers, ese. Kill the fuckers."

"Quiénes?"

"They're L.A. Capones, man," said the other boy. He stood tall, older than his friend, about eighteen. His acne-pocked cheekbones and lanky shoulders emphasized the beer belly already hanging over the creased pants. His mottled forearms were blue with tattoos: tigers, handcuffs, chains.

"Shut up!" Bobby barked.

"That's who they are, Bobby," said the boy slowly, puzzled by his reaction. "L.A. Capones."

"They'll be pones when I finish. Little greasy lumps," Bobby snarled. He gestured toward my belly again with the gun barrel; his bony wrist flexed.

A cold seemed to have misted my skin. The hair on my neck stood up.

Bobby saw it. He grinned crazily. "It don't matter you're so big, eh, pendejo, you got a magnum aimed at you."

"Bobby. What do the Capones want?" asked Ramón.

"What?"

"Nobody shoot por no razón."

"The fuck you know? You ain't in no gang!" His face flushed. The gun began to bounce against the dark blue fabric on his hip, as if a thing coming alive all by itself.

"No. No gang, ese," said Ramón softly.

"La Junta!" The other boy turned with interest. "You in La Junta, eh, Ramón?" He looked at Bobby. "I heard about that, ese. My brother's in Huntsville. He went in same time as Juan. Hey, Bobby—they mean, ese. La Junta. That's the Mafia Mexicana. My brother, he been hung up by those guys."

Ramón glanced away, deadpan.

For a second Bobby stiffened. His upper lip lifted under its delicate flocking.

"*Fuck La Junta!*" he choked out. "I don't give a fuck about La Junta!"

"It's Jorris," the other boy said reasonably to Ramón. "Is why all this shit happening, man."

"Shut *up*, Jesus!" cried Bobby, voice cracking.

"Jorris?" asked Ramón.

Bobby swallowed hard.

"Lives down on the corner. Jorris the dealer, man. He got no legs, they got blown off in Vietnam. Bobby, he's his runner," explained Jesus. "Is how come Bobby's house got lit up. Bobby, he was supposed to give Jorris's stuff to the Capones after he take their money. But he never give them the stuff."

In the silence following I heard only the chugging fan.

"You keep the money?" Ramón asked Bobby.

"No, man. I pay Jorris, same as always." Sullenly he blinked from Ramón to the wall.

"Where's the stuff?"

"Jorris ain't give me it. He say to wait."

Ramón paused, meditating. "He set you up."

"No! He was waiting on a delivery, man," Bobby defended.

"Why would Jorris do that?" asked the tall boy. Genuine bafflement lent his pitted face a naïveté.

"Well, who does he work for?" I asked.

It was then that all three turned.

"Jorris works on his own," said Bobby automatically before biting it off. But Ramón's stare hardened suddenly on me.

"Stay here. Don't move," he snapped to Bobby. "Comprende?"

Bobby's jaw dropped. He nodded. Then he wrapped both hands tightly around the gun butt. Ramón wheeled, strode out the door and down the hall. It took two whole seconds for Jesus and me to catch up with him.

THE GRASS SEEMED to breathe heat as we moved up the block through the bright humid noon. I was walking a few paces behind Ramón and Jesus, not wanting to draw too much attention to myself. A lowrider Chevy rolled along the street, its tires making hardly any sound on the hot asphalt except when it crunched over a couple of beer cans, the stereo jolting a deep arterial beat through the sealed doors, like a distant rumor of chaos. Its pink ball-fringe shivered above the back shelf. Jesus nodded in greeting;

through the smoked windows I saw a ceremonial hand rise before the car slid under veils of shade.

"That's his place." Jesus stopped, pointing.

The white frame house had a sloping ramp fitted over the front steps. Yellowing lace drapes hung at the windows. Scraggy flower bushes grew on either side of the porch. A sprinkler stuttered on the lawn. By the curb was parked a green Dodge van, recent model, a handicapped license plate above the rear bumper.

"He's home." Jesus collapsed into a sitting position on top of a fire hydrant, hunched over, elbows on knees.

I peered at the house. "Is he married?" I asked as one of the drapes stirred and then shifted back into line.

"Not no more. His wife, she left a long time ago."

"So he's alone."

"Un perro," said Ramón.

At his words a German shepherd the size of a Harley-Davidson raced around the carport corner and smashed into the cyclone fence encircling the yard. *Ah-oooo!* it howled, then stood on hind legs, forepaws rammed against steel, barking like a kettledrum roll.

The sound triggered my dizziness. For a second the dog's head spun like a pinwheel as I tried to steady. Slowly I walked up to the fence, balancing along the way, until I reached the place where I saw his nose condense, black and glittering, hard as diamond. I stopped and whispered. "Hey, fellow. Hey."

"Raorf!"

"Good old fellow. Good guy." I curled my hand inward against the wrist, offering it.

"Are you crazy?" Ramón asked softly. Glancing over my shoulder I saw his expression. But Jesus said nothing; he sat watching, smiling his shy dolphin smile.

"He's all right," I said, as if I really knew. A hot breath basted my knuckles. The teeth gleamed, the brow retracted. Then the German shepherd swacked the hand with a tongue like a flag, his cocked head revealing his own startlement at this betrayal of bloodthirst.

Ramón murmured, "I thought you don't like dogs."

All at once the phantom on the dark patio on Cozumel quickened to life, the clicking nails, the hammer panic. I remembered how I'd steeled myself for the bite, never imagining I was being observed. Looking down, I stroked the dog's head, the hard dish of skull, and smiled to myself.

"Let that dog alone!" said a voice. "He'll rip your goddamn arm off."

"What?" The dog gave a little whine of appreciation. I glanced up at the porch. A wheelchair creaked into movement.

"You want to test it out?"

The soft ears pricked. Moaning threaded from the dog's chest as his conflict swelled. "He's okay," I reassured.

"Moose!"

The head jiggered under my hand. "Steady there. Hey. Don't worry," I urged.

"*Kill!*" yelled the voice.

"Moose. Whoa, Moosey," I murmured. "Hey, good fella." I stared into the yellow eyes that, though troubled momentarily by the clash of desires, looked clear as marbles.

"*Rowse,* I said!"

But he was too late. The choice was made.

"You turd-eater," growled the man, slapping his wheelchair tire in futility. "You worthless tub of mange. You goddamn carcass."

"Where'd you get him?" I asked.

The wheels swiveled abruptly. He started to go inside. Then he paused before the open door, apparently reevaluating. It was when he turned back around that I saw him clearly for the first time.

"You know what? None of your goddamn business."

He had a chin notched like a milk carton. The eyebrows looked thick from this distance, pelts stuck on with glue. Black hair lay oily and uncombed over his ears. From his chest a massive gut swayed down into his lap, and the unbuttoned shirt on either side of it parted like stage curtains around a prize pumpkin.

"He reminds me of one of those army dogs. Trained to attack spies, sniff out explosives, something like that," I said ingenuously. "He sure is mighty handsome. You must feed him well. Good coat. Strong." To point out his warm, friendly nature would have been overkill.

"He's a pussy." The humiliation smoldered. He spat on the floor. "Bag of garbage."

"Why, I'd think you'd be proud of him."

"You'd think, huh?"

"Sure."

"Well, you just think on." He clamped his mouth; the folded trouser legs twitched a little. From the corner of my eye I caught sight of Ramón's expression, which read plainly as a telegram—this marriage of hatred and maimed flesh intimidated him. He didn't know where to begin. Not until now had I dreamed that Ramón could ever be knocked off balance. But then inspiration hit: this was what Jorris counted on; this reaction was his chief weapon, an advantage that served him every day.

Oh, Granddaddy, I thought, thank you for sending me to school with cripples.

Just then Jesus pulled himself to his feet. "Hi, Jorris."

Jorris squinted as if he had only now noticed him.

"What are you doing here, Jesus?"

"I come with them."

"Why?"

"Because of the house getting lit up last night."

Jorris chewed this over, calculating as his cold lips worked. "House lit up last night—there a drive-by?" He tipped back his head. His eyes looked like blue grommets punched with holes.

"Yeah," nodded Jesus. "The Capones."

"Well, I'll be. Didn't hear a thing. I was setting inside listening to the TV."

"There's a dead baby today," I added.

"What's that?"

"A baby girl shot to death. A few doors down at the Hidalgo house. You know the Hidalgos," and then I opened the gate and stepped past the fence into the yard.

Ramón made a quick intake of breath.

"Hey! What are you doing?"

"Coming to visit."

"Get off my property!"

I continued up the sidewalk. Moose loped to my side and growled. The growl cut short as he nudged against my thigh, looking for another little scratch. Jorris must not give him any: his mistake; army discipline, no doubt. Ramón was following me now. I sensed his movement, and the shuffle of Jesus's boots as he came behind.

"You deaf or what? Stop right there."

I shook my head. "Nah."

"You want me to call the police?"

"If you want to."

"You better know it." He started to ram the wheelchair around as I reached the foot of the ramp, the handicap phoning in for his protection rights.

"I don't really care. But it might be interesting. Considering your profession around the neighborhood."

He stopped. "What profession? I ain't got no profession," he said evenly.

"Oh. What is it, a hobby?"

He stared at me. The blue eyes burned. I could feel them on my face. But I was just as aware of Ramón's eyes gouging my back.

"I'm retired."

"Hm. Easy retirement."

"You asshole. You think I can work? After what the U.S. Government did to me? Look at me!" He sneered first at me, then down at his own stumps, a volcano of theatrical self-pity.

"Yeah, well." I shook my head musingly. "That's never stopped my old high school buddies. Monkey's a mud-wrestler, his legs are like dead logs. Rick won a fly-fishing contest recently. Old Chelmsford the Third, he's already got himself three Taco Dia concessions—he's a real go-getter, though."

"What in goddamn fuckball Christ you talking about?"

"Your business deals," I said.

Emotions churned across his face. I ambled up the ramp's slope.

"Back *off!*"

I shook my head again.

"Why don't I just shoot you for trespassing." From the space between his spine and the wheelchair he reached back and pulled out a sawed-off shotgun.

It occurred to me then that perhaps psychology wasn't Jorris's chief weapon after all.

"Ugly piece," I said.

"*Taylor—,*" murmured Ramón.

"I'd sooner go for your police suggestion."

"In this state we're talking justifiable homicide," said Jorris.

"If you're willing to risk it on your own front stoop." Now I was standing over him, looking down at his hair: dandruff. He poked the gun barrel into my belly. The metal had a curious feel, warm through the shirt; it made me recoil to think of his sweat and clamminess on it. But conceivably the recoil might have stemmed from something more.

"Your buddies'll witness you trespassed. They'll have to swear it in court. They'll have no choice." He grinned, revealing a stylish gold tooth pierced with a nude woman's silhouette, like the steel cutouts you see on eighteen-wheelers.

"Hey, Jorris. Why you set Bobby up?" asked Jesus suddenly.

"*What?* Move, Jesus. I'm going to blow your big old moron friend here to New York City."

"This guy ain't my friend. I don't hardly know him. Bobby's my friend, Jorris," said Jesus. All at once he was looming next to the wheelchair, his face still reflecting the bewilderment that had rendered him so childlike in the Hidalgo house.

"Bobby and me'll do our own talking. It ain't your business. Now go, Jesus, get on home." I saw Jorris's spare hand grip the pump action. It slid into place. Then I understood two things: that he regarded Jesus as simple, and that he would kill me.

"You know, is my business, chico," spoke Ramón at last.

"Oh yeah? And why's that?" Jorris turned.

But Jesus was still pursuing his lone thought. "You told Bobby to sell that stuff to the Capones. You took the money. Then you never give the stuff to him."

"If he told you that, it's bullshit! Little wormy spic. Bobby's a liar. Now go on. I don't want to have to use this on nobody but him." The barrel prodded my abdomen.

"Bobby don't lie. Not to me, not to his bro."

"Looks like he do, Jesus."

On Jesus's other side Ramón flanked the chair's rear. I could see his eyes: he was getting ready to grab the gun and yank it clear.

"His baby sister's killed," dogged Jesus.

"It's nothing to do with me, damn it!" Jorris roared.

"I think Bobby's okay," said Jesus, as I reached down to do what Ramón had not yet done. Gripping the barrel between my hands, I was twisting it sideways to wrench it free when Jorris fired.

A FISSURE APPEARED in Jesus's thigh as fabric and flesh merged and quaked apart; a bright red wing flew through the air, the hole blossoming deep inside the secret muscle, ragged-petaled, a zinnia of fire.

At first I just stood there in shock. But three seconds after he hit the floor I moved. Wrestling the shotgun from Jorris's hands, I shoved him up against the wall. My fingers found his throat. Its curve welcomed me: the little hard larynx box, gristle and skin giving way like new-baked apple pie. By the time Ramón pulled me off his tongue was lolling out, but after he'd swallowed a few times he caught enough breath to scream, cussing as the patrol car and then the ambulance arrived.

A funny thing: all this time, Moose stood in the yard yowling like a banshee. But he never came near us.

THE AMBULANCE RUSHED Jesus to the hospital. At the police station, after they'd grilled us and taken our statements, they let us use the shower to wash our faces. Clothes were another matter. For the first time I discovered how blood has a smell all its own.

We got back to Oak Cliff in the late afternoon. "God, I'm sorry," I said to Ramón. "I'm so sorry."

Ramón looked down the street at the silent house on the corner. An eeriness hung about its drawn drapes and closed blinds, the sprinkler still twirling on the grass. From this angle we couldn't make out the mess splattered against the porch railings. "It's not your fault."

"Yes it is. If I'd grabbed the gun sooner—if I'd just tried—"

He shrugged. "You would have got shot in the belly, man. Dead."

For a split second I thought I saw one of the lace drapes twitch aside and fall back into line. I must have imagined it. "Maybe."

"Seguro. For sure. Ahora, Jorris es terminado."

"So's Jesus." I shook my head. The memory of the gun blast still rang in my ear. Jesus would probably lose his leg. "Somebody should tell the Capones that."

"They know." He reached out and patted my shoulder. "Mira. Jesus listened to himself, his friend. He choose." He glanced reflectively at the Hidalgo house next door. "Now the Capones know Bobby is not cheating them, they feel maybe sorry, maybe not."

"Christ—do *any* of these people ever feel sorry?"

"Bobby, yes. He's now sorry, I think."

I looked down, stung.

As we walked up the path to Ramón's uncle's door, Ramón took the steps ahead of me and reached for the handle at the instant the door opened wide.

"Hola," he murmured to the person inside. Then he shouldered on past through the front hall.

"Hello," I said after a moment.

She stood very still just beyond the threshold. Her face hung half rimmed in shadow. The slanting sun picked out the gleam on her eyes, that was all. Flicks, sequins of light. Her black hair streamed down. The only thing I could think of as my heart bumped was the musk of violence clinging, and the impulsion that grew overwhelming—to step up and reach for her, press, feel her close—which was what I was fighting so hard without understanding why.

"Taylor?" she said. Only her lips moved.

So I stopped fighting and did it.

As I touched her a pain ripped through my groin, and my brain closed off. I crashed down the steps. "Gringo estúpido! What are you doing?" dimly I heard her yell.

I lay writhing on the cracked ground while nausea engulfed the world. Floundering in the dust, nerves white-hot, head whomping like a clothes dryer, I clutched my balls and tried to haul back together the chunks of Oak Cliff that pain had flung to every corner of sky. After a minute she stepped off the porch. From my deathbed I could make out the whirling toe of her sandal.

"Why'd you *do* that?" Her voice floated, disembodied.

"I don't know." Pieces of Texas spun away like asteroids. I rolled into a fetal roll.

"I didn't want to hurt you. It's reflex." She sounded exasperated. I looked up. A slab of the house roof clapped back into place. "Guys got no business grabbing me."

"No kidding."

"Can't you talk clear? I don't understand you."

I took a deep breath. "I can't move."

She frowned. Then she bent and reached down, seizing my elbows; with a spine-wrenching heave she brought me to a stand, tottering a little as I stumbled sideways. I planted both feet in the weeds. Halfheartedly she brushed dirt from my shoulders, then stepped back, nipping a stickerburr off my shirt. Her hand rose to my collarbone to pluck a twig. The twig dropped. The hand's sudden heat felt clean on my skin inside the heat of evening. We both stared down at it.

She licked her lips. "Why are you here?" she asked.

6

The backseat was dark.

"Does it still hurt?"

"No."

She reached down to touch.

"Lo siento."

"It's okay."

"Pobrecito," she mocked lightly. "Pero mira. See? He's okay, qué no?"

"Yes."

"Much better." She chuckled, then her voice went husky. "How about here?" She reached up to the bite marks on my neck, flicking the one on my earlobe; her breasts rose beneath my hand. Tracing their soft weight, I felt her skin glide so smoothly I had to keep stroking. Slowly I brushed her nipple with a palm. She moaned and, despite herself, despite all her sparring, her haughty defense, her caution, arched and wrapped around me once more.

WHEN I WOKE it was to thunder. The stars burned on the gulf. Toward the horizon a cloud curtain flashed orange, stitched by lightning. Breeze rattled through the cornstalks. We'd left the rear door of the Escort open so my legs could stick out. The scent of rain steeped the field.

"Teresa-Maria. Teresita," I whispered, and rubbed her cheek lightly, watching her eyes open. Presently the lightning moved off and insect song and the faraway highway surf filled the cornfield.

Sleepily she murmured, "I heard what you did, Taylor."

I held her, staring at her beauty, feeling Jorris's throat under my hand. I knew what she was going to say.

"Going after Jorris." She paused. "Have I embarrassed you?"

"Oh, no. No. Not at all."

She gazed candidly up at me. "Jorris sells drugs for La Junta."

At first I couldn't speak.

"You didn't know that. Did you? Nobody is supposed to know."

La Junta, I thought. "How come you know it?"

"Juan told me. Last year, when he got out of Huntsville and got sent down to Cozumel."

"But Bobby's not in it, is he? Surely not. He's only a kid." Fuck La Junta, he'd said. So defiantly. I don't give a fuck.

"So?" She scowled, disgusted. "He's been running drugs for Jorris since nine years old."

The thunder rumbled faintly.

A picture coalesced, one of polluted childhood: the cunning, misery, the uneasy bondage, the squalid after-school errands, the excitement, the daily sense of death. I thought about the skinny kid with the shaking hand and the bloodstains on his shirt. I recalled my afternoons in the backyard azaleas, all my sweet safe solitary geek hours. I thought of her little brother Ricardo. Of Jesus's wound. Nine. I swallowed. "So what will happen now?"

"Someone else will come in for the business. Take Jorris's place. If the police keep him in jail." She said it with contempt. "Burglaring. Holdups. Smoking drugs. That's what they do with their education!"

"But not you, huh?"

She looked at me, eyes narrowed. "I don't live like these criminals. I have a job, comprendes?"

"Yes." Yes, I thought. You're very strong and fierce. You are what I want.

"I got home to Dallas last night. Only twenty-four hours. My vacation! From working hard from six in the morning to eight at night every day, no day off, training for a serious tourism career. Now already I want to fly back to Cozumel." An edge of lunar light glittered under her eyelids.

"Don't leave," I whispered. I gathered her and held her tightly.

She whispered back, "What's going to make me stay?"

"YOU WIGGLE IT in the lock, soft, like this," Ramón explained. With his index finger he gingerly rocked the tip to and fro. I knelt beside him, studying the manipulations.

"Where you get all these picks?" Bobby demanded.

"Made them out of wire. Coat hanger. Also some eight-, ten-, and twelve-gauge. The shanks and patterns I got from a book."

"They got books on *stealing?*" Bobby laughed like a woodpecker. "I'd steal a book like that!"

"It's what they call an underground publication. Not one you can find in regular stores."

"Those things ain't no good for real jobs." Bobby frowned, squatting beside the Yale keyhole in the flimsy panel of flaking paint and sun-rotted wood at his parents' back stoop. "This door is old, man. Piece of shit. Rich houses got dead bolts, alarms—fuck. They got everything!"

"So what are your favorite tools?" I watched as Ramón drew the pick from the lock, twisted the latch, and magically pushed the door open.

"Crowbar. Hammer. Fist." He grinned.

"What's the hammer for?"

"Break a window, man! Same as fist. *Pow!*"

"Too much noise."

"Not if you smother it in a blanket." He held out his hand for the pick ring. When Ramón gave it to him, he rattled through it, held one or two picks up to the light, then slung it down in disgust. It landed on a fire ant nest tucked in some weeds against the back steps. "Fuck. I got the best burglar tool you can have, man. Right here in my pocket."

"Which is what?" I bent to retrieve the ring and shake off the ants.

"My baby." Stuffing his hand down his baggy pants leg, he pulled out the gun he'd pointed at my heart the day we'd met.

Ramón snorted. "You going to jimmy a door with it, ese?"

"It's a cleanup tool, ese," Bobby snapped.

"Where'd you get it?" I asked.

"Jorris give it to me. Un regalo. Last year." His face darkened. Then he changed course. "Hey, Taylor, what you shoot, man? Three fifty-seven? Forty-five? Uzi?"

"I've never shot anything."

There was a silence.

"Wah!" roared Bobby. "You never popped *nothing?*

"To be honest, I've never handled a gun."

"You shitting. Ain't you got *none* in your *house?*"

"Well, my grandfather has a couple of deer rifles. Shotgun. I think a twenty-two." There had of course been training at school, but the shooting range was designed specifically for the paraplegics. The lethal potential of a bullet fired from within my vortex even now prompted a shudder. In the sudden churn of vertigo, where would it fly? The ceiling? The instructor's eyeball?

"You could use *them,* man. Take his ones. I would." He pondered a moment, weighing the gun in his hand. "Hey. I tell you what, ese. You want one of these? I'll take you where to buy a good one, real cheap."

"For why would you want one, man? Nothing but trouble," said Ramón.

"Yeah. Probably," I said. But the picture of Bobby standing beside me somewhere out in the country, of facing a row of bottles arranged on hay bales while he instructed me in the art of sighting down a muzzle, had its own peculiar romantic appeal.

THE STREETLIGHTS ALONG Commerce glowed like South Sea pearls, a line of soft-edged radiances floating in air. Cruising toward the dark end of Deep Ellum I could smell moisture wafting in through the open window.

"Step on it, hermano," Bobby complained. "You go too slow, you ain't no vato."

Without replying I held the speed that I'd come to adopt as general downtown policy, although at this godforsaken hour there weren't many other cars or traffic hazards around. Conspicuousness never pays. When we'd stopped for gas at an all-night convenience store and I'd seen the night clerk's white face turn automatically toward the glass like a weather balloon, catch sight of Ramón and Bobby, and then stare doggedly down at the cash drawer the whole time we pumped the gas. Even when he counted out my change, with Bobby roaming the candy displays and flipping through comic books, he'd kept his eyes trained to a narrow perimeter, all his gestures carefully limited—clearly a man whose survival depended on what he could ignore. We'd left after the most cursory trans-action. But I knew he wouldn't forget us in a police lineup.

"Close the window, at least," grumbled Bobby, shivering in his tank shirt. "It's freezing, man."

"It's just damp," I said, and rolled the glass up halfway. It was the end of June. After two days of sheeting summer rain, the black asphalt shone like enamel. We were sliding by a block of office towers obsidian and metal green in the half-light. Here and there a bright square showed on a higher story where some computer jockey or cleaner was working late. Ramón darted sideways glances right and left, as if their alien business rhythms posed a menace to the life he knew.

"Damp, shit. It's like a iceberg in here," growled Bobby.

I rolled the window up the rest of the way and paused at a deserted intersection, waiting until red turned to green. Tonight Ramón was finally going to show me how to disable a burglar alarm system. We'd already picked out a house in a North Dallas development, empty and waiting for new owners but plastered with alarm company warning decals on every window. I'd been practicing alone using devices I'd bought from a mail-order catalog, but an actual hands-on site was a different story. As soon as Ramón completed his errand we'd be on our way. My fingers tensed in anticipation. Directly on our left stood an older building, a sore thumb among the modern skyscrapers. From the corner of my eye I noted its fine points: an excellent example of Southwestern art deco architecture, heavy as a citadel, nine stories tall. The expanse of pink granite shadowed black where the streetlamps' light tailed off. I could make out its old-fashioned lobby's revolving door, now a dark fan of glass; the original building's title cut in gold-polished brass; the sole window, burning like a fiery hole punched into the stone face. Above the entrance marquee a familiar capital *D* loomed twice as large as the four block letters that followed.

I glanced down. A whole building with his name. A whole empire.

Whose light? I wondered.

"Down this alley," Ramón said. He pointed with his cigarette between some buildings in the next block, then stubbed the butt out on his boot heel.

"Okay. What's behind?"

"A store."

"We busting in?" asked Bobby from the backseat. His mouth was stuffed full, chewing; when he spoke a fragment of bean burrito flew out and struck the windshield. "I ain't got only a socket wrench with me. No crowbar or nothing."

"How come you got a socket wrench?" I asked.

"Borrowed it from the Circle K. Man, I love that Circle K on Mockingbird—they got a whole tool display. Last time I scored two tire gauges and a gas cap."

"You don't got no car," Ramón said.

"No, ese." He cackled and slapped his knees. No wonder, I thought, the night clerk had kept his eyes down.

The alley tunneled between two high walls, empty except for a dumpster and a lone cat that scampered off as soon as our headlights brushed it.

"Qué pasa?" asked Bobby.

"Meeting," said Ramón.

"With who, the cat?"

"Somebody inside. Cómo dice?—counting. Inventario."

"At two o'clock in the morning, man?" marveled Bobby. "Hard worker." He crammed the last wad of burrito between his teeth and peered out the window.

"Park here."

I braked and looked down the lightless brick vista. A few yards away a shift in blackness broke its line.

"Espérame. Muchas gracias." Ramón opened the car door.

"What do you mean, wait? Ain't we coming too?" Bobby demanded. But Ramón ignored him, slipped out, moved toward the cavity in the wall, and disappeared.

After a minute of silence Bobby smacked a fist. "Fuck this."

"He won't be long. Be patient," I said.

"What you say? You talking to *me*, puto?" He glared. His eyes glinted against the dark. "I ain't sitting here like a duck." He climbed over the seat back, opened the door, and slammed it behind him.

"Hey! Wait!" I said. But already he was jogging down the alley, slowing as he passed Ramón's vanishing point, craning sideways to see what he could see. A few more paces and he'd sidled around the corner, thumbs in pockets, his elbows cocked out.

I cussed under my breath. There was no sign of Ramón, no change in the cavity's darkness. My isolation was total. There was nothing to be done. I waited as the seconds ticked by and stretched into one minute, two.

Then, all at once, from somewhere in the distance there came a crash. What was that? I nearly yelled aloud. But instantly I knew.

Glass.

Shoulders rigid, head tensed, I listened without knowing exactly what for. It wasn't until the sirens streamed across the humid wind that I understood what might happen next.

A figure shot out of the density like a rock, hurtled toward the car, smashed into the door, then grasped the handle. "Go!" he barked, and threw himself into the front seat.

"Can't. Bobby!"

I was already gunning the accelerator. He looked around. "Dónde?"

The sirens were very close now. Any second they'd turn in. I shoved the gearstick into first without switching on the headlights. "He took a walk."

"Ándale!"

My foot crashed down on the pedal. The Escort rammed ahead. Just as we reached the far corner a figure flapped into sight like a rangy chicken. I slowed down enough for him to leap inside as the siren swelled to an intolerable pitch. Sweat pricked; blood banged in my temples; my hands clutched the wheel as if the flesh had welded to it; the gold shank bit into my knuckle. The Escort screamed around the block. I cut on the beams just as two spears of light pierced the alley darkness behind us.

"IS NECESSARY I go to Mexico," said Ramón.

I broke from the reverie of a yellow window searing the night, a solitary figure reading papers at a desk. "Why?"

Under the patio roof shadow he sipped his coffee. A gust of leaves scuttered against the plastic ridges overhead. Teresa-Maria twisted around in my lap, her face troubled.

"Por Juan?"

Ramón nodded.

"I thought he was coming here," I said.

Ramón looked into the cup. His self-containment seemed remarkable considering the getaway only half an hour before. My breath still stopped short, my heart was still pounding. Ramón shook his head.

"You reckon he got held up? Or changed his mind?"

"He is disappeared," said Ramón. He tipped back and poured the last of the coffee down his throat.

"What do you mean?"

"Tonight I hear. Three weeks ago Juan start from Cozumel to Monterrey. He meet some people in Nuevo Laredo. From there he was going to cross at Laredo."

"Arrested?"

Ramón shook his head. "The connection knows who gets taken. He was still okay when he left Nuevo Laredo. Hiding, secret ways, not the main big road, you know. At some place between the town and the border—" He flipped his hands up.

For a moment nobody spoke.

"What are you planning on doing?" I asked

Against my neck, Teresa-Maria's arm tightened. I heard her breathing go still. I could feel her shaped weight, light and limber in my lap. A tiny lamplit vein jumped under her temple.

If Juan came back to Oak Cliff I would eat dirt sooner than lay eyes on him. He'd harass my life every minute of the night and day. He would make the simplest pleasures a misery; he'd find out what I was up to and then bully or blackmail forever. Ronnie Dean Jordan, I thought, was a hayride in comparison. Plus I was dating his sister; I spent my hours in the bosom of his family. Juan had to be conclusively the biggest pain in the ass I'd ever met. Never mind what I felt about Teresa-Maria. And what possible gain lay in his return? His own neighbors and relatives shook their heads over him in sorrow. He was a convicted felon, a deportee, someone who could get everybody in trouble just by showing up. Teresa-Maria herself had denounced him as a criminal idiot. Only his poor old father held out, nursing some forlorn hope that he might discourage his little brother Ricardo from gang membership—an optimistic delusion if ever I'd heard one. Then there was also my future.

Ramón didn't have much left to teach me. He'd now schooled me pretty thoroughly in the basics; his old Monterrey skills were almost exhausted. Besides, he had no wish to pursue burglary. He'd only consented to take me on because he was my friend. Between him and my private studies, I was at last almost ready to enact my plans: the building, the office at the top with its bright window, the violation poised on my fingertips, ready to devastate the man inside.

Ramón leaned back, shrugged, and closed his eyes. All at once he looked tired.

"Well, sir. I guess we'd best go find him then, huh?" I said.

SOUTH TEXAS IS like being on the ocean. You climb a crest that seems like the edge of the world but proves to be only shoulder high, and suddenly the horizon shifts one hundred miles to the south, lipped beyond a wilderness of mesquite, false willow, creosote, blackbrush, and towering castles of prickly pear. The landscape seems flat but it swells and rolls, troughed by water catchments and rippling with scrub humps. Heat wavers across the bitten stones and dirt washes. There are occasional fences. Sometimes you see a windmill.

Mostly it's empty.

The sky had turned first green and then purple and black like a widespread bruise that night as we neared Laredo. Ten miles away the city lights glowed like phosphorous spilled across the desert floor.

"Extraño," said Ramón.

"Pretty weird-looking," I agreed.

We gazed at the landscape before us, the desolation of brush, the rising space tented by cloud. We could see in the distance a hypothetical strata where Texas air blended with the state of Nuevo León.

"You think we'll find him out there somewhere?"

Ramón glanced at me, and then wordlessly lit a cigarette.

So for the third time in my life I entered Mexico.

7

The land where the posse couldn't go is now a frontier of industry. You cross the Bridge of the Americas into Nuevo Laredo, past the big new maquiladoras along the river that churn out sweatshirts, machine valves, air bags, and the artifacts of lust, past the zapaterías and bars and Golden Fried Chicken stands, and come to a stop in the century's paradoxical heart. The visible signs of legend are gone. The colonias with their tar-paper shanties and untreated sewage look nothing like the village in *The Magnificent Seven*. Cantinas blaze with neon. Scrap garbage litters the plazas. Yet ultimately, temporality reigns. Persisting beyond all this recent human crust lies the soil steeped in blood, Indian and European, bison and iguana, the country where the elements bond with the flesh and bathe and chastise it; where thorny leaf swords imprison a cache of sweet juices, where blistering sun and parched wind command the surrender of the body's will to their own finalities. The landscape sucks you dry and renders you up.

We drove until we found a McDonald's, where we bought some tacos. Sitting in the parking lot, sipping a Fanta, I looked out over what I could see of the streets and stores and thought about what lurked underneath, below civilization. Afterward Ramón pulled out a deck of cards, and we sat playing poker and drinking beer in a bar near the polluted river's edge until eleven o'clock, when sleeplessness finally caught up with me and I couldn't stay conscious any longer.

We spent the night in the car, stretched out each to a seat, parked on a lane of cement and adobe houses near the railroad yards. In the front I lay humped over the console with knees jammed against the dash. When I woke up just before dawn, roosters were crowing among the houses. I cranked down the window and looked out at the graying world. An agave stood ghostly green next to a wrought-iron fence. Lights burned in windows. From the switchyard a freight train created a foundation of sound for the street noises—babies wailing, a truck with a bad muffler, a grandmother calling the family to breakfast, a man who stood whistling cheerfully as he pissed into the dirt beside his front door. I could smell frying tortillas, sausage, coffee.

In the backseat Ramón stirred.

"Buenos días."

"Uhh," he replied.

"Where do we start?" I asked.

He grunted, blinking awake. With the back of a hand he wiped his mouth. "A man. We find a man."

"What kind? Young? Middle-aged? Any old guy?"

"Near the mercado. His name is Rafe."

I peered out the window. Two children stepped into the patchy garden of the house next door. They wore shorts, no shirts, and broken beach thongs. The boy picked his nose; the little girl was singing a song in a high, rapid voice as she seized a bucket near the gate. They flicked us curious glances. Then the girl closed her mouth with a snap and ran back inside, the bucket banging against her legs, while the boy squatted in the gritty dust and grinned at me.

I grinned back. "Does Juan know this Rafe guy?"

"Everybody knows him. He don't know nobody."

"Oh, of *course!* Naturally!"

"He can tell us maybe where Juan went to cross."

"Even though he doesn't know Juan."

"Rafe is prudente," said Ramón with simplicity. "In this country is necessary. Is his business."

WE LEANED AGAINST the threshold of a yellow cement house. Ramón spoke softly to the woman who'd answered our knock; she was peering at us through a curtain of colored plastic strips. "La Junta," he said.

She nodded.

Ramón rubbed the back of his neck.

"Prisión?" she asked with sweet idleness.

"Huntsville."

Her eyes didn't move. Her face stayed impassive as carved soap. "Un amigo?"

"Mi primo. Hace dos, tres semanas. Con Rafe."

"Ahora viene a Rafe?"

"Sí. Por favor."

With one spare and delicate hand she lifted a cigarette out of her skirt pocket and stuck it between her lips. The dark eyes remained on Ramón while she took out a kitchen match, scratched it with a thumbnail, held it to the cigarette tip, and then expertly shook out the flame. It looked incongruous; in her housedress and fuzzy pink slippers she seemed too domestic to be acting the style of a movie gangster's moll. "En la fábrica," she said, exhaling two plumes through her nostrils. "La sombrerería." She glanced down the street toward the corner where the market began. Her voice had the throaty burble of the long-term smoker.

"Verdad?"

"Sí."

"Gracias, señora."

"Nada." Already tired and bored, not bothering to take the cigarette from her mouth, she stood watching us as we walked away, one leg crooked out on its muscular calf.

The hat factory occupied a corrugated iron shack on the next block. A sign nailed on the wall outside said in curly but fading script, SOMBREROS CELESTE. We paused, caught up in the bustle of people at the edge of the market stalls, around us the din of voices bargaining, boys selling Chiclets, radios blaring out dance music, the morning news, a soccer game. Near my leg a toothless young beggar woman with a baby looked imploringly up. "Por favor," she said. Her baby lay still as a doll in her rebozo, his eyes shunting like ball bearings. Searching through two pockets I found one quarter, three nickels, and a penny. I dropped them into her hand. A tumult of footsteps rang out as a pack of children stampeded through the crowd on their way to school. My dizziness stole back for a second; I tilted sideways. Then I leaned against a stall hung with cheap leather purses reeking of tanning fluid. The odor was rich as fresh manure.

"Rafe, he's the one to connect," said Ramón. He pointed to the hat factory. "People find him aquí. He meets them with a coyote."

"Coyote?"

"Sí."

"You mean, like wild dog?"

"A veces," he said cryptically. He eyed the factory door. A dozen or so red sombreros stitched with gold braid dangled above it in the breeze. "El coyote—he takes you over the river. Illegal. You pay."

"Oh." Inside the open door we could see movement. People passed back and forth, carrying things: piles of felt, boxes, a hat stack taller than the girl who balanced it in her arms. The shop seemed very busy. It was obviously a tourist success story. Beyond the counter stood one motionless figure. After the hat girl walked out of the way, I could see it was a man loitering, his arms folded over a big stomach. He sported a lot of gold. Chains dripped around his neck like tinsel on a Christmas tree, two or three bracelets glittered in his elbows' shadows, a brooch hung pinned to one of those cotton shirts with tucks down the front. The shirt was red. A pair of gold eyeglasses perched on his nose, lending him the air of a shady tax accountant. It had to be him, I thought. But then I changed my mind; it was impossible to miss his resemblance to one of the gaudy sombreros overhead—a proprietor's advertising. Although he seemed to be taking stock of nothing on the street, I realized he was watching us.

"Does Rafe work in there?"

Ramón shrugged. "It's his friend's place. He stays sometime."

"So what do we do?"

"Ask for him."

"I don't think we'll have to ask far." I glanced toward the red-shirted man.

Without reply Ramón started up the curb to the door.

The interior felt only a little hotter than the street outside, but once we'd crossed the floor the stuffiness hit our noses and mouths like a velvet drape. I had to drag for breath. The man watched us come. He stood motionless, his eyes magnified to moist dark bulbs by the glass lenses, and the tiniest frown chased his forehead as he glanced from Ramón to me and back again. To his left yawned a huge doorway through which I could see some women working at benches, stitching beads onto hats. A boy no older than Dodie stood at a machine, fitting colored felt circles into place and then dragging the lever of a steel press. Steam rose through the air. A scent of chili sauce and hot, wet dog hung everywhere. The racket was terrible.

"Buenos días," said Ramón.

"Buenos días."

"I'm looking for Rafe." To my surprise Ramón spoke in English.

"Quiénes Rafe?"

"This is business."

The man shrugged, his arms still crossed. "No sé."

"I come from La Junta."

"La Junta? No sé."

Ramón arranged his most serious face. "Miguel Tracon sent me."

Then it struck me why he was speaking English. He was making his strengths and alliances plain.

For a second or two the man rolled his tongue around his teeth. The tip came to the right bicuspid and stopped beside it, probing. I watched as he inserted a little finger and wedged in the nail, mining some food fragment left over from breakfast, which he removed and examined in the light with scientific interest. "Quiénes Tracon?"

"El jefe."

"Qué jefe?"

"Con uno huevo solamente," Ramón said patiently.

The man looked at him, blinking. Well, I thought, you'd have to know this jefe pretty damn tight to know a thing like that. After another moment he dabbed the fragment back onto his tongue, swallowed, then nodded at a door. "Okay." Shifting almost imperceptibly on the balls of his feet, he turned away from us to oversee the factory entrance.

A small, wizened man stepped out into the room. "Hola," he said.

"Hidy," I answered.

He wore a khaki shirt rolled up at the sleeves, a pair of rumpled jeans too long for his shoe tops, and a brass belt buckle. Cocking his head, he looked us over. We watched as he squeezed out a jovial smile. "What you want?"

"Are you Rafe?" asked Ramón.

"Sí."

"My name is Ramón Vizuelos."

Rafe nodded.

"We want to go to the river. We want to see where to cross."

"Por qué?" He stopped, wheezed, coughed, and smacked his chest. "You are both legal."

"How do you kn—?" I started to ask. But Ramón nudged me and I bit my tongue.

"To find the coyote who helped mi primo. To ask him where mi primo went after he crossed."

"Por Miguel Tracon?"

"Sí."

"Miguel Tracon is your friend?"

"My boss."

Rafe kept the smile plastered on his face, which was still tipped quizzically. "Qué es el nombre de su primo?"

"Juan." No last name.

He gave a lazy shrug. "Muchos Juans come, they go. Yo no los conozco. And many coyotes I do not know, also."

"No es peón."

Rafe said nothing but perked his birdlike head a shade higher. I would have sworn on the Bible that he knew every coyote working the Texas border from El Paso to Houston.

"Habla inglés."

"Sí, sí. Muy gran número hablamos inglés. Seguramente todos," Rafe agreed.

"This Juan, though—he went to college in Texas," I said.

The comment seemed to catch him off guard. The smile tightened just a fraction.

"I meet many people. Many customers, many strangers. Then I unmeet them." He shook his head. "Is dangerous, you know."

"You remember him, though, don't you? He would have been different from the rest. More sophisticated. He would have mentioned La Junta, too, I imagine." He wouldn't have been able to resist.

Straightening pensively, Rafe weighed the description. "Yo no sé. Perhaps I think I can remember someone like that. About six weeks ago? Or seven, perhaps?"

"Three," said Ramón.

"A-hem." With a knuckle he kneaded on his throat to clear it of phlegm. "Did he have much money?"

"Two hundred dollars."

"For crossing."

"For everything."

"Hmph." He frowned. Then his eyes brightened in ingenuous recollection. "Ah. Ah! Perhaps. A one with a barbilla much—?" Raising a twisted finger he tapped on his chin, then made a tiny contracting circle between finger and thumb.

"That's him," I said.

He nodded. Wisdom relaxed his features into sunny kindness. At no time during our chat had he and his friend the sombrerero traded the slightest acknowledgment. They hadn't even acted like they knew each other. "Yes, yes. I remember. There was a person I found for him. I send him to the blue house."

"Where is the blue house?"

"Las Cruces Rosas."

"And where's that?"

"A place. Down by the river about fourteen kilometers."

"A village?"

He shrugged, still smiling. "Two or three houses."

The girl with the hat stacks came through the cavernous door from the factory. This time the stack she carried was green and black. Kneeling down, she placed the hats carefully in a cardboard box, closed it up by tucking the flaps into one another, stood up again, and peeking shyly at us, walked back into the steam-clouded gloom.

"That's where we'll find the coyote Juan hired?" I asked.

"You can meet him there."

"How do we locate the blue house? Who do we ask for?"

With a forefinger Rafe stroked his lower lip. "I will guide you," he said after a pause.

I felt the atmosphere change. A prickle of sharper attention radiated from the fat man behind the counter. His stance, however, could have been molded from a fibreglass front-yard Santa.

"You'll come with us now?"

Ramón waited, silent.

"Yes. I will do that."

"Well, let's roll." Suddenly I wheeled around, flashing a big surprise grin. I met the Santa's eye. With indifference he twitched his mouth down, looked away, uncrossed the arms, and leaned forward, pressing both fists against the countertop, so that at last I could ogle red shirt, rings, bracelets, his watch, all his hoard in its detailed and golden amplitude.

"IS THIS ROAD," said Rafe.

"Okay."

He sat smiling in the seat beside me. I had decided that the smile must be a freak of facial muscles; how otherwise to account for its permanent bonhomie? It was pleasant rather than alert; it lacked the craft I'd presume automatic to his trade. As we cruised down the seamy avenues of Nuevo Laredo's outskirts I cataloged it with similar smiles I'd met in the past: the weekly chirp from my fifth-grade Sunday school teacher; the drunk lep-rechaun king in *Darby O'Gill and the Little People;* the jolly rue of Bueller, the mentally retarded janitor at military school, when Chelmsford III cleaned him out of his Saturday movie money with yet another round of Go Fish. If Rafe's eyes hadn't softened like the cobbler's while he watched the elves completing last night's shoes, I might have thought him an elf himself.

"Isn't this kind of far from the highway?" I asked as he steered me through an intersection. The pavement had run out. We were now driving on dirt.

"No highway to Las Cruces Rosas."

"How many people live there?"

"Not so many. Only one truck. No car."

"Why did you send Juan to a coyote so far from town?" asked Ramón behind us.

Rafe answered to the windshield. "He say he was deportado. The Rangers arrest him. It was how he know La Junta, from prisión. Las Cruces Rosas is safer."

"Safer than Laredo itself?" I asked.

"Not so much routes, but not so much patrols. You can go at night."

"You remember him pretty well now, huh?"

Rafe raised his brows, good-natured. "I am pay money to forget all people. Is the best training. Sometimes it works more better than I plan."

"Fair enough."

He turned and spoke over his shoulder. "Su primo, he should have come to you two weeks ago."

"Sí."

"Maybe the Rangers get him after all?"

"No," said Ramón.

"Seguro?"

"Yes."

Rafe settled back into the seat, shrugging again. "I send him to a good man. He would cross safe. After the crossing, we promise nada."

"What's the name of this guy?" I asked.

"I do not say."

"Is that because you're protecting him?"

"You will meet him."

"I will talk with him," said Ramón.

"Sí, sí. No problem."

"So long as we can't call him by name," I said. Rafe eased down, his eyes half closing in the strong light.

"So now what am I supposed to do? Just plow right through all this stuff here?" The road was quickly vanishing. We cut along a path that looked no more than a faded stripe in the weeds.

"Las Cruces Rosas is a few more kilometers only. You follow the river."

"When I can see it."

"Behind the trees." He glanced out and pointed to the ledge of false willow on our left. With a metallic crunch we fell into a dip, then swam out again, breasting the scraggy mounds of grass. Birds rose from the hard pans and cactus clumps around us.

"I hope this doesn't totally trash the car." I could taste sweat trickling down my cheeks. Air-conditioning didn't help. The heat was a presence inside, live, insufferable.

"No problem." Once again Rafe nestled his head back and closed his eyes.

"I will fix the car," said Ramón unexpectedly.

"Nah. No need. I was just kidding."

"Oh."

"It's doing fine, to tell the truth. It's a solid gold jewel of a car, this thing. You know? Runs like a gold wrist watch."

"Okay."

Rafe's eyelids quivered next to me. He coughed, reached up, and gently patted his chest.

"Yep, she'll make it," I said. "But thanks anyway."

"De nada." A distance sounded in Ramón's tone. I glanced around. He was staring out at the acres of desert, his eyes no doubt tracking an imaginary figure wading its dry brush as we bumped along. I had no way to tell him anything. There was no means to tip a signal in the rearview mirror; he sat directly behind Rafe's head. From the time we'd left the fábrica to now, I'd been desperately trying to construct a code adequate enough to circumvent Rafe's omnipotence and reveal what I now knew.

"So. How did old Juan look when you saw him?" I asked Rafe.

"Qué?"

"How'd he look? Was he healthy? Excited? Pleased to be heading north?"

"Excited, quizá," he opened his eyes, shrugged.

"Yeah, I'll bet. That old boy sure does like it up in Texas. He's got some sharp plans, I can tell you. Mr. Tracon'll be real happy to hear where-all he's got to. That old dog."

"Ah." The eyelids drifted down once more.

"Yep. We'll be sure and tell him what a big help you've been, dogging him down and all, once we get hold of him."

"Muchas gracias."

"Mr. Tracon's been a tad worried. You might imagine."

Rafe said nothing. Behind me Ramón grunted, then cleared his throat.

"Hey. You know what?" I said, plunging recklessly on. "Maybe you and Mr. Tracon could even work out a deal for the future. Like, due to his gratitude? From now on you could be the guy who arranges all the tricky border crossings for La Junta, the one they go to right off. A specialist, kind of. You ever think about that?"

Rafe opened his eyes. I turned to face their cold surveillance. "I am," he said.

Well, whoops, I thought.

"Taylor? Please—you must concentrate on the driving," said Ramón.

"Yes, sir. I guess you're sure right," I said. I stirred up as much obsequiousness as was possible at such a hair-trigger moment. To play the hired chump seemed my sole hope. "Whatever you say, Mr. Vizuelos."

"Muchas gracias." He sounded only a little puzzled.

"Sorry. I should know by now when to shut up, I guess," I said, and set about rendering the goopy moron. "It's not like Mr. Tracon appreciates it when I start using my brain. Shoot, what brain? 'Drive, Taylor,' he says. 'That's your job. Not thinking.'" I nodded vigorously, laughing: *har har, snork*. "'Taylor, you cannot think,'" I quoted. Now I shook my head like a dog. The sweat spun out in rain and slapped the dashboard. "He's right. If I just stick to orders and don't horn in, I'll be fine. Stay professional. Shut up and listen."

Rafe was listening to me in icy stillness.

"Sí," Ramón concurred. "Por favor."

"He has a heart of gold, really. Doesn't he, Mr. Vizuelos? That Mr. Tracon. Pure-dee *nugget* gold. You should just *watch* him sometime."

"*Taylor.*"

"Yeah?"

"Here is Las Cruces Rosas," said Rafe.

There was a silence. Ramón leaned forward. "Dónde?"

Rafe knocked his arthritic knuckles against the glass.

We had entered a hedge of willow, cenizo, and mesquite. Cactus sat scattered around the field like furniture. Stretching on a curve to either side, the brush screen obscured our view; we were corralled in its U-shaped trap. The grass like a sea scraped against the Ford's undercarriage, lush, thick, rippling in the breeze, watered by its proximity to the river.

"This looks like a lot of nowhere," I said.

"Aquí," said Rafe. I followed his finger. A portal stood open before us, whether natural or machete-made I couldn't tell. Looking closer I realized that some of the vines grew like blackberry brambles, woven among the many branches. I pressed the accelerator. The car nosed through it with a squeak of thorns.

"Fuerte," said Ramón in appreciation.

Rafe said nothing.

Beyond the gap in the hedge spread a river bottom planted in mesquite and oak trees. We slid to a stop. Pools of shade lay blue on the hot ground; a cane thicket edged the banks to the left. Over its top we could just see the current sparkling against the mud brown eddies and sandbars. A gravel island jutted up from the shallows on the side nearest us where the water ran clear, but beyond it the depths turned jade green. The far banks looked empty, a field of littered flint and mesquite. The island was fringed with weeds. Six-foot-tall cane hid the center.

"Mira. Mucho corrientes," said Ramón.

"Sí."

"People cross here?"

Rafe nodded.

"Pero no sé puede."

"Is why you need a guide with a boat."

"Is that what you call that? A boat?" I gestured at the island. Drifting along its shore was a metal shell that looked at once strange and familiar. Someone had anchored it with a piece of rope.

"You can walk to the island. But not past it to the Texas side."

"Good God Almighty." I had recognized the shape of the vessel in its quirky cutwork: two auto hoods welded together to make a coracle. "Would you look at that! Can it actually be safe for humans?"

"Claro," said Ramón. He sounded slightly fatigued.

"The dangerous time come when Federales wait on the other side with guns. You must be careful then."

"Guns," I said. "Well, hey. Technically speaking, is the island in Texas or in Mexico?"

"Ninguno. Is in the river. Is nowhere."

We contemplated the no-man's-land for a moment.

"So then is this here the blue house you were talking about?" I asked through my idiot's persona, nodding toward a shack set a few yards back from the brush hedge. "Not exactly blue." It was half crumbling adobe, half tin. Old planks shored up a lean-to where a fire burned pale in the noon-time. Plastic bottles and broken steel cluttered the yard. A door hung open. No one was visible.

Rafe gave me a glance.

"Ven conmigo, por favor," Ramón said to him, opening the car door and politely waiting for the older man to climb out.

I pulled at my door handle.

"Taylor, you stay here."

"Well, I think I ought—"

"Stay," said Ramón flatly.

There was shit-all to be done. The stooge act had discouraged him; I couldn't get us alone for a second. Watching in frustration as they moved toward the house, I noted how heedlessly Rafe stumped along, as if he didn't have a thing on his mind, and how each step drew him fast to Ramón like a shadow.

They reached the door frame and tapped. The *thunk* of rotten wood sounded across the bottoms. We waited.

After a couple of minutes it grew clear that no one was going to answer the knock. Rafe and Ramón stood conversing in murmurs. Ramón looked uncertain. Rafe spread his hands palms up and then inevitably shrugged as they walked back to the car where I still sat.

"Taylor, the man is not home."

"He is on the island, fishing," said Rafe in a reasonable tone that hinted at repetition.

"I don't see him," muttered Ramón.

"Cómo mira el? He always fishes on the Texas side. That is where to find the fish. You see the boat." Rafe gleamed with common sense.

"How will we go?"

"Walk."

"But the rapids."

"The water is not deep. When it come strong is necessary to lift your foot solamente un poco." He demonstrated, mincing his worn cowboy boots sideways in a crab scoot across the grass. "No problem."

"You have done it before?"

"Sí, sí. Muchos veces."

"Muy bien," Ramón sighed.

Rafe ducked down and peered through the driver's window. "You are coming?"

I don't know what alerted me. I looked at him: the guileless poverty of the boots, the tarnished tobacco smell that drenched his clothes, the glibness of his invitation, the good nature with which he'd shown us the way out here. It all suddenly combined to make goose bumps rise on my arms. Straining a grin, I spiked it with just a touch of sulky resentment. "No, thanks."

"You will wait here?" asked Ramón.

"I believe I prefer to, yeah."

"Come if you like."

"Nope. One slap's enough, thank you. Believe I'll just keep my seat."

"As you wish," said Ramón. He shook his head slowly. "Lo siento. Pero es mejor." Then he turned alongside Rafe and started toward the river.

When they reached the edge of the canebrake, they sat down to take off their shoes. Ramón began rolling his pants up to the knees, but at a handflap from Rafe he ceased. "Vano," Rafe said. His voice carried, reflected against the cane like light on the water. "Está calado en dos minutos."

"Ah."

"Secarse rápido."

"Sí." Ramón stood up and let the pants legs drop. Then, tentatively, he stepped into the cane that walled off the water. Rafe followed.

I waited until they vanished before I got out of the car. Standing on the running board I could just see over the feathered tops of the cane. Sure enough, in a moment Ramón reappeared, inching precariously through what must be a tough channel current, with Rafe right behind him. In no time they were soaked up to their waists. It took them about five minutes to struggle over to the island's shore, where they quickly grasped the tufted weeds and heaved themselves onto the gravel. Neither of them glanced my way. Ramón turned to Rafe and asked him something. Rafe threw his thumb over his shoulder to indicate the opposite shore. Regaining their feet, they parted the high cane, entered it, and for the second time were swallowed by vegetation.

Instantly I jumped off the car and ran toward the bank, fumbling to kick off my Nikes as I moved. The cane scraped at my arms and neck as I fought through, but I ignored it; there was no time to lose. Once in the water I braced both feet on the rough, stony bottom. To raise them seemed impossible, the resistance was like a huge weight fixing me in place. Cold currents lapped around my crotch. Their force disoriented; they tugged relentlessly toward Laredo, swirling like a dream into consciousness and reawakening the black vortex that had slept for so long. Then fear arrived. Groping for precious seconds, I prayed for the dizziness to go, but my lips seemed as numb as my brain; the cold shot through and through. I began to fall. It was at that instant that memory of the Yucatán snorkel returned to me. The tide pushed and tore, pulling me out to sea, I strove leadenly toward the water's surface, fighting for breath into my lungs, rolling against the whirl, until I raised one arm to steady myself and then felt rather than saw the ring's gleam on my finger: *Deeds,* it said. The thought of where my doing would end if I failed stung me back into clarity. Focus returned. I blinked, gravity centering me like a rock. Before me the sky arched huge and bleached pale with heat. The canebrake on the island stood motionless, a jungle unshaken even by the wind. When I started out again the river's voice drowned my splashing, except once as I slipped and got swept downstream, floundering along for several yards before I found the bottom and dug back in. Even then the core did not desert me; I imagined the red shirt of the sombrerero, the neck hung with chains; I saw the ringed fingers, the fat arms under their crusting of gold, the hideous unmistakable nuggets that made up Juan's watch as it tick-ticked away on the wrist propped over the counter.

The island loomed above.

With both hands I seized the weeds and hauled myself from the sucking water. There I crouched, totally still. No rustle disturbed the noon ambience. Not even a bird came flittering out of the cane. I listened to the silence. The river washed against the island banks, burbling, lapping, yet no breeze whispered inside the leaves. Then, as I tensed to move, Ramón's muffled voice floated through the brake. Rafe's wheeze answered. Relief flooded me. It occurred to me that perhaps my fears were groundless—perhaps Juan had simply traded the watch in exchange for his passage. Rafe was obviously as harmless as the creases in his boots and was acting in good faith to help a fellow countryman find a missing relation. All I had to do was stand up and holler, tell them I'd changed my mind, I was over my huff, I'd come to join them. I would convince Rafe that I'd been trying to inflate my own importance with all that talk about the one-balled jefe of the Mexican Mafia. Juan was an asshole. Probably he'd crossed right over from this nowhere land to Texas and caused a stink-mess of trouble somewhere. Knowing him, he'd argued, bragged, made a nuisance of himself, no doubt finally provoked somebody into shooting him. But the moment this thought swung home, I understood what had happened.

I stared out into the rushing green-brown water. A tightening in my belly held me.

Something trembled in the jungle's heart.

The crepitation came from off to the right, buried deep among leaves.

It changed to a swish that then turned into footfalls, the syncopation of two people churning through heavy brush. A pause. Silence.

"Aquí," called Rafe.

"Okay," Ramón said.

Levering to a stand, I parted the cane with both hands and stepped inside.

The trick was to move without noise. Any touch could rattle the dry stalks and inform the prey. With all the burglar's stealth, with all my practice, I still couldn't help stepping on a twig now and then, or hitting the tiny branches that stuck out and seemed to crackle louder than cellophane. There was no path. I was moving blind. Cane smacked my face and ringed me round, the only aperture the sky, the only footprints those of small animals in the muddy layers of old growth. I had no machete to slash the way. It took concentration to keep the direction of Rafe's voice, all the while creeping toward what must be the exact spot. A foot or two would miss them. But even so it grabbed me by surprise when all at once I stood three feet from Rafe's back.

His shirt was dark with moisture. He stood at the edge of a small natural clearing. Dead leaves cluttered his hair. I could smell oil from his head, I could smell his rank sweat, and I couldn't imagine that he didn't feel my hot breath hit his nape as he poised there behind Ramón. Ramón's back was turned toward him. I froze.

"Eh! No viste? Sentado atrás de los árboles?" he said.

"No, no observa. Dónde?" asked Ramón, shading his eyes to peer ahead through the canebrake. Rafe's hand stole down to his waistband and drew out a knife.

"Mira, cuidado."

As the steel blade drew back and then rose, I lunged.

The knife leaped ahead into Ramón's flesh, its stab so weakened by my blow that it skittered across his ribs like a snake burrowing under packed sand. It had been aimed below, left of center up toward the heart. Blood spurted and ran in a widening stream. Ramón staggered sideways under the point. Then he tumbled face down, smashing into the cane stalks. I heard him grunt and sigh his wonderment. By then Rafe had already withdrawn the blade and flown about to see what thing had knocked his arm. He looked bewildered but turned angry, his black, still eyes locking down, when he found me facing him. The blade cut arcs of silver across the air as it passed and I saw winged light like butterflies, then a bird that swooped close as if to rest on my shoulder but dropped below instead. I flinched just in time before Rafe tipped to ram the blade home. It grazed sideways, catching and ripping my shirt. It missed me. He stepped back for another thrust. His lips were sealed tight on his teeth. The anger had transmuted to a look of solemn calculation, the eyes not aggressive but considerate, aware to what should soon be foregone, pacing mechanically through the steps to finish it and make it real. He had danced this dance before, I saw. Many times. Times beyond counting. He pretended to jump. It worked like a matador's feint. I jerked the other way. This was what he'd planned for; whipping out the battered toe of his boot, he struck my ankle, and for the millionth time in my own life I began wheeling toward earth, tripped by yet another surprise, thrown into the familiar spin, so that his feral eyes contemplating me sparked with a slow-motion luminosity of triumph that became startlement when I flipped troutlike in midair and twisted away from the knife once more. The island felt springy beneath. Not like the UT trampoline, or the wrestling mats at boarding school. When Rafe dove I was ready, his arms like wire snapping taut, and I evaded with another twist and roll so that I butted his stomach and pushed him off my body and straddled him with a wrestling hold, the knife hand flailing until I could wrench it still and double it against itself; I then bent it so that it flexed tight in defense next to his ear, ready to pop forward and stab, and I could see plainly what his silent eyes intended. So, leaning with all my weight down and to one side I pushed until suddenly before I realized it the razor point was spindling his throat, piercing the artery, and he let out a scream and then two more as blood geysered up and up. The blood fell back into his open mouth. It jetted my cheek. It sprayed my eyes. Gathering beneath us, it sank like black fluid from a broken pipe. It wasn't like the leg, I thought, not like Jesus's leg. The screams grew garbled. In his bed of smashed cane Ramón groaned; I could feel as if it were mine the muscular space behind his heart pouring life out through the wound. Still the heart pumped defiantly; it banged inside my ears, louder than Rafe's ragged gasping, louder than the gurgle in his throat that overtook and became one with the gurgle from the river. Rocking back into the decayed matting, I smelled a stench. The smell congregated. I looked a question at Rafe; his eyes found mine, they were hardening against it in protest, then they stilled and went glassy, their depths closing like mica on that endless vacancy, and I realized the thing they usually don't tell you about death, how his body had released itself and was now sagging into its own shit on the springy layer of dead cane, into the lake of blood, the living cane encircling it like the sides of some ancient sacrificial pool, and that if I only stood up, just scrambled up, just heaved right on up, I could leave him and it behind forever. I tried.

Then the odor of the rawhide purses from the market stall in Nuevo Laredo came rushing back and I bent over and vomited across the clearing.

I GRASPED RAMÓN'S shoulder. He moaned.

"Hey," I whispered. I glanced down at my sticky hand, then at the corpse, fearful of what our voices might wake. The darkness welled and seeped into the ground. Nothing stirred.

"Come on," I urged. "Come on, old buddy."

Ramón remained silent.

"We've got to go." I stooped beside him, lifting the arm that lay so nonchalantly flung over the stalks. I wrapped it around my neck. "Come on, now."

His head turned from its nose-down position. He drew a deep, sawing breath.

So I raised him up and stumbled through the thicket with him in my arms.

WHEN WE REACHED the bank my strength was failing. Both my arms shook. Spots drifted black against the blue sky. Looking down, I saw Ramón's eyelids twitch, but there was no question of helping him to limp or even to stand; the blood strapped around his chest like a red scarf. I sat down in the gravelly weeds at the edge of the river to rest. Air gashed into my lungs. The accompanying thirst felt unbearable. Laying Ramón's cradled head carefully to one side I squatted at the river, dipped my hands in, and started to fill them, but then caught sight of the blood skein unraveling and knew that it would be impossible to drink from that cup. The black spots wriggled. I thrashed and thrashed the hands until their threads slipped away. Still when I raised them dripping they stank of death. They weren't mine anymore; I had to get clean. Frantically I shoved my face into the water so his blood would peel off. The current swept by, tugging at stiff brows, licking forehead and cheeks, the cold, fine, swift current. I held down as long as breath permitted and rose gasping, then looked around for something with which to dish a drink for Ramón. Scrabbling through the weeds made the odor of death grow stronger. So I forced myself to lift the tufts that overhung the river, where a cluster of big, useful leaves had snagged. But when I saw the thing that lay caught within them I knew the smell was not coming from my hands.

A human foot floated, gray, pulpy. Someone had chopped it off at the ankle: a dead creature all on its own. The flesh lay shredded a little off the bones, which glowed green just under the water's surface.

I racked both arms under Ramón's shoulders and yanked us straight down the gravel, tucked his head in my elbow's crook and towed him out into the green-brown shine.

The water buoyed him up. That was how we did it. Otherwise, how could it be?

Now when I think about that crossing, to describe it seems the hardest task of life. The act won't shape into language. My mind goes dark. I move once more inside the dream: time merges with swirling waters, the river churns deep, mysterious, filled by a hollow roar. Words swim through its murk and flip away again, and I must reach into the cold darkness to fish up each one, hook fingers around each firm, solid body, and haul it to the light, before it can stand alongside the others.

His body tore away over and over. Only the chin notched against my arm kept us together. Several times I slipped, pulled by the sodden weight into the maelstrom; several times we went under. Water poured from his mouth. Afterward, froth. Then the rapids dwindled, the shallows rose up under my feet, I dragged us onto the Mexican shore.

He wasn't breathing to speak of. His wound had been invisible, but when I turned him sideways to empty the lungs, I saw it. The passage had rinsed it clean and raw. Even the shirt now molded white around it. I had to mash his rib cage and pump what he'd swallowed back out so he'd start breathing. But I couldn't press against that shark's-mouth slit. I couldn't. Luckily he didn't hold much water; it came trickling from his throat and nose onto the stones. After the first few coughs he began to gasp air.

I slumped over in exhaustion. Nothing worked anymore, arms or legs or even the neck holding my head straight. Every part quivered. The sound of the river had fallen to a trill, the roaring gone. All I wanted was to lie down in the mud and sleep through deliverance. It seemed best, sleeping, to drift numb under broad daylight and forget what had happened, forget the body on the island and the one lying next to mine. But rest wasn't in the plan: I had to determine how deep.

The knife had run sideways under his skin, then upward like a letter opener, cutting a long, thin slash. The shirt hung plastered to his back. Its rent exactly matched the open-lipped place beneath. Rafe had sliced through the fascia wall, but how far below that and the ribs I couldn't gauge. The wound between my fingers lay spread hygienically graphic so that I could see skin layers and muscle and slanting rib cross-sectioned like an anatomy drawing. I stared in desperation. He'd lost a lot of blood; that was all I knew. Even now the cut was brimming red again.

"Hey," I whispered.

His face relaxed into weary peace. He frowned, eyes opening.

"You're alive."

The lips moved.

"Ramón! Shit—you're alive!"

He blinked and winced, not prepared to discuss it. Galvanized, I leaped up and pulled my T-shirt over my head and wrung the river water out, then tore it in strips to make a bandage. Slipping it under him seemed a challenge. But I didn't know what else to do; the sense of not knowing what to do was crippling. "Sorry. Sorry, buddy, I'm sorry," I said over and over, kneeling there. "You'll be okay. I promise you're going to be okay. You'll be just fine," while I wrapped and tied and concealed the unspeakable slot in his back so as to bear to think that something claimed out loud might be true.

After we'd finished he closed his eyes, sprawling on his side once more. I didn't speak again. I touched his hair, the sweat drops on the temple. He looked like a child after a hard morning in kindergarten. After a minute I stood up to peer over the canebrake. On the bottomland near the hedge, a filament of smoke still spiraled sideways out of the lean-to next to the blue house. My car sat where I'd left it, parked halfway to the adobe walls. The scene looked precisely the same.

Why did I feel someone was near? Where was the person who had lit the fire?

"Listen."

Ramón's eyes fluttered as he wafted in and out of consciousness.

"I hate to tell you this. But we've got to go."

He looked trustingly at me. In his face shone the transparent water-marks of pain.

"You need a doctor bad. Now don't worry, you'll be okay. But you've got to get stitched up, maybe some other stuff, too, I don't know. Antibiotics. Shots." I preferred not to speak my fear of the house.

"Sí," he croaked after a moment.

"Can you move?"

"No sé." Already the lips were parching in the sun.

"I'm going to raise you a little. Then you try and test your legs to see if they'll support."

"Sí."

"It might hurt some. Here, give your arm." Once more I folded it around my neck. He licked his lips, gazing unquestioning straight at me, and kept his eyes fixed as we straggled to a standing position with me grasping his waist and him leaning like a toppled pillar against the unreliable wall of my side. I stepped slightly ahead of him, shouldering and shoving cane as we passed. When we reached the open space, I searched around quickly to see if anyone was there. The house stood as before, door hanging wide. The fire had died down to coals. No sound. No truck, nothing.

We limped the rest of the way. At the car I negotiated Ramón into the backseat, settled him down as comfortably as possible, and climbed behind the wheel. Just after I'd turned the key, just as my foot stomped the accelerator and the engine revved and the Escort bucked and skidded across the grass toward the gate, I looked back at the adobe doorway and glimpsed, materializing from its interior like two dim pearls, the fearstruck faces of an old woman and a little girl.

8

The U.S. Customs officer who motioned me over to a bay looked like one of those ancestral Scottish types: widemouthed, sandy-haired, with little blue eyes and deep gullies trenched around his mouth. It was two-fifteen, one and a half hours after Rafe's attack. Here on the border it was limbo hour. Heat drifted like some bright, stale precipitant across car hoods and bridge pavement, sifting onto the tar roofs of the International Station buildings. Ramón was bleeding to death in the backseat. He was going to die.

I turned to the officer and flashed a smile. "Hello, sir, how you doing?"

Shaking his head, he rapped on the window.

"Sorry—I thought you sounded a little muffled," I chuckled, rolling it down.

"You American?"

"Yessir, I sure am."

"Who's that you got with you?"

"Oh. That's just a good buddy."

He bent and peered beyond my shoulder into the backseat. "Show me your passport, please?"

"Oh. Yeah, sure. Right here." I patted around my pants, scrounging for my wallet.

"Why don't you step outside." He opened the door.

It wasn't until I stood on the asphalt beside him, unwedging the wallet from the still-damp jeans pocket, that it dawned on me to worry about Rafe's blood. It was too late to check in the rearview. Could there be dried streaks in my hair? Flecks on my ears? On my shirt? *Murder*, the word whispered up. There had been blood everywhere, rimming nostrils, coating wrists. I could still smell it. But of course, I thought: no spot could have survived the Rio Grande. I glanced at my hands. Two fingernails shone crescented in rust.

Heat rushed through my face.

"Why's it so wet?"

"What? Oh—you mean my wallet?" I splayed the wings of soggy leather and flapped them negligently in air. "Man. Well, um, we been, you know, kind of fooling around at this, you know." He waited. "Aw—a whorehouse."

"Yes?"

"Yessir. Anyhow. There was this bathtub?" He stared. "Our other buddies—it was a frat weekend, you know. All KAs. Anyhow, they figured I was too sober because I'm the designated driver? So those scumsuckers took aholt of me and threw me in that tub. Bunch of bozos." I coughed. "Damn thing's full of the nastiest old water. Lord knows what-all else was in it. Every damn stitch I have on's soaked."

"Your passport, please."

"Oh. Sorry." It dawned on me that what he'd asked for wasn't in my wallet. I dredged through my other rear pocket and pulled the loggy mass of paper out, before realizing what a miracle it was that it too had outlasted the river.

"Taylor Troys. 4120 Maple Drive. Bernice, Texas."

"Yes, sir."

"What's his name?"

"Who, him? His name's Ramón Vizuelos. Don't worry, he's a U.S. resident."

He bent forward. "Hey, there! Wake up!"

Ramón didn't move.

"What's his problem?"

"Oh, you know. Too much partying."

He sniffed. The fumes of the tequila I'd sprinkled all over Ramón's clothes and poured into his wound to disinfect it laced the atmosphere. His face lay blanched against the seat, sweat-glazed. Mustache growth peppered the grayish skin of his upper lip. The officer sniffed again with slow finesse, as if separating the odors into more precise weft.

"We're both pretty rank." I laughed apologetically. On the outskirts of Nuevo Laredo I'd stopped at a hole-in-the-wall bar for the tequila. I'd come close to feeding some to Ramón as well, until I'd remembered just in time alcohol's danger for injured nervous systems. "But shoot, we can't help it."

"Hey there!"

Ramón's eyes opened.

"Climb on out, Ramón."

"He doesn't feel too good. He threw up about ten gallons of booze back there in the road."

He ignored me. "Come on now, chico. Ven conmigo."

"Here—his green card's in his right rear pocket, he showed it to you guys when we crossed over last night. I'll just—" I started to crowd into the car past the wide plank hand, which grabbed the nape of my neck.

"Back off."

"He's legal, I swear to God. We've got to drive back to Austin by tonight, we promised his mother—"

"Debhart?" he called across the bay. His colleague had been standing inside the open booth, watching the proceedings while he ticked through some papers on a clipboard.

"Yo."

"One in here for quarantine."

"Okeydoke."

"Better bring the dogs out while we're at it. What's he got?" he turned to me. "Overdose? You said vomiting. What else? Diarrhea?"

"He's been stabbed, goddamn it!" Suddenly the outrage burst its banks. I stood trembling.

"Stabbed." The officer quirked a brow. "How'd it happen?"

"I don't *know!*" My fists knotted. "In the damn street! Some damn drunk cut him. All the hell we did was go pay to get screwed and some punk comes on us with a knife. We couldn't go to the Mexican police. You know what they'd do. Look, please just pull his green card out and let me get him to a hospital." I was beside myself. I wanted to rip the officer's face off.

"Let's see the wound."

"He can't fucking be *moved!*"

"Where is it? In the back? Ribs?"

Debhart sauntered up and stood beside the door, one hand resting lightly on his holstered gun.

"You want to give me a hand?" the officer asked him.

"Long as he ain't contagious."

"He's bleeding to death! What you smell is blood!"

"So that's where you got it, huh?" The Scot nodded toward my chest. I looked down. There was no shirt.

With fingers shaking I touched the bloodwreaths Ramón had left on my skin. It must have happened when I'd bandaged him. With my shirt. After, while we'd struggled to the car. Drops freckled each arm. Dried red dapples flaked the belly, roses tattooed. A smear of fine cilia crossed one nipple. I studied it. At first glance I might have mistaken it for a feather.

"You're not in too good a shape yourself, are you?" the officer said more gently. "Hey, there, sit down. Sit on that counter before you faint. We're calling the paramedics. I think we'd better get you both to the hospital."

IT OCCURRED TO ME, sitting in the ER waiting room drinking Cokes for shock, that maybe I'd done the wrong thing. What if Ramón's green card was forged? What if La Junta had provided it? Had I accidentally set him up? Should I have tried to ferry us across illegally, or sought underground help and risked somebody wondering about Rafe? Or what? The fatigue quavering through me sent my hand into a spasm that jerked the Coke can out onto the floor. I sat, tears running down, unable to raise the shuddering hand again to wipe them.

"Mr. Troys."

I turned. The Scot stood there. "How you doing."

"All right."

"I just want to tell you you'll be free to go."

"When?" I swallowed and tried to disguise the tears, hunching my shoulder, leaning forward and bracing my face in my fists.

"The nurses' station said your friend should spend a couple of nights here. Once they release him you two can take off home."

"He checked out okay?"

"Yes he did." He paused. "They also said to tell you that the bank phoned. The money you asked to be wired for the hospital bill has arrived. From a Judge Peter S. Troys in Bernice?"

"Ah. Oh. Thanks."

He watched me with a bright, flinty gaze. "It's just my business to be curious."

"I know that."

When I didn't add anything else, he said, "You know, we have a serious problem around here. Maybe you're familiar with it, maybe not. The magazines and papers report it sometimes, those TV news shows—*60 Minutes, 20/20.*"

"You mean to do with all the illegal aliens."

"No. I mean with the drug cartels."

I sat silent.

"Pushing dope across the border, cocaine in particular. Supplied by the Cali through Mexican druglords." He paused. "We went over your car real good. We also ran a check on you. Not even a traffic ticket. You're clean. So's your friend Mr. Vizuelos, apparently."

"I know it." I closed my eyes. Safe, I thought; safe. Within the darkness visions floated, the dead face staring with its two drilled night holes, roses blood-petaled, the rose blossom tattoo on the arm of the Tulum taxi driver as he took me into the jungle toward the cenote. The sombrerero's fat wrist cinched with lumpen yellow metal. A one-balled Mafia chief, face covered in scars. A severed foot bobbing.

"What I can't figure out is why you didn't just tell us in the first place."

"What?" I opened my eyes.

"It looks kind of suspicious, don't you think? You showing up all wired with panic instead of just explaining he's been mugged." The canny eyes raked me up and down.

"Dumb, maybe. But how could something so stupid be suspicious? If we'd been trying to smuggle or whatever, would we have come over that way? Wrecked up?"

"You'd be amazed at the things we see."

"Well hell. I didn't know what to do." As I spoke the relief of offering one pristine fact threatened to overturn all my credibility.

"You were in shock. Just a country boy in over his head. Trapped in a foreign situation." He nodded sympathetically, deceiving neither of us.

"You could put it that way."

"Well, sir." He put on his hat, tapping it squarely in place. "I'd best get on now."

"I really appreciate all your help."

He nodded once more. "De nada. Maybe next time you'll steer clear of the bordertowns if you're wanting a binge, huh?"

"That's for sure."

"By the way. You mentioned Mr. Vizuelos's mother. And you've obviously informed your family of where you are and what you're doing."

"Yes, sir."

"Well, you might want to also let Mr. Vizuelos's wife know about his condition."

The automatic ER door opened and closed with a hiss. Somewhere nearby an elevator bell rang.

"Oh. Yeah," I said. "Of course I will."

"Apparently she lives in Dallas."

"Yep. That's right. She sure does."

"Northwest Dallas, the address on his record suggested. Out toward Arlington." He paused. "Far piece from Austin."

"I'll go call her."

"She might be worried. After all, seeing as how she's the reason he got his green card in the first place." He smiled, tipped his hat, and walked heavily across the linoleum. Right at the entry to the waiting room he turned. "God protects fools and children, Mr. Troys," he said.

"WHERE ARE WE?" asked Ramón.

I looked around for a sign. "On the interstate right outside of Belton."

"I think I need another pill."

I scrabbled around the console and handed him the Percodan bottle and a Dr Pepper can.

"You talk with mi tía today?"

"Yeah. She knows you're okay." I hadn't told her about Juan. His fate quivered inside the car between us like a mirage in a desert canyon.

"Gracias."

"There's someone I did fail to contact, though, since I don't have the phone number."

"Quiénes?"

"Señora Vizuelos."

Outside the window three cars zoomed past.

"Ah." He licked his lips. "You mean mi madre? En Monterrey?"

"No. I do not mean your mother." Then he had the decency to duck his eyes downward.

I accelerated hard toward the inside lane. "So where did you two meet?"

"In the hotel three years ago."

"How convenient!" At once Dodie's furious tear-streaked face appeared, pinched with despair as she watched Eduardo saunter away. A little silvery dart chilled my blood.

"She learned I want to go to University of Dallas."

"Ah. Romantic, too! Who is she? Some idealistic little Texas girl? Some fine-hearted humanitarian Baptist, doing her bit for education?"

"Why are you so much pissed off?"

"Well, it's not something you've exactly confided about, is it?"

"She's just trying to help," he muttered.

"Great!" I nodded energetically. "Hell! Not great. Wonderful!"

"Con matrimonio I got legal after two years. Also Dallas residence, exclusive. For the cost of state college. She helps me to do this."

"Perhaps she hasn't heard of some of your more piquant connections. Darn. Come to recall, I haven't yet contacted that other good pal of yours, either—Mr. Miguel Tracon. At his Huntsville residence, exclusive."

He didn't speak.

"Look. You know what, Ramón? I don't give a rat's ass what you do."

He looked out the window at the road verge.

"But that's the point, isn't it? Of friendship? You can do what La Junta hired you for. A true friend won't dream of asking questions."

"What are you saying?" he said.

"You know. Your job. Hauling cocaine back over the border for the Cali cartel."

A truck roared past.

"Isn't that right?" I prodded.

"You don't know nothing."

"Oh, I know all right."

"Shut up, Taylor, okay?" His eyes closed.

"It took me a while," I mused. "I finally figured it out. Not until our friend from customs explained, you understand."

He made a sound.

"That little rendezvous you had in Deep Ellum that night? 'Got to go look for Juan.' That little run over to Jorris's that morning? Family loyalty. Great! Look for Juan, who's disappeared while toting merchandise. For the likes of Jorris. *Wasn't* he? And you were supposed to find it *and* him, and then bring them both back yourself. You, the mule." I rolled down the window and hawked some phlegm, jetting it into the tearing wind. "With me as your driver."

From the passenger's seat came silence.

"I guess my stooge act with Rafe wasn't so far off the beam, was it? Old Taylor, tame dummy. Smart as Mrs. Vizuelos herself."

"Stop," he whispered.

"Only you didn't know the first steps. You were another chump."

"No."

"The thing is, even though I admit we both got interested in each other on a need-to-know basis, something just sticks in my craw. Like, I thought we'd moved beyond friendly user somehow. You know. You use Mrs. Vizuelos. Susie, Heather, whatever her name is. They use you. You lie, use me. You nearly die."

He turned his face away.

"I owe you," he said after a minute.

"Nah. Fuck no! Near arrest and long-term prison are reward enough." Keeping the car to an even sixty-five, I turned over the widening spread of possibilities. "Not to mention setting up some nice girl who only wanted to help you for jail."

"I *had* to do it. They pay me already. They bring me to Texas. If I don't they kill me."

"They just about did, didn't they?"

He didn't answer.

"And after all, I owe *you* for teaching me to pick a dead bolt."

It had all appeared so mysterious. So dangerous—Ramón down in Cozumel, in his slick black thief's outfit, calmly bullying his asshole cousin. I'd been magnetized by my own inspiration, the dark potentials that our connection had implied. But even the fine art of burglary turned out to be something practiced with a bludgeon.

As I sat weighing up all the lies told to further my secret inner life—to

Mother, Grandfather, by omission to Ramón and Teresa-Maria—I realized that there was really no way to justify this moral pique against Ramón. I'd done exactly the same thing he had. I just hadn't actually planned to set my friends up with prison sentences if I got caught. But that's what would have happened, I thought. It could have. Staring through the windshield I saw fields, a farmhouse, the little towns with their water towers. They all seemed anachronistic, paralyzed by sleep and television. That was what I'd rebelled against. Who out there remembered the liveliness action confers? Overhead the sky stretched wide open, empty as a tablet page. Every tree, every grass blade and fence post and cow stood out crisp against the infinite distance. No line could blur on such a space, no action look equivocal. But on the cathode screens ethics had no outlines anymore, only a perpetual jittering fist. This was the world my father had given to my mother, the world she'd passed on to me to cup in my hand. Chaos. Betrayal of friendship. Betrayal of love.

When I inspected this vision, the urge to harden, to climb above the stew of corruption rose up in me, breaking through the skin. But first, I thought, I had to plunder his life.

"Taylor," he said.

"What?"

"Lo siento."

I drove a few more miles before I replied: "Forget it."

On the island the body sprawled in the clearing, buzzards circling and landing, picking at his chest. I saw the eye lock onto mine, the fear's final imperative before the shutter snapped closed.

"WHAT DO YOU think happened? Where is he?" asked Teresa-Maria. She warmed her hands around her coffee cup. In the next booth a family suddenly burst out laughing, each member in turn having tried to spoon-feed a high-chair toddler with a pirate's rolling eye who kept spluttering their offerings onto the table. "Could he have gone home to Cozumel?"

"No."

"No, of course. He would phone Mama and tell her at least." She sighed. "Maybe he missed his ride and had to walk."

"No."

"Why not?" She peered sadly at me, then down into the overflowing salsa bowl, trimming the excess with her finger. I remembered the way she'd run it down my chest. I had only one longing: to lie down with her, erase what was about to come or leap beyond it, feel the camber of her thigh, make her happy. It was, like so many others, an impossible goal.

"There's a particular reason we couldn't find him."

"Claro."

"We did find his trail."

She looked up. "You haven't told this."

I nodded.

"You've been home for three hours. Why didn't Ramón say this?"

"He's feeling too sick to talk much."

"Was it when Ramón got hurt that you stopped following the trail?"

"Yes. But not just because Ramón got hurt."

She stared uncomprehendingly.

"Juan is dead," I said.

"Eee-yow!" screamed the baby, dredging his hands through an enchilada plate and tossing the results around. His chin glowed, smeared with orange sauce. The father of the family laughed and toasted the baby with his beer bottle. The teenage daughter seized and manacled the wrist of a silent child who was placing sugar packets, tacos, tamale wrappers, butter pats, and saltshakers on the high-chair tray and then peering at the baby with a researcher's expectant curiosity.

"Jesus, Maria Madre," whispered Teresa-Maria.

"I'm sorry," I said, grasping her hands.

"How do you know?" Her eyes filled with tears.

"We found the man responsible for his death."

"Qué?"

"The one who cut Ramón."

She gulped. "Did you—" A resistance impeded. "Did you see—," she tried again, shook her head, and then licked her lips.

"I saw enough to convince me." Truth, I thought: honor. But there was no need to describe that disjecta membra to her.

"A . . . body?"

"Well. Yes."

"You think Juan? Pero no seguro?"

"I'm pretty sure."

"Where was this? In Mexico? How could you see a dead body and not see who it was?" She'd begun to tremble.

"I saw another guy wearing his watch."

"Maybe it was not his watch." She sat weeping silently, no sobs, no sniffs. The tears spilled down her flawless cheeks, lacquering the beauty mark, mingling on the upper lip with the run from her nose. She didn't move. A drop splashed onto my wrist. "Watches can be all the same, they can look alike."

"I know. Teresa-Maria, believe me." I paused. "It's conceivable that Juan might have traded it or got it stolen off him, but that's not what really happened. For sure. Do you think I would tell you this otherwise?"

"Why would someone kill him?"

"Because he got obnoxious."

Her face contracted with horror. She snatched her hands away. "Bastante!"

"I'm sorry. It's the truth." I sighed. "I guarantee it. Those guys down there don't put up with any bullshit. They're not going to take extra risks, it's too dangerous. If somebody's a hassle they get them out of the way quick. No mercy. Believe me." The baby began squalling. The teenage girl tried to cajole him with a tortilla, which he slapped away like a bug. Teresa-Maria was staring at me openmouthed. I saw again Rafe's turn, the knife cutting brightly through the air. "You know Juan. Cocky. Bragging. Petty-minded. Smart-ass. He must have smarted off somehow. Remember what he said to you that night back in Cozumel? 'Buzz, buzz, the mosquito'?"

She closed her mouth, opened it. The tears seemed to have frozen on the skin.

"You can imagine what happens in a situation like that." God knew I had. "People paying to cross over illegally every day. No tracks, expendable, worth only whatever hard cash they have. Juan wasn't just illegal. He actually had a record with the U.S. Feds. These guys are ruthless. They don't tolerate Jonahs messing with their business. So they—"

"Bastardo," she hissed. Her lips trembled, she kept trying to close them against the snot.

"Yes. They're true bastards. Scum." The venal, murderous resonance of the world I had stepped into now echoed through my ears. "But I promise you: The killer isn't there any longer. He won't be doing anybody else. Do you hear me? No harmless family men trying to make a living. No kids on the run. Never again." It was my solo solace: the justice braided into that island afternoon. The only offering I could give.

"Bastardo! Hijo de la puta!"

"Honey—they're scum. Listen. Would you like to go outside?" Maybe, I thought, it would be better if she didn't have to sit publicly under the harsh café lights, her grief peeled back, the waitresses hurrying past, couples and families eating, the jukebox playing New Age Nashville. I caressed her hands. They'd clenched into hard knots. She uncrooked the fingers, stretched them out, rotated them around within the shelter of mine, and dug ice picks into my palms.

"Ow!"

"You arrogant gringo bastard," she whispered.

"What?"

"How dare you? How dare you say these things about my brother and then use us to get what you want?"

My jaw dropped.

She slid out of the booth and stood up. Her eyes had turned to black fire. She puckered her lips, gathering tautness, and spat in my lap. "Pendejo. Go to the devil in hell."

FOLLOWING BEHIND HER steel-armored back, inching along the five blocks from the café to Lee Street, I watched her jerky-legged walk home. Her skirt switched from side to side, her heels made the clicking sound I'd first heard in a tropical hotel lobby. She looked so slim and proud with her hair piled high that my heart was breaking.

"Hey," I tried once, leaning out the window. The Escort bumped forward. "Please get in. I swear—you just don't understand what went on down there."

I saw her lip lift over her teeth.

"Teresita. Please. Let's talk," I said. Her speed never faltered. Everything about her body spurned me with contempt. When we finally got to Lee Street I parked as she strode up the flagstones. By the time I'd jumped out she'd marched into the house and slammed the door.

I sat on the curb. Well, I thought. Goddamn it.

I didn't want to talk with Ramón. He was sleeping by now, anyhow, full of painkillers. Nor did I want to overhear the wailing when she told her parents about Juan.

Anger swilled through me like acid. Every muscle and tendon burned. A television was blaring through the open front door of the house across the street. I could see the family inside huddled around it like Neolithic Man around the cave fire. From this angle the Hidalgo home looked blank, its boarded windows ominous, the shattered wood rotting already. Suddenly I wanted to punch somebody.

Two lowrider Chevies roared past, their exhaust pipes belching and grinding sparks on the potholes while Latino rock blasted from their stereos. Three weeks before, some gang had shot out every single streetlamp within a ten-block radius. So far the city had only gotten around to fixing one or two toward a lot where a vacant house loomed behind wildly overgrown shrubbery. I started walking along the asphalt in the hollow darkness.

At the corner something soft brushed my hand.

"Hey!" I recoiled and looked down. A whimper mewed behind me.

"Moose!"

He had come out of the shrubbery and was sagging back on his haunches, his tail scraping the cement with each wag. The huge tongue lolled over the jawteeth as before; I could just make it out in the orange aurora hazing the leaves. When I reached out to pat him he leaped up and jammed his head under my palm.

"Hey boy. What are you doing here? How you been?"

He shoved my thigh, panting like a cardiac victim. "Are you on the loose?" I asked.

"I'm taking him for a walk."

The voice drifted through the dark, thin, delicate as fretwork. I turned. There was no one to see.

"Has he been cooped up lately? I haven't seen him around."

"I don't like to let him out in the daytime. People get scared of him, and all them little kids chuck rocks."

"Well, heck. That's ridiculous. Moose wouldn't hurt an ant." I searched right and left through the shadows. The only obstacle was a big shrub climbing a telephone pole on the next-door lot, bushing out lushly around its base.

"I know that. I ain't never claimed he would. Daddy's the one."

"Ah." I paused. Moose nudged harder.

"Taught him to bark so loud like that."

"Yessiree. He sure can bark. He's a real barking champion."

She didn't say anything.

"Are you hiding inside those leaves?"

"I know who you are," she said.

"Oh." Slowly Moose sank back to his hind legs. I rubbed the pointed ears, scratching the head between them. "Is that right?"

"Yes."

"Uh-huh, I see. Well, that's good, isn't it?"

"You got Daddy put in the jailhouse."

"Well, not exactly."

"Tried to choke him to death."

"Um . . ."

"Took out his big old gun and thought he'd just shoot you to pieces. Then he hit Jesus instead."

"He, um, got him*self* arrested, actually." I cleared my throat. "But I'm sorry I had something to do with it, if it's hurt you."

"Taylor Troys."

"Yes—that's right."

"Is Jesus okay?" A hesitation, of fear or something else, made her slightly breathless.

"He will be." I paused, remembering the barrel's heat scorching my grip. "Sooner or later."

"Will he walk again?"

"They're giving him a new leg. He'll be home from the rehab soon, I think. Walking, even. But first with crutches."

"How can they do that? Give him a new leg?"

"An artificial one. Fake. You know, like maybe you've seen on TV? Plastic, or with metal."

"Plastic?" She pondered. "It won't look nothing like Jesus's real leg, will it? No skin, no hair. No kneebone." She went silent. The silence lasted a long time. I scratched Moose's muzzle. "Jesus got a scar on his ankle, playing tag one time. Fell down on a piece of glass. That's gone now, ain't it? They never give Daddy none of them legs down at the VA."

"I think it only works if you still have some of your own one left."

"Do you know if he's mad?"

"Who, Jesus?" It was the question I asked myself every night. "You mean with me?"

"No. Not you. Daddy, I guess."

"He hasn't mentioned it when I've visited him. He's remarkably cheerful, in fact, considering."

She let out a tiny sigh.

"I have an idea. Why don't you come out?"

The leaves rustled. Then they stilled.

"Moose, could you please maybe get her to come out?" I asked.

Moose whined and licked my fingers. "He can't make me do nothing, that dog," she said with startled scorn.

"I guess not. Can you, boy?"

The leaves rattled again. She stepped out into open air. "Ha!"

"Hidy," I said.

"I can do it my own self, thank you."

"So I see."

"Daddy was the one always made *Moose* do things."

She stood tall, gangly. Her crown came even with my chin, which is unusual for a girl. I judged her to be about sixteen. Her skin gleamed pale in the scanty light, with a skim-milk translucency to the legs poking out like stalks from her cutoff shorts: the kind of unnaturally white skin that records each minuscule encounter with outer objects—holding indelibly the lines from a dragging thorn, preserving in red a finger's pressure, showing the imprint of a towel texture, the blush or heat rash, the blue veins underneath. Her hair looked copper. It fell to her shoulders in thick terraced waves.

"What things?"

She looked sideways toward me. "You know."

"No, I don't."

She glanced off, inexplicably lightened. "Oh. Well, then. Just crummy old things. Barking real loud. Carrying on."

"That's what dogs do generally."

"He taught him, though. With a dead rabbit."

"A what?"

"Yes. Rabbit. You heard what I said." She paused. "He made me get the rabbit from the pet store. Give me the money, told me I could keep it for my own pet. Little soft, sweet bunny. I brung it home, so he used it still alive on Moose. Then when Moose wouldn't hurt it he killed it and bopped Moose on the head with it a bunch of times. Later on he skinned it."

"That's mean." That's psychopathic, I thought.

"He's a mean man." She shrugged. "He likes doing that. Skinning animals." She paced around me a little way, making a show of looking me over. "You look sad."

"I do?"

Diplomatically her eyes strayed off up the street to the sky. She scowled at it as if she could make out the stars above the city's glow. "Looked sad standing there a minute ago. Soon as I saw you."

"I guess I was."

"It's that girl, huh? Me and Moose saw you chasing her. She's mad at you, ain't she?"

"Yeah. I guess."

"She is. Hoo, boy."

"She's just upset. Period."

"*Period?*" she cried, scandalized. Then, "What'd you do to her?"

"Told her a true thing."

She frowned, her nose wrinkling, and rubbed her elbow sideways against her pelvis point.

"It's just something between her and me."

"Well la-di-da."

"No. I mean—she's upset about her brother."

"Goody for her."

"I'm just telling you. In case I sounded rude."

"Think I care?"

"No."

"Good. Cause I don't." She licked her lips with the flat of her tongue. Then she raised a finger to scratch the inside of her nose, her gaze wandering absently to the houses opposite. It struck me that she was someone who spent her time utterly alone. All at once I remembered the drapes twitching aside the day we tackled Jorris.

"Tell me. Have you been inside your house all this time since your daddy went to jail?"

"Well, I live there, don't I? I have a right." Her elbows jutted out sharply on the skinny arms.

"Is there anybody there with you?"

"Of course not. Me and my daddy been by ourselves for as long as I can recall."

"How about your friends?"

"Friends from where?"

"School."

"Ain't got any friends. There's only just us." She stopped still. Her thin face and turned-up eyes went shy. Her bare feet nearly disappeared under Moose's butt; she leaned into his fur, as if seeking safety. "I'm glad you done that," she murmured.

"Done what?"

"Gripped him upside the throat. Turned him in to the police."

For a moment surprise stopped me from answering.

"I'm glad they locked him up. It's real nice not having him around."

"Is he hard on you?"

"I don't like what he makes me do." Awkwardly she bent down, rubbed her ankle, and moved closer to me. "Red bugs," she explained. "Chiggers everywhere. He makes me be mama."

"You mean, like, do the cooking? Clean house?"

"Heckfire. *He* cooks breakfast. He can cook good, don't you worry. He says my food tastes like K rations. Then he tans my hide."

"Good grief." I looked at her. There was something almost feverishly carefree about her hopping from foot to foot on the sidewalk in the darkness, swatting a mosquito, or digging her toes around on Moose's hip. When a car drove by she squinted at it like it was some monstrous creature she'd never seen before. She seemed far younger than she should. I wondered if she was quite right in the head. Then I thought, with a father like Jorris, of course not.

"I'd rather he hit me than make me be mama."

"How does he do that?" I pictured Jorris making her pamper him like a baby, comb his hair, feed him, clean up his table messes, tuck him in at night.

"If I felt like telling you I would." Incongruously she began to whistle. I recognized the tune: "Button Up Your Overcoat." Moose's ears pricked. A momentary sound down the street behind us made her pause and tilt forward to peer over my shoulder: a metal door slamming, or a garbage lid banging down. Then suddenly the same two lowriders raced around the corner side by side, rpms at top volume, the booming mufflers dragging the street. They shot past us, and I watched their headlights hone the dark like razors. She turned to watch, too. Then as she pivoted back she threw her full weight against me; both arms clinched tight around my shoulders. "'Be mama! Be mama!' Unzipping his nasty old pants," she mocked shrilly.

"What?"

"But don't worry. You fixed his wagon."

I gasped. "I did?" She knocked the breath out of me; for a second I failed to apprehend fully what she'd just said.

"*You* did! You and Jesus and that other boy. Then when the police come I know it—he won't be doing that no more to me!"

I was speechless.

"I love you!" she cried.

"My God—wait—"

"I love Jesus. I love him most. His poor poor leg. He lost his poor leg when Daddy shot him. But him losing it saved me. His poor little scar. I think about his scar all the time. Now he's half like Daddy because Daddy made him that way. But Jesus can mess with me. Any time. Daddy can't ever mess with me no more."

"No."

"But I love you, too."

"No," I whispered.

"I'll do whatever you want."

I shook my head.

"You want it? I'll give it to you. I will. I won't fight or kick or nothing. Any time. Any of you. You're the ones." She smelled like rinsed rice and florist flowers. My mind teetered toward what he'd done to her. Then the tender terror seizing me seemed to turn inside out; I had to force myself not to shove her away. "I can leave the house come night. Or you can come on in. But don't let's do it in my room, he might be waiting there in his mind. He might could see. Even from the jailhouse."

"Listen." I gasped a breath. "I want to help you."

"Don't worry. He won't come back no more. *No more.* That's what that policewoman told me. She asked me to come with her, but when she heard I was eighteen my last birthday she said I could just stay put. I have a right."

"Yes," I whispered.

"Do you love me? Please love me?" She moved in close and nuzzled my neck. The skin on hers glowed softly. Moose gave a yip. Then he settled back at her feet. I could see the frail down in the little scoop at her clavicle, a place where he'd touched, where his unspeakable acts had defiled.

"I'm going to get you some help." The down glowed silver. My voice shook. My arms crept up; I held her there. Her face tilted to mine. Thin ribs arched through the thin skin against the thin cotton shirt. Every vertebra felt distinct, fragile.

"You already did help me."

"More, I mean. More help." The police, I thought. No; a therapist, some kind of counselor. An expert. The down was like silk, the skin smooth and pale.

"Stay here with me. Please." She ducked and buried her mouth in my chest, her fuzzy hair brushing my chin. My eyes closed. "Taylor. Please don't leave me all alone."

"Shit, no. Don't *leave,* pendejo."

I looked around.

Teresa-Maria stood watching, no more than a pace away, her face filled with nightmare outrage. Tears sheeted her cheeks in a mask of ice. Dimly they glistened as her head turned back and forth. "Don't leave," she repeated.

"Teresa—"

"Ramón told me, 'He save my life. Juan is dead but Taylor save my life.'" Her teeth bared. "You take your little puta. You hijo de la puta. Fuck your little buddy." Her voice was dull, mechanical, grinding like a metal cog.

Jorris's daughter fell out of my nerveless arms.

"Teresita—"

"Fuck your puta," she hissed, raking me hard with her spread-out hand. Then she went running up the street. I gathered my wits together and chased after her. But before I could catch up she'd dashed into the house, slamming the door, and when I tried to leap those two little steps, the vertigo I thought I'd finally defeated rose up again at last like marsh mud, swamping me, and I whipped around and crashed to the yard dirt beneath the gritty, tired mimosas, right where I'd landed the day she first kneed me in the balls, and lay there spinning in the hot, buggy dark.

By the time I managed to haul myself up and look down the block, it was empty. Jorris's daughter was gone.

"YOU JUST DON'T know the way women's minds work," Mother had said to me.

No kidding.

With one sprint I jumped into the Escort, started it up, and squealed away.

The rage boiled. I clutched the steering wheel. "To feel like that about somebody is the sweetest thing you'll ever know," she'd said, and I'd believed her. Frustration, anger—after I'd done everything I could for Teresa-Maria, for her brother, her family, even nearly getting myself *killed*—

all churned inside. But the indignation was smoke. Under it lay another, more terrible and furtive knowledge.

Checking the rearview mirror I caught sight of my own face. Revulsion surged. Crunching the gears into third, fourth, fifth, I gunned up the expressway.

She was right. I'm no different, I thought. I'm the same as the others. Rafe, Eduardo, Jorris. Ramón, who married some do-good innocent just to get legal. My stepfather Ben, who'd controlled my mother's life, nailed his daughter's love, and then hauled off and died. Women users.

I careened like the outlaw lowriders around blocks, up McKinney Avenue's antique shops, past Turtle Creek mansion lawns, onto the tollway, while all the satanic defects of men slid through the dark inside my head. A woman at a dressing table, surrounded by jars and pots and tubes and bottles; a girl crying as her lover strolled off through the pyramids; two faces hanging in a dusky adobe doorway; a girl crossing a lobby while a man leered in lust; the child crouched behind a closed curtain, arms buried in dog's fur, huddling through her long night, alone.

The same as him.

"I just trusted him," she'd told me. Then, "Men like that are often very ambitious."

I didn't want to think about the endless justifications behind other men's goals. They made me retch. So this is my real inheritance, I thought: to be driven like him; to do what he'd done. Was ambition all that mattered in the end? Did everything get skewed to its service? Was it in fact the sweetest thing he'd ever known? Sweeter than my mother's pain?

At 1:00 A.M. I drove through Deep Ellum, turned right, and parked the Escort down the alley where I'd let Ramón out five nights before.

METROPOLIS

On the eighth day . . . he arrived in Athens.

—Plutarch

9

A cat scrambled over the Dumpster and leaped into shadows.

The indigo sky hung between the buildings, a pink stain at its edge. I climbed out of the car and slammed the door. Then I unlocked the hatchback and grabbed the attaché case from within.

The alley lay deep between two buildings. Its dark gave enough cover for a complete change of clothes. It took only a second to fumble inside the spare tire recess for the cache: a black turtleneck sweater, gloves, a pair of leotard tights, rock-climbing shoes. Unbuttoning my shirt, I dropped it to the ground. Next fell jeans and underwear. When at last I stood naked I knew that, although this wasn't what I'd planned, it was correct.

The time was here.

One by one I donned each article of my chosen vocation. Then I ran my hands across the fine-grained new leather and popped the catch. Inside, the black polypropylene ski mask lay curled like a sleeping animal waiting to flex, to be filled with another flesh, another species.

Unrolling it, I slipped it over my head.

The tools I selected were these: a small titanium crowbar; the ring of lock picks; nylon rope; two electronically magnetized steel plates with battery-powered bases; a tension wrench; a Magno-Probe; a flashlight; a screwdriver; a credit card; a stethoscope; a liquid-filled compass; wiresnips; a chisel; the gun I'd bought from Bobby—my honorary criminal souvenir.

Each item had its scabbard fitted onto the black webbed belt—all except the gun, which I positioned in the small of my back under the tights' waistband, over the turtleneck's hem.

Next I pulled on the gloves.

NO ROOM IS so dark that the cat burglar's eye cannot eventually frame distinctions within it. Even if you're blind, objects have a way of radiating their own presences so that your subliminal radar picks them up. There lies a density within the hollow, the lump of coal within the ink, and sooner or later, patiently, you will sense enough outline not to stub your toe. Of course, it's true that the longer you remain in pitch blackness the more disoriented you'll become, mistaking hollow for substance, lending shape to the empty dark. But only when you lose your nerve does such a hazard loom large. Slipping behind the Dumpster, I considered this fact and its correlation to the human heart. Darkness is like falling in love. Or like any other strong emotion: a circumstance that cuts the normal scope of perception and then distorts it. For the likes of me, in whom disorientation was a lifelong condition, it presented a strange, inverted opportunity. The trick in both cases rested on focus.

Ever since I'd embraced this skill I'd realized I possessed an advantage. Now as I moved from doorway to doorway up the alley the adrenaline leaped through my blood. My heart pounded. And it was precisely because of the old, old habit, the friendship of my handicap, that I was able to pause, draw a deep breath, concentrate, and defeat twenty years' worth of fury hampering my every step.

Bastardo, she had called me.

Two blocks up I slipped into the side porch entrance of the Deeds Building.

• • •

NO LIGHTS WERE burning in the top-floor windows. The citadel stood vacant, a husk containing relics. But these would reveal more about his life than anything else, and this was my deepest desire: to read that life and then empty it.

I had counted on three things: old alarms, the building's age, and the fact that it was on an office block. I knew what it contained. The only things inside worth money were furniture and computers. No valuable goods lay housed here, no portable assets stored, ripening for the black market. There was nothing to steal but knowledge.

When I found the alarm I felt jubilation but no surprise. Its quaintness was touching, in a way. Childlike. So few walls to his kingdom—such ragged little sentries at the gates. It took me three minutes exactly to do what I'd practiced so often in the last few weeks on test dummies—disable the connection. What a fool! I thought. His self-confidence seemed too humble to believe.

Once the door shut behind me I clicked off the flashlight for a moment and lifted my eyes up the fire stairs into the vaulting dark. The fluorescent fixtures marking each landing had been turned off. There was no draft, there were no ducts leaking cool oxygen, only the stillness of a narrow absence six stories high. Absence. Beneath the mask clammy sweat sprang out on my upper lip. The stairwell enclosed a smell both musty and dank, like dried mouse droppings, like cement dust, like forgotten ventures recorded on foolscap and locked in stone. It was an aural event as well; it held the deadness of old tombs newly entered, of trapped silence suddenly released that poured toward the straining ear. I stood in this underworld, registering each nuance of his threshold. The tools' weight clung around my hips. Retinal images burst and died, soaking up the blackness. Then, when I'd felt everything there was to feel, I lifted my foot and touched the first tread, then the second, ascending toward my father's throne.

On the ninth floor I stopped in front of the last door, a pulse thundering hard through my head. Pulling the flashlight from its loop, I switched it onto the pressbar to see where I stood.

There were no wires at all.

A prickle of warning brushed my arms. Be careful. There are probably hidden detectors everywhere. You could trip a beam, step on a mine button. Wall panels may hold video cameras. The handle will prove heat reactive, the door hollow could have eyes. Even the flashlight might sting some circuit into life. Standing back about six inches, I held my breath, counted to three, then flicked the switch.

Nothing happened.

Slowly I played the light over the door, scoured the landing, then turned to the lintel and searched down the frame, peeling off my right glove for more sensitivity.

At that instant footsteps sounded on the other side.

I stopped breathing. The flashlight froze.

For perhaps ten paces the footfalls crossed the area just beyond the door. Heels squeaked on floor wax, louder. I hadn't been able to find out about a night watchman. My research had consisted of sneaky visits in sunglasses to the lobby to scan the building directory and the men's toilet, gloss over black marble walls (quarried Italian), check behind potted palms, under the aluminum clock (thirties deco), and between windowsills for alarm boxes, while the elevators opened to glimpses of mahogany. He'd restored the original decor from his grandfather's time after he'd made his fortune and bought the building back. Moisture dripped down my chest. My fingers vised around the flashlight. The footsteps paused.

A metallic tink scratched as a key came too close. A door squeaked. I jerked back. The darkness continued unbroken except for my own beam.

The footsteps stopped: carpet. Off in the distance someone rattled a drum, dropped into a chair, rolled some casters, clanked cutlery. Then another hush. It lasted either sixty seconds or a hundred days. The chair wheezed, the footfalls caused faint vibrations across the rug, the door sang loudly as it closed. The lock snicked. The footsteps smacked back down the hall. An elevator bell dinged. Bronze doors slid wide with a rumble, then shut. Dead silence.

I gasped for breath.

Was it a second burglar?

But then I reevaluated the sounds: they had all rung too casual, too customary. The person on the other side of the door was without question an habitué. But why at this hour?

Should I leave? I wondered. Adrenaline banged my temples. No, to hell with him. He was gone. I waited for another fifteen minutes of silence, then cautiously uncramped my muscles and began to tackle the lock.

The door swung open.

Soft shaded light blurred the parquet floors of the corridor. For one moment a swinging dizziness dragged my sight. Wood tiles rose. I smelled the fear in my own sweat; the earth bucketed and I clamped my head and held it fixed, both hands, mask black against eye rims, while all competence leached away. Then the wavy tunnel fell into dim golden particles that tightened to make walls, floor, doors, ceiling. I blinked. Focused. And at last stepped out into this new order and moved toward the sole door.

The plaque said A. J. DEEDS. PRIVATE.

Behind it lay files, records, letters, life, history, the blueprints of a character. The carpentry of his empire.

The lock required a pick I'd nicknamed the Bumblebee No. 17. It slipped in smooth as grease.

And as soon as the door opened I knew the mistake I'd made.

THE WOMAN STOOD just inside. I faced a dark, wallpapered vestibule. Before I could turn to run, she said, "A.J., we've got a burglar. Call the police."

She spoke quietly, without moving her eyes. The throaty voice sounded easy yet intense. Her nerve turned my knees to butter.

"What do you mean?" He moved toward the spot in the doorway's center where she stood. He came into view, slid into view, hove around into view, and then he was there, sighting me through the blond-gray strand over one eye.

"I've got a gun," I said.

"Do you? All the more reason for the police." She tapped his elbow. "I don't see it, personally," she said, nodding toward what must be a phone cradled on a table out of bounds in that bright telescoping radiance. "I told you those old alarms are crappy. Now I guess maybe you'll listen and get them replaced." She crossed her arms with a relaxed air, regarding me. For a split second her fingers jerked.

"What do you want?" he said.

You, I thought.

"Well?"

"To come in."

"Ah."

"My, that's new. I didn't know they said that." She licked her lips, slowly. I watched that tongue travel, plump, pointed, over the thin curves naked of lipstick.

"They usually don't." I realized neither one was moving, but watching, hanging fire, and then I realized it was me they were waiting on, my aggression because of what I'd said about the gun. They were testing the weather. They were waiting for permission.

That's how this gets played.

"Why do you want to come in? There's nothing much here."

"Yes there is."

"What?" He looked around the room as if puzzled, trying to see it with a stranger's objective valuation. His eyes moved away, unlike hers. He was unafraid.

I took the step into the vestibule. She gave a tiny indrawn hiss. Her complacent gaze meant control; all power, all strength, depended on it, and I understood suddenly that she was grooming him in her own mind to tense and pounce.

But he came back to me as if sliding slowly through raw amber.

"I live here," he said. "It's not fancy. Just an office apartment."

The doorway framed only part of the room. A high wooden monk's table, a maroon sofa back, the wrought-iron chandelier. I stepped all the way inside now as if he had invited me and saw that what he said was true: this was a large living area, mostly empty, with a single desk way down in one end. Branching off to the left lay another room. Through its door I could see a bed, a wooden nightstand, a painting of what looked like colored flags in luminous hues.

His stuff.

"You live here," I said.

"Yes."

"Not on Turtle Creek. Or in Highland Park someplace."

"No," he replied, bemused.

"He doesn't have a gun," the woman said, moving swiftly forward.

I reached my right hand behind me and pulled it out.

She stopped. They both stared.

"What is it you want?" he said.

I had no answer ready. The gun hung lopsided in my hand. They had locked into the positions of people in a front yard statue game, and the insight came to me that my silence frightened them.

Yes.

Using the gun barrel, I motioned to the two streamlined chairs angled toward the sofa.

As they settled stiff-kneed, for the first time I took notice of their clothes. He wore a tucked white shirt, stud loose at the neck, with black bow-tie ends draggled limp around the open collar, and black tuxedo pants. Her red sleeveless blouse and velvet skirt looked dressy. Gold and diamonds twinkled on her ears. She was in stockinged feet. I grew aware of an awful heat singeing my cheeks and forehead, the polypropylene cooking, condensing the damp. How could they not hear my heart? With the left hand I pulled off the ski mask.

Her eyes flared once, as if jolted. Then they narrowed.

"You're very young," he said quietly.

I didn't respond.

"Is this a kidnapping? Is that it?"

He sounded tired. He was older. Naturally. I had for two months now pictured a man to fit Mother's description: the tanned lean face, the young skin, the candid eyes. The eyes were the same. They examined me carefully.

"No. Not a kidnapping."

"Okay." He paused. "If you're from the Beeville crew, then I can't see what you expect to accomplish. Once the court's decided the judge won't change his mind. You're just getting yourself in hot water here."

With an inner shock I realized I knew what he was talking about. This amazed me—so soon into our conversation, so much ground and time spreading us apart, and already we touched familiar themes. Of course! The clan of illegitimate relatives my mother had told me about, the sons of that woman in South Texas. The one his father had lived with. Bastards. They must still be giving him legal trouble. Even after all these years. I even remembered their name: Palantido.

I remembered everything.

"This is nothing to do with Beeville. Or anybody from down there."

"You look a little too got up to be a chance break-in." He pointed to my belt.

"I'm not."

For a short space he leaned forward, elbows rested on knees. "Was it Minamoto sent you?"

She opened her mouth. She was watching me so closely that I felt burned by her gaze. But a calculating look hung about her, and it was plain she'd now suddenly swung onto another track far off his.

"I don't know Minamoto."

"Hm," he smiled dryly. "You don't have to."

A sound broke off as she started to speak. Next to her chair stood a small table. A couple of boxes, an ashtray, a lighter, a book were arranged on it. "Hey," she said.

"What?" It was all I could do to lift my stare from him.

"Do you mind if I smoke?"

"No."

She reached toward a flat red laquered box. Then she withdrew her hand, considering.

"If that's who's hired you, you can tell him it won't help," he said.

"I'm not hired." The gun felt heavy. I wanted to put it down. The wind seemed to leave my chest all of a sudden. "Are you married?"

Surprise showed on his face. "No."

"A.J.," she warned tersely.

He turned to her, smiling a little. "We're not. Not yet." Then he looked at me. "This is a peculiar burglary. Why do you ask? Unless you *are* kidnapping somebody."

"Does 'not yet' mean you're planning on getting married?" His voice, the deep, light timbre, had started a tremor through my gut. I watched him reach up to poke back his pesky hair and recognized the gesture as my own.

"Yes, we are," the woman said. Her lips compressed.

"I see."

"Do you." The accent sounded Yankee, New York. Her eyes, a clear, pale green, had heavy black brows that emphasized their bones and matched her thick hair. She looked alien, as if she didn't belong in this room with him. Her body seemed raw and commanding. Long legs crossed each other under the short skirt. "Is it a criminal's business?"

"Maybe." The anger stirred. She was a witch. I swallowed to hold down the lurch.

"How old are you?" he asked.

"Twenty."

He tilted his head a little as if listening to something. An interest began to kindle his face. "Tell me. What are you doing this for?"

"Now, that *is* my business."

"Which is getting tiresome," she snapped. But still he sat poring over me while his eyes seemed to search for a remote memory, a long-gone moment that he might reel in closer and closer to the present one. I watched him pause bewildered, fumble, nearly find it. The eyes warmed.

"Are you some kind of adventurer?"

"You could say that."

"A hobbyist? On a dare? Practicing burglary? Since there's nothing really much here to steal." He nearly smiled. "I don't think you're planning to steal, though, are you? Gun or no gun."

"Oh, yes." Suddenly his calm sparked my anger.

"What?"

"Information."

The brief moment died. The memory vanished. His face closed into an executive surface; when he looked at me again there shone only a hard sizing-up. "You can tell Minamoto forget it. He won't get a scrap. Strictly the rules of agreement—our choice. Now take your gun and go play with it." He turned away in contempt.

That ignited the straw. "I don't know any Minamoto. I already told you. And I'm goddamn sure not interested in your scraps, you can count on that." Laying the gun down on the carpet, I said, "I want to smash you. Put you through the shredder. Eat you alive. But before that I wanted a single fact. I've found it. And it's not worth piss."

His eyes moved from my face to my empty hand.

"I believe I'll have that smoke now," the woman said, and quietly reached over to the red box on the table. She picked it up, brought it into her lap, turned it sideways and busied herself with the catch.

"No!" he screamed. Lunging, he grabbed her fingers, smashing the box from their grip. She cried out. The box flew into the air, bounced sideways off the back of her chair, landing top down in the red carpet pile.

I stared at the flashing buttons. A voice called out from the tiny grid at one end. "Hello? Hello? This is 911. Can I help you?"

My father knelt down, picked it up. "Sorry, our mistake," he said, and punched the Off switch.

"A.J.," she murmured.

He turned to her, his face bleached white.

"Your heart."

"Hush," he replied. Then he stood up and looked at me. "Where did you get that ring?"

I looked down. My right hand was bare. The glove still hung from the belt where I'd tucked it for safekeeping on the landing.

"This?" I said. My mouth was dry.

"Yes," he whispered.

"From the center of the earth."

He peered at me in the roaring light. His face began breaking up, shifting, while the planes of the room grew large and his eyes brimmed, and the light came down to where we stood face to face and swallowed us whole.

THERE ARE DREAMS that you sink through in the night's small hours, long treks in which all the streets are one-way, where every event tunnels, and even in your sleep you know to predict the final drop from the window ledge, or the fly-away of love, or the car's screeching brakes with the dog run over, and the dream's inevitable end. And then, all at once something changes and you discover that even in the most relentless, repetitive dream there is the possibility of surprise.

"What's your name?" he said.

"Taylor," I said.

"Taylor. Why'd she call you that?"

"Oh, for goodness sake," said the woman, grabbing the gun from the floor in front of me. "Chatting with a felon. Let's get him arrested!"

"I don't know."

"I'll tell you why. It was my grandmother's maiden name."

At last. The missing link from the phone book parade.

"She lived on a little farm outside Bernice."

"I know it."

"You've been there?" I nodded. "When?"

"Right after I first heard about it. Quite recently."

"Didn't—didn't Alicia tell you any sooner?"

I just looked at him.

He stared. Then, sighing, he sat down. "Medina—this is my son."

"Blow me over," she said.

I didn't want to look at her for some reason. She held her hand, the one he'd smashed the box from, kneading the fingers gently. The gun was now wedged into the upholstery by her side.

"I just can't believe you're here." He shook his head.

"No."

"It's so unexpected. Well. One doesn't really expect to meet one's son for the first time." He smiled artlessly. "I mean, it's something you imagine would take care of itself at the start."

"Yes."

"Or at least when you'd planned for." He shook his head again, wondering. "I thought I'd see you when you turned sixteen."

Settling on the couch, I pulled off the other glove. "Sixteen," I said.

"That was what we agreed. When your stepfather and I talked."

"When you talked," I repeated.

"I could respect his argument that I keep clear until then, even though I didn't have to like it. He'd assumed responsibility as your acting father. He genuinely thought it was in your best interests. But I always hoped that might change well before sixteen."

"Oh." Trust is so precarious. It falls one way, then another.

"Tell me. Was the reason you didn't come before to do with him? Ben Sikes?"

"Ben died when I was eleven."

He winced. The woman noticed.

"How?"

"Car wreck."

"All these years . . . nine years," he murmured, then paused. "So—it was Alicia?" he asked tightly. "Her preference?"

"No."

"Yours, then?"

"She didn't even know you wanted to see me."

Some instinct must have warned him that I didn't wish to betray my mother. He frowned. Then he glanced for an instant to the woman whose eyes rested coolly on us both. "She didn't know," he said.

"No."

"But—what about the globe?"

"She wasn't sure what you wanted. She thought you'd just meant it for her."

"For her." He frowned again, and I knew he was recalling his words when he gave it to her. The words in his letter. "But I told Ben Sikes as well. I asked him."

I shrugged.

"So," he said, "when she gave it to you, then that was when she showed you what was hidden inside."

"She didn't know."

He blinked. The surprise twisted into a troubled look as the import of this sank home. I could see him at once begin to imagine the scenarios. "Didn't know?"

A stubbornness made me balk.

"Didn't know what I'd left with—"

"She thought it was empty," I said.

"Empty!" His face went blank with shock.

I glanced toward the woman. She watched, calm, assessive.

"Well . . . at least once you opened it, you saw what it meant."

"It meant that I finally knew my father's name."

"*Ah!*" This time his pain gasped out. "She hadn't even told you *that?*"

I said nothing.

"What have you thought all this time? That Ben Sikes was your father?"

"I've always known perfectly well Ben wasn't my father." I paused. "She held off marrying him until I was already two years old."

"I see," he said levelly after a moment.

Can you? I thought. *Have you ever been the kind of bastard I am?*

"My! This all sounds quite mysterious." The woman smiled at me with ironic falsity, lolling back in her chair. "'Accomplished criminal breaks into alleged father's office. Yet another dubious claimant to the Deeds's . . . family considerations.' You might have to join the queue."

A.J. turned to her. "I've told you quite specifically about my son."

"The burglar? Sorry." Her smile changed, now lazy, complicitous, and sensual. She picked up the lighter from the table, pressed the button, watched the little flame spring and die.

"Why burglary?" he asked.

I thought about the explanation. "I was pissed off," I said.

"Ah," he said.

"I've been training."

"Training!" Medina laughed. "Sweet. Don't you think? Such advanced hardware. Tell me, how do you use a . . ." she cocked her head, reading the label, "Magno-Probe?"

He ruminated. "Couldn't you have looked me up?"

"I had to see whether you were somebody I wanted to meet." I couldn't bring myself to say the word *revenge*. I couldn't bring myself to say *hatred*.

"Of course I am."

"Why should I bother to meet you at all?"

"That's an interesting question," said Medina pointedly.

"Because I've been waiting to see you for eighteen years. Since the minute I knew you were alive." He paused. "I'm your father."

THE TURTLENECK I was wearing made a ring of sweat; tugging at it I glanced down. The belt with its row of instruments looked clownish. Slowly I unbuckled it and took it off.

"Would you like something to drink?" he asked.

"I don't care."

"Medina?"

"I'll have white wine," she said.

"I wonder if I could please use your bathroom." The request sounded embarrassingly childish to my ears.

"Sure. It's through the bedroom. Here, I'll show you."

"No. Thanks."

"I'll get the drinks, shall I?" she asked, and smiled.

"All right. Whiskey for me." He watched while she straightened her long legs and rose from her chair to walk to the alcove beside the desk, disappearing through a doorway. Then he turned.

"At least let me check there's a towel." He stepped forward. It was, I saw, with an eagerness. I followed him. The bedroom looked as austere as the living room, the walls bare except for the bright painting and a hat rack holding one Stetson and a feed cap. The bed was still made, not a pillow-slip crease out of place. Inside the bathroom he pushed a wall button. Lights jumped on. We stood, the two of us, side by side before a mirror.

For a moment neither spoke.

"Well."

In the mirror's depths, the walls of the room shone aquamarine. Another mirror hung at our backs, reflecting doubly into a watery infinity, and despite the variance in our clothes and staggered heights and doubled contours of our bodies we could have merged into one person, replicated down that corridor over and over forever. The same face peered back at us from two places, one young, one more haggard, plainly tired. In the fluorescent glow time was eradicated, his gray hairs regilded, wrinkles chiseled, my stubble erased. "Well." He breathed deeply. The identical thought appeared on our faces.

"I didn't know," I said. You don't stand in front of a mirror for hours. Not if you've got things to do. You don't know your own looks nearly so well as any other person's.

"How could you?"

He raked back his hair, almost at the same second that my hand rose to do so. Then I remembered. "Mother told me. She said I looked like you."

"That's an understatement."

Suddenly I knew the moment the resemblance first clarified. "She gave me your globe because of it, I think."

"Is that right?"

"Funny how *we* missed it." I stared into the mirror.

"Yes. Though I guess, not truly surprising."

And then I realized why Medina's eyes had widened the instant I'd taken off the mask.

"I wonder why she—" I didn't finish. He knew who I meant.

"I guess, maybe, she preferred not to notice. At least not before—" Then he too fell silent. We both recalled the long fingers lifting the phone, dialing the number, summoning the police.

I made a sound.

"We've been involved for several years now," he said quietly, as if to excuse the dark implications of her fallibility. "She's a vice president of one of my companies. A smart woman. Dynamic. A lawyer." Once again I saw her sitting there, crossing her legs, whetting her lips as if they had an appetite.

"Efficient," he added, and frowned.

"Well. Good thing you saw the ring."

"Yes."

"In time, I mean." I looked down at it, not wanting to look at him.

"Hm."

"Once called they probably wouldn't back off so easily. I'd be in jail by now."

"Well, your gear might be somewhat hard to explain."

I thought of the border I'd left two days before. I thought of the attaché case in the car, hidden at Teresa-Maria's until Ramón and I had returned. I thought of customs combing state records for my references, writing up their report.

"So," he said, and drew himself up. "Well. I tell you what. You go ahead in here. Take your time. There's a little something I want to see to." His thoughtful expression deepened.

"A.J." The name dropped from my mouth like a sinker, strange and hard to form. But my head began to swim with lightness.

"What?" he said.

"This ring? You know how you gave it to Mother . . ."

"It was my great-grandfather's." He nodded gravely. "But of course, it was always supposed to go to you."

BY THE TIME I'd washed my face, flushed the toilet, fiddled with the shaver, run some water, and dried my hands, the loudest sounds of argument had stopped. One short shout burst against the silence. A door slammed. When I stepped back into the living room, she was gone.

10

"Where are you living?" he asked.

I tallied up the nights I'd slept on Ramón's uncle's living room floor, the backseat of the Escort, Teresa-Maria's clandestine bed. "Officially still with Mother and Granddaddy, but I haven't been home in a while."

He sipped his whiskey. "Do they still live in the same house?"

"Mother and Ben moved us in after Grandmother got Alzheimer's."

"Alzheimer's. Damn." He frowned, absorbing this news. "I'm sorry."

I shrugged.

"So what all did she tell you?"

Now we were at the meat of the evening. For twenty smoldering years, I'd wished him dead so I wouldn't have to see him missing. There is a skill to framing such information so that it falls of its own weight onto the soul.

"That you disappeared, no forwarding address."

"Ah," he said. Then silence.

I stared. He nursed the glass, rounding it with his hand.

"I did leave her one," he said slowly.

"She tried it. It was obsolete."

A spasm crossed his face, followed by a wake of old, deep sadness.

"I'm not asking for explanations."

He raised his chin. "You have a right to them."

I glanced around the stripped-down apartment. "I'm not asking you for a damn thing."

He finished the whiskey, went to the kitchen alcove, came back out with the bottle, and poured another glass. "But you need to know why that address quit working." He sat down on the sofa and tilted the glass as if to swig, but then pulled it back and placed it carefully on the wooden table. "I was in prison."

"What?" I said.

"For three years."

For a minute there was only the chink of ice melting. I tried to take it in. I rolled it over, around in my mind. "Couldn't you maybe have written a letter? Don't even prisons have postal service?"

"Not in Iran."

I swallowed.

He grinned wryly. "It was nip and tuck to negotiate a stamp."

"How did it happen?"

"Wrong place, wrong people. An oil venture. Not for the firm I'd been with in London, which is how come they fobbed your mother off like they did."

"Some other firm?"

"My own."

I sat folding my hands in my lap, gauging. Over three years in his twenties, it had been. Three years of his life. "Did they—do anything to you?"

"Yes."

A single glance closed the question.

"You might have at least told her where you were going."

He shoved his hand through his hair. "There are bridges you always have to cross to make things happen. Risks. Turning dirt to gold." When he looked at me now, the likeness seemed so obvious that I took my own amazement for granted. This is how I'll appear in twenty-five years, I thought—mouth, eyes, jawline. "I never meant to hurt her. Of course, I had no idea that she was—that you—"

"It's a result that does happen."

He frowned and shook his head. "I truly loved her. Maybe that's why."

I stared. Such naïveté coming from a grown man sounded absurd: the unexpectedness of love's taking root in the body. My anger stirred.

"Maybe I still do," he added, bemused.

"Excuse me for saying this, but you don't know her."

He looked at me, then down to the bottle set on the carpet.

"She's no longer the same person."

"Isn't she? How's that?"

"We changed her." I paused. "You and me."

He closed his eyes. The hand with the glass sagged.

The mystery of one's parents' congress, their secret currents: most children prefer such matters to remain invisible. Ever since the night Mother had first told me about him I'd had no choice but to brood on those revelations.

"She never blamed you. Not once," I said.

"How could she not?"

"Why didn't you take her along? You were going to England, weren't you?"

"She didn't even ask such a thing. I wasn't just going to England. She knew I'd be gone awhile. And *I* knew it would be to places that were possibly dangerous."

"Oh."

An exhaustion slid over his face. He rose, paced to the kitchen, opened the door, and stood meditating. "You know, there's an extra bedroom off here. Never even been used." He turned. "Why don't you sleep here tonight?"

"Here?"

"Well, yes." He smiled, grimacing. "It's your home."

• • •

I WOKE TO dishes clanking. The room I'd slept in had more furniture than my father's and the living-room office combined, as if everything of consequence or pretention had been hustled out of sight. Maple burl antiques filled the corners. The bed was canopied walnut. White silk draped the window, which was at this early hour ribboned with light. Spinach green wallpaper framed an array of oil paintings. As I lay under the high ceiling looking around me, one picture stood out: a portrait of a brown-haired woman with head seductively dipped, her throat closeted in pearls, her palms pressed against the wall beneath a frieze of bright yellow dragons. It took a minute before I recognized Medina.

The door opened. "What do you eat for breakfast?" my father asked, standing just inside the threshold.

"Uh—toast, thanks."

"You drink juice?"

"Yes. Or whatever's going, really."

"Okay." He disappeared back into the kitchen. "Two toast, two orange juices, and some coffee, Martha," he said.

"Yes, sir," somebody replied, and then I heard a door shut and the sound of water running. By the time I'd pulled on my turtleneck and the ridiculous black tights, he was back, carrying a silver tray.

"I thought it'd be wiser to breakfast in here so we can see what the deal is." He nudged the door shut with his toe. "I don't know your plans. But I'm due at a meeting by nine and it's seven-twenty now. It looks to me like there are things to ascertain before I leave."

"Okay," I said. "What?"

"Like what do you want."

I gazed down at the bedspread. "You mean—here? With you?" Here it is, I thought. The push-off. The finale to the fairy-tale evening. A bad taste climbed up my throat. "I told you last night what I'd wanted. I've gotten it. No sweat. I'll take off now."

"You will? Why?" He looked disconcerted.

"Well. Because." Get in first, I thought. Don't let on.

"I thought we—I thought you wouldn't—might not mind staying here awhile."

"Staying here?"

"Well of course. It's your home, like I said." He paused, sat down on the mattress, and with stiff deliberation spooned two sugars into his coffee. "Although I can appreciate how you might not want to feel that way."

I couldn't answer.

"Naturally you'd wish to at least find out more about who I am before committing yourself further. I understand that. It's up to you to decide where we go from here. Either way I won't blame you." The spoon stirred the dark fluid. His face set into a bland, tense inertia.

"You'd want me to stay?"

"Well of *course*—" He put the spoon on the white saucer and looked at me blankly. "Why do you think I left that ring with your mother?"

For a moment I sat there. My eyes moved to the portrait over his head. The woman stared evenly back, her pearls luminous under the hump-backed dragons. I thought about the night before, the treacherous fingers on the keypad, the yell as he'd leaped toward the phone. Then her disappearance afterward, that one sharp shout.

"Do you think I went to all this trouble to just read your appointment diary?" I said.

"I don't know." He looked at me.

"I could have been planning to steal you blind. You can't ever be sure I wasn't."

"Oh yes, I can," he said.

A KNOCK SOUNDED as we finished chewing our toast. "What is it, Martha?"

"Your first call is in two minutes," called a woman's voice muffled through the door.

"Please reschedule everything I've got now to five o'clock this evening and tomorrow morning first thing before the Alacra Annual. I'm going to be tied up all day today with the legal department, I don't want to be disturbed."

"It's Mr. Matsudo."

"Oh." He reflected. "I'll phone him back."

There was a long pause. "Okay," she said dubiously.

"Thank you, Martha. Good-bye." After a moment we heard footsteps padding away from the door.

"So what is it you do exactly?" I said.

"Well, how much do you know so far?"

"Seventeen years ago you bought this building back from some company that was ready to tear it down and put up a mirrorscraper. I know that from going to the newspaper morgue and reading an article about how your Grandfather Deeds built it in the 1930s after he struck oil wildcatting in West Texas."

"Well, that's enterprising of you. The newspaper."

"It wasn't much. It said you wouldn't give them an interview."

"Speaking of grandfathers, how's yours?"

"Still on the bench."

He nodded. "I heard that." It made me wonder how until I remembered who administered my trust fund. The lawyers must have been in communication all these years, I thought. On my behalf. Keeping to the limited subject.

"You probably knew where they sent me to boarding school," I said.

"No. I don't really know much of anything at all."

So Ben had been thorough. Which meant he didn't know about my condition. "Well, now I've flunked out of college."

"Have you?" He eyed me. "That's interesting. You flunk out on purpose?"

"Sort of."

"You intend going back when the probation's up?"

"No."

"What are you going to do?"

"I'm not sure yet."

"I see." He laced his hands around his knee. "Well, we'd best get down to it, then. Let me tell you my business."

"I studied your lobby directory downstairs."

He made a face, shook his head. "That won't disclose much. I'd be better off listing some things. I own five hotels, a cattle ranch in Hawaii, a ski resort, and a chain of fast-food restaurants."

"Oh." I sipped the orange juice, swallowed. Then I swallowed again.

"That's leisure and service industry. Also there's a baseball team."

"Yeah?"

"The Lubbock Chaparrals. Then one TV and two radio stations, couple of oil independents, a medical research facility."

"Is that all?" I asked after a hush. He'd turned inward, concentrating on something while a frown developed on his forehead.

"Oh. No. There're two or three things more." *He knows exactly how many*, I thought. *Make no mistake, Taylor.*

"What are they?"

"They're in the way of projects. Electronics, et cetera." His frown deepened.

"Oh."

"I'll tell you more tonight." He got up. "Will you stay here today? Or meet me this evening?"

"There's somebody I should try to see."

"How about suppertime then? About eight-thirty?"

"Sure. That'll be—that's great."

"Come to the main lobby. You can let the alarms alone, I've already told the superintendent to get new ones. Unless you're wanting to keep your hand in." He smiled, contradicting Mother's word about his sense of humor. "Tell the security guard, he'll let you up."

"Okay."

"I look forward to it."

"Yeah, me too."

He reached the door. "Step out here and meet the help."

I followed him through the tiny kitchen to the living-room office, where a girl who was sitting behind the desk before the glowing computer monitor looked up as we came in.

"Did you reach Wilson and Intel?" he asked.

"Yep. They're rescheduled for five thirty-five and six-fifteen today."

"Good. Here's somebody I want you to meet. He's going to be living in this dump from now on."

"Hi," she said.

"Hi," I said back.

"I'm Martha. A.J.'s personal assistant." She was dressed in jeans and a large white T-shirt. She looked maybe twenty-two years old.

"My name's Taylor," I said, and paused. "Taylor—"

"Deeds," said my father.

MARTHA LOOKED AT my tights. "You a bike racer?"

"Nope."

Glancing toward the door my father had just passed through, she tapped something on the keyboard and watched the monitor change. "His kin?"

"Son." The word clung to my tongue. It felt hard to release. I'd never used it before.

"I kind of figured that."

"How come?" I paused, savoring this new moment: the first public acknowledgment. "Because we look alike?"

"Yeah. Or else you might could be one of those Palantido brothers from South Texas. Only he'd never let them in here, much less to live."

"He didn't exactly let me in either."

"He didn't?" Curious speculation lighted her eyes. A gold pendant hung around her neck on a thin chain against the T-shirt material, and I felt an urge to try to decipher its inscribed device.

"I came calling at an inopportune time."

"Oh. Was she around?"

"You mean, Medina? Yeah, she was."

"How'd you get rid of her?"

"I didn't."

"You must have. Otherwise she'd never have left." Turning from the keyboard, she scanned down a printout column on the desk, then typed a few words.

"She pretty much got rid of herself."

"Impossible."

"Do you not like her?"

"Heck, how'd you guess?" The telephone rang. She answered, listened, said, "Not Tokyo, New York. The number's programmed, just punch Recall Seven," and hung up. "So where did you live before?"

"You mean where have I been all these years?" She waited. "About forty-two miles south of here. In Bernice."

"Bernice. Y'all don't see each other much, huh?"

"Not yet."

"Guess you will now. Roommates!" She opened the top desk drawer, took out a stick of gum, unsheathed it from its silver foil, stuffed it into her mouth. Her arms and nose were freckled and matched her chipped blond hair and tomboy style. I could imagine her riding a horse, most likely a pinto, most likely bareback.

"Are you here every day?" I asked.

"I come in at 6:30 A.M. I make breakfast, run A.J.'s central computer systems, coordinate his schedule, synthesize whatever he needs, and leave here at six at night. Everything electronic passes through these hands." She peered satisfied down at their short nails and smacked her gum.

"You been working here long?"

"About a year. Thirteen months, nine days. Ever since graduation. I work weekends too if he needs me, which is generally. But that's okay. I live outside Dallas with my parents so I've got no home to keep up."

"Oh." I took a few paces around the room. A dissonance had seized me as I'd watched my father leave, which I could neither identify nor shake. I was here. She'd recognized me right away. The years of anger were over. Why did it seem so inconclusive?

"You want something to do?" asked Martha.

"I don't know. Graduation from what?"

"Huh? Oh. MIT." She clicked an overlay onto the screen with her mouse, checked it, closed the file, and opened another.

"Good grief! What are you doing working as a secretary?"

"In this position? What do you think?" She gave me a look, then pressed the mouse; the printer began to hum. "I would say conservatively that I know as much about this core data system as anybody at Deeds Headquarters, probably in the whole conglomerate. That's not bragging, just the reason I was hired. Hacker at an early age." She smirked. "It's hardly like I'm sitting taking dictation from some pompous old geezer, is it?"

"I guess not."

"Do you go to school?"

"Not anymore. I went to UT Austin. Then the Vizuelos Academy of Extended Studies, majoring in Domestic Annexation."

"Shoo. I don't even know what that is." The second phone on the desk buzzed. She picked it up. "Two seventy-five," she said. "I'll give you back to Merle in Central." She hung up.

"For a secretary you don't have to answer many calls."

"There's a whole roomful of people who do that downstairs. Important calls get filtered through three layers of top management and none of them reach me. I'm strictly A.J.'s pulse checker."

"Well, I guess I'm standing in a privileged spot."

"Apparently so."

I looked down, ashamed of the clod-headed banter, a little put out by my own uselessness. "I'd probably better be going now."

"Scoot on out."

"See you later."

"Yep." She was already back to the screen, cursor scissoring, thumbing down the selvage of industrial action.

"MOM?" I GRIPPED the receiver. The phone booth felt hot as a pizza oven.

"Taylor! Oh, Taylor, thank goodness it's you. Honey, where have you been?"

"I'm in Dallas."

"Your granddaddy said Mexico! What were you doing there? He said something about a Laredo hospital and wiring money from your trust. Are you all right?"

"Yeah, I'm fine. A friend of mine had an accident. But everything's okay, don't worry." Outside on the street the cars flashed by, slinging down the expressway. All at once I felt a little queasy.

"A car accident? Oh, God. Was he badly hurt? Did he not have insurance?"

"It's all right. He'll be okay. Everything's taken care of."

"Thank goodness! Are you back at your job now?"

"No, not exactly." I cleared my throat. My hand was shaking. "The fact is, Mother . . . I'm meeting A.J. tonight."

"A.J.?" she said. She sounded vacant. "My—A.J. Deeds?"

"Yes."

A silence dropped.

"We're having dinner. I'm staying at his place."

A tiny whimper carried through the earpiece, so dim and distant that it could have been made by a child out on the sidewalk down the block.

"Mom, it's okay. We've met each other and it's all okay. I like him. He's a nice guy. A good person. We're getting along fine."

"Oh, Taylor."

"Please don't cry. I'll be coming down to Bernice in a few days and I'll tell you all about it."

"Is he—what does he look like?" The tremulous question disclosed an entire panorama of memory and pain.

"He looks like me," I said.

AS I HUNG up the phone and went toward the alley where I'd left the car, I thought about calling Ramón. I'd awakened with a desperate longing for Teresa-Maria—to feel her against me, hold her, smell her, retrace the geography of her breasts. The Lee Street of my mind basted in its despair. There was nothing more I could do, nowhere to go. I was stranded halfway between the past and the future.

"Where's the meeting A.J. went to?" I asked Martha as soon as she opened the office door.

"Downstairs in the legal department." She looked at the attaché case in my hand.

"I'm going to change clothes."

"Be my guest."

I went back into the green room where Medina gazed tilt-lidded from the wall, her motives veiled but her heart avid. Opening the case, I took out my pants and peeled off the turtleneck. As I buttoned last night's shirt, something tickled my throat. Craning sideways, I peered down at my collar. There, woven accidently into the oxford cloth, lay a long wavy hair the copper of a Levi's rivet.

11

Lee Street dozed in the sun, empty of life except for some toddlers playing in the yards. Ramón's uncle's old '76 Buick sat parked in the driveway with its trunk lid sprung. Next door the Hidalgos' house looked dead.

I U-turned the Escort just as Ricardo came limping out the front doorway, manhandling a big twine-tied suitcase far too heavy for him. He dragged it along, struggling through the grass, wearing a plaid Sunday jacket with a little bow tie jutting sideways under his chin. His feather hair stuck up everywhere. When he got to the Buick he heaved the case into the trunk, stood for a second staring at it, then started back toward the house.

At that instant Teresa-Maria appeared carrying a bag. A canvas duffle was slung over her shoulder. Her father stepped down from the threshold, pacing carefully beside his wife and holding an elbow to assist her hesitant, wobble-headed gait. Behind them followed Ramón.

I braked against the curb.

Ricardo recognized me first. His features rucked together; he ducked his gaze to the ground. His sister took one glance, opened the back door, threw herself and her two bags inside, and then slammed the door shut and locked it.

Her mother looked up. She stopped in her tracks. "Taylor!" she moaned, a mournful sound as I climbed out.

"Hi."

Her dumpy waist seemed to have shrunk. She wore a navy dress with a wide belt cinching it tight. Wings of hair hung dry and snaggled along her temples. When I reached her she grabbed my hand, patting mechanically. "I'm happy you come."

"Yes, ma'am. Me too."

"We're riding on the bus to Mexico today."

"I'm so sorry," I said.

She gave a quick, tremulous sigh, gazed at me, then off at the Buick. Tears began to leak down my cheeks. "Thank you for finding about Juan," she said.

"I just wish I could have helped. I'm sorry."

"Ramón say you save his life."

"Sí," said her husband, nodding, rheumy with tiredness. For a minute we stood there. I wiped my nose on the back of my wrist.

"Are—are all y'all going?"

"Pedro will stay here. He has to work."

"I will stay," confirmed her husband.

"Ramón is coming."

I turned to where he stood. He gave a short jerk of his chin.

"Well, I hope you'll have a good trip, at least." All words had become irrelevant. Her head thrust forward; she pecked me on the cheek, crushed my hand.

"Shh. No llora mas," she said, touching my cheek, and then tottered off toward the car.

Ramón walked up. "Hola, ese."

"Hi. How's the back?"

He nodded. "I told Teresita what happened. But she's pissed off, man. Por que no sé."

"I made a mistake."

"She ain't going to let you clear it up."

"Maybe not now. But later?" I thought I might fall on the ground and cry.

"No sé, hermano. She's stubborn." He shook his head, sorrowful and perplexed. "I'll write you a letter."

"Here. Take this address," I said. I reached in my jeans pocket and pulled out one of the Deeds Headquarters' business cards that I'd picked up off Martha's desk that morning. "There's a fax and phone number, too."

"Deeds Incorporated," he said, reading it. Then he frowned. Looking down, he studied my ring finger.

"A relative," I said. After a pause he nodded.

"Maybe you can pass the number on to her. To phone collect."

"Maybe." Then suddenly he clasped me. "Hasta luego, joven." I could feel the tape and bandages under my palms. He let go, pushed me away, walked around to the other side of the Buick. His uncle started the engine.

Ricardo lifted his head. His limbs started to work, one foot, the other foot, as if swimming through a dream to the car door. Before sliding in he paused, gazed at me. For one long second he registered my red eyes. Then the dark isolation filled his face once more, and he sank like a deaf-mute into the glass box.

I DROVE BACK downtown to the Deeds Building. It was only one o'clock, but I entered my father's apartment exhausted. Martha sat talking on the phone. Her eyebrows rose as she continued her conversation, so I went straight through the kitchen to the green bedroom and shut the door. The bed had been made. I pulled down the coverlet, mashed my ear into the pillow, and lay there listening to the hum that throughout childhood I'd mistaken for a far-off night train, air-conditioning, a plane's drone, but which I now recognized as the sound of my own ceaseless and circular blood.

. . .

I WOKE TO total darkness. No light penetrated the drapes' heavy lining. I stumbled past furniture to the door while my equilibrium reeled like the state fair Yo-yo. The kitchen was black, but Martha had left a pinpoint reading lamp burning on her desk next to the computer screen. I headed toward it. Then I realized that the lamp didn't burn because of Martha. The monitor screen flickered, scrolling through pages, then tripped to a graph display. Somebody was sitting there.

I'd been so silent that she heard nothing beyond the clicking mouse. Not until I stood above, inhaling her rich perfume, did she sense a watchfulness and look up.

"Ah, the burglar boy," she said.

"Hello, Medina."

She pressed a key. The graph went blank. "Have you burgled in with your special instruments? Or did A.J. give you a key?"

"I've been home awhile," I said.

"Home. Really."

"In there." I nodded backward.

"Doing what?" I could tell how she disliked her own hastily concealed surprise; she hadn't thought to check.

"Taking a nap."

Coolly she snapped off the monitor, leaned back, crossed her legs, and sat fiddling with the mouse. "Apparently you're authentic now. Publicly proclaimed as the new heir apparent throughout the Deeds legal system. Congratulations. Fast work."

"I am?"

"Naturally."

"How do you know?"

"I'm one of his lawyers." She paused. "Also a corporate vice president."

"Oh."

"So in a court of law, that now makes you sole beneficiary to a seventeen-billion-dollar holding."

It knocked the wind out of me. Which is no doubt what she intended.

I stood there, the room looping, contracting, whirling, while the door frame went elastic and I grappled for a still point. I hadn't thought. He'd acknowledged me, that's what I'd heard him do. He'd called me son.

"Cock, aim, fire," she said.

"It isn't—what I'd been thinking."

"I suppose you were looking for male bonding? Grand larceny à la Robert Bly? Or," she smiled dryly, "perhaps a trophy to take home with you. Solid booty. An engraved ruler. A Deeds Co. pencil."

I didn't answer.

"It does lend your father's achievements a certain moral substance. Empire plus continuity. Every tycoon's dream. And such a cute bedtime story! Less than twenty-four hours after a masked stranger breaks into the magnate's office he's inducted as the long-lost prince who will inherit the kingdom. This is all abstract, of course. Not strictest jurisprudence. But what a killer opportunity for the press."

"I guess."

"You guess? Don't you watch TV?"

"I just wanted to know," I said.

"I imagine you've got a pretty clear picture by now. I certainly do." And oddly enough, it was this that made me realize how rapidly she'd been dropping her bombs, painting her pictures.

She fake-smiled as if to an idiot.

"So what are you doing? Catching up on other work?" I said ingenuously. As far as I knew, she had a perfect right to be there. But the furtive mouse clicks, the fugitive paleness, the stream of talk, suggested otherwise.

"Tying up some loose ends." Uncrossing her legs she rose and stretched. Her arms clasped high, a working girl at the end of her day. The computer's A-drive light blinked off and on. There was a disk in there.

"A.J. will be home soon. Are you sticking around for dinner?"

"I have other plans."

"But A.J.'s counting on seeing you, huh?"

"I would hate to intrude on your evening. He's let me know how important it is." Seizing her jacket from the back of the chair, she folded it over her arm. A briefcase stood open on the carpet below the desk. She dumped a couple of tablets and some papers into it and then, swift as a bird, touched the button that ejected the disk. "So I'll bid you good night."

"Well—okay. Good night, then."

"But there's one thing I'll advise first."

"Shoot."

She turned, the diskette in her hand. "Don't underestimate his enemies. You might wind up wishing you'd never been born." Her eyes gleamed, a cold quick fire. I felt hackles rise on my skin.

"Is that—are you threatening or warning me?" But just then something metallic sounded in the foyer.

She whipped around. The briefcase snapped shut simultaneous with the front door. When A.J. walked in, one hand loosening the tie knot under his collar, he saw us and stopped.

"Hello, Medina."

"Hello."

"Did you want something?"

"Not really, A.J." She gripped the briefcase handle and threw back her head. "I just dropped in to say good-bye."

"I thought we already did that."

Her face was neat and matte as an egg. "I didn't want it to end on such a sour note. But I can see you're busy. So I'll go." She started for the door.

"Look." He reached out and clasped her forearm. "I'm sorry, too. It's bad. It's been a bunch of years. But after last night—and then today—"

"Are you sure?" she interrupted in a low whisper. Her voice had that deep, unnerving throatiness again. "Is this really what you choose?"

He frowned.

"Treating me this way? Repeating history? Like your father? And his father? Like you did before?" She tipped her head my way. "Does it run in the family?"

"It's not the same. You know damn well. Don't twist it. You stood there last night and asked for half my busi—"

"Is it worth it to you?"

He stared. "Yes," he said simply.

"Then know you'll both pay for it," she spat, and wrenching her arm away, stormed out through the vestibule. The door crashed.

My father looked stunned.

For a second I said nothing. Then I realized.

"Wait!" I croaked, thudding to the door. "Stop!" The doorknob seemed alive under my hand. Wrestling it open, I skidded across the parquet into the hall, looking both directions through the golden sconcelight. The elevators stood closed, the call buttons dead, the old-fashioned dials set for the first floor—all except one, which was how A.J. must have ridden up.

No one was there.

I rushed to the fire door at the end of the hall. It swung open at my push. I leaned over the landing into the darkness. No sound. Nothing.

Clanging the door shut as if going back to the corridor, I crouched down and waited.

When at last I stood up and uncricked my legs I knew she'd gone another way. But which? The closed elevator? A separate office? I remembered the sounds I'd heard the night before, the squeaking chair, the clink of forks. Or had that somehow been amplified from my father's apartment?

"Sorry. She's gone," I said to my father when I returned to the living room.

"That's all right. It doesn't matter." He sat down on the sofa, tired out, and scratched his head.

"I think maybe it might." I crossed the floor to Martha's desk. Sure enough, the computer light still shone green. "She was doing something on this when I found her. She took a disk."

"Oh, hell." He lay back on the cushions, arms spread-eagled. All at once he looked very middle-aged. "Well, we'll just have Martha check in the morning. God knows what she's been up to."

"Yes, sir," I said, sitting in the chair opposite. "Whatever you say."

12

What stands out most sharply about those first days, when I bring them living to my mind, is one specific moment.

Throughout the long rowdy summer of introductions—to A.J.'s company directors, lawyers, bankers; to Deeds Building personnel; to the socialite women who urged us to their cocktail parties and barbecues; to his friends and hunting buddies—throughout the whirlwind crash course in business, the receptions and museum openings and the drop-jaw amazement of everyone who saw us, the walking Before and After exhibit; throughout the interviews with Dallas magazines and newspapers heralding a new son and heir, the "crown prince," as some jackass journalist named me, our hours were always haunted by a groping uneasiness. Between us seemed to stand a barrier that neither time nor growing acquaintanceship could remove.

I didn't know what it was. I thought I did. I wasn't angry anymore; I felt that, considering the circumstances, we'd both come out pretty well. But once or twice in the midst of our friendliest moments, it would happen. Out of nowhere he would frown. We'd lapse into awkward silence; he'd grow absent, turn away, busy himself with papers; at his withdrawal I'd stifle the sudden need to clear my throat or in any way call attention to myself, and proceed to watch him from the corner of vision. The nature of it, I thought, was simple common sense: neither of us knew how to act like father and son. We'd had no practice. What could be normal in these situations?

While he pored through geology reports or photos of a hotel site in Chile, I'd lean into the soft leather of the Rolls backseat and listen to the underwater clicks his cell phone made. Who are we kidding? I thought. He hasn't got time for family. I'm a mascot, an aide-de-camp. Junior in training. Somebody he needs to make things up to. How can we ever learn each other? Say what needs saying? Do we just ignore the last twenty years of missed memories, or race to fill them in? It was too late, I felt. We were both already men. I'd pluck at my lower lip, wondering suddenly what I was doing here. I had the curious sensation that we were living not in the present but at the rim of the future, that every conversation was geared toward transcending a hump that never got any closer.

"I tell you what. Let's get out," he would say. "Go on a little jaunt some-place. Listen to some music." He'd close the file, his forehead etched with preoccupation.

"Sure," I replied. "Whatever you like."

So we'd sit through a symphony at Symphony Hall, or head off to a honky-tonk in one of the little towns near his ranch outside of Fort Worth, and I'd think, Okay, maybe this is it: here's the answer! And we'd swig beer together and stamp our feet whistling during the applause and eat pork rinds and smoked brisket, and then get back to the Deeds Building about midnight, smile good night at one another, and close the doors of our rooms, alone once more in the insularity of our private thoughts.

Not once during those weeks did he ever mention Medina. Nor did I tell him anything about Teresa-Maria.

• • •

ONE NIGHT IN early August we flew in his jet to Houston for the premiere of an opera.

Outside the opera house limos stacked up along the entrance, disgorging people from Tucson, L.A., Atlanta, Paris. Shouldering through paparazzi snapping their cameras in a lobby full of chiffon and tuxedos, trying to remain anonymous, we made our way to our reserved box. The production, *Madama Butterfly,* was one A.J. had helped finance. Voices I half recognized had hailed him as we pushed by; some tried to stop him and bend his ear. But he'd just waved, nudged me ahead, and forged on. Now the chandelier dimmed, gloom fell, the orchestra tuned up. The curtain rose. All at once I turned to where he sat rapt in the opening blare of horns and discerned through the twilight his thin temple, the tired lines, the hard jaw with its faint silver beard, and my heart nearly cracked in two. I reached out toward his hand, then pulled back and dropped mine into my lap. He smiled briefly with a look of no surprise at this hesitant, unmanly gesture made in the stealth of the dark.

"TAYLOR DEEDS, ISN'T it?" said a gravel-voiced woman at the post-opera buffet table, drifting to where I stood alone forking grilled salmon onto my plate.

I turned.

"I won't ask your other name. The first, legal one," she said.

Since the night I'd broken in A.J.'s office hallway I hadn't experienced serious vertigo. But at the sound of her voice a dizzy twist hooked my head; clumsily I dropped the fork, reached for it, watched it bounce off the silver candelabra arm and fall to the carpet. I stooped to pick it up. "Yes, ma'am. It's Taylor Deeds," I said.

"You know what they're saying, don't you?"

"Who?" Slowly I rose, gripping the table's edge to steady myself. A.J. was across the room, facing the other way. He hadn't noticed.

"Folks." The woman wrinkled her tortoise face into a close-lipped smile and then, sipping from her champagne glass, deftly picked over the buffet platters for titbits.

"No, ma'am. I guess I don't."

"They're saying it's a good thing for old A.J. that nobody ever filed a paternity suit. One glance at you and the judge would have sent him to the cleaners."

"Oh. Is that right?" I said, stiffly polite.

"Yes. Of course, not all of them say that. One human being at least implies something very different." She scrutinized my face. "But I suspect your mama must get quite a start every time she sees you. Talk about reliving one's youthful moments."

"I guess I can't judge about that."

"Now where have you said she lives?"

"I didn't."

"Darling, I've known your daddy for more years than I care to quote. He's a slippery thing. But I usually get him to confess." She wore her bleached blond hair pinned behind both ears. Her wrists clunked with gold. The hideous dress showed off a scrawny bosom. Coral-and-diamond ear clips like sinkers dragged her lobes into long fleshy tongues. I'd seen her kind before, but none with quite the same crackle of confidential danger. "Your daddy's always been labeled a loner. Mighty rich one, though. Only the best catch in several states."

"I see."

"Tell me. Have you met Mrs. Medina Semple?"

I stared. "Yes, ma'am."

She paused and nibbled a shrimp. "You know, your sudden appearance *is* so romantic. Just showing up out of the woodwork. A.J. definitely never struck me as a one for secret marriages."

"Hm." It was all I could think of to say. The drill of her eyes went spike-sharp.

"And I've seen him through many a season. In the public scope. Although I must confess he's not looking all that wonderful right now. Working too hard would be my guess. Or maybe making up for lost time, trying to keep up with the younger generation—you aren't running him around all the nightclubs, I hope? Those techno places? But you know, I once wrote an article on him when he himself was still a young buck, predicting a bigger comeback for the Deeds family than anybody could guess."

"Do you write for the *Dallas News*?"

She cocked her head, quizzical. "I used to."

"I think I read your article."

"Now, isn't that nice? Although I don't see how you could have, darling, it was before your time. You didn't even know your alphabet yet—and I know full well A.J.'s never kept a clipping service."

"No."

"Hardly the self-aggrandizer, is he? Very Texan. We get full-out braggarts or the strong silents, either way it's one riot, one ranger. But maybe you saw it somewhere else." The bright probe came quick as a dart.

"Possibly so."

"Romance and tragedies. Aren't we lucky. Life's so full sometimes it's hard to believe we might escape scot-free. Lord knows they're mother's milk to some spiteful people. Or snake venom." She gazed at me, sipping from her glass, and the brightness, although cold, was not unfriendly. "By the way, darling, just so you know. I don't do a column anymore. I married well enough to quit, then he widowed me."

"Oh. I'm sorry."

"That's all right. He was old, we had a good old time. I live here in Houston now. I've always been real fond of your daddy. Handsome as a bloodhound though he be."

"Is that a drawback?"

"He hasn't leaned on it. That's a plus in my book. Not that I'm going to write one." She finished pecking on her plate and slipped it onto the tray of a passing waiter. "You don't count on it either, I can tell. No. You just keep your mouth shut if you want to. Everybody claims to hate a mystery, but they really love them in their souls. Do you go to school?"

"Not right now."

"But you've mastered a trade."

"Well, I—"

"Besides the one your daddy's grooming you for."

I was so thrown I had to track backward through her litter of clues.

"Now don't fuss. I may be old, but I can find my own champagne. You just stay put and stay careful. There are plenty of creatures out there, not all of them jealous liars." She paused. "Those I wouldn't spit on if they were thirsting to death."

I started to speak, but she laid a hand on my arm. "Oh, look, there's a Hunt. Isn't he looking stout these days! I'd better offer my greetings or he'll hope I've forgotten him." She slouched off, her glass draggling empty at her side. I stood watching her go.

My father stepped up after a moment. "You've been talking with Rita Jo Moseley."

"Is that her name?"

"I would have introduced you if I'd had time before the Montforts pulled me away. She's some girl. Tough as barbwire. She'd have loved to meet you."

"She did," I said.

"You mean properly?" He mused. "Well, of course. She'd know who you are. What's she been pumping you about?"

"I'm not too sure. To tell the truth I think she's been more telling me something."

"Now that's intriguing." Watching her trail through the clumps of merrymakers, he added, "Well then. Whatever she says, listen close. It's true."

• • •

"MARTHA, WHERE'S THE list?" A.J. strode through the doorway after a conference on the second floor with some electronics firm executives and their
lawyers.

"Which list?"

"Which do you *think?*"

She flinched. I watched hot color shoot up her cheeks. I'd never seen
her flustered before.

"Here." She bent down, took a strangely shaped key from a zip compartment of her purse, unlocked the top file drawer in her desk, removed
a computer disk, and held it out.

"Go on, crank it up."

"Now?"

"That's right." He paced to the window and twitched a blind. Then he
prowled back, pausing to snap off a dry ficus leaf and frown into the waste-
basket. During the last hour I'd noticed he'd begun to droop; at one point
during the negotiations he'd almost seemed to slip into a trance. Several
times someone asked him about a company agenda and he simply failed
to hear. But now he was storming with energy.

"Okay." Martha glanced fractionally my way, then pulled the old disk
from the slot and inserted the new one.

"You've been killing the modem and wiping the data each time?"

"I'm not a moron." She scowled, typing instructions onto the keypad. Then she muttered, "Everything's tighter than a gnat's throat in
here."

"Let's see what we got." He bent over the screen. "Shaver. Willis. Okay."

"Thomas and Orvitz."

"Not Orvitz. He's moving over to IBM."

"He is? Since when?"

A.J. was still watching the appearing information. "Delete him."

Jumping up from my chair, I stepped toward the desk. "Stay back, Taylor!" He didn't so much as turn around.

I sat back down, nonplussed. Martha didn't look at me. She murmured, "But Orvitz was—"

"He's in love."

"Love?"

"With a hometown girl. He thinks he might have gotten her pregnant." He added in an afterthought, "IBM owes me."

"Oh my Lord." She shook her head slowly, her eyes wide. "Does he think you're firing him?"

"Does it matter?"

"It will to him."

"Put in 'Dubrevsky, Ivan John' as an interim entry. Then check his job record against the personal notes. See if he'll score." He stood up, suddenly tired again. His face looked bleached and cheerless. He was working too hard, I thought as I tried to stifle my resentment. The woman at the opera buffet had been right. He hadn't looked this bad when I'd first broken into his apartment. Clearly I was a strain on him; it must be because, as he'd just so sharply demonstrated, no matter how much he planned to include me, he wasn't used to sidekicks; he was a one-man show. Then I remembered what else Rita Jo Moseley had said to me, about trying to keep up with the younger generation.

"Taylor," he said. "Are you ready for tomorrow morning? Have you gone over that stock report yet?"

"Yessir."

"You've got to be prepared. Every facet of this conglomerate counts. You never know when lightning will strike."

"What lightning?" But he shook his head, frowned, and told Martha to book two reservations at the Petroleum Club for dinner.

After he left for another meeting I asked Martha if he seemed like usual.

"I haven't known him very long. It's hard for me to tell." I went to the same blind he'd twitched aside and peered through the window, trying to hide my disturbance.

"What do you mean, like usual?" she asked.

"Well—is he crankier? Maybe a little more jumpy than he was a few weeks back?"

"People have moods, don't they. Sometimes cranky, sometimes not," she shrugged.

"Come on, Martha. You know what I mean. We were in bed by ten o'clock last night. This morning at breakfast he looked like he hadn't slept in a week. Has he always been like this?"

"A.J. has a lot on his mind."

"So what's new?" She wouldn't answer. Her fingers darted over the keyboard making an old familiar sound, *chic chic*.

ON A MID-AUGUST afternoon, the day after this discussion, I drove to Bernice.

The front door was locked. I'd forgotten my key and had to use a credit card. The door opened onto silence. "Mother! Granddaddy!" I called out, but when I entered the wintry climate of the foyer nobody answered. The pine panels, the silk flowers on the credenza, the fruit prints and brick floor and potpourri, evoked that spooky feeling I'd often noted coming home from boarding school: Whose house was this? Had it shrunk? It felt like I'd been gone for fifty years.

I stepped into the den and plonked down on the couch. Idly I wondered where Dodie might be, but then remembered she'd just gotten her learner's license. I hadn't phoned ahead. Granddaddy would be at the courthouse. Mother, most likely, was out playing bridge or planning some dance at the country club with the golf alcoholics' and doctors' wives who made up her circle.

The brass clock ticked loudly over the fireplace. Grandmother's potted African violets smelled earthy and damp. Somebody must have just watered them. If I closed my eyes and felt their velvety leaves I was always reminded of Grandmother's skin. So persistently alive were they that I felt she must be somewhere in the house—she might have left this room right after straightening the coffee table magazines. Her body warmth hung on the air, her last footfall just stifled. Surely she was upstairs pulling back the covers for her nap, or in the kitchen polishing the dessert service, or coming back in to pat my hair part and say, "Now Taylor, I want you to do Grandmother a sweet favor. You know that garden hose in my daylilies? Can you move it over to the rose bed without tripping or falling and getting yourself wet, like a big boy?"—instead of lying dead under the cemetery dirt.

I was about to go make some iced tea when a motor sounded beyond the circular drive. As I peeked through the sidelight, Mother's Lexus rolled into view and stopped off. After a moment she climbed out, her arms loaded with shopping bags. I opened the front door.

"Taylor! Oh, my Lord have mercy, what are you doing here?"

"Let me take those." I grabbed her packages. She threw herself against me, strangling my neck in a deadly hug.

"I'm so glad to see you! I'm going to faint. It's been weeks. Oh, my what a surprise!" Smearing lipstick all over my chin, she pulled away long enough to guide me back into the den, tossing the bags on Granddaddy's TV chair as she passed. "Here! Sit right down this instant. Oh, Taylor. What in the world?"

Sinking onto the couch beside me, she let go my neck, gave a hiccuppy sigh, kicked off her pumps, and sprawled backward. Then she bent to massage her feet.

"Where have you been, Mother? You seem tired."

"Oh—all over! You know. No place. Just out for a little squander wander."

Immediately I came alert, glancing at the store names on the bags: Cole-Haan, Polo, Neiman Marcus. She saw my look. "Picking up a few things for fall," she added airily.

"Have you been in Dallas?"

"Just Highland Park Village." She gave a sugary little laugh.

"You're kidding."

"What's so special about that? Don't act all strange, Taylor. I've been shopping in Dallas my whole life long, thank you very much."

"I—just—well, shoot, Mother. We could have had lunch together."

She frowned, squinting at her anklebone. "I don't think so," she said.

"Sure we could. Why not?"

Evasively she pursed her lips. "How could you know I'd be there?"

"Well, I didn't."

"See?" Her brows rose as if she'd just won a debate point.

"But that's what I'm saying. Why didn't you call? Get in touch?"

"Well, I have no way to."

"Mother! What are you talking about?"

She didn't reply.

"You've got my number and address. I phoned you just last week, remember? Every time I call I double-check to make sure you've got A.J.'s private number."

"Oh. I can't use that."

"Of course you can. Don't be silly." My reaction, I realized, sounded top-heavy; I was feeling slightly guilty.

"No." She studied her stockinged soles, kneading them with ringed knuckles.

"I don't see what's the problem."

"Yes you do." Her eyes lifted, meeting mine. Then they dropped. "For one thing, people might think."

"Think what?"

"Things."

"Things? Like what? Who?"

"Secretaries, maids. Receptionists. People—working. They might assume I—" She broke off.

"That's ridiculous. They wouldn't even know you'd phoned." Then I thought of Martha, and hastily rationalized: she didn't count. Besides, she wouldn't assume.

"It's just not an option, Taylor. That's all."

After a moment I reached out to rub her shoulder. "It isn't how you imagine, Mother. You'll really be surprised."

"I don't imagine a thing. I've got my own life to live. Don't think for a minute I don't. It's perfectly good. Right now Dodie's away at cheerleader camp in Kilgore. When she gets home next week we're going to Galveston with the Frickers." Her voice quivered.

"Well, that sounds fine."

Then she burst out. "I've been shopping up there almost every single day. My credit cards have nearly hit their limits."

"For how long?" I murmured, after a little while.

Wiping her eyes with the hem of her blouse, she gave a long, hard sniff. "The whole last month," she laughed shakily.

"Why didn't you *tell* me?"

"Oh, honey, I just—" Her eyes squeezed closed. The tears continued to trickle a little out the corners. "To just know we were in the same city, with you-all so nearby . . ."

"He wants to see you."

"What?"

"That's one reason I'm here."

She turned, staring. "He doesn't. How could he?"

"He's never forgotten you. He's loved you from the start."

For a moment she didn't answer. "Then why—"

"The first night we met I said something to discourage him from contacting you."

"Oh, Taylor!"

"I was wrong. I'm sorry."

I think every child in the world ultimately dreams of his parents' perfect union. He longs to see them face beside face; he longs to know they were truly meant for each other, perfect for one another, no matter what's happened in the meantime. He wants their love to form bedrock, to make an eternal seal. He wants all this without a risk of their mutual recoil. Parents cannot part. The node of engenderment lasts forever. Thus he can count himself balanced, an authentic result, confident in that greatest of all birthrights, his own virtue.

Which was why her words made my heart thud.

"I forgive you. But no," she said.

At first I couldn't speak. "What?"

"I can't see him. Not yet."

"But—why?"

She let go of the feet she'd been clenching so tightly, and stretched out her legs. "It's been too long. I'm not ready."

"No, it hasn't! You'll be great, Mother. You're—you're wonderful. Listen—"

"I have to think of Dodie."

"Dodie!"

She nodded. The tears had spilled, making wreckage of her mascara, but now they were drying.

"This is my father. Mine! We're talking about him. Not Dodie's. She doesn't have a thing to do with it. She's not even relevant!"

"She has to do with me," said Mother quietly. "Just as you always did."

"You've got no reason! This is important, this matters more than—I want you to see him. He's *always* mentioning you, he asked me to—I mean, finally I have a father. *Finally!* Don't you understand that, Mother? Don't you get it? He's called me his son, he's named me his heir." And maybe this was it. This must be it: the missing part, the answer.

She reached out and clutched my hands. "I know. And I'm so happy for you, honey. So happy."

I had begun to break. "We're even in the newspaper. In magazines. Together. Interviews. Asking about you, where you are, who, what kept us all apart, what happened."

"I don't think it's anybody's business what happened, do you?" she said.

"I think he's sick," I said, and bent over, crying. Suddenly I felt as if everything that had transpired over the last four months was rising like a black oil from my stomach up my throat. *I killed a man!* I wanted to cry out. *I stabbed him with a knife! He's dead! Teresa-Maria hates me, she's gone. Jesus nearly lost his leg. A.J. won't let me get close, he's wasting away, I can't stop it, I can't stop all that's happened, and it's my fault,* the words beating in my head, *I'm helpless, I'm trying to keep up,* but Mother knelt over me and rubbed her hand up and down my back. The sobs rose with the black substance, great retchers that doubled me up until I couldn't pull a breath anymore and I had to choke or stop.

"It's okay," she murmured. "It's all right, honey. Don't cry anymore. Don't." Then, when at last I shuddered into silence, she said, "Now. What did you mean? Sick how?"

So I told her.

"GIVE ME FOUR weeks," she said.

"Why four? Why not one?"

"If you think he's getting worse and you can't get him to a doctor, then call me and I'll come sooner. Otherwise, for my own sake, I need a month." She sat back, still holding my hand, and touched her other pinkie to her lip corners.

"What if it's serious?" There was something I was trying to remember, some words ringing in the back of my mind. They filled me with dread. Yet I couldn't recall them, I only heard a woman's voice—Medina's voice? Martha's?—smudge their blank hollow with sound.

"Then we'll see." She sighed. "Twenty-one years, Taylor. Nearly twenty-two. It's a very long time."

"Yes, ma'am."

"You were right that he looks like you, though."

"How do you know?"

"I've seen the papers." She smiled.

"Oh."

"I meant what I said. About Dodie. I need to weigh what's best. She's been very troubled, she doesn't need more upset."

"This is my father," I repeated, but quietly now.

"Hers is dead," she answered.

13

"Mr. Matsudo," said Martha, offering my father the phone receiver.

He peered at it as if it were a plug of excrement, then took it from her hand. "*Hai*, Hiro-san."

"Hey. I remember that name from somewhere," I said. "Who is he?"

"Not up to me to say," said Martha, flipping grimly through the computer screens.

"I told you our agreement stands," said A.J. He held the phone close against his ear. "The total's five. Our lottery pick." He frowned, listening. "No, I do not consent. The contract is quite specific. Any international law court would uphold it. And Mr. Matsudo—blackmail does not become a man of your employer's stature." His mouth clamped into a straight line.

"Jesus," said Martha, hammering on the keyboard. "Why did he ever go public?"

"What blackmail?"

"Shh!"

"No, Matsudo-san. I made a guarantee of good faith and I stick by that, both ends. The candidates get compiled and drawn as always. My concerns are that none of the personnel we've sent respond to their relatives." He sat listening. "The indifference of family Ameri—you son of a—"

For an instant his equable control dissolved. "Mr. Matsudo, I'm not interested in sociology. Here's a simple remedy. If everybody's so happy then
make sure they say so." Then, his face stiffening with rage, he slammed
down the phone.

"Next time he calls make him wait twenty minutes before you even tell
me he's there," he snapped at Martha.

"Yes, sir."

"Who's Matsudo?" I asked.

A.J. stood, nostrils tightened. "The president of a company called Kan
Nai, Inc."

"Where is it?"

Over on the table in the living area the private red lacquer box phone
purred. A.J. strode to it, yanked it up, held it to his ear and listened. In that
split second I thought: Mother.

"How did you get this number?" he said evenly. I froze, pulse ratcheting.

"Which woman lawyer?"

Martha smothered a gasp. He gripped the phone, knuckles blooming
white, his features shifting from tautness to flat, mineraline concentration.
"Listen carefully, Matsudo. First of all, Medina Semple is no longer in my
employ. I'd advise you to regard all data she supplies as obsolete from this
moment on." He paused. "*What? How* do you know who's on it?"

Martha stopped breathing.

"No, Orvitz certainly will not. He's no longer available. I don't care
how fine his credentials are. That information is confidential. And this, Mr.
Matsudo, places you in breach of contract. You had no rights to that list
until the draw was completed."

He listened. "Blackmail again?" he said crisply.

"Why didn't I catch it? Why?" breathed Martha.

"Congratulations—on my what?"

Martha sat stock-still.

"How dare you," he whispered. His face drained. It was like watching
the last sand pour from an hourglass.

"Now listen to me," he said, his tone level, deadly. "My family is none of your business." Martha's eyes rounded. She whipped halfway toward me, then back to the monitor.

"I don't give a damn. I won't tolerate it. Get that clear." Yet despite the fury of this absolute statement, he kept the receiver raised to his ear, and did not put it down until the finish from the other end.

"I'll get the number cha—," began Martha.

"Don't bother. They've got the high-code file. We'll have to start over."

"You want the list?" Her fingers shook slightly, curved like talons ready to pounce on the keyboard.

"No." He brooded, rubbing the phone lacquer with the ball of his thumb. "Hold all my calls. I want to think."

"So what's going on?" I asked.

My father looked at me bleakly and smiled. "Nothing. Forget it," he said.

THE ROOM WAS congested with darkness that night, the way it had been when I'd found Medina at the keyboard. This time I didn't stumble into any furniture. My door hinges opened silently. In the living room no lamp shone beside the monitor; the screen was switched off, but beneath it the computer exhaled its ceaseless electronic sigh. Two green glowing numbers branded the dark.

I pushed the screen button and watched it leap into light.

Then, kneeling, I took the three picks I'd bound together to simulate the wards of Martha's strange key and started on the drawer.

"WHAT'S A *KEIRETSU?*" I asked Martha the next morning as she stood in the kitchen cutting oranges for juice.

She paused in midslice, knife high.

"A what?" The knife lowered. "I don't know. Why ask me? I thought you had a sore throat."

"Swollen glands. I want you to tell me."

It was Saturday. A.J. had flown to Galveston to look at some old sal-
vage ships. I'd begged off, too sick. Martha dropped the knife and stood on
tiptoe to heave the juicer from its shelf. Quickly I reached it down and set
it on the counter. "Do you know what this is?" I said, holding the lock-pick
bundle in her face.

She stared.

"How about this?" I pulled the disk from my bathrobe pocket.

"Oh, hell."

"What's a keiretsu?"

Her hands fell to her sides while the oranges lay leaking juice on the
white cutting board. She mashed her lips together.

"A keiretsu is a squad of Japanese corporations owned and run by dis-
parate groups that are all united by one concern—loyalty," she said as if
quoting a textbook, then angrily picked up an orange half.

"Loyalty to what?"

"To each other." She slammed the hemisphere onto the juicer cone. "In
every decision they act as allies, mutually supportive of each other's interests."

"So why is my father sending Kan Nai, Inc., in Tokyo his choicest
employees?"

"Oh, for God's sake." The motor whined, the cone biting pulp. "You
heard him on the phone yesterday! Blackmail."

"What for?"

"The head of the keiretsu is threatening to seize his companies through
hostile takeovers."

Why? I started to demand. But the question that burned most came
instead. "Why hasn't he told me?"

She lifted her gaze. Her eyes shone clear and hard. "If you were a
tycoon," she said slowly, "who'd built a whole multibillion-dollar conglomerate all by yourself using nothing but bare hands and wits, would
you want to admit to your only long-lost son that some creep was forcing

you into a corner to sacrifice innocent human beings?" Her mouth curled. "I imagine he's ashamed."

"HERE'S HOW IT works. Every two years, one single company inside the Minamoto keiretsu skims a top layer of young talent from Deeds."

"You mean, like, corporate piracy?"

"They have A.J.'s permission. Eight years ago he signed a deal."

"So how come he's pissed off?"

"At that time he didn't know the consequences." She clattered the juicer parts into the sink, turned on the faucet to rinse them, and handed me my glass. "You want some soup or toast?"

"No thanks."

"Damn it, Taylor." She glared, her hand bunching to a fist; she started to punch my abdomen. All at once she looked like Dodie. "Are you going to tell him you stole that disk? Or do I have to?"

"I'll tell him."

"Give it here."

"Once you've told me the rest."

"You're a pain." She opened the fist, wiped her palm on her tennis shorts, tugged at her polo-shirt hem. Stomping to the couch, she flung herself down. "The firm is given the right to check through a special lottery draw from a personnel list. Those people get hired to Japan."

"Okay. So?"

"The hirees must meet certain criteria—high qualifications, some experience proving their value, under twenty-five years old, single."

"Yeah." When she didn't go on, I prodded, "They need to be virgins as well?"

"Ha, ha." She flopped over. "They're whisked off to Tokyo into corporate housing. The office and lab complexes sit right next door. The job descriptions fall perfectly within their fields of expertise. The firm hiring is a leader with world standing—pharmaceutical research, electronics—and owned by one single man. Each of the young people has a certain brilliance, cut for success."

"So what's the problem?"

She pondered, brooding at the rug. "They vanish."

"THEY STOP WRITING letters." Martha leaned back and jerked her pendant around and around on its chain. "They completely fall out of touch. Don't phone, don't visit. Sometimes they might fax their parents, but the faxes sound unnatural—too polite or something."

"Well, hey. Maybe they simply get involved in new lives, which is very easy to—"

"No," said Martha with finality. "No cards. No phone number. No snapshots of weekend ski trips or a restaurant table. No Christmases home. Only maybe one stupid Thanksgiving video, sitting there dope-faced and making goofy remarks like a zombie."

"How come you know that? You sound pretty sure."

"My brother got hired two years ago. That video's been the only time we've laid eyes on him since."

I blinked.

"It's how A.J. first started finding out. Mom contacted Deeds Head-quarters, worried out of her mind. Red had worked for Deeds for half a year. He was designing a new test system at the med center when they took him. The biggest bragging, teasing, blabbermouth mama's boy ever to graduate from Planeau High," she closed her eyes, "and he shut up like a clam the instant he set foot on the Minamoto corporate jet."

"What did he say on the Thanksgiving video?"

"Moron stuff. How he's working hard and misses us. A real Boy Scout crack about losing his chance to vote in the presidential election. Some presents came with it, with 'Love, Red' on the tags." She swallowed, stood up, started roaming the room. The desk phone buzzed. She stopped and stared at it.

"It's Saturday," I said. "You're not even officially supposed to be here." After two rings the phone fell silent.

"He's never voted his whole damn life," she said. "'Love, Red.' He always signed everything with a joke poem poking fun at the person. Even a get-well card."

"Tell me one."

She sealed her mouth tight.

"Okay then, don't."

"'This present may be little bitty, but I picked it out to match your titty.'"

"Hm. Yeah. So, was he drugged? Mutated?"

"Not visibly. Just boring."

"I mean when he wrote that poem."

"Ha ha," she said again and wrung her hands together. I realized I had never seen anyone actually wring their hands, as if they were squeezing water from the fingers. "You're a crack-up."

"I'm sorry."

"A.J.'s tried and tried to find out what's happening. The American consulate's checked it out, gone to the workplaces, interviewed a few employees, talked with managements. Everybody said, No, no, we're really happy here. Kan Nai's a terrific place. Minamoto's great to work for. It's all legit." She strummed her gold chain. "They got him on contract. It's how they hooked them all. How long they have to stay, conditions, everything. See, nobody can legally quit, they have to give a long-term notice lasting *years*."

"Why would anybody sign on?"

"They pay a mint. And promise huge R and D."

Suddenly I was remembering the night I'd broken into this apartment, a question my father had asked. "Minamoto."

"That's what I said. Ito Minamoto."

"Is that a person? The head of the keiretsu? Who's threatening the hostile takeovers?"

"Yes."

"Why?" I scratched my head. My throat hurt; the sunlight glaring through the windowpane prompted a shudder of vertigo.

"Revenge."

"What did A.J. ever do to him?"

"It's not just A.J. It's the United States."

"The whole country?"

"At least certain establishments. But yeah, the whole country. He goes after people all over."

"Some kind of bloodlust?"

"I want coffee," she said, jumping up. I clambered to my feet and followed her to the kitchen. "God, you are relentless."

I sat on the counter, clamping my head to still the giddiness, and watched her spoon pulverized beans out of the grinder. "A few years back, the pride of Ito Minamoto's life came to the United States. His only son, Anjiro. He was twenty-two years old then. Very bright. After graduating from Todai he'd landed this fellowship at Rice, in the doctoral physics program. His Japanese professors thought he was pretty special because he had a real gift—an innovative mind."

"Ah," I said.

"Well, at Rice he published some papers, made friends, had a good time. He also invented a new mathematical sentence—the Minamoto sentence." She paused and filled the kettle. "By the end of the year the department announced he'd won the Tollinger Grant."

"What's that?"

"An award given every two years for outstanding new work in astrophysics."

"Then his father should be happy."

"Two other students had been in the running. Americans. No doubt they'd counted on winning, which would have made their careers. But they were Anjiro's buddies. That night after the presentation banquet all three decided to go barhopping to celebrate, cruising down Montrose getting drunk. About three in the morning they crawl out of a beer garden. These thugs waiting out in the parking lot must have been loaded. They started bashing them around, demanding money. One of the Americans pushed Anjiro forward and used him like a shield. 'Ask him! He's got the money,' he yelled. 'His daddy's the richest man in the world!'"

For a moment Martha paused.

"Anjiro was just this foreign guy, standing there scared and confused. Can you see it?"

"Yes," I said. "Oh, yes."

She shook her head. "He couldn't answer their questions right. So, they hit him, knocked him down, kicked him over and over in the head and gut."

I closed my eyes. I saw the landscape as she spoke: The asphalt plane zooming in, starred with gravel. The humid Houston night. Teeth-jarring fire as the boots landed, the grass at the lot's edge, his event horizon, yellow stems on the lip of light; the blood, the jabbering, hysterical voices.

"And then one reached down, pointed his gun, and shot him."

My eyes flew open. She stared.

"Sirens sounded. There'd been another robbery up the street. The gang ran. By the time the police got there Anjiro was dead."

Into the ensuing quiet came the whistle of the kettle. She reached over, turned off the burner, then stood clutching her arms as if cold.

After a long pause I asked, licking my lips, "Where are they? Where are the two American guys now?" Where was Ronnie Dean Jordan? the tormentors since?

"One teaches quantum mechanics at Stanford. The other went into construction. He's a boozer. The last A.J.'s been able to trace him he was working on the Houston docks."

"The one who shoved Anjiro forward," I said, certain.

"No. The one who stood and watched."

Silence hung. Under the bathrobe my skin prickled with goose bumps.

"So, was he telling the truth? Is this Ito Minamoto really the richest man in the world?"

She turned to pour the water into the pot. "Damn close."

"HOW'D HE GET so powerful?"

"The keiretsu." We were on the street now, hiking toward the art museum. Claustrophobia had driven us both out to fresh air. Hardly any cars rolled past; Saturdays downtown were always deathly quiet.

"What does that mean in practical terms?"

"For instance, say there's a restaurant company." She sighed. "Then say an American distributor wants to sell them beer. Well, he won't have a prayer, because somewhere in that company's keiretsu is a brewery. Every single person working in the keiretsu—banker, car maker, textile weaver, engineer—drinks only that beer. You can identify the loyalties of any salaryman in Japan by his beer label."

"That's ridiculous. What if he doesn't like that kind?"

She shrugged. "He'll also root for his keiretsu's baseball team. Which will be owned by a department store, tied to the auto firm, so the team players all drive that brand of car, and only one beer's sold at the games. And the cars will be covered by an insurance firm belonging in the same keiretsu. As will the salaryman's house and belongings. You get the drift?"

"Yes." She crossed against the light. I had to run to catch up.

"There used to be groups called *zaibatsu*. Just as powerful, even more interconnected. Like royalty, passed down from fathers to sons like the old feudal system. After the war General MacArthur busted them up. They'd helped fund the Japanese nationalist military. The keiretsu replaced them. It's the same thing, though."

I shook my head.

"Usually one company stands biggest—say, a banking house like Mitsubishi—and often it has a hereditary head descended from the zaibatsu families. Total obedience, respect, and trust. More powerful than a head of government. In fact, he helps run Japan." She paused.

"Ito Minamoto is one of them. That's what you're telling me," I said.

We'd reached the museum. I followed her into the courtyard, which sweltered like a hot box under the end-of-August sky.

"Yes."

"Why does he hire these particular Americans?"

"They're some of the smartest people here. They give America its edge. Japanese firms are always searching for brains. That's his rationale." She paused before the big glass doors. "But they're the same type of brains that Anjiro Minamoto had."

"But how can he hold them?"

"Contracts. Cast-iron, lead coffin."

"That wouldn't nail them, would it?"

"Minamoto's real old-fashioned. He has them sign these heavy rice-paper scrolls with seals, one copy each. Matsudo told Red they're like Imperial Court decrees from nine hundred years ago. He trots them out whenever there's some international law question. No one over here is allowed to tip the candidates off to what they're committing to, or else A.J.'ll lose his companies as a penalty."

"And they're the only proof binding these people to Minamoto?"

"Maybe not the only. But the most legally crushing. One-way tickets."

I chewed on this a moment. "Tell me. Where are these contracts kept, just out of curiosity?"

"How would I know?" She pushed on the glass door. A rush of cool air hit our faces as we entered the pale stone hall. "Mr. Matsudo tells us every time, 'They are very safe. Please don't ever worry. No earthquakes or fires will destroy them. Thank you.' As if we cared."

"Obviously they do."

"Do I give a damn how they feel?" she said.

SITTING BEFORE A Frank Lloyd Wright panel of stained glass in the museum café, I watched its colors jolt and quiver; my dizziness flowed in, triggered by fever. "You look sick," Martha said. "You'd better have some soup."

"I wish he'd told me."

She picked up her glass of iced tea.

"It's eating him alive," I said.

"Yes."

"For a while I thought it was my fault."

She looked perplexedly at me. The waitress brought a basket of rolls. The smell hit my raw throat.

"He could have trusted me." I took a roll, crumbled it. "How did Minamoto pick *his* companies?"

"I asked him that. You know what he said? 'Entrepreneurs note each other.' Minamoto's gone after other companies with solo directors. The individual doesn't seem to matter. Except that A.J.'s been the first one to fight back. And he's from Texas." She toyed with the butter knife.

"Anjiro died here."

She nodded. "I worry about his health. It's not just this time. It's next time. And now that you're in his life, I know that when you finally take over he doesn't want to hand you . . . that."

A bowl full of steaming tomato-basil soup was set before me. I stared down into it. "That would be a long time from now. Decades," I said.

She didn't answer.

"When is the final list due?"

"Next week. We draw the last names Wednesday night."

"From how big a pool?"

"Forty-nine." She met my eye, pushing the tip of the knife again and again into the butter. "At midnight Wednesday they get electronically transmitted to Tokyo to meet the September first deadline."

"You have access to the list until then?"

"I make the transmission."

So obvious, I thought. Fate hands a card, fans out the next, the ineluctable suit falling one by one onto the table, until at last you sit staring at a royal flush. All the faces in order: king, queen, ace, knave in the hole.

"There's something I want you to do," I said.

"What?" She looked up. But unlike Ramón's puzzlement the time I'd used almost the same words to ask him to yield his secret skills, I knew: she must have seen it, too.

"THIS IS CRAZY," my father said, staring at the scroll.

I watched him. He hadn't been prepared. That's what I told myself, seeing his face go gray as ash.

"It's a setup. By Matsudo. And Medina. Well, that's it!" He began to snort, rifling through the contracts in their long brocade boxes, already witnessed, sealed, and ready for delivery by special courier from Martha's desk. "He knows he's only allowed our picked list. They can't change the names. Did he not think I'd review these contracts before they went back to Japan?" Any moment now the anger would start transforming into relief.

"I've already signed it," I said.

He looked up. Then he stared. "All agreements are terminated. Starting now."

"No sir, they're not." I stared back. The room began to teeter. "He hasn't changed any names."

"Of course he has!"

I shook my head.

"I won't permit it. Your name is not on here. It does *not* belong on this list. It will not be on here," he said, crushing the rice-paper scroll in his fist.

"It does."

"I saw the list! Five minutes before you sent it!" He turned on Martha. "What's he talking about? Have they sabotaged us electronically? How is this possible?"

She blinked and looked down.

He frowned. Slowly his head cocked. "What have you done?" he said.

She just sat there, hands folded neatly. He drew himself erect, crashed over to the window, strode back. "*Taylor!*"

"Yessir."

"Do you truly imagine I'm going to allow some kind of trade-off?"

I looked at him. "I don't—"

"I've waited twenty years. Twenty years! Do you really dream for a second I'd let you go?"

"Sir," I said. His hand flew up. He raked his hair wildly. "That's why I have to."

Abruptly he sat down. "I—what?"

I waited. He looked sick. When he remained silent, I said, "It's not Martha's fault. Don't blame her. I forced her. That Rice mugging had nothing whatsoever to do with you. Or the other companies Minamoto hires from. But you're the ones paying, and so are the people you've handed over."

He scraped his forehead with his knuckles as if the pain were indelible. "Somebody's got to do something."

"No."

"He must have quite a brain drain sitting there under his roofs."

He leaned forward, head between hands.

"What kind of products has his firm been coming up with as a result?"

"Zero," murmured Martha. Something in her calm tone made me look at her more closely.

"Show me that list of contracts," I said.

Wordlessly she handed it over. I scanned down the rows of names. There. *Deeds, Taylor Thaddeus.* Side by side with the elaborate résumé of credentials we'd cooked up.

And just below it: *Franklin, Martha Racine.*

"You're on here," I said.

"Of course. Did you think I wouldn't be?" She smiled sweetly, her blue eyes clear as ice.

"*No!*" my father cried.

"I'm sorry. It's done," she said.

"Listen." I sat beside him and touched his arm. The night in the Houston Opera House, that touch uncompleted. The truths I hadn't yet told him, about Mother, Dodie, my early life; the things I'd hidden: my infant meningitis, its legacy. "Remember how we met?"

"Of course."

I glanced toward Martha, steadfastly preparing to disappear from her own real life. Then I turned back. "What do I do best?"

LABYRINTH

Not long after this there arrived from King Minos of Crete the collectors of the tribute which the Athenians paid them . . . [this tribute being] seven young men and as many virgins. [These victims were taken by ship to Crete,] where, wandering in the labyrinth, and finding no possible means of getting out, they miserably ended their lives [some say as food for the Minotaur].

—Plutarch

14

Looking out of the plane window at the architecture of the clouds, their pillars reflecting on a silver sheet, I at first mistook the flatness for sky but then realized it was water, the icy floor of upper space, the ceiling above the sea.

"Have you ever been this high so long?" asked Martha.

"Yeah. Not over ocean, though."

"Scares the shit out of me."

"We won't crash. Don't worry." She bit her lip. I patted her shoulder, then turned back to the cloudscape, stretching outward like my father's empire, its stacked ornate masonry painted in the colors of oysters. For an instant the image darkened. I saw his face once more saying good-bye.

"Excuse me. Do you have a watch?" A tall, gangly man leaned over us, one hand on Martha's headrest.

"Hi, Thomas." I flipped my wrist. "Six P.M. Dallas time."

"I was wondering when they'd start the next movie."

"After dinner, that steward said."

Still he remained tilted above Martha, mashing a strand of her hair, oblivious to her wince. "I was just talking to Shaver and what's-her-name."

"Becky Willis?"

"They told me they haven't been to Japan before."

"Is that right."

"I assume you have."

"No, actually I never have."

"Since you're A. J. Deeds's son I find that surprising. I thought you could answer a couple of questions."

"Sorry."

The plane hit a trough of turbulence, bouncing him forward; he righted himself just before conking into Martha's crown. "What were you wondering about?" I asked.

"Food."

"It's probably the same as a Japanese restaurant back home, don't you think?" said Martha, pointedly tugging her hair free. "Sushi, tempura."

He stared at her shoulder, then switched his dozy gaze back to me. "I don't eat raw food."

"From what I hear you can get anything in Tokyo. Pizza, Big Macs, spaghetti," I said.

"The enzymes give me hives."

"Well, I'm sure you'll find plenty of alternatives."

"Or fish. No seaweed. No soy."

"Our apartments have furnished kitchens. And there's a cafeteria that serves Western style," said Martha, but he pretended deafness.

"No rice. No noodles."

"Hm. How about grits?"

He hesitated. Then with a sudden twitch he let go the headrest and sloped off up the aisle, his shrunken khaki pants flapping around his knobby ankles.

"What a freak." Martha glared, rubbing her scalp.

"Now, you know he's charming."

"He hates women."

"That's his sad, sad loss," I shook my head, and then climbed over her to go use the bathroom.

At the toilets I ran into Steve Shaver, enclosed in cigarette smoke. "Hidy!" he said. When I'd first met him that morning he'd lurched into the departure area, his pudginess gaiting him like a bowlegged sailor, a tweed jacket buttoned tight over his damp blue shirt although the sky still threw heat like a nuclear test. He'd said the same thing. "Hidy!" he'd cried. "Real pleased to meet you."

"Nice to meet you, too," I said.

"Whew! We're all in this together, I take it!"

"Looks that way."

"Pretty exciting, huh? Boy. I'm sure trusting one of you folks speaks Japanese."

"I don't," said Becky Willis, a willowy Cal Poly cum laude engineer whose loss A.J. had lamented. "Do you?"

"I haven't had time to learn. *Konichiwa!* That's the total. I only found out I was going for this job six days ago. Whew! I mean—hired in haste, fired at leisure!"

"It takes years to become literate," intoned the tall man, lifting an upper lip like a camel's.

"You'll pick it up, no problem." Cheerfully Steve whapped a *Scientific American* against his thigh, then hitched one short shoulder high to stop his vinyl tote strap from slipping off.

"I'm hopeless at foreign languages," said Becky.

The tall man turned away and crossed his arms. In his heavy-lidded eyes lay a sedimentary indifference, as of someone whose highest ambitions had been gratified at too early an age.

"So hey. What's your name?" Steve asked.

"Mine?" The man turned fractionally.

"Yeah."

"Thomas." He didn't add either Christian or surname.

"Are we all going to work for the same outfit?" said Steve.

"I'm Kan Nai, Inc.," he replied distantly. "Director of Modeling and Optimization."

"Oh, those are the testing and formulations systems, right? Neat! How long have you known you'd be coming along?"

"They've experienced some emergency. They made me a short-notice offer I couldn't refuse."

"Whoa, I figured six days was plenty damn short."

"I had to sublet my apartment in that time, not to mention farm out my dog," said Becky.

"What kind of dog you got? I love dogs."

Turning, I caught a glimpse of Thomas's aloof face, which held a look that said, Of course you do.

"He's a Staffie named Pooch. My parents took custody."

"Pooch. Well, that's a good, regular guy kind of name."

"He went with me all the way through grad school. He doesn't know anybody else."

"Hm! Smart dog. What'd he get, a master's? Don't worry, you can always visit him during vacations."

"I guess," she sighed.

"How about you?" Steve turned to Martha.

"Information Integrator."

"Yeah? Who do you work for?"

"A. J. Deeds."

"Heck! Don't we all?" He was sweating under the tweed, a powerfully advertised truth that did nothing to diminish his goodwill.

"His private office."

"Well—hey there, honcho!"

"Not exactly."

"Where have you been working, Steve?" asked Becky.

"I'm Chief Technologist for the MedRay facility over in Athens, Texas. That's where I've been living, in a little cabin in the piney woods. Real pretty."

"You doing anything special?"

"For the last nine months I've been culturing a new potential form of biocomputer."

"Culturing. What—you mean living tissue?" Her eyes lighted.

"Living genetic intelligence. Kan Nai has a lab set up for the next phase. I'm not sure yet of all the details, but it sounds real promising." Martha shot me a look. I remembered the elegiac note that had crept into my father's voice as he described Steve: *He may come off sounding like a fool, but within his field he's remarkable.*

"Pet computers. Wow," said Becky.

"The attendants are calling us," Martha said.

"Oops! Here goes. Glasses. Billfold. Inhaler. Crosswords. Anagrams. Passport," Steve muttered, slapping his pockets. "Passport?"

Thomas stooped for his carry-on. Becky rummaged through a leather handbag the color of a human prosthesis. Surreptitiously I gripped Martha's elbow. For the tiniest second she shrank down, huddling inside her shirt like a sparrow. Then her shoulders stiffened, her face tipped to the last of the blazing Texas sunlight; she joined the queue, magazines stuffed under her arm.

The one person no one had asked about was me.

"SO, YOU LOOKING forward to a change, Taylor? I've always lived in the Lone Star, myself."

"Me too."

"Born down in Refugio. Becky's from Port Arthur. Thomas comes from the Midwest somewhere, he won't say where." Steve paused. "I think maybe there're a few health problems. I feel kind of sorry for him." He frowned and plunged his cigarette into an ashtray beside the toilet door, marked MINAMOTO CORPORATION AIRLINE. "Well, at least he'll enjoy the beer. Japanese beer is great."

"He doesn't drink, I believe."

"Did he say that?" His eyes popped. "Holy cow. Poor guy!"

"It's a pity." I shook my head.

Shyly he ducked. "You know, I've actually met your daddy. I wasn't going to mention it. Over in Athens. He interviewed me personally once this offer from Kan Nai came in. I thought that was pretty conscientious."

"He probably didn't want to lose you."

"No, he acted real supportive. He said he just wanted to make sure he'd cleared the deal with me, that I was okay with the venue change. Asked me stuff about my family, my parents and all. All kinds of details. He's a real nice guy."

"Yeah. He is."

"A. J. Deeds." He looked up with regret. "I'm sorry I won't be working for him anymore."

"Well. You never know."

"No, you don't, do you?"

AFTER OUR LUGGAGE was discharged, we trudged through passport control, emerging into the sterile glory of Narita Airport. Immediately a man stepped up. "Mr. Deeds."

"Yes."

"Please come this way. My name is Hiro Matsudo, president of Kan Nai Incorporated of the Minamoto Group. Welcome to Japan." He bowed, then proffered his hand.

No one could have faulted the pinstripe suit. Dovetailing with his black haircut, natty ears, lustrous shirt and tie, and wing tips polished like volcanic glass, the suit finished off a piece of seamless craft. He exuded cultivation like an artifact. My own dishevel was in itself a purist's achievement: my enormous hand blundering into his, some meaty livestock herded there by a redneck in stale jeans; my landmark height an American Statue of Something. Three other men stood ranked behind him, each in a blue suit. They too bowed, but despite this deference I noted they didn't exactly warm. Not one of them looked directly at us. At a discreet little distance from Matsudo's left elbow stood a girl wearing a hot pink dress with a short jacket and an emerald bracelet. Her gaze fluttered, then dropped to the carpet. Her eyelids were curved like pale shells. One temple as tender as paper had a wisp of black silk loosed against it. At first I had assumed she was a bystander waiting for some passenger. Only when she remained near

Matsudo's elbow did I realize she'd come with our greeting party—a secretary, maybe, or assistant, although if the bracelet was real, her salary must afford serious vacations.

"I recognized your voice," said Martha.

"Ah—sorry, sorry. Yes, Miss Franklin! Of course you would."

"Nice to meet you, Mr. Matsudo," I said.

"I hope you had a good flight," he said.

"A little longer than expected, thanks. Some turbulence."

"Oh, is that so? How unfortunate. The Minamoto jet is of course invariably on time. Excuse me now please while I find Mr. Shaver, Mr. Thomas, and Miss Willis." Swiveling, he glanced toward one of the blue-suited men, who glanced sideways and down; then he skimmed the crowd pouring through the doorway from customs. I felt a chill watching his small, moveless, urbane eyes, so tight-set in their modeled bones.

"There they are, coming through now," I said. "The tall man, the girl with white hair, and the guy in tweed." Little lambs.

One of the blue-suited men bowed and dashed away, sidling up to Steve through the flow. They spoke briefly. Steve lit up with his smile. Thomas followed. His boredom seemed even more false in the rush of glad arrivals. Considering that his sleep mask still dangled around his neck from its elastic like a giant bow tie, the languor looked a touch oversmug.

"Please, we have cars waiting for you outside," said Matsudo. "But first I will introduce you to these gentlemen. Here is Yoichi Oshima"—the one directly behind Matsudo bowed—"this is Nagisa Kawai, and here, Kiyoshi Imai. They are each managers in Kan Nai Incorporated."

"How do you do." We all spoke at once. Steve attempted a bow, which although well meant transformed him into a choleric frog.

"And this young lady is Ayako Minamoto."

Instead of stepping forward, she stood motionless. The dress reflected on her throat. Pink glowing against new cream. She glanced halfway, bowed five times. She looked at me. Looked down. Looked at me again.

"Hello," I said.

"I am honored," she murmured.

"Me, too."

"My father is happy you are here. Please, welcome to Japan." Her face remained blank as empty water.

"Thank you. We're all honored." I came toward her. Still she didn't move. Even as my hand extended and she stared at it, her palm slowly rising, inserting into the loose clasp to shake, no muscle inflected, no fingertip quivered. There was only limp weight, a silent pause.

"My own father's less thrilled, but he'll be glad to hear you've greeted us."

She peered into my eyes, her sole manifestation of question.

"Aha! Good. Finished here now, I think? Please come this way to the automobiles," said Mr. Matsudo. He quirked a brow at one of the managers, who instantly launched up and hurried toward the exit doors. "I will have the drivers carry your baggage."

"Don't got much, but thanks!" said Steve. He gave his plastic shoulder tote a thump. Matsudo regarded it impassively.

"I'm afraid I have tons," said Becky. "You do too, don't you, Thomas?"

His answer, obvious from the steamer trunk and three suitcases on his airport trolley, was slow in coming. "I need a few books."

"That's okay. I'll carry my own," Martha spoke up. She clutched her magazines to her chest as if they were last relics. Gripping the small suitcase, she started toward the exit.

"Oh, one moment, please. Please let our drivers help you," Matsudo insisted.

"No thanks. Really."

"Please. So we may honor your arrival properly." He nodded infinitesimally. Blue Suit Number Two rushed up, bowed, and gently began prising the suitcase handle from her clenched fist.

"Is this one yours, Mr. Deeds?" Matsudo indicated my duffle.

"Yes. But I'm quite able-bodied, thanks."

"We wish to provide every service. We're glad that you are joining us at Kan Nai."

With both arms I hoisted the duffle. The three drivers were striding up the concourse alongside Blue Suit Number One. They wore chauffeurs' uniforms out of a 1920s English movie: black livery, jodhpurs, gold-buttoned coats, visored caps. In my defended-tower state they looked like the U.S. Cavalry. I steeled my feet into place, then, groping recklessly, found inspiration.

"Mr. Matsudo, I'd be much obliged if you will allow me to carry my own bag. In fact, from now on I'd really prefer to look after myself entirely."

"Mr. Deeds?"

"I wish to do this out of respect to Mr. Minamoto. You see, it is my father's deepest wish that I show Mr. Minamoto and all his people every possible courtesy, and dedicate myself completely to their service. That's the reason I'm here. That's what I came for. So, for the sake of these people now officially working for Mr. Minamoto," I gestured to my travel companions, "and out of obligation to my father's name, I'm sure you'll understand my duty to take this position."

Matsudo paused, nonplussed.

Next to him the blue-suited manager swung around with a look of uncertainty. The drivers hovered, waiting. The other two managers seemed caught in a dream. My fellow Americans blinked, recoiling; Steve grinned nervously. Beside me Martha sucked her breath.

"Mr. Deeds." People were pressing close, stepping around the knot we made, peeking sideways in polite curiosity.

"Yes, sir," I bowed again.

He hesitated. Then he said, "I respect your position."

"Thank you." I gripped the duffle. One thousand war movies—soldiers' honor, lives mangled, Toshiro Mifune, banzai pilots hurtling, my father's tutelage—resounded in a clang of brass.

"I would like to carry Miss Franklin's bag too, please. Also Mr. Shaver's. My father requests this as a token of—his humility. Although I'll have to forgo Thomas's and Becky's—I don't think I'm quite up to the Olympics. But I know my father will forgive me."

Matsudo's mouth closed. He bowed again.

"Are you jet-lagged?" Becky whispered to me. In wry befuddlement Steve was trying to strap his carry-on across my shoulder.

"Not really. Just doing my job."

"Interesting task description," murmured Thomas, stretching his neck. The sleep mask waggled to and fro.

"You'd be surprised," snapped Martha. But at my small headshake she pressed her lips tight. Matsudo's men were already walking a few steps behind him to the outside doors. The duffle with its freight rode securely in my arms, Martha's suitcase banging my kneecap at every step. Beside me Steve humped along, smellier than a wet Clydesdale, but I couldn't criticize; my knit shirt clung with sweat, my shoulders strained against the weight, I struggled to keep upright as the load sent my vertigo churning, I felt crude, awkward, slovenly, exultant. A snappy tune played over the loudspeakers. I wanted to whistle. It was only when I followed the procession through the doors that I risked glancing toward the girl in the pink dress.

Her eyes, so demure and self-contained, could have sliced off my skin with their swerve.

THE INSIDE OF the limousine felt like a sauna. We'd already been driving for more than half an hour. I craned around to view through the smoked gray windows. There didn't seem to be either electric buttons or crank handles, and I could scarcely make out the fields and groves, the city roads and factory clusters in the evening dusk.

"If you would like some fresh air I will arrange it," said the manager on the seat opposite mine. Unless I'd made a mistake he was the one named Kawai. He was taller than the other two, and his suit seemed a shade darker. He was the only one wearing glasses.

"It's a tad stuffy," I admitted. He nodded, touched a button on the console beside his leather lounger, spoke low. Immediately the temperature dropped.

"I have heard that Texas is very hot," he said.

"I won't argue that."

"We wish you to feel comfortable."

"Well, heck! You do a good job. This might just as soon be July on the Gulf right now," said Steve.

"The Gulf," mused the manager. "Ah, yes. The Gulf." He nodded sagely. "Of—Persia?"

"No. Mexico!" said Steve. "You know. Corpus Christi? Galveston?"

"Ah, is that so? Oh, yes, one moment! The song. 'Galveston oh Galveston.'" The manager, gratified by his success, spoke in hurried dabs of English. "Ah, yes. The Gulf!"

"Do you happen to know that from singing karaoke by any chance?" asked Steve.

"Yes, yes, karaoke."

"Now you've named one of my favorite kinds of entertainment."

"Ah, yes, is that so? You like karaoke?"

"They got a machine in this little bar outside Athens? Where I drink beer? A few of us get together sometimes after work. We have a blast." He beamed fondly. "Hey—I always meant to ask. Do the karaoke machines here show lyrics in English?"

"Oh, yes, yes." The manager nodded, relieved to be so helpful. "American songs, thousands! At least, you will find them in Minamoto Mansions."

"Mansions!"

"You will be living in Minamoto Mansions, expressly designed for Western taste. There are several hostess bars and restaurants." He smiled, nodding. Outside the window Tokyo was gliding fluidly by, a traffic canal with huge neon signs in colors too filtered by the glass to read. The headlights in the adjoining lane were dim fireflies, the streets winding, sinuous, and multicornered once we pulled off from the expressway. Two other limousines followed behind us like great white sharks. Oshima escorted Becky, Martha, and Thomas in the the second one. Matsudo occupied the third with Imai.

"Well, hey then! Maybe you'd like to come join me, sip a few some night. Lubricate the vocal cords. Nagisa, isn't it?"

"Yes, Nagisa, yes. Nagisa Kawai."

"Well, how about it, Nagisa?"

"Ah, that is a good thought. I would be most interested to join you perhaps. Some time in the future."

"Great! You just name it. When?"

Kawai gazed modestly down at his manicured hands. "Thank you. I will make every effort. I don't know yet when I can be free, but it would be a great pleasure."

"I'll pass you my number once I know. Heck—you probably have it already, don't you? When you're ready, just phone. I look forward to it. We can sing 'Galveston.'"

Kawai's gaze stayed fixed on his hands, deflected but radiating assent. Only the most stringent self-control kept me from jeering out loud.

"In fact, here's some trivia—did you know there's a whole ton of songs with Texas towns in the titles?"

"Really, is that so?"

"Sure! Far more than any other state. 'Abilene.' 'Amarillo.' 'Streets of Laredo.' 'El Paso.' You can play a great beer game. 'San Antonio Rose.' Wait, I'll head north—'Did You Ever See Dallas from a DC-Nine at Night.'"

"Ah, sorry, I do not think so."

"No, it's a song."

"How about 'Going Back to Houston'?" I said.

The girl looked up.

She had sat propped on the other lounger behind the driver like a glazed vase in a cushioned box ever since Matsudo had bowed her in. All this time she'd remained silent, legs crossed at the ankles, high-heeled shoes arching her instep. Sometimes she stirred to peep out through the fuzzy glass. Then she would study the upholstery logo, trace the fabric of her lap. Sometimes she adjusted her bracelet. Never once had those eyes opened wider than halfway, or strayed in a human direction. Her hands lay curled like flower buds. She sat facing me.

"You know that song?" I asked.

The eyes alighted on mine.

"Dean Martin. He's the one who sang it."

She bobbed her head in a way that I instantly understood meant no. "I'm very sorry."

"Lousy tune. You haven't missed much."

"Excuse me, isn't that 'Going Back to Memphis'?" asked Steve.

I peered into the black eyes' luminous surfaces. She sat expressionless, letting me. "Houston," I said.

"Well, yeah, I guess it'll scan," said Steve, amiably doubtful. "But you'd be cheating, you'd get disqualified."

"This is a different game."

"Now hold on, wait a minute! Shoot." He hummed a snatch of melody. "You know what? I believe you're right. It *is* Houston. Doggone. That's one beer on me, once we're in the spot for it."

"Have you been to Houston, Taylor Deeds?" asked the girl softly.

"Yes," I said.

"Ah. Do you know it very well?"

"Not very."

Her eyes roved tentatively over my face, stopping at this point and that, like a woman inspecting inch by inch a length of sale material. But other than the minute click of pupil, the iris's glisten, her own face didn't move. The dark gaze drifted back to mine.

"Houston has a reputation for many things. Money, scholarship, art. Industry," I said.

"Ah, really?"

"Unfortunately its crime rate has always been bad. This sometimes results in terrible tragedies. We grieve over the well-known fact in my home state." I couldn't credit I was telling her this. I couldn't believe she was here. Nor I, for that matter.

She perused me for a moment, then meekly glanced down. "My father says that a country forms its own people. It does this by the standards it expects of them. In this way the nation is responsible and must be held answerable for how its people behave."

"Now there's a thought."

"This is true of states, provinces, and cities also, he says."

"Do you believe it?"

"My father says this."

"It might prove interesting to apply that theory to society here in Japan."

"Society in Japan is very orderly. Not much trouble," Kawai chimed in.

"So I've heard. But try it out. For instance, when explaining your mafia. What's it called? *Yakuzas*."

Her head lifted.

"You wouldn't want to have some innocent little old lady pay the price for their crimes, now would you?"

"Yakuzas are outside society," said Kawai.

"Not when they're paid to harass a stockholders' meeting. Or blackmail and manipulate politicians."

"Ah, how interesting. Where have you heard of these activities?"

"Around. Here and there. I suggest that any criminal element is an intrinsic and inevitable part of its society. Such has been my experience."

"Is that so?" asked Kawai politely. How could a tycoon's son, he was wondering, have experience?

"So how about yakuzas?"

Kawai parted his lips as if to answer, then closed them again.

"You might consider them the country's dark side, the secret—the private face. What's the word? You have a special term for it, don't you."

He looked down, smiling strainedly.

"After all, isn't that precisely what Mr. Minamoto is claiming?"

For the first time she shifted in her seat. I watched the legs uncross, the pupils shift and recalibrate.

"But please don't assume we're not naïve to your culture," I said to Kawai. "Of course we know nothing, really. We're pig ignorant. It's just we hear items on the news or read the papers."

He bowed slightly, murmuring some pleasantry. Nobody had instructed the poor sap to ignore us. You don't hobnob with the prisoners. Not if somebody might actually communicate.

"Are you ignorant, Mr. Deeds?" Minamoto's daughter said.

"Yes. Sure. Of course," I said.

She fastened her eyes on me.

"You think Houston's bad, you should try Chicago. Whew! I stayed there last summer on vacation. Talk about crime! And heat!" Steve fumbled out a handkerchief and mopped his forehead, the picture of a good boy who'd been mother-reared to change the subject when the talk got tetchy. "Hey, that reminds me. How's about a real dandy—'The Folks in Paris, Texas, Sure Ain't Poor!'"

"Now that's terrible," I replied.

"You know it, huh?"

"Nope."

He grinned, then laughed and turned to Kawai. "By the way, Nagisa, where's this you're taking us?"

"To a hotel where Kan Nai Incorporated will welcome you with a small honorary banquet," said Kawai. "We arrive there soon."

I stared. She didn't falter. When I moved away she drew me back, curious, innocent, teasing me as a magnet does iron filings. Under her lids her gaze brushed mine, each touch stinging like a fizz of naked wire. But upon her downturned, transparent face lay oblivion. And in the midst of such subtle art I had to wonder why, after the last two whole months spent avoiding girls, being left unmoved by the most beautiful flirts in Texas, feeling Teresa-Maria's memory sit on my heart and suck away all desire, I was now electrified by the daughter of my worst enemy.

THE HOTEL SAT halfway down the block from a big park. Pines marched along its perimeter, in contrast to the tall office buildings across the street.

"What's that place?" asked Steve.

Kawai smiled.

We entered the lobby through hot, smothery air, in the bright night-time of a city still entrenched in summer. I had barely grabbed the luggage before Matsudo and the managers hustled us up the steps past the glass doors and into a lobby of beige marble, with geometric carpet designs beating against my eyes. The lobby sported the same plush institutional decor found in urban hotels from Beijing to Beirut to Minneapolis. The gold lettering on the doors said GRAND IMPERIAL PALACE.

This was my first clear glimpse of Tokyo.

She had already moved like a sleepwalker to Matsudo's side. He bowed, gave my load a stony look, and said, "Please accompany the bellboy. We will telephone your rooms and give instructions after you have changed yourself. The banquet starts at nine o'clock." He watched as a bellboy ushered us into an elevator by waving white-gloved hands, followed by a second with a trolley top-heavy with luggage. He was still watching when the doors closed.

"Can I have my bag now, please?" asked Steve.

"Oh. Sure," I said. I unslung it from my shoulder.

"Thank goodness. I was afraid you might have to carry it all the way to our new home. Minamoto Mansions! I need my razor and aftershave."

"And deodorant perhaps?" said Thomas. Steve turned, for the first time dismayed; I realized he felt embarrassed in front of the girls.

"The people of this country are often offended by foreigners' smells," Thomas added. "It's not fair to aggravate the problem."

"Well, I appreciate the tip, Thomas, thanks very much," said Steve.

Becky turned to Thomas, earnestly kind. "You might want to do something about your breath since that's the case."

"Oh, my, yes. For the sake of diplomatic relations," agreed Martha. "Definitely. Like before dinner."

Thomas stared.

"Here's your bag too," I said to her, handing over the suitcase. The elevator slowed.

"Thanks. And many, many, *many* thanks for carrying it, Taylor."

"At your service." She smiled at me, blinking her lashes.

This is insane, I thought. What do I think I am? Mission Improbable?

In the room I set the duffle on the bed, ignoring the luggage rack anchored beneath a recessed light fixture. There was no way of knowing where the cameras were hidden. But so far I'd succeeded in blocking access for an X-ray scan and a real luggage search; I wasn't going to make it easy now. Pausing, I stretched ostentatiously, knuckled my eyes, yawned, and then reached down and pulled off my shirt, which fell as if by careless accident, draping halfway over the duffle's zipper. Touching my toes I bent one knee, the other. The air-conditioning chilled my bare skin. I stretched overhead once more, turning, twisting, hands behind neck. Then lazily I yanked the zipper so that the duffle split clean wide as a watermelon, its interior concealed under the half-tent of shirt. Reaching inside I dug around as if looking for some inconsequential item: a toothbrush, comb. When I pulled my hand back out it held a T-shirt and a pair of clean under-wear, which shrouded the tiny tool case cupped deep in my palm.

I WAS STILL in the shower when the image of Ayako Minamoto returned.

The soap lather slipped down my chest. Once more the slim knees, the perfect fine-tuning of her features, ghosted through my consciousness. She was so small. Had I ever seen a girl that small? She wouldn't come to my middle ribs. I could have wrapped a hand around her wrist double; her bones looked neat and delicate as ivory. That silk hair. What had she meant by those looks?

All at once I remembered an afternoon when Chelmsford III and I had driven to San Antonio so he could order a pair of expensive handmade boots for his eighteenth birthday. The boots were a real symbol of man-hood; Chelmsford III bragged how he planned to stroll into the frat houses during Rush Week the following fall with these genuine signed future heir-looms under his jeans. I knew what he really hoped for was to draw atten-tion away from his webby fists. We found the shop, then spent some time waiting for the famous boot maker to measure Chelmsford's feet, which luckily were normal. Lined on a shelf behind the counter sat finished specimens ready for pickup. As we stood admiring the workmanship, Chelmsford pointed to a pair stitched in violet ostrich capped with snakeskin toes, dainty as a child's. From where we stood we could read the tag on the bootstrap: Mrs. Linda O'Dell. Chelmsford smacked his lips. "Man, I'd sure like to lick the leg that slides into those," he said.

There was no certainty that she'd meant anything whatsoever. But then what was I but a burglar feeling around in the dark?

THE BALLROOM WAS hung with shadows.

In the middle of a long white-clothed table sat Ito Minamoto. There was no question in my mind. Flanking him were Matsudo and Ayako. Two of the managers lurked down the far peninsulas, the acreages between interspersed with empty chairs. The third manager, Nagisa Kawai, had disappeared. We five sat arranged boy-girl-boy-girl-boy around a small table in the middle of the floor. "Our hosts consider five a lucky number. Four, six, or eight are unlucky," said Thomas, condescendingly. Nobody answered.

The ritual flavor bore down inescapably. Silence coagulated in the dim spaces. Clinks of silverware sounded vulgar, an unnecessary and intrusive counterpoint to the mute chopsticks ballet going on beyond our heads. Occasionally we glanced at each other. Even Steve manfully tried to curtail his slurps of champagne; I almost volunteered my napkin to wrap his fork, the way outlaws in the old days used to muffle horses' hooves in feed bags.

Our menu differed from the head table's. We ate chicken Kiev, mashed potatoes, and salad. They were eating small things from tiny dishes on trays. Whatever else Minamoto had in mind, I saw, he spared himself with home cooking. I sat watching Ayako's chopsticks rise and fall. I didn't even try to eat. Not once had she raised her eyes.

The man sitting next to her held my deepest attention.

He was old. This was the first, most confounding discovery. I hadn't

expected this effigy with duck down patching his skull. His wrinkled walnut face seemed to have recorded experience like the surface of a brain. The
black suit flowing over his torso hung robelike; bent fingers emerged from
the sleeve ends to raise a teacup or pick at some rice. Vigorless lips chewed
methodically on a morsel forty, fifty times before he swallowed. It was hard
to imagine his power. He seemed an emblem, perhaps the papier-mâché
idol representing some obscure religion; when he sipped from the cup his
hand trembled, and once he'd put it back down he slumped, listless, apparently preferring to ignore further tidbits and the single murmur Matsudo
risked leaning over to release into his ear. But a few moments afterward his
head lifted. When he glanced our way, his eyes held the embers of a private
rage.

Matsudo stood up.

"I am happy to welcome you to Japan. On behalf of our daimyo Mr. Ito
Minamoto you are honored as his new employees and his guests," he said.

Next to me Becky cleared her throat. Minamoto muttered something
low. Matsudo bent, listening.

"Mr. Minamoto wishes you to be comfortable. He understands that
you are each at the peak of your abilities. This information satisfies him
very much. He receives pleasure in hiring the most talented tip-top people
from United States. Your work helps the benefit of all people. In this way
we cooperate together, enabling nations to find proper places in world
order. So now all countries can discover their true and right stations." He
paused to allow the effect of his proclamation to sink in. "Mr. Minamoto
would like to toast the future with sake for this special occasion." Matsudo
bowed, then nodded toward the shadows behind us, the deepest fathoms
of the ballroom.

A woman stepped forward into the light. Her hair stood piled in black
varnished domes; her face shone stark white. A kimono worked with wis-
teria was tied by a wide gold obi. Between her hands she carried a tray with
a blue pottery bottle and several tiny bowls. When she reached the head

table, she knelt to the ground in theatrical collapse, placed the tray in front of her, and then bowed until her face hung suspended maybe four inches from the floor in a way that made my spine ache.

Minamoto grunted.

After a long moment she seesawed to an upright position and recaptured the tray. Then, crouching like a hunchback, she put the tray on the table before Minamoto, bowed once more, and crept backward until the shadows devoured her and there remained only an ectoplasmic glimmer of gold and mauve, like a fish in pond waters.

"It's a movie," whispered Becky.

"Commonplace tradition," Thomas dismissed.

"Disgusting," muttered Martha. "Crawling on your knees."

"She didn't crawl. *Form* comes with *formality,* in case you haven't noticed."

"You're so damn didactic, Thomas. Don't you just make yourself sick?"

Matsudo stood silently waiting.

Ayako got up from her chair, walked around the table to the distant spot where the geisha had knelt. Compared to that artificial revenant she looked like a discotheque dancer. She bowed. Bending forward, she carefully poured steaming liquid from the bottle into a cup. Then she bowed again, presented it to her father, and murmured something. He made no sign. She poured and presented three more cups one by one to Matsudo and the managers, who responded with a phrase. That the daughter of someone as exalted as Minamoto had been conscripted into menial service bewildered me.

After that she poured five cups in quick succession. Then she picked up the tray and walked to our table. The legs moved palely under the short skirt, flashing in the darkness like ivory scissors when she came round to each of our places in turn, her attention seemed to numb. I watched the black eyes. As she bowed each time when we helped ourselves I realized again what I'd seen in the limousine: this mask was a strict firebreak behind which life smoldered.

She served Becky first, then Steve and Martha. Only Thomas hesitated,

frowning before lifting his cup. At last she reached me. I brushed my wrist-
bone against her fingertips. They stiffened like silver casts; she stood in
that same sleepwalker quietude, only a telltale gleam revealing what she'd
felt. When we'd finished she slid the tray onto our table and walked back to
her seat.

"Now Mr. Minamoto officially awards you the Minamoto Grant. This
lifestyle money he gives in memory of his son Anjiro Minamoto, master-
mind scientist, the champion best of your country. It is your research
employment prize. May you work for him forever," said Matsudo.

Martha strangled a sound.

He held his cup high, then moved it to his lips.

"Hear hear! Let's hear it for world cooperation. Viva Kan Nai!" called
Steve. Tipping his head he chugged the sake down. Everyone at the main
table stared unsmiling.

I shoved back my chair. "I would like to answer that."

Matsudo winced. From the managers' solitude came an involuntary
rustling. Minamoto raised his terrapin head and looked at me, his features
immobile. His eyes held cold contempt, the remote regard of a fanatic.

"Taylor, you're not supposed to stand taller than he is," declared
Thomas.

I smiled and shot him the finger.

"On behalf of my father, the former employer of these people, and of
Deeds Holdings, I propose a toast—may this enterprise bear fruit as yet
unsuspected." I held up my hand, within it my untouched sake cup. I put
it to my lips and drank. Then, as they watched appalled, I pulled the ring
off my finger and brandished it high in the air.

"This gold ring bears my family name. By its word I will carry out my
duty to my father and his former employees, serving Ito Minamoto in all
the best possible ways, so long as I am in Japan." Then I rammed the ring
back on, raised the cup again, and tossed off the rest of the sake. My throat
smarted with heat.

"Yay! Hear hear!" hollered Steve, reaching for the bottle.

"I wish you'd stop doing that," said Thomas.

"Moushi wake arimasen," gasped Matsudo, bowing to Minamoto franti-cally. I heard him distinctly. *"Moushi wake arimasen, Soushi!"*

Minamoto gathered himself and stood up.

"Ta*ylorrr!*" whispered Becky.

For one second only he stared. Then his head dipped no more deeply than the twitch of a willow leaf. Turning, he muttered to Matsudo.

"Mr. Deeds," cried Matsudo in a fluster. "Please sit down with the oth-ers. Please all drink sake in respect for Kan Nai Incorporated. Then walk to the lobby where the driver waits to take you to your new apartments. The dinner is finished."

"Uh-oh," murmured Martha. "I think you've just made a manners boo-boo."

"Nothing I trust they'll forget," I replied.

Minamoto turned. Ayako bowed in her seat until her father barked a word; rising, she followed him from the ballroom in a pink shimmer. She didn't look back.

None of them did.

When we reached the lobby our bags were stacked by the front doors. This time we climbed into the same limousine. The doctored alcohol must have penetrated our brains the minute we sank into our seats, because for the next two hours, as we rode through narrow streets around looming walls, past black buildings and colored blurs, twisting down the maze of Tokyo in a jet-lag fog, we could hardly strain toward the smoked windows. There were no interesting sights. Only smears of shadow. By the time we arrived at the compound our stupors were complete; my vertigo bucketed; we stumbled out and someone guided us reeling up flights of drugged nightmare stairs to bed.

15

One morning when I was five years old something strange happened to the grass.

Mother was driving me to kindergarten, and just as we passed the park playground I noticed through the car window that some quality had changed: silver shimmered on the swing sets like they'd been coated in mercury, the cemetery pickets jutted up like strong black spears outlined in light. At the same time objects grew an extra dimensionality. Tree bark looked gouged, the ridges stood out sharply; metallic gleams ran down the cracks. A brownness drenched the air. Movement quickened in unexpected places. The earth was swarming with lines and bright coins. It took me a second or two to understand what made the difference: all the shadows had flipped inside out. Leaves glittered beneath the pecan trees, but they were really leaf shadows, shining instead of blotting. As I watched they became half shines cusped in blue. The real leaves above them grew haloes. At first I felt wonder: my imbalance was taking a new form! All the world's familiarity had got sucked up into the dark hole and poured out again backward. But then I grasped that this change lay outside me. Mother slowed down, then pulled over to the curb and stopped the car. "Oh, Taylor, just look!" she cried. "It's the eclipse!"

• • •

I WOKE WITH a headache.

Someone was knocking on the wall. Each blow synchronized with the pulse inside my skull. First I had to drag out of bed, stumble over a threshold into a blinding inferno, then claw around searching for the doorknob. The pounding kept up, my feet sank into a sludge soft as cake icing; I bumped into blunt furniture, the corner, my fingernails scrabbling for a bump, hinges, any clue at all, before I found the frame's edge and realized that the door was built to slide open. I must have made noise. The banging stopped.

Thomas stood there.

Instantly I reeled back, heels sloshing through the deep wool carpet, almost tripping. I was in a strange room in a strange apartment halfway around the world, wondering how in hell I could feel this hung over, dizzy, and cripple-headed when I'd drunk so little and kept so wary. But Thomas was scarier by a long chalk.

"You look sick," he said.

"Ah. Thank you."

He scrutinized the wrinkled clothes I'd slept in, glanced down at his watch. "It's two-seventeen in the afternoon."

"*What?*" I swung around through a dancing nebula. The window shades had been left open and I could see the sun hanging just past zenith. "Hell. I like that seventeen touch."

He poked his nose up. "Eighteen now, precisely."

"I've been asleep for twelve hours?"

"So have Shaver and those other two."

"Why haven't you?"

He shrugged. "I'm abstemious."

"I saw you drinking something last night, didn't I?" But what? I scrubbed my scalp, the memory of Thomas with a cup to his lips floating around in a jumble of hotel scenery. What had happened? I hadn't been this confused. I'd been clear—drowsy but lucid—up until we made the drive to wherever we were now. Then it suddenly dawned on me why my head was throbbing and why my mind lay in a shambles as great as the world's. "The sake."

"I feigned two sips only out of courtesy," he replied. "As it was a formal occasion."

"No—I mean that's why I'm so wrecked right now."

"I really wouldn't know. My allergic sensitivity set in, as I knew it would." His equine upper lip stretched.

Whatever they'd laced it with had reacted like Thorazine with the jet lag and champagne. As I brooded on this he stepped through the swirling motes to the table, sat right down, and made himself at home. "I'm surprised at you, Thomas, already checking on whether the girls are awake."

"We're supposed to report to work today."

"So were you seeing to it that they made it?" There was a small kitchen alcove near the table. I began pawing through cupboards. A notion seared through me that coffee might be crucial; I had to find it or die. A box rattled in the cupboard's rear: green tea.

"I was inquiring to see if they got the same welcome I did. For which, I might add, I regard you as culpable."

"What's that?" I paused. The tea was in a tin caddy tied up in two layers of fancy paper, another of colored cellophane, another of brown paper, and a double twine bow, knotted. It looked like a wedding present.

"I regard my reception this morning, here, at Minamoto Mansions in the Kan Nai Research Enclave, as your fault."

"That's pretty much what I thought you said." The knots seemed less convoluted than he did. I struggled with them until I was ready to bash them with a hammer.

"My treatment is obviously a direct result of your ludicrous behavior. You have affected my professional status, therefore my effectiveness. This is unforgivable."

"Thomas, what are you droning?" I held the twine and paper to my teeth and ripped. Then I threw open the other cupboard doors, looking for a pan.

"Just because you are the son of a self-made tycoon with a gambler's habits does not give you the right to obstruct serious science."

"Thank Christ. You want some tea?" I held up the kettle I'd found under the stove.

"You alienated Minamoto," he denounced, and sneered.

"Now that's first class. You're getting really good at those sneers, they're almost art. What have they done to you?"

"The facts should have become obvious last night to anyone familiar with Japanese culture."

"Are you familiar with Japanese culture?"

"In a desultory way. I've read a little."

"Does anyone know this?"

"Who is 'anyone'?"

"Well, exactly!" I filled the kettle at the tap, then plonked it on the stovetop.

"I hardly qualify as a student." Which meant he'd been able to prevaricate on his résumé.

"What facts irked you last night?" I had to lean against the counter, sagging from the hairline down.

"Several irregularities in protocol."

"Tell me, Thomas. Explain," I urged. Please God, drip coffee. IV coffee.

"First, there were no gifts."

"Gifts?" I pondered. "Maybe they consider all this a gift." I waved at the luxuries in the room: leather sofa and chairs, genuine reproductions of van Goghs, china knickknacks, stuffed bookshelves, an anorexic floral arrangement of one thin branch twisting above a rock. I held my head sideways, squinting at titles: biographies, romances, cookbooks, art books, coffee-table books. Sans coffee.

"Don't be stupid. It's presentation," he said dryly. "On arrival. Gift-wrapped items."

"Ah. The tea!" I scooped up the paper mess and shook it.

"The sequences in the dining room were wrong. The seating. The way she served us sake last straight from the tray. In fact that was actually a deliberate insult."

"Is that right?"

He stared, silent.

"You think it had to do with me."

"After your airport display? Of course." He discharged a thin breath through his nose. "But far worse was your toast and its consequences today."

"Which are?"

"I have identified myself at the apartment reception desk. They recognized me, of course. They were perfectly friendly, very polite. They said yes, someone would show me my new office in the Kan Nai Building. No doubt a person would call for me soon, the department probably assumed I was still sleeping after the flight. But when I then went to the front doors to take a stroll the security guard prevented me from leaving. The doors are electronically controlled. I told him I must. I insisted. I wished to find my way around. He said yes, of course, sometime soon, no doubt I could then. The Japanese scarcely ever say no, you understand."

"No, I didn't."

"It's an invisible word."

"What do they say instead?"

"Body language. In their vocabulary a vague deflective gesture should suffice, even if the person continues to affirm verbally. Signs are explicit yet subtle."

I thought through my pounding headache about the subtle yet explicit signs I'd gotten from Ayako Minamoto last night. Had I dreamed them? Mistaken her? Probably. I'd never see her again anyhow. Why had she been there?

"Do you understand what I'm saying, Taylor? He denied me egress."

"Did he say a flat no?"

"He sat at his post, smiling, without opening the doors."

"Did he speak English?"

"Only enough to say, yes, later, soon, of course. Obviously rote."

Like so much of Thomas's conversation, I thought. "At least they speak it at Reception."

"Only enough to repeat the same."

The kettle boiled. Thomas watched disdainfully as I poured water into a cup and stems and leaves swilled to the surface.

"I next asked for directions to the breakfast café. When I said 'eat' they finally understood me."

"This sounds challenging." I bobbed the debris around, held the vapors to my face, closed my eyes, and took a sip.

"There's something else."

"What?"

"Thanks to you my luggage has at some point been searched and certain possessions removed."

"Thanks to me." I drank, scalding my tongue. "Like what?"

"Dictionaries, texts, reference books, maps, journals, and magazines."

I finished the cup and poured more water. "Well, maybe they got stolen en route by baggage handlers. Confiscated by customs. Contraband!"

He sneered, witheringly. "You have placed us under suspicion. You have damaged our first workday with your antics. By association we're implicated—lumped with your *gaijin* boorishness. The Japanese system is inflexible in certain respects. How can they possibly take us seriously?"

"Why would they want to cut their own throats by treating new employees badly? How is that productive in the long run? Especially such important ones as yourself?" What a good question! How long would it take this fool to ask it? But meanwhile I was looking around for bug locations. On the other hand, the bugs placed here would be so advanced, so subtle yet explicit, that the likelihood of finding them was minimal. "By the way, I hope they had some food you could eat."

"Dry gluten-free toast," he admitted, frowning.

"Oh, terrific."

"I think you should apologize."

"Beg your pardon?"

"A letter will do it. Written to a proper format. Perhaps followed by a personal visit to Matsudo to declare penitence."

"Have you ever considered a career as a Jesuit?"

"No."

"Get out."

"I have some idea of the traditional wording."

"You don't want any tea, get out of here, Thomas. Go complain elsewhere." I pushed away from the counter and started toward him, prodding finger extended. He glanced at it. He glanced up at me. He must have seen in my face that I was taking him seriously. He started walking backward, eyes for once wide awake, fixed first on my finger then on my face. I could feel my temples suffuse with blood, drip with the hot clammy sweat of anger and overdose, and I jerked at the sliding panel, half expecting him to warn in that flat reedy voice that he knew judo. But he flinched, turned, and hustled out the door. "You'd better fix this, Taylor."

"You've been a profound loss to the Inquisition, by the way." I shoved his shoulder blade the last few inches and rammed the panel closed. But this, I knew, was not productive.

Nevertheless, the magnitude of Thomas's vanity surprised me. How could a trained analytical scientist be so one-eyed? It hadn't occurred to him to wonder why someone as deitic as Ito Minamoto, who owned multiple companies, who was daimyo of his keiretsu, who controlled an entire media network, suggested favored outcomes to the prime minister and the Diet, mingled closely with the emperor, and actually claimed descent from the original shogun family, would bother to appear at a minor welcome for a clutch of lower-level gaijin labor. Thomas assumed he deserved it.

I shook my pounding head, pressing it between my palms. To hell with Thomas. My father's and Martha's research had uncovered only so much about Minamoto. I needed to know more.

I looked around the apartment for a phone that didn't exist. The air-conditioning was frigid. Condensation had formed on the window glass and the ceiling paint near the ducts. A TV with a built-in VCR sat in one corner, but when I switched it on the screen remained blank, waiting for a tape: no antenna or cable connection. I couldn't find a radio, although the stereo system in its chrome stand looked expensive. A rack full of CDs and videos stood under it—innocuous oldies rock, classical, Hollywood action and comedy movies. The whole setup seemed a showcase designed for generic middle-aged Americans. Everything, of course, brand-new.

I went back to the bedroom, strenuously avoiding the bed. Instead I peeled off my shirt, wrapped the top sheet around me, went to the tiny bathroom, bumped my elbows against the walls as I slipped my pants off underneath, washed, brushed my teeth, and climbed into a set of clean clothes, all the while keeping the sheet in place, a modest, well-raised Texan boy. To my relief the tool case was still strapped firmly to my inner thigh. Nobody had ravished me while I slept.

My shoes were waiting in the little alcove outside the front door. Certainly I hadn't left them there the night before. The hall lay empty. Marshy gray carpeting stretched from end to end, blending with the blue color scheme and terminating in the staircase under a chrome sconce. There were other doors up the corridor, all closed. Who knew on which floor my companions had been installed? I didn't even remember what this one was.

Three flights down I reached the main lobby. A desk the size of an ocean liner, gilded apricot, took up most of the space. Two women sat behind it. They smiled and nodded when I appeared. *"Ohayo goza-i-mas!"* they cooed—a pair of nicely groomed suburban California housewives. Another glass stall stood by the entrance, with a uniformed man inside sitting over a control panel. I went over to him first. Stooping and mashing my face to the glass, I breathed a fog chrysanthemum right at eye level. He looked up from his comic book, saw me, snapped a little bow, switched his gaze down when I straightened up, meticulously twiddled some knobs, and then stiffly resumed reading.

I wandered to the main desk. "Hidy. Where's everybody gone?"

"Good afternoon, Mr. Deeds," said the taller woman. Both were dressed in navy blue suits and yellow blouses, their hair cut chin-length. But their faces looked very different. The shorter one was almost gaunt, her smile less authentic, her teeth discolored. "You sleep well!"

"I'm flattered you think so. Can you head me toward the café, please?"

She consulted the shorter one, who said something in Japanese, then turned to me. "Eat?"

"Yes. Eat. Where?"

"Ah, so—eat! Yes, yes." She nodded encouragingly. "There." She pointed to a hallway like a greenhouse. "Good afternoon!"

"You bet." I sidled past the desk. The sun was blazing through glass, but the hallway, forested in bamboo, offered a cool, leafy illusion. At its far end squatted a hollowed-out boulder brimming with water. A wood ladle rested on its edge. I stopped a moment, dipped my hand in the water, flicked moonstones at the leaves, then opened the door to a cafeteria.

The floor was cluttered with tables. Muzak trickled through the air, a soothing, sweet mulch of jazz. The color scheme transmuted to baby blue. The seven or eight people sat mostly alone, nursing cups, eating, reading, with the exception of one couple who bent over to nibble on each other between coffee sips. Nobody spoke. The only people to acknowledge my entrance were the dark-haired servers who peeked over the food troughs behind the tray lanes, their white coats burning with a surgical radiance.

Then I saw someone I knew.

Studying his Thanksgiving video, watching him over and over, I'd eked every detail from its limited frame. Red Franklin—same freckles, same fiery brush—seemed just as glazed and spiritless lolling in front of a piece of pie as he had when projecting those vapid jokes toward an inaccessible world. During those last six days I'd pored over other photographs of sacrificial victims. But he haunted me most. The despair camouflaged by his stutter, the hazed and haggard look in his eyes, shredded my peace at night; it was like watching a Save the Children film. He resembled his sister. If his sister had passed into a coma.

Nonchalantly crossing the floor, I pulled out the next chair. My hands were trembling. "Hey there, Red."

"Huh?"

"How's it going?"

"Fine." His shoulders slumped. He looked up. "Do I know you?"

"Nope."

"Oh."

"I know your sister, though."

This news from the stratosphere seemed to dawn on him very slowly. He licked his forefinger, rubbed the table edge, then crumpled his forehead and tilted back.

"Which one?"

"Martha." Damn, I thought. She'd never told me she had sisters.

"Yeah? Where from, Boston or Dallas?"

"Dallas. She's not in Boston anymore."

"She's not? When did that happen?"

"She graduated a year and a half ago."

He sat up. He levered his fork, which was stuck in some purple pie goo, let it drop, *clank*. "How's she doing?"

"She's okay. Probably a little slow right this second."

He stared at the fork, woggled it. Embarrassment nullified his tone even more, as if he'd been caught forgetting somebody's name. "How's that?"

"General circumstances."

"Martha's never been slow a day in her life. If you really knew her you'd know that. So maybe you don't really know her." His eyes turned flinty. He sat up again, suspicion congealing. I got the impression his days were lived in a state of two extremes: either total apathy or utter paranoia. "So just fuck off back to your master and leave me alone."

"I know her. She's a pistol, all right. Give her trouble, she'd blow your head off."

"So?"

"So I know her."

"Anybody could know that or call her any name they choose."

"She calls you a bragging blabbermouth mama's boy."

He looked up. "Fuck you!"

"Hey, it's not my definition. I've got my own little sister."

He paused, rethinking. "She called me that." A trace of smile, more a painful spasm, touched his mouth. "I guess maybe you might have met her somewhere," he conceded.

"To my cost."

"Why? You interested in her or something?"

"Put it this way. Her deepest interests coincide with mine."

He mulled it over, gently shook his head. "You just get here, or what?"

"Last night."

"That's too bad."

"Why? Seems like a great opportunity."

"For?"

I shrugged. "Work!"

"Hm." The dull guardedness returned. Meeting his eye, I found a glint of pity. "Don't get too thrilled."

"I've been real curious ever since deciding to come," I said, as if he hadn't spoken. "Martha couldn't tell me much. She said your family hadn't heard from you in a long time, so this place was a mystery."

"Yeah, well."

"They miss you a lot, though."

He hesitated. "Did she happen to say why they reckon they haven't heard from me?"

"One or two guesses." I shrugged again: none of my business.

"Are they, well, pissed off? Or—anything?"

"Heck, I don't know. Ask her yourself."

"Nah," he mumbled, looking elsewhere.

"Sure. Why not?"

"Yeah, sure." He was still fighting it: whether to enlighten or let me discover the truth.

"She's only about five hundred yards away," I said quietly.

The last thing I'd wanted was to hit him hard. The room's climate made me edgy. "You can check with the main desk for her room number."

"She's *here?*"

The backlash came harder. His eyes sharpened, his jaw flexed. "You're bullshitting me!" He thumped his fist on the fork's handle, flipping it high so it landed on his water glass. Instantly he drew back, glancing around toward the servers, ceiling, potted plants, in trepidation. No, I thought: definitely not drugged. The other people in the room hardly stirred.

"She's hired by Ito Minamoto. She was working for my father—"

"Who's that? Your father? Who are you?"

"My name's Taylor Deeds."

He flushed. His lips pulled back from his teeth. "Deeds!" he said.

"Yeah."

"That bastard!"

"Nope. Wrong generation. But she got herself picked—"

He stood, chair crashing. "You telling me she's been *working* for that shit-eating son of a bitch? Your father's A. J. Deeds? Goddamn it, I'm going to fucking kill him, I'll kill *you*, you goddamn fucking prick—"

"Settle down," I said. "What do you think I'm doing here?"

"YOU'RE THE REASON she works for my father. He knows about you."

"Yeah. Like a killer whale knows about a minnow." He'd picked up the chair, sat down, and started pushing his fork through the pie, crushing it to a gelatinous pulp.

Two years is a long time to sit on the boil. I sighed and shook my head. "Listen. He's been stewing longer than you have. This whole thing makes him sick."

"He's sending us, isn't he?"

"Yep."

"That's enough."

"And I'm here with you."

For perhaps a twentieth of a second he looked nonplussed. "Where is she?" he asked.

"Still sound asleep, I'd think. We drank sake last night at—"

"—dinner at the Grand Imperial Palace Hotel. Don't tell me." He grimaced. "Same routine. Big feed in a big room. Table full of guys. Minamoto lording around. Little tiny high school chick pouring out the booze. Lackeys sucking up their emperor's sushi. Total dead silence. He does it every time."

"She's not in high school anymore."

"What?"

"I think we should ask at the main desk for Martha's room."

"They call them flats here. Which just about says all, in my opinion."

I glanced through the barnlike, antiseptic room. It must be miked, I thought. By this time it was possible our shirt buttons held mikes. "Hey, listen. Do me a favor and show me around. You know a comfortable place to talk?"

"Comfortable?" He stared.

The exits from the cafeteria opened up onto a shopping mall no bigger or more elaborate than Bernice's main street. In fact if you'd taken Boise D'Arc Avenue and squashed it, you'd wind up with the shopping district of the Kan Nai Enclave. The mall was two stories high, narrow, with a clear plastic roof collecting visible bird droppings and leaf scurf, and cement block pavers planted with plastic dahlias. We walked past a sporting goods, a department store offering a cornucopia of kitchen tools like eel skinners and celery juicers, nylon lingerie, paper umbrellas, and boring trinkets made out of exotic materials: ox horn, pampas grass, kola nuts. The window displays looked like the flotsam off a Galveston beach. Apparently local marketing opinion held that Kan Nai, Inc. employees must favor shopping in last-stop bargain discount basements with names like Dollar Squalor. Beyond the department store we came to a grocery, a men's and women's boutique full of expensive French designer jeans, two coffee shops, a café, a delicatessen, and a bar. No wonder Red didn't enjoy sending presents home.

He led me to a vestibule at the far end. "We can't go outside, can we," I said.

"Outside? Yeah, why not?" Pushing the steel doors he let in a wedge of clean daylight, and smiled sardonically. "Be my guest."

I stepped out to a walled garden. Flowering shrubs banked the edges, their tops leggy as a bad haircut. Vines runnered around benches and trees. The landscaping reminded me of a cramped movie jungle. It wasn't like the pictures I'd seen of Japan's gardens. The only clear space was the sky above our heads.

"Here you go! Outside," said Red.

"More like a shaggy room."

"You know why, don't you?"

I turned to him. A battle of emotion played over his face.

"If you mean we're prisoners, then yes."

He collapsed on a wooden bench, suddenly looking exhausted. Perhaps no one had ever put it into words before. No fresh and objective newcomer, that is.

"I just don't yet know enough beyond that," I said.

"Jesus Christ."

"It's a good thing I've run into you. You can fill in the details."

"Which ones?" he asked bleakly.

"Well, like where we are, specifically."

"We're somewhere outside Tokyo, Japan."

"Narrow it down a little."

He smiled. "Good buddy, that's as close as it gets."

THE NIGHT BEFORE I'd left, my father had come into my bedroom where I was packing, weaving through the logjam of furniture to sit on the bed.

"This is crazy."

"Listen. We've gone over it. It's going to be okay. Martha's got the electronic stuff we need. I'm taking my tools. The minute we're out safe I'll phone you on your private number, just exactly like we've arranged. Don't worry. I'll be back within a month." I took a big breath. Sooner, I thought. Three weeks, two. Having proven everything beyond question. And then Mother would arrive, and I'd finally confess to him about the handicap, and we'll all three laugh together at the absurd joke it had played on us, separating us for all those long years—a joke that was now over, transcended at last. "I'm looking forward to it."

"You're my son."

Carefully I rolled up a pair of khakis, stuck them into a corner of the duffle. "I have to do this."

"Don't be ridiculous! Good God, you're twenty years old!"

I looked at him. He looked so pared down all of a sudden, sitting there on the edge of the bed with the spread crushed underneath him and the pillows in their white Irish linen cases tumbled askew. He hadn't meant to insult. He just wasn't used to disadvantage, or forfeiture, or tight spots. Except maybe the Iranian jail. But then I thought: Wait. How much tighter can it get than that? How much longer can this shadow be? Perhaps tight spots are some kind of inner flaw he carries, some lure of entrapment that he feels drawn to. Sometimes despite the human stink the tiger just can't resist the tethered goat. And how many others suffer the results? Our best plans fray; we neglect some important consideration, miss some signal, let a crucial chore slip our minds, and then everyone pays. There are many paths to choose. You can't always tell.

"I just know," I said.

My father sighed and rubbed his eyes, then pinched their bridge of flesh. "Have you ever walked around in the Bernice Cemetery?"

"Yes," I said, and paused. The bright light and blue shadows of that late spring day wavered before me, the mown grass smelling sweet under the crape myrtles, the dogwoods and magnolias blooming above the gravestones where I searched for the slab on which I'd been conceived.

"There used to be an old wooden case in one of the family plots, a kind of display box. I don't know if it's still there or not."

"It's not," I said.

"That's—oh. A shame to hear—" He didn't finish, but took my hand where I loomed above him, holding it for a moment in his own.

IT HAD NOT occurred to me that Minamoto's strategy could be so simple.

As I sat down on the bench beside Red I began to comprehend the elegance of Minamoto's revenge, how its workings ensured so beautifully the seclusion of his son's living competitors. Because that was how he saw us, I realized. We were all accountable for Anjiro Minamoto's death: the young, greedy, ambitious people who slipped into this trap to further their careers.

"At this moment in time the Japanese are the richest people on earth," Red said.

"That's true."

"Now, I know for a fact there are plenty of good, nice, kind people out there in this country. I'm not stupid. I may be sick to death, and I'd like to crush somebody to pieces or shoot them, but I'm not stupid."

"I can see that."

"He's got us penned up. That old man you saw last night. But hell, if you're A. J. Deeds's son you probably know a lot more already. We've had to learn the hard way."

"Wait." I held up my hand. "Is this place bugged?"

He just looked at me. Then his lips pulled back in a snarl, frightening in its bitterness. "You kidding? Why would they bother? They've got us by the short and curlies, boy. Coming and going."

"Okay. Then tell me what you've learned."

"Bugged." He snorted, shaking his head. "The work he hired us for is legitimate. There's just no point in doing it."

"Why?"

"Because," he said tiredly, "it's playwork. Patty-cakes. It could be done by low-grade lab techs or pencil pushers. There's five main office buildings, plus high-security labs and test centers. Kan Nai is the hottest research spot of Minamoto's enterprises. But we never get near the real deals. All that stuff about ongoing projects? Forget it. It's crap. At least we *think* it's crap." He looked troubled. "We can't tell completely, that's the thing. We work on little bits, but basically we suspect they're phantom projects, going nowhere. We sit here waiting, or we piddle on these make-work things, or go on drinking binges, or just lie around, while everything we hoped for and trained for gets wasted away, straight down the drain. They look after us real good, no arguing that. But they aren't using us right. We can't keep up in our fields because we're so isolated we don't know what's going on. When we ask why, we're told the company's run in their special way, and we could never understand it. When we complain they just look at us. Complaining is considered indecent, so it alienates the person we're talking to. And what's more, we're locked into contracts we've been told by lawyers are virtually unbreakable—so much so that if we broke them and actually left here, we could expect serious criminal charges from the Japanese police, accusations of theft, all kinds of stuff. We'd never get past customs. It's crazy."

He hunched over, prodding a clump of dagger-leaved plants with his toe. "A couple of people got out in the last few months. They had no money. No cash. All our salaries are paid into the Minamoto Bank. We can't touch them. Anything we want to buy in there," he pointed to the doors to the mall, "is charged on credit to our bank accounts." Suddenly I recalled what my father had told me about the parking lot murder of Anjiro Minamoto: the demands for cash he no longer had, the useless credit cards, the declaration of his father's wealth, the spurs to his killers.

"So this guy named Maxwell Chang was able to invent a way to bypass the electronic security system and leave. But he didn't have one single yen on him for cab or train fare. He didn't think it would matter. Once he got to the subway or whatever, he'd punt—ask for help, talk his way through, phone the consulate. Only he never got that far."

"Why?"

"You want to know what's out there? I'll tell you." Sitting up, he grabbed a handful of tendrils from the jasmine awning above our heads and began to shred them savagely. "Nothing. Nothing's out there. Nothing we can relate to, nothing we can find our way through. Just mile after mile after mile of flat, identical plain, with the same apartment house over and over in block after block of these cramped-up, winding, skinny streets. The streets don't even have names. Can you imagine that? The streets of Tokyo, unless they're big major ones downtown somewhere, have no names."

"You're kidding."

"No." He laughed.

"How do people find their way around? How do they find addresses?"

"Who knows? Chang sure didn't. He said there are numbers on the houses and buildings, but they aren't even in a linear sequence. Like, number 52-721-97 will be right next door to 26-0-184, which he said is right next to a noodle shop or a factory or a nursery. And you can't ask directions. First of all, hardly anybody speaks English." He laughed again, this time with a rusty sound; he held his sides cackling in real amusement. Tears edged his eyes.

"Or if they do, they won't show it," he gasped. "Nobody! Not even the people inside here." He poked a hand full of clawed-up jasmine at the mall. "A few in the offices can. They're the ones polite enough to fill us in on why Maxwell's attempt got thwarted. But they sure won't speak to us in Japanese, or teach it to us."

"I see," I said.

"No you don't. It's too big. You can't imagine how totally foreign this place is. Even if you had the name of some place to go to—say, some place famous, like the Ginza. How would you get there? Say you bought a ticket and caught a train, any train. And you made it to the Ginza. Then, where would you be?"

"The Ginza."

"Yeah, but so what? It's just a name. If you have no context, you're shipwrecked. If you don't know what the Ginza means, or where to go from there, it does you no good at all."

"Surely people there speak good English!"

"No doubt plenty. And there would be signs. But hell, you're never going to get that far. See—most people who live around here either work for one of Minamoto's companies, or their relatives do, or they depend on his patronage, or just plain respect him so much they would never risk offending him. Why should they? So they're not going to break etiquette and give you a hand." He shook his head. "We're stuck out here in the middle of nowhere. This is Limbo."

I recalled the drive of the night before, the wandering, dark-windowed vistas.

"God knows where the train station may be. There has to be one for commuters, right? But what happened to Chang was, when he stopped people on the street to ask for help, they just shook their heads. They were trying to understand him. This one old lady tried; she tried directing him every which way. But she was being nice. He walked for miles." He sighed. "Then he finally stopped this businessman who was obviously on his way home from work. Chang said the words 'train station.' The guy understood him! But then, he mentioned Minamoto. All of a sudden the guy clammed up and looked serious. So Maxwell offered him his gold watch." He shook his head and wiped his eyes, which were watering still from the raggedy laughter. "That was the big mistake."

"What happened?"

"The guy got really upset. Horrified. Chang may as well have said he wanted to pay to screw the guy's wife, he'd insulted him so bad. The guy turned away and started marching off down the street. So Chang chased him, waving the watch, trying to give it over, begging and yelling and crying. He'd been walking all day by this time. He hadn't eaten or drunk anything, just trudged through this concrete wasteland. So he lost his head. And if there's one thing you don't do here, it's cause a scene."

"What happened?"

"The guy went running as fast as he could from this lunatic sticking a gold watch in his face. The next thing Chang knew the police had picked him up and brought him back here."

"Where is he now?"

"Dead."

The surprise took me so completely I couldn't speak.

He started shaking his head again; he went on nodding, hunkering over almost double with his elbows on his knees, glaring down at the battered scraps of vine and foliage and the torn-up dirt clods rooted with gritty hair. His head bobbed like an automated dog's in a rear car window.

"How did he die?" I asked finally.

"A few days after the police brought him back I found him in his apartment. Excuse me, *flat*. He'd hung himself."

"*You* found him?"

He kept nodding.

"God."

"Shoot. He was depressed." Once more the lips pulled back in the rictus.

"You said there was another one. Someone else who'd got out."

"Oh, yeah. That other old boy. He went nuts. He's not been the first. It also happened to this girl from Berkeley. She spun out, they locked her in the infirmary. But this other guy, he managed to break through the doors, jimmy them somehow, and then when the guard stopped him he went to punching and kicking and just about cracked that guard's head open. The police arrested him for assault." He paused. "The law is, if you get arrested just on *suspicion*, you can be held without bail and interrogated for twenty-three days. We were told this at the office. I guess they wanted to make sure they don't get any repeat performances."

"So where's the guy?" I asked.

He shrugged. "Jail. He assaulted a citizen." He stood up, pacing the four or five feet of garden width. The sun was already starting to drop toward the horizon, the tangled shadows elongating over the stones. "That's just it. When people get here and first start understanding the situation they can't hardly believe it. Bright people, hog-tied and dumb-founded. The thing is, why is he doing it? Keeping us here? It's just money! For nothing!"

"Not entirely," I said. "Just nothing rational."

"WELL, GOOD MORNING, there! I brought you a present."

"Taylor. Oh, God. I think I'm going to throw up." Martha's skin looked harsh in the blue tint of the hallway, pasty white where the westering sun-light struck. Her freckles stood out like pepper. Behind her lay a room exactly like mine in every tedious detail, down to the fruity grained colors of the van Gogh reproductions. With the back of her wrist she wiped her puffy mouth.

"It's five o'clock in the afternoon."

"Why'd you say good morning then?" Her voice sounded like sand-paper; I could smell a yeasty bread odor. Her T-shirt dangled just above her bare knees. She yawned hugely, turned, and trudged toward the window.

"Hi," said Red.

She screamed.

Then she was whirling, flying to his arms, jumping like a terrier, whacking him back and forth, her elbows jutting out sharp as boat cleats.

"Sisterly love," I said.

"Wait!" Her voice broke. She pulled back, turned and ran through the bedroom, eyes stricken, hand clapped to mouth. The bathroom door slammed.

"I guess she's glad to see me," said Red.

"Yeah. I don't think my sister would deliberately seal herself in a barracks with no Neiman Marcus, eight thousand miles from home, just so I could make her vomit. You must have done something nice when she was little."

"I cut her hair once with a lighted sparkler."

The bathroom door opened. Martha emerged dressed in a white cot-ton robe, a little color returning to her cheeks. "Red! You scumball. You look just terrible."

"You, too. What are you doing here?"

"What do you think?" She smiled tremulously, came up and kissed his cheek. "I've come to get—"

"*Ahem,*" I said, pointing to the walls.

"—some real-life experience and earn a salary bigger than my brother's."

"Yeah? How do you plan on doing that?" he said.

"You kidding? I've got what it takes, boy. It's in the bag."

"I wouldn't count on that." I glanced through her bedroom door to where her suitcase lay open on the floor, its contents disgorged in stacks of clothing, underwear, shampoo bottles, the pink satin lining razored out and folded neatly like a retired flag beside a pair of Reeboks. I knew that pink lining. I'd watched her tape a MicroDeeds prototype wallet computer below it, then stitch and glue it back into place against the Samsonite lid as if fresh from the factory.

Turning, she followed my eyes. *"No!"* Her palm slapped over her mouth.

"Don't tell me you're going to throw up again," I said loudly.

"Get ahold of yourself, now," said Red, and rubbed her neck.

Her eyes turned back to mine, brimming and tragic above her spread fingers.

"You know, I've come to decide Texans can be pretty naïve travelers," I said. "You don't want to mess around with a bad tummy. I reckon we'd best sit down and revise our little sight-seeing adventure."

EARLY THE NEXT morning I squeezed into the bathroom to brush my teeth. Sink, shower stall, floor, toothbrush holder, towel bar, bulb recesses, and medicine chest: the entire cubicle had been molded in a continuous extrusion of shining blue plastic. A mushroom stool sprouted through the floor, its bowled water perhaps the natural accident of rain. I marveled at such economy of vision; no doubt I'd find a capsule exactly like it in each flat on each floor of each building in the enclave. Nothing is separate, this shrine announced. All distinctions work toward a single unity. And re-member, the flusher is computerized.

Stepping into the living room, I poured some cereal. Breakfast took no time. Afterward I prowled around the glaucous interior like a lone guppy in a tank, rehashing all our discussions of the night before. The tool strap chafed my thigh. Now that Martha's secret wallet was confiscated we'd need more help. The electronic complications downstairs required keener knowledge than a brief skim through *How to Bypass Burglar Alarms,* and more complex equipment than Martha's Waterpik. We were to report to Nagisa Kawai at the main desk at 8:00 A.M. for our first day's work. For lunch hour we'd agreed to meet in the cafeteria to exchange plans. My watch still said only six. A stale light diluted the window, blanching patches on the wall, printing the sofa pale as mildew. As I paused to fill the kettle for tea, a knock sounded.

I didn't know what to expect. If it was Thomas I'd have to kill him. But this time the rap fell too faintly even to shiver the frosted panes. When I slid the panel back Ayako Minamoto stood there.

"Hello," I said. My heart jumped.

"Taylor Deeds," she said.

Although the alcove still hung dark, her hair shone lavender black, lucent as gun oil. She was in fact just tall enough to reach my middle ribs. When she looked at me I couldn't have looked away.

"I didn't wake you?" she asked.

"No."

"So. That is good." She glanced modestly down the hall, then back. Her shoulders squared, expectant. Her face lay impeccably still. I saw the boss of her eye shifting under its shallow lid, the upper lip violin-shaped, the lower lip full, glossed cherry.

"Please, may I come in?"

"Oh, sorry! Of course. Yes. Please. Please do." I shook myself and moved aside.

"Ah. Thank you." She hesitated. All at once I had the feeling that she'd bucked some inner resistance, breached some code, to ask that question. Her mouth corners turned down. Then, stepping to the threshold, angling sideways, she shucked off her shoes. Her feet slid from the calyxes like pale buds, shatteringly naked.

"Don't worry. You can keep them on. The carpet's not *that* clean." She looked up in surprise.

"Oh, wait, sorry, I forgot. Shoes off at the door."

She smiled. "Yes, that's right."

"Here. Let me close this." I snugged the door back into its frame.

"Okay."

We stood there, still looking at each other.

"Good morning!" she said.

"Yes. Good morning. Would—uh, would you like a cup of tea?"

"Ah, tea. Very nice."

"I was just about to put the kettle on."

"Oh, really? I will make it for us. Thank you."

She walked past me toward the kitchen with a tight, jerky grace that at first I took to be self-consciousness. I followed right behind. To watch her walk that short distance was strange, like observing somebody on a tightrope learning a new skill: subtly contracting her body, tucking her head low, fastening her arms to her sides. It looked very different from the fluidity of the hotel ballroom. And when she stumbled on the step down from carpet to tile I realized such awkwardness was alien, she was actually thrown off balance from holding in some tense, compressed emotion. I caught her elbow. "Oh! Thank you," she said.

"Sure." I cradled the elbow in my palm. So slim. The fabric of her shirt, knitted silk, rose and fell. Whatever she was feeling, I could sense its energy: sealed, but radioactive.

I swallowed.

"How are you? Are you well?" she said.

We stared. I let go. It was like holding a tiny bird, then letting it free, seeing it stay instead of flying off. "Yes. Fine, thanks."

"You are perhaps wondering why I'm here."

"Uh, sure. Yes." I cleared my throat. "No, not really."

"You are not surprised?" she asked.

"Yes. Yes, of course I am." I didn't want to sound rude. She could be spying. She could be making a hospitality call. Whatever reason she might supply would certainly not be the main one.

"I wanted to see you."

She bent to finish filling the kettle. It overflowed, water purling off the lip. She let it run a moment. Both of us stood watching that fluted crystal sheathe the metal. Then, reaching over, she turned the tap, poured out enough to even it off, set the kettle against the burner, and pushed a button. The gas caught. She looked up. The brushing glance tingled as it had in the limousine.

"I'm glad you wanted to," I said. It was hard to talk. My voice sounded husky.

"I know how to use this type of stove," she said.

"I can see that."

"All kinds. I learned in my school cooking class."

"Great. That's great."

She paused. She considered the closed cabinet doors, poising her fingertips on the countertop. "Do you have tea?" she asked.

"Oh. Yes, sure, in here." I prised the door open and reached for the caddy.

"Thank you." Carefully she took the caddy as I handed it down to her, her fingers tapering white against its lid.

"You're welcome."

"And a—teapot?" she asked, still with that considering note.

"Um. Next cupboard." Craning over her, I opened the door. To get to it brought me a few inches closer. Her head was just under my lifted arm, her face almost against my chest. She didn't pull back.

Slowly I grasped the teapot and brought it down.

Her face tilted up. "You have teabowls too?"

"Teabowls." It was like looking into a flower. No, a smooth velvet petal unfurled, staring straight down at it from the height. "Oh. Cups? You mean cups?"

"Yes. Cups."

My head swam. I couldn't get my breath, it caught short in my chest. It was stuck, everywhere else coming alive. Her chin just grazed my solar plexus; her eyes half closed, she tipped so far back there was no room between us at all.

"The kettle is boiling," she said.

"Yeah. Yeah, it is."

For a second we stayed there. A billow of steam hissed up behind her.

"Here they are." I reached back to the shelf. Her eyes opened. Gently she stepped away, only a step, to push the button off. Her arm slipped lightly against my side.

"I haven't prepared the tea," she murmured as I set the cups side by side on the counter. She picked up the caddy and tried to pry off the lid. Again her movements faltered. The lid sprang, flying through the air, bouncing with a tin quiver against the stove's edge, landing clattering on the floor. I felt that same tension encased within her body, barely contained, almost unmanageable.

"Oh! I am sorry," she laughed softly.

"It's okay. No problem. Look, see?" I bent to retrieve the lid.

"I have not come to visit you for tea," she said, breathless.

"I know."

"I came here to take you out."

I straightened and stood up. "Out. Where?"

"Into Tokyo," she said, her widening eyes lifting to my full altitude, her lips parted, waiting.

16

A lone man in a blazer sat upright at the reception desk, hands crossed peaceably on the rose-gold surface. By local standards his hair seemed a little tousled; dandruff drifted in the part. His shoulders and pouchy face looked broad as a boxer's, with a porch-roof brow that squashed his eyes to grooves. For this reason it wasn't until we'd crossed the narrow isthmus between the desk and the sentry booth that I realized he was asleep.

The guard was not.

At his glass panels Ayako stopped short. He was a much older man than the one I'd seen yesterday. Gravely he looked at her and bowed. She bowed and said something in Japanese.

He turned. Inch by inch his gaze traveled from my waistline up the shirt placket, skidding across jaw, socket, temple, hair—an eerie deflection, as if his eyes slipped on ice, or he was surveying a natural landmark just enough to satisfy a tourist obligation.

He asked Ayako a question.

"*Hai,*" she said.

He asked something else. Wordlessly she reached down into her little handbag, pulled out a piece of paper, and slipped it through the round port just above his console. With a labored sigh he ticked through a series of handwritten characters that I could see perfectly well from my vantage point. Stamped at the top left-hand corner was a round red inked seal, spiral-mazed like a thumbprint. Below it, another red seal, this one of a flower. Refolding the paper he pushed it back through the port. Ayako took it. He bowed, murmured, spoke the name Minamoto.

"*Arigato,*" said Ayako.

Then, bracing her bag to her side, she stepped toward the tempered early morning light. The glass mausoleum door rumbled open. Before us stood a chute filled with smog-yellow day, screened by a high wall, and roaring from the other side with car motors, bus tires squealing, a horn tooting, a clang unidentified—the world.

AS WE MOVED along the white flock of Toyota and Minamoto sedans in the staff lot she groped through her purse. Odors blew sharply on the heat. Others muffled the air like invisible pillows. I could smell chicken roasting on charcoal, exhaust, sesame oil, bleach; woodsmoke, plus a strange, clogged perfume like rotting gardenias. In contrast the rooms inside the enclave had smelled arranged: dead with chemical lemons and false pine. Even in the cafeteria a sweetness unrelated to food wafted through the ducts, surpassing the highly colored blobs we'd been fed in both texture and pungency.

Chinks pierced the plaster wall at intervals like arrow slits. Stooping, I pressed my eye against them. Each view was a quick take through an old-timey movie projector: one scene at a time, cropped tight, bridged solely by the sky. In the first a mob of kids in sailor suits stood on the corner just outside the wall. Their clothes looked identically antique from top to bottom: a row of black braids, faces, then white, then navy, pale knees, kneesocks, black shoes. At the next slit a street appeared, alive with traffic. Cutting across a yellow warehouse darted a shiny new Ferrari. An old lady bicyclist wobbled along the curb. I failed to catch up with her at the following slit, which revealed two stamp-size yards, a stubby tree limbed in green wads, and bushes corralled beside matching cinder-block houses.

Blue roof tiles glittered watery in the sun. An apartment tower stood twenty stories high, combed with tiny balconies like teeth. Clotheslines hung stiff in undershirts, a record store advertised Michael Jackson—a nightmare of aridity, interrupted by a stoplight at the next intersection. So this was where he'd hidden us, the neighborhood through which Maxwell Chang had trudged and foundered before returning to the enclave to kill himself in despair. All in all, it seemed perfect.

Twisting, I studied the building we'd just left. On the right, the glass corridor to the cafeteria, mall, offices, and lab buildings snaked like a fat boa's midsection, glittering with panes. The bamboo grove inside stood in ghostly pikes.

"We must go," said Ayako politely. I turned. She stood waiting a few yards away beside the open driver's door of a red Mercedes 600SL, her keys clutched between her fingers.

"All right."

The passenger side was unlocked. I tamped myself down into the leather seat. She got in and touched a button; our tinted windows climbed the burled walnut frames. She didn't look my way. The engine started with a hollow *brummm,* fine as a chord of music.

They must have known her at the main entrance because the ten-foot gate, webbed with sensors and for all I knew fatally electrified, swung out at a wave of her hand. Looking back at the gatekeeper's box I saw a genderless figure, obscured behind reflected clouds, bowing good-bye.

WE WERE ON a big expressway. Below the elevated roadbed, buildings streamed past in gray and colored piles, each street shortly dead-ending or turning a corner. Watching the landscape tripped my vertigo; every minute or two I had to look straight ahead to clear its orbit. Sometimes in the distance train tracks cut the scene, raised to our level or dropping into earth. Once we rode directly above them, and I stared down that black maw before we hurtled beyond. A little farther on, the tracks laced between blocks; a train thundered by, curving away like a steel ribbon as we veered.

Through the pallid air I could make out dim mountain outlines. Occasionally we passed a sign poking up from the buildings: giant neon tulips or Gothic cathedral spires with PACHINKO written in roman letters. I felt a jolt each time I recognized their familiar shapes. But mostly the signs flashed in Japanese—hatched lines, splashed dots, incomprehensible pictures of a language. Twice we crossed bands of water that turned into rivers lined with weedy sandbanks.

I didn't try to guess direction. Ayako concentrated on the traffic, which seemed to be growing more sluggish. Her fingers dented the steering-wheel leather. Insinuated against that window backdrop, her profile stood out: dark silk, cream curve, slope, notched lips, rounded chin, throat stem. Once she flipped her hair back over her shoulder with a rigid hand. But still she stayed silent.

So did I.

Since leaving the apartment we'd hardly spoken. After that moment in the kitchen we'd silently gathered ourselves together, and headed straight for the door. Our departure had been so abrupt she barely got her shoes on. It was as if panic had gripped us, and now, once we started talking beyond bare-bones pleasantries, we were going to have to admit how bizarre all this was: my presence in Japan, inside her car, her motives, our designed getaway, our purpose.

For well over an hour we nosed down the miles of lanes before she finally glanced at me. "We have left Chiba," she said.

"Is that where it was?"

"Yes."

"What's Chiba?"

"It is a—" She frowned and nibbled her lower lip. "It makes a leg around Tokyo Bay."

"A peninsula?"

"Yes. Also, a city."

"Looks like we're still in it."

One of those furtive flicks, then back to the windshield. "Now we have come to Edogawa-ku. Afterwards Kōtō-ku."

"Is that where you have in mind?"

"Pardon?"

She was so small that I could have perched her on my lap like a bird. She wore the pale knit top, narrow black pants, two gold bracelets, and a short string of pearls whose lunar glow mingled alchemically with her skin.

"Is Kōtō-ku where you're taking us?"

"Oh—," she laughed. One hand covered her mouth. "We will go to another place."

"Okay." The traffic was now almost at a standstill. "Where's that?"

She hesitated. I wondered if after all she acted on some plan designed for me by her father. Or maybe her innocence was so complete that she really believed she was merely picking up a new employee for a little fun and taking him on an outing. How much could I tell her? It would be insane to tell her anything.

"What do you like?"

"What do I like?"

"Yes." Her voice fell low and shy.

"You mean, where would I like to go?"

She nodded.

"Well. I don't know Tokyo at all, except for the lobby of that hotel."

"Ah, yes. But it's good if we go somewhere else."

"Fine with me."

"The grounds of Imperial Palace are over the street from the hotel," she said tentatively.

"That park we passed on our way? Opposite all those big office buildings? Is that the Imperial Palace?"

"Yes." But she didn't add more.

"Tell me, Ayako. Where is your father's headquarters?"

"Headquarters?"

"The main building he runs his companies from."

"It's on the street from the Imperial Palace also."

"Ahh."

She glanced at me, a quick dark stroke that I could feel. "You come from Dallas?" she asked.

"Roughly. I was actually born in a little town about thirty-five miles from Dallas, called Bernice."

"Your father lives in Dallas?"

"Yes, he does."

"And he knows my father?"

"Only on paper," I said dryly.

"Ah, he's a daimyo in the United States?" she inquired.

"You could say that, from what I understand."

"And he's given you to my father, because of Anjiro? For payment of *giri*?"

"No." So there it was, I thought. She knew. "Not for giri or money or work or any other commodity."

"You are here," she said, almost whispering.

"But he never gave me."

"You decided to wear the *on* yourself, for your father? You and Anjiro are in the same—the same place to your fathers, is this so?"

"I suppose if you put it like that, then yes. Their only sons. But let's just get this straight, so there won't be any doubt or question. Don't think for a minute my father meant to send me. I came here on my own. I'm not paying back a thing."

"That's what I have thought," she said. Under its softness her voice edged with a deep, satisfied finality.

"I owe your father no debt. Neither does my father."

"I understand," she murmured, and smiled at the windshield.

I felt a shiver run up my spine.

"Tell me. Are you very well acquainted with your father's setup out there in Chiba? Do you know what he's doing, and why?"

"He hires Americans to work in his companies," she said limpidly.

"I don't reckon they call it work. But the point is—is all this solely out of revenge for your brother Anjiro's death?"

She swerved around a Nissan stalled in the far lane. Many yards ahead I could see the cars locked bumper to bumper, fluming exhaust. "My father has other reasons for his actions. These reasons are very complicated, but they join together."

"Give me an example."

She bit her lower lip again. "America always makes large scientific progress. Japan makes progress now, also. Many intelligent people work here. If my father brings the intelligent people of the competing American companies, they won't be so strong."

"He wants to handicap U.S. competition? That's kind of naïve. He's already ahead. And he's not stupid, he must know there are whole oceans full over there ready to replace whatever he skims off the top. The removal of a few clever people won't do much damage."

"That's what the other keiretsu presidents now remind him, I think."

"Does that mean somebody's objecting?"

"No one would object to the wishes of the daimyo."

"Right." I mulled this. "So he has other reasons."

She said nothing.

"Is that what you're telling me?"

The dark head dipped, as if checking the speedometer.

Suddenly the interior of the car felt far too snug. My shins were crammed against the dash; my head mashed the soft top each time we went over a bump. Although she sat embedded in the leather driver's seat her thighs and hips lay only centimeters from my hand. I looked at her arm arched toward the wheel: the inner elbow, soft and exposed, its taut satin.

"Do you often take the tame Americans out on little field trips like this?" I asked.

"I have seen them at the airport and for the sake ceremony." Her eyes fixed carefully on the road.

"What about later?"

She shook her head.

"It's a risk for you, isn't it?"

A tiny breath lifted her nostrils.

"I'm glad you've done it."

"We must choose a place to go now." There was a tremble in the note. She clenched the steering wheel and stared unblinking at the exit sign in front of us.

"Wherever you like."

"I have told you something," she said then.

"Yeah? What's that?"

"A lie."

"You've told me a lie?"

She turned and looked at me. Her eyes had gone liquid with a tender, brazen fear. "I have lied," the words rushed out, as if she were leaping some obstacle that required great surrender and strength. "We have not been in Chiba. We haven't come to Edogawa-ku or Kōtō-ku. Kan Nai Incorporated is in Saitama, the other direction. North."

After a moment I asked gently, "Why did you lie, Ayako?"

"The location is secret."

"Yeah, I figured that."

"I didn't know if you understood where you were."

"You were testing me." She shook her head, agreeing. "You wanted to see if I truly was lost? Or if I was who I seemed to be?"

She glanced at me, as if surprised by such acumen.

"And am I?"

"I have confirmed my impression on this," she said, turning again to the windshield.

IN THE MIDDLE of the dense city buildings and underground parking garages we wandered along gravel paths through trees.

"What's the name of this place?" I asked.

"Ueno Park."

The trees overhung the paths and woods to either side, full of leaves, not yet autumnal. The day had turned hot and muggy. Cicadas whirred in the bushes, crows cawed loudly back and forth. Shade fell in stripes across the faces of morning strollers—young mothers pushing baby carriages, old men pacing sedately, prim housewives in twos or threes, a knot of swarthy black-bearded men who looked unmistakably foreign. They were, in fact, the only non-Japanese I'd seen since we'd climbed the steps from the street. They stood clumped beside a food vendor's stall, chaffing loudly in another language, their wavy hair and shrubby mustaches bristling. Cheap rayon shirts clashed against red or green pants and striped Nikes. For a moment I felt a forlorn twinge of camaraderie: what was Bobby up to these days? The men stared appraisingly as we walked past. "You want phone card?" one called out. "Buy two! Six hundred yen only!"

"No, thanks."

He frowned. The man next to him muttered and then laughed. People shrank away to the path's far edge, avoiding proximity. A few yards farther on I asked, "Where do those guys come from?"

"They are Iranians," Ayako said.

"What are they doing here?"

She peered up at me. "I think perhaps they come here to work. Making buildings? What is the English word, please?"

"Construction?"

"Ah, yes. And they become lawbreakers, selling drugs and other specialities." Ramón, I thought, Ramón. What would he make of all this? It wasn't until we'd rounded a corner that I realized how strange my question had been. Would I have asked it in Dallas, I wondered? Mexico? But she'd known exactly who they were. Everyone in the park would know. At no time in my life had I been in a public spot where diversity seemed so obvious, grating, and out of kilter.

I looked down at the six feet between my chin and the ground. I caught sight of my gold arm hair. I turned to Ayako, gliding beside me.

"Where can we go?"

"We can go to the museum. Many tourists go there from other countries." Instantly she'd understood.

"Listen to that." Music was jittering from a grove close by. Searching under the shade I found a group of people gathered around a blue-suited man with a portable tape deck. He seemed to be playing requests. He loitered by his little table, fingering the cassettes and gulping huge gouts of cigarette smoke. A scrawny old woman in a black wig, red lipstick, and white wrinkles tottered up to a microphone, waited for him to start the music, and then started warbling in a high nasality, nodding her head graciously at her audience. We stopped to listen. The mike relayed her plaintive tune into the trees, looping them with sounds tight as wire. On their folding chairs the audience seemed to be having a good time. One old man in a cotton kimono, straw sandals, and white socks started dancing. His white hair fluffed out in the breeze under a headband. Almost he looked small enough to be a dwarf, waggling his pleated fan back and forth, tiptoeing coquettishly. When the woman finished her song she beamed and bowed. Everybody clapped. Someone shouted a remark, prompting much laughter. The next man rose to take her place, easygoing, dignified, naming his choice; the little dancer grinned and fluttered the fan in delight. Reaching down I grasped Ayako's hand. It was the first time I'd deliberately touched her. Without looking at one another we started off again under the leaves; long after we had passed, the music still meandered toward us.

"The museum is through this way," said Ayako.

"Do you know the park very well?"

"I've come here with my school for *sakura matsuri*. Ah—'cherry blossom parties.' Also I studied in the museum for an art class at Waseda University." We both felt very conscious of our hands.

"You're in college?"

"I have finished."

"In art history, right?"

She glanced up to me. "History of Western Culture."

"Oh, really." That, I thought, could explain her fine English, although no doubt Minamoto had made sure she'd been meticulously educated. "Did you enjoy it?"

"I learned very much." She paused. "My father wished me to take a degree in this subject."

"How come?"

"He says we should know our adversaries."

I stopped.

On a post beside the path stood an enormous crow. He shuffled a little, flapping his wings, the sheened feathers rustling like a stage costume. Eyeing me, he jabbed forward, opened his pincer beak, screamed with fury. The beak clacked shut.

"For Christ's sakes! Who does he think we are?" I exclaimed.

She bit her lip. Her fingers shook slightly between mine. "I have enjoyed learning very much about the United States and its customs. Also I studied other Western countries, in Europe, Africa, and South America. Please come into the museum now. I would like to show you some statues of ancient Japanese art."

I pulled her back, closer to me. She halted. "Have you ever been to the United States, Ayako?"

"Someday I hope to visit there," she said.

"Millions of Japanese go every year. Did you know that?" She nodded. "Skiing, Disneyland, Hawaii. Golfing, sightseeing. Your fellow countrymen now own Pebble Beach. Plus Rockefeller Center, a chunk of Hollywood, and whole blocs of our university systems in the form of endowments. I have a good buddy named Rick whose parents these days run their old family ranch out in West Texas as a dude ranch. Do you know who it's for? It's for Japanese businessmen to come and play cowboy for a weekend."

"Yes," she said.

"It's very intriguing, given your background, that you haven't yet traveled to America."

She looked down. The crow belted out another vicious caw, right near her ear.

"Would you enjoy the museum now?" she asked.

"Sure." I let go the tug on her hand. "Of course, I'll go to the museum now."

Instantly her hand relaxed and then crimped smoothly into mine.

LIKE MANY OF the other metropolitan buildings I'd seen so far, it was designed in an Oriental Western style. But the architecture—gray stone, lofty flights, monolithic balustrades—could have been found in plenty of large American cities, except for the pagoda-peaked roof.

Our hands broke apart. Ayako paid our entrance fees before I could scrape the yen notes out of my pockets. I only had a few thousand, anyhow; the rest of my cash was still hidden back in the apartment, a total of $100,000 in yen, so far undiscovered. Enough for a planeload of tickets. That was when it hit me, suddenly. By taking off on this surprise jaunt I'd left myself wide open. For certain they'd search my apartment while I was gone.

For certain Martha and Red would start worrying by lunch hour.

For the first time it occurred to me to wonder: what would everybody do when they found out I was missing?

I looked at Ayako peeling notes from her wallet. By now Nagisa Kawai knew I'd missed our appointment together to report for work. Matsudo was in charge. Nobody before had ever been allowed out of the enclave. How far did Minamoto family sanctions extend? Who would the boss's daughter account to, but the boss?

"We go this way." She handed me my ticket. We walked through a large, empty hall, past a bench where a tiny girl lay asleep with her dress rucked up, her thumb plugged in her mouth. The hall seemed very quiet. Except for the ticket seller no adults were in sight.

"Aren't her parents afraid to leave her by herself like that?" I asked Ayako.

"Afraid for what, please?"

"Well—kidnap. Strangers."

She looked perplexed. "Kidnap? Ah, yes, I see. Child sleeping nap! But—strangers?"

"Never mind." I shook my head.

"In this gallery we find the very old temple statues," she said, leading me through a large doorway. Now that I was no longer touching her, my palm felt abnormally empty. I hung back to watch her walk ahead, hips shifting neatly in her black pants, scapulae outlined against the knit falling down her back. At a glass case a few yards away stood two Westerners, Swedes or Norwegians. They peered closely at the wooden figure seated inside and spoke in musing murmurs. The man stood nearly as tall as I in his brown fisherman's sandals; the woman looked middle-aged, a cheerful crinkle-haired intellectual. Ayako glanced toward them, cocked her head, and smiled meaningfully at me. Here on neutral ground her step had grown lighthearted. I couldn't guess yet what would happen. She might not be serious, she could still be merely trying out a little adventurous rebellion. The uncertainty made my stomach clench.

We halted before a statue with multiple arms. "This is Nyoirin Kannon," she said.

"So he is."

She laughed. "You know who is Kannon?"

"The ancestor of a camera?"

"You shouldn't say disrespect! Kannon is a very holy representation of Buddha."

"Handy, too. Maybe he's got insect blood."

"It was made in the early Heian period. And these are holy objects, from bronze but later period." Playfully she moved along the display. "See this one? The plate for food offerings. The incense-burning cup."

"Is this stuff still used in Zen ceremonies now?"

"Oh yes. All traditional items still used in worship." Unlike the gutting knives of the Yucatán, I thought.

"Here is the priest's bell, and the—please, what is the word?" Deliberately she ignored the placard, smiling sidelong up at me.

"I'm a total ill-educated, ignorant fool. I have no idea whatsoever." I squinted at the sign, which had clear English printed below the Japanese: GOKOSHO, THUNDERBOLT. "Baby rattle?"

"Here is a vessel for candles." Abruptly she turned.

"A vessel."

"A candlestick, very old, from Nara. A vessel." She scrunched her chin down.

"Are you okay?"

"Okay? Ah, yes! I am okay." Her voice sounded small, breathless. She giggled without mirth, mechanically.

"I'm sorry. I didn't mean to offend you." I reached out a finger to brush the tips of her hair.

"This comes from Nara also," she said after a moment.

I nodded, glad to change the subject. "What about this man?" I stepped to the glass case that the two Scandinavians had just abandoned.

"Ah, yes." She paused, tilting her head to read the card. "He was a famous monk, the abbot of a monastery in Kyoto."

"He was a real person, then?"

"Yes, ah yes. He lived eight hundred years ago." Lightly she pressed her hand against the edge of his glass box.

"He's beautiful." I stared at the elderly face so calmly carved, pellucid with character. The bald dome. The paint had rubbed off in spots. Whorled wood grain lay underneath. He might be breathing. Every fold of his robe swung with volume, alive to the potential of meditational shift.

All at once I had to shut my eyes to blink back tears.

Squeezing the lids together, I crushed memory into that crowded darkness. When I opened my eyes she was peering up at me.

"You are moved by an image of such wisdom?" she asked softly.

"I—well. Yes." I cleared my throat. *Granddaddy. Granddaddy,* I thought.

"I was taught only Japanese can understand this." She turned back, very still.

"Well. You never know." Feebly I wiped my nose. Then I went over to the next case, where I stared hard at a standing bronze Buddha, slender and definitely female. After a brief space she joined me.

"Kannon."

"Where are all the arms?"

"A different Kannon bodhisattva," she smiled again. Now the smile looked different. "In the Zenjoki type. And nearby, Amida."

"I didn't realize there were so many different kinds." I inspected the Amida on his gilded lotus flower, his pinecone hair stuck on top. My eyes were still watery. Rambling ahead, I turned the corner into the next room. "Hey. Now here's a guy who makes an impression."

She walked up behind. The smile evaporated. A life-size statue of a demon, surrounded by cutout yellow flames, loomed over the dais. His blackened face shone with eager hate, his eyeballs bulged in ferocity. "Man. How many souls do you suppose he would usually eat for breakfast?"

"It is Fudo Myoo," she said.

"You know him personally?"

"He is the messenger. But since I was a little girl I recognized his true self." She stood, shoulders rigid. Her eyes never moved from his. "He is my father's *honsho.*"

"His what?" Deep down it seemed, watching her, that this was what she'd really brought me here to see. And somewhere, from some lesson, I knew the word.

"The private face of my father."

OUTSIDE IN THE park we stopped at a stall. Ayako selected five skewers of rice and fish and some rice balls filled with sweet bean paste that the chef, a toothy, sharp-spoken woman in an apron, laid out in a plastic coffin. Under a marquee stood several machines vending canned or boxed cold drinks, labeled in English as well as Japanese: TeaTime—A Custom of Relaxing for that Right Fashion Afternoon; Asahi Beer; Pocari Sweat; Tomato Juice; Oolong; Kirin Beer; Mucos Sport; Coke; plus a variety of others. A cigarette machine had a picture of Roger Moore on it urging "Speak Lark." We sat on a bench beside a tree tagged with hundreds of paper streamers. The tags wavered a little in the breeze, frail and temporal as their written prayers. Looking at them Ayako said, "We could go next to Yasukuni Jinja."

"What's there?"

"I'll show you where the prime minister must come every year to honor the dead."

"That sounds okay." It sounded off the track. Rock music blared from somebody's ghetto blaster farther down in the hot sunlight. I hadn't dared ask what came after this.

"When you see it you will understand more of what perhaps you wish to know."

"How do you know what perhaps I wish to know?"

She glanced sideways at me and then looked down, sprinkling her skewer with soy sauce.

"All right. What exactly is Yasukuni Jinja?"

"It's a Shinto shrine. But different from other Shinto shrines."

"How?"

Demurely she bit into the fish-rice daub and chewed, not answering.

"THE IMPERIAL PALACE Garden is over there," she said. It was just past noon. Again the thought of Martha and Red struck me, the futures I was now risking. We were climbing up a hill alongside a wide, busy street after parking in another underground garage, this time a hotel's. Lunch crowds hurried past. Across the intersection people poured from a subway entrance.

Idlers milled around the palace grounds, pointing to the duplicate pine trees, rubbernecking the stone bridge arched over the moat, licking ice cream. The noise was unbelievable. Loudspeakers blared from the tops of trucks, motorcycles darted through the packed traffic, music crazed the air, buses wheezed, taxis stopped and started, the humidity seemed to din in my ear. Each person looked well dressed. No one appeared even slightly casual or sloppy or shabby. But for that fact, it could have been an afternoon in Los Angeles, a New York boulevard, maybe, with a hundred thousand office workers rushing toward their sandwiches or pasta salad.

"What's that big building over there?" I asked.

"That is Budokan. Stadium and concert center."

"They've built it directly above the Imperial Palace."

"Ah yes."

"Hey—I thought you didn't want us to enter this neighborhood."

"This neighborhood is very busy. Do you think so?"

"Well, I sure wouldn't argue." The awareness of her physical presence moved through me in a wind. Its honeysuckle fragrance dazed the senses. Walking uphill I could feel her cheek close to my bicep, even.

"My father has flown to Osaka for two days," she said. "He's meeting with some others for a conference."

"When did he go?"

"Late in the night. Last evening."

I weighed the news while we walked. "Is this the place?" We had reached the upper slope of the hill. Trees and shrubs clustered below a huge gate. Cicadas sang through the heat; their shrillness climbed as we entered the green shelter facing a gravel aisle.

"Yes," she said.

The sweep inside the trees was lined with stone lanterns. Yards of path led up to a massive pillar thrust high. On its top a bronze statue stood poised: a lordly man dressed in robes and kimono, sword ready at his waist.

To the left lay a paved parking lot with three or four white cars. A bus took up a stretch of curb. Two sound trucks stood under the trees. Just then another rolled in and braked to a stop, motor idling; the driver got out and lighted a cigarette. The few people in the lot were all men, all wearing suits. Two of them also wore sunglasses. I was the only foreigner in sight.

"Why do I get the feeling this isn't a prime tourist venue?" I asked.

"It's very historical. We will go into the shrine. You will perhaps find it picturesque?"

"This is pretty picturesque."

The two men in sunglasses turned their dark lenses my way. They stayed fixed for a moment. The driver of the third truck did, too, his face stern; then he drew on the cigarette, removed it, folded his arms, and looked off into the trees.

"Shall we go in?" said Ayako.

"You bet."

She stepped hastily past the stone pillar before I had a chance to read its plaque further than the roman letters OMURA MASUJIRO. Following down the gravel strip on the statue's far side, I heard my footfalls crunch through the buzzing summer silence. Ayako glanced over her shoulder. We hurried to another torii gate. Gravel changed to pavement. Ahead stood a roofed wall with two open wooden doors about twenty-five feet tall, each studded with a raised golden chrysanthemum.

Ayako stopped.

"This is it?"

"Yes."

"Who were those guys back there?"

"They are very strong patriots. Members of Japan's nationalist groups. The American term is—'right wing'?"

"Uh-huh." I glanced back. Mercifully they were now invisible. "Isn't that the emperor's crest?" I pointed to the gold medallions.

"Yasukuni is His Imperial Majesty's special shrine dedicated to the memories of all people who gave their lives for Japan. Since 1869 they died. The emperor came here to pray the night before he declared the last war."

"Here? Right here?"

"Yes."

"You mean—before bombing Pearl Harbor?"

"We'll wait here a moment," she said uncertainly.

"Okay. Why?" I wanted to get farther from the parking lot.

"Pilgrims are having photographs taken."

"Yes, I see that." A large gang of elderly women accompanied by three or four old men with medals pinned to their lapels sat composed in the sunlight before the doorway, smiling as a photographer bent over his tripod. Their smiles stayed plastered in position while he fiddled and adjusted; even after he'd pressed the button and shouted with triumph they continued, markers of time and occasion, until at last they gradually dissolved into the lapping tide of sound, the cicadas' trill, doves burbling, crows cawing, the click of folding chairs being dismantled. The pilgrims dispersed, their polyester dresses fluttering in the breeze, and headed off toward a big walk-in stall selling bags of rice crackers, key rings, votary objects, and tasseled toy swords.

"Are they war widows?"

"I think yes," said Ayako. "From a town far in the country perhaps."

My uneasiness grew. We climbed the steps through the doors, past the photographer's billboard displaying more veterans, a young couple with small children—the granddaughter or grandson of some sacrificial soldier, moonfaced and happy, absolutely right in having made the trip to honor a dead forebear. Other devotees were walking through the courtyard. Fathers pushed baby strollers, a pair of teenagers stood purifying themselves at a stone trough with bamboo ladles. Among the old people's throng a feeling suddenly came upon me that for them I was defiling the meaning of this place; this was the spot where their lives had once centered, and then pivoted forever. Even the trees tagged with paper strips, the white doves boiling around under their shade, seemed to reject my actual corporality.

"What's that building through there?" I pointed to the first truly Japanese-style structure I'd seen. A large banner stamped with the chrysanthemum crest hung from its eaves. The roof arched and peaked above it.

"The shrine where worship is made."

"They hold memorial services?"

Ayako moved toward the shrine. Then, laying her fingers on my arm to bid me to hold back, she went to the stone trough, picked up a ladle, poured water over her hands, took a sip, and set the ladle down. Returning, she climbed to the highest stone step before the veranda, bowed twice, slowly clapped twice, and bowed her head. A young man in traditional Shinto clothes—loose, wide pants and sashed jacket—passed her up the steps, leading a group to a waiting priest in a shiny black hat. I could see them kneel on the floor through the open shoji screens. Every human here was Japanese. The power and intent of Yasukuni Shrine, the focus of its visitors, felt unmistakable. Ayako bowed one more time and came down the steps. I looked at her. She was an utter stranger.

In an L shape to the left of the shrine ran a long row of linked wooden cases paneled in glass. Each box held a single flower arrangement. Walking down the line of *ikebana* plumed with fern, or five stalked orchids, or a bird-of-paradise or bulky dahlia, I asked, "Are these for honoring the war dead?"

"Yes. The families have put them there."

Involuntarily I thought of the Bernice tricycle above its owner's grave. My father sat on the bed's edge, bending his head, remembering that long-gone child. *What are you doing right now, this minute?* I thought. *Have you told Mother? Granddaddy? Do they know yet where I am?*

I turned. She had trailed patiently after me, keeping pace with my strides.

"Why have you brought me here?"

She stood very still. A stout, tough-looking man in a wheat suit strolled by. He stared at us, narrowed his eyes, looked at the shrine, paused in contemplation. Then his hands lifted, his arms curved overhead in a gesture like the Buddha's, fingers touching together.

"My father lives here," she said.

"Here? What do you mean?"

"This is the home of his spirit."

And peering through the vaults of empty air between the buildings, at the burnished gold, the giant bronze torii, the flower colors echoing down the rows like ghosts, the tags' susurration on the trees, it came to me what she meant.

"SO WHAT'S NEXT? Are you driving me back?" I had to force myself to ask. Wheeling out of the parking garage, she looked demure, enclosed. With her body a handspan away I suddenly felt more isolated than ever in my life before; the risk was now completed, my oversight fatal.

"Back?"

"It's getting late. I guess they'll be missing me." How had I ever hoped? What had I been dreaming?

"You cannot go back."

"What?"

"I thought you understood," she said politely.

I turned too fast. Just as we swung sharply around a corner into an office tower's shadow, my vision sank without warning between two black cliffs. In reflex I whipped my head toward the sky, granite edges, any still point through the buckling dark. The world dipped. We were speeding up the avenue, past the Imperial Palace grounds, jiggering pines, elastic walls, bobbing bridges. If I hadn't been sitting I'd have crashed onto the street.

"Are you going to drop me off somewhere?" I tried not to gasp.

Her pale cheek oval glimmered on the darkness. She didn't look at me. Her left hand gripped the wheel, her right gathered her purse close. Graceful fingers slid pensively up and down its shoulder strap. "We will go to a love hotel," she said.

17

A sound wove through the afternoon twilight.

When I listened carefully above the rush of my own blood I could make out dim piped-in music. "What will my Mary say?" Johnny Mathis was arguing tenderly. *"Don't go,"* pouted the girl. *"If I don't leave I'll be sooor-ry,"* sang Johnny. You're damn right, I thought.

The sound came from a fountain in one corner of the room where water trickled into a scallop half shell; a pale troglodyte figure teetered on its plaster hinge. Stepping closer I saw it was a cherub pissing into the fluted basin, watching his own stream with clinical interest. A few drops spattered onto the carpet. The walls behind him were crushed red velvet, rich, corpuscular. The mirrored ceiling compounded their effect. Centered below it lay the bed.

"Do you like this room or a different room, perhaps?" Ayako asked.

"I don't know. How do you feel?" The round king-size mattress was made up in black satin sheets.

"They are versatile, I think. Like the pictures in the hall?"

"Yeah, I saw those."

"Please, if you like another we can request."

When she'd motioned us up the street of garish architecture to a three-story parody of Sleeping Beauty's castle I'd followed her into its front hall, feeling the knot double in the pit of my stomach. I was sweating. I could smell it. "What's this place called?"

"The name is invisible. This is so people will not have embarrassment to go into a love hotel."

"So all these other buildings are plain, regular hotels?" I pointed to the fantasies out of Disney World propped around the sloping streets, their neon signs flashing.

"They are all love hotels," she replied, laughing behind her hand. "Many people come to Shibuya for privacy and fun."

"Oh. Right." I nodded.

She pushed through the glass swing door, apparently unconcerned lest she might be seen entering a love hotel, discreet temple for privacy and fun. In the hallway leading to the lobby she paused to open her purse. A bank of framed photographs decorated the wall: theme bedrooms, each with its own fixtures in tasteful yet didactic coherence, each labeled in Japanese and English. The Pirate Schooner. The Princess Coach. The Commodore. The Pink Cadillac. The Buckeroo. The Elvis. All with decor that depended heavily on various phallic objects to emphasize the point, such as the gold-tipped longhorns wreathing the Buckeroo chandelier, or the fat, round-capped candles surmounting the Princess Coachman's lanterns. The beds each replicated some nostalgic vehicle. I figured locomotion must be the hotel specialty. Elvis's '59 Chrysler sported leopardskin upholstery, fins, ruby red bullet taillights, and a convertible top. I got the same feeling I'd had on the street when we passed first a noodle shop and then a sushi bar, their show windows filled by realistic wax models of five-course meals.

"What do we do now?"

Her self-assurance made me jumpier. "Please wait a moment." After taking out a ream of bills she carefully relatched her purse, then walked up the hallway to the tiny chrome lobby booth.

There was no desk.

"Is anybody there?"

"I pay through this." She nodded to a slot in the wall with a buzzer beside it. She pressed the button. Someone spoke through a microphone.

"*Hai*," said Ayako. She asked a question. The microphone answered. A metal flap opened. Carefully she counted some bills and then slipped them through the slot. "*Domo arigato!*" A metal-ringed plastic card came out.

Ayako took it. "Come this way," she said.

Our room was on the second floor. When we'd breached its uterine interior I realized the truth: she'd paid no attention whatsoever to her many options. Certainly this wasn't the Commodore. Despite the marine touch with the fountain scallop, I found the whole scheme a shade eclectic. I looked up at the gold-webbed mirror in the ceiling.

"You wish to change?" she asked again.

"No, no thanks. This is fine." My mouth felt dry. A tic had started leaping inside my wrists. I steadied them by casually jamming my hands in my pockets.

"Here is television also. And VCR."

"The viewing selection might prove a little limited." I hadn't felt this nervous since the whorehouse those years before in Matamoros. Now there was no one to ask, no drink to buy, nothing to break my fall.

"Ah, really, is that so?" Politely she bent to the rack and examined some titles. "Ah yes!"

"Pretty amazing, uh, stuff," I said, nodding at the fountain. I wished we were still holding hands.

"Do you have rooms like this in American love hotels?"

"We don't have love hotels. At least, not per se." I cleared my throat.

"Oh, really? Is that so?" She seemed genuinely surprised. She went to a wall knob, an experimental look on her face. Electric light flared yellow as butter. Shadows vanished; the cherub glared like fishmeat on the scallop cusp, poised upon his continuing mission. "The lights are adjustable," she observed.

"Would you like to sit down?" I asked. Suddenly the mixture of anchorlessness and panic peaked to an almost unbearable erotic drive.

"Yes. Thank you." Neatly she perched on the edge of the bed. "Ah, see? A control to make it go in a circle." She pressed a button on the bedside console. With a crank and whirr the whole black satin plateau started to rotate. She laughed, pushed it again. The carousel shuddered and stopped.

"Not my style, I think," I said. An orbital bed, just what I needed. My head began to rock. "So—is there room service?"

"We can order." She smiled and indicated a telephone receiver.

"The thing is—" I shuffled around. I squinted at the main light, shaped like a long, smooth, pink rocket ship. I looked away. "The thing is—"

"Would you like to sit down, please?" Her voice quavered. She tilted her head at the satin shore beside her.

"Yeah. Okay." I walked up to it and sat down.

"This is a good place. Do you think so?"

"Um, well, sure."

"I tried to think of one."

I looked up. "You did?"

"Ah yes. In Tokyo, places where you could have no questions."

"Where I could have no questions—to ask you?"

"To answer to others."

"Oh." Slowly a picture began to dawn.

"In another hotel are many questions. You perhaps write papers with information?"

"You mean, like—fill out forms."

"Forms." She nodded.

"You picked this place because it's anonymous!"

"At the Prince Hotels you must tell your name," she agreed.

"Of course!" I sat back. "Or give them a fake one," I added, enthralled.

"A fake one?"

"Yeah. You know. One that's not really your own."

"Is this possible?" she looked puzzled.

"Ah—no, never mind." She glanced at me. "So this is probably one of the few places in the whole city where nobody expects an ID. *That's* why you brought me here."

"It is perhaps simple for some corporations to check all hotel registrations with computers?"

I stared. "Jesus."

She cocked her head.

"You're brilliant," I said in wonder.

"Ah, no, no." She turned away, laughing mortified, holding her palm up as if a barrier.

"Without a base I can't hide out."

"Yes."

"No one will trace one horny American tourist. No way. There's probably hundreds of us." My mind was racing.

"If you like food or drink we can call."

"Maybe in a little while. First, tell me a couple of things."

She looked down at the purse on her knees. She bent and placed it on the floor. Her lids lay so smooth I could scarcely see the eye curve.

"What will happen when your father gets home from Osaka?"

For a second she didn't respond. Then, very slightly, she shook her head.

"Okay." Maybe she honestly doesn't know, I thought. Since this is without precedent. Or maybe she knows exactly. "So how long can I hole up in here?"

"Hole up—"

"How long can I stay?"

"The rooms are usually rented for two hours."

"Rats. That won't work."

"Also for the night. I told the—desk keeper? pay person?—that we would take the full night and tomorrow morning, maybe two more."

"Whoa. Man. He must think we're pretty rambunctious."

She looked uncomprehending. "It is a lady."

"Oh." I smiled. Suddenly I felt like laughing out loud. But I would have ripped out my tongue rather than embarrass her. And a more serious problem lay waiting. "There's something I need to find out."

"Okay."

"Well." I looked at her. "It means snitching on your father."

"Ah, so?"

"Yes."

"Yes, okay," she said.

Studying her immaculate face, serene and unreadable as a porcelain cup, I leaned forward.

"Never mind." How could I even consider? Even in distraction? "Forget it. It doesn't matter."

"Not matter?"

"Hell, you wouldn't even know what snitch is."

"Oh yes. I know."

"You do?"

"It's in movies." Her expression cooled slightly.

"Oh. Yeah, right." *Dunce,* I thought. *Moron—idiot, Taylor.* The shame mounted. "Well, anyhow." In chagrin I bent over and picked at my shoelace.

"You wish to find out something?"

"Really, I guess I just need to think. Figure some moves. Pull some facts together. See, I've left everybody—I'd hidden this money . . ."

"Perhaps you will tell me?"

"I think probably it'll be better—" I was mumbling now, aware of her sitting so close. Her perfume wove the air: roses, lavender, sandalwood. She smelled female. "It'd be better if you don't plunge any deeper. Than you already are. I mean, I'd just as soon not get you in trouble."

"Oh, yes. I understand."

"Yeah." Alternatives would show up, I thought desperately. They'd have to.

"I already am," she agreed.

"What?"

"In trouble." Then she raised her hand. She ran it down my throat. She slipped inside my shirt. She stroked my chest, the ribbed wall, my nipples, she slid her fingers through the hair. They paused. She closed her eyes.

"YOU'RE SO BEAUTIFUL," I murmured.

Drowsily she peered up and smiled.

The deep crimson saturated the gloom like a breathable substance. Outside the tiny window hatch dusk was falling. An hour or so earlier she'd reached over to the console and switched off the lights. Now I lay looking into the ceiling, watching our reflections fracture in the gilt-shot glass, our limbs ripple through those murky quadrants. We looked pale against black, pale as underwater creatures on the Yucatán seabed: shell, rubbed coral, bone.

"You are awake."

"Oh yeah. Absolutely."

"Tell me, please." She turned over. "Are women here very different from American women?"

"You mean, are you very different?"

I swiveled on the pillow. She inspected me again, gravely.

"Yes," I whispered. "Very different." I kissed her, combed my fingers through her hair.

"How are the ways?"

Lips, eyes, voice. Scent. Neck. The contained walk, the childish grace, the intelligence, mystery.

"You're unlike anyone in the world."

"From Japanese?"

"Anyone."

She shook her head, forearm sliding up my chest. She brushed her wrist lightly against the fur, back, forth.

"I'm only different inside," she whispered.

"What do you mean?"

But she smoothed her palm over my bicep, then rested the wrist and wouldn't answer.

"Do I seem very different to you? From Japanese men?"

"Oh yes!"

"In what ways?"

"You're hairy."

I stared. She started laughing. Her eyes half closed. I could see their gleam. "Men in Tokyo aren't hairy. Young men often remove the hair of their bodies."

"You mean, like shaving their *legs?*"

"With wax. Or—lotion? In the salon."

"You're kidding." I held her hand, unfurling the tapered white fingers one by one. "Why?"

"It's fashion. Girls like it better."

"So what am I? A big hairy barbarian?"

"Ah, yes." She laughed harder.

"You mean it! Is that how you saw me from the first, out at the airport?"

She nodded, giggling, mashing her face into my shoulder. "You are the giant of hair," she said. "Barbarian!"

I pushed her head up. "Now listen!" I said. "Now listen here—" Slowly, softly I kissed her mouth.

"ALL MEN ARE hairy in America, is that so?" she said a little later, this time with a more academic inflection.

"Not really. I guess some." I yawned. "Depends on the genes."

"In Western movies it's so, isn't it?"

"You watch a lot of those, huh? Wyatt Earp? Billy the Kid?"

She shook her head. "When I go to Narita to meet the Americans I've noticed sometimes how the men look."

Pushing myself up on one elbow, I squinted. "Is that so?" She smiled. "Do we all look like barbarians?"

"You the most. Only you." With her fingertip she flicked the tuft curled just below my clavicle. "In Dallas, Texas, do you carry guns?"

"Good grief. What do you think we—" Then I halted. It struck me that

it wasn't an outlandish question. No doubt she watched the news. A hot
breeze blew through my mind, tinted with asphalt and the false scent of
rain. Sirens erupted down the street; my hand closed around Jorris's
throat, the police arrived, the shot blasted out. The weight of the metal, the
waistband of my tights popping back, when I pulled forth the muzzle to
point directly at my father.

"Yeah. Some people carry guns. Sometimes I've carried a gun," I said
and looked away. The rush of the last few months suddenly reeled through
my head thick as dizziness, those bright, sharp actions.

"Have you seen a person shot?"

"Yes." I thought of that red wing flying, feathering out across Jorris's
porch. Jesus on the boards. The crater opening to pour molten blood.

"You have shot one?"

"What?" I swallowed. "Yes."

"And you killed a person?"

"Yes."

I lay, still seeing the shotgun flower fire as I gripped it, Jesus's thigh
fragmenting, Jesus foundering, the blood corsage imprinting my chest as
I stood at the border station. At first the shock of my admission almost
went unnoticed. I closed my eyes. I opened them. The seismic rumble
started faintly deep inside my body, like stone boiling within the earth's
core.

"When did he die?"

"What?"

"The person whom you shot with the gun?"

"Die? He didn't die. Thank God."

A cloud passed over her face. She stared.

"What made you think he did?"

"You have said you killed a person."

"I have said—" The bed went silent.

"Your answer. You said you killed a person."

The singing droned from the stereo speaker. My heart pounded. The hammering swelled, faster, harder, deafening me to all but itself. The rumble broke.

"I have. I have killed a person."

"Was it a man?"

"Yes. It was a man," I whispered. I couldn't breathe. It was strange—the loosening in my chest, heart bursting and slowing, brainpan emptying, the hollowed flue of throat through which air could not flood in and out, breath utterly impossible. "Not with a gun."

"You killed him another way?"

"Yes."

"Your hands?"

"A knife." I gasped. "My hands."

Her eyes went wide.

"He was harming my friend. He'd stabbed him. He was going to kill me." She nodded.

"My God." I closed my eyes. A great gust deflated my chest; I drew one back in, deep, filling myself as I hadn't been filled for so long, letting go at last the thing that had crouched there, the thing I'd tried to tell Teresa-Maria, wanted to tell my father, couldn't tell Mother: the dark churn of river water, the corpse under the buzzard's beak, the slime in the weeds.

"In every country sometimes this happens, I think," she said, as if confirming something. "But especially America."

"I don't know."

"Yes. Like Anjiro." Then she climbed on top of my body and spread herself across it full length, silk ironing against grain, globe filling dent, cup sliding over boss, holding me into her consolation, kisses penetrating even that black pain; she thrust her hand down through the pain to reach me and pull me out, and she did this without asking for another single detail, and so it wasn't until much later that I realized how little she'd been surprised.

HOURS LATER WE lay listening to the fountain trickle in the darkness. The bedside console glowed phosphorescent against its knobs. Johnny Mathis had long ago given the floor to Frank Sinatra, who was ineluctably singing "Strangers in the Night."

"Ayako," I whispered.

"Hai." She was nearly dreaming.

"There are some papers I have to get from your father's headquarters."

"Some papers?"

I didn't want to tell her. I realized as soon as I said it. Our complicity of the flesh, this sweet, relieved amazement, would be corrupted by my slightest intention, which was the last thing in the world I desired.

Yet I had to go on from here. Where could I do so? Without abandoning my purpose?

"I'll say to you now. Before we spend any more time together." Because I had fallen in love. In the instant of thinking, I knew it. The confession couldn't be betrayed. That was what it meant.

Love.

The air wove in and out of sound, in and out of our slippery sheets, her satin pores, her limbs, my lungs.

"For me to accomplish what I've come to Japan for, I have to defeat your father's plans."

"Yes?" she said, her voice soft and broken with sleep.

"I have to rob him," I said.

She said nothing.

"You should know. So that you can get out. Warn him or whatever you need to do. I'm not deceiving you. And I don't want you thinking your loyalty's compromised because of me." I breathed out and lay still.

"You will rob him of what, please?" she asked.

"Some papers he's holding. On my friends, the people out at Minamoto Mansions. Their employment contracts."

"You are a robber?"

"Yes." I breathed in. "I'm a cat burglar."

"For your father?"

"For all of us."

"You have promised this robbery?"

"Yes."

"And you keep your promises?"

"Yes. I do. If humanly possible, I do. Of course." There, I thought. I've done it.

"My mother died when I was very little," she said.

I paused. "I'm sorry," I said. *That's why the lady is a tramp,* Frank intoned in the distance.

"Anjiro was oldest, ten years older than I. When I was three years old came my sister, Seiko. Then when I was five years old, when my mother was giving birth to another boy baby—" She swallowed. "It killed her."

I didn't know what to say. Her head stirred against my arm. This was her truth. This was her confession to me, the wound, the only tradecloth she could offer from her innocent life. I kissed her hair.

"Since her death my father has called me to pay back her giri."

"What do you mean?"

She bit her lip. "You understand giri?"

"Not really."

"My mother wore an *on* before she died. She owed a great debt to my father and his family."

"Why?"

"Because the boy baby was her lover's child."

The fountain burbled, unfailing as a pool at a river's edge. *My kind of town, Chicago is my kind of town,* Frank sang through the speaker.

"If people had known of my mother's lover, then my father would badly lose face. It was a secret. My father claimed the baby as his child. He gave my mother his word that he would keep the baby safe when it got born. But his mercy and generosity made her wear an *on*."

I closed my mouth, opened it. "How about the lover?"

"He was a *sumo-tori*."

"Sumo." She nodded. "You mean—a *wrestler*?"

"Yes," she said. "Ushi-zuki was a champion who trained in a *beya* owned by my father's keiretsu. Minamoto Television shows the tournaments." She paused. I felt her chin dig into my shoulder. "My father felt vanity at Ushi-zuki's fame. He . . . took it personally."

"I'm not sure I understand."

She frowned. "As daimyo my father hadn't given special attention before for any other wrestler. This goes against *jicho*."

"It's unprofessional, you mean? To take such a personal interest?" I hazarded.

"Inappropriate," she said with decision. She pondered, closing her eyes. "But my father was proud that such a winner came from his beya. So, when my father told my mother to accompany him to the autumn Tokyo tournament and Ushi-zuki took the top trophy, a company president introduced them."

"Then what happened?"

"Then, secret meetings. The pregnancy came. The baby got born. My mother killed. Too much blood. But the baby's true nature was seen before she died."

"His true nature."

She ungrooved her chin and burrowed under my armpit, burying her face in the pillow.

"What nature?" I asked.

When she didn't answer, I said, "Ayako?"

"My father named him Ushi-oni," she whispered, her voice muffled by black satin.

I ROLLED OVER onto my side. She stayed stretched facedown, eyes concealed from my sight. Now it had grown too dark to discern our bodies adrift, floating through those fathoms above. "Did the baby die too?"

She shook her head. The room expanded in the dark. "He had no human mind, no right body. The human parts were broken. Like an animal."

"What do you mean, broken?"

But she merely nudged more deeply into the bed, shivering.

"Your father couldn't live with that? As part of his promise?"

She raised her forehead so that I could see her eyes. "So much shame," she whispered.

Then she began to weep. I lay stroking her shoulder blades, wiping her tears with the slick sheet, imagining that dying woman: her grief, her hopelessness as they held up the baby for her to see in the last glimpse of light. The broken child. As my mother had once seen me.

Was this why she was here?

"Ayako. Tell me. Why were you sent to the airport with Matsudo to fetch us? Why were you serving sake? Like the geisha? In front of his employees?"

The sheet slipped from my fingers. I let it. Her face stared at me, twisted in pain, no longer immaculate. Her eyes burned.

"I wear an *on*," she whispered.

"Is that how *on*s get paid?"

"When Anjiro was killed, my father couldn't forgive that the only son left was the one my mother gave, to carry his name." Her hoarse voice paused. "My father is old-fashioned. Traditional. Not like other rich fathers. He fought in the war. *Bushido*. After his wound healed he was head officer of a prison camp for Americans and Australians. I wear the *on* for my mother, for the promise he made before she died. It's my duty to repay what can never be repaid. Not one-tenth of one ten-thousandth."

I took her. I held her between my hands, both shoulders. I stared into the eyes, that blaze of humiliation.

AFTER A MOMENT she spoke. "One person knew," she said.

"My mother had a friend," she said. "An architect. He came from South America, Buenos Aires, and lived in Japan many years. When he started working for my father, drawing buildings for the Minamoto companies, he became my mother's only friend. She told him of her lover. It was in his house that she met secretly with Ushi-zuki."

"She trusted him? Even though he wasn't Japanese?"

"Because he was not Japanese."

"Ah."

"During his career time he designed many of the official Minamoto buildings. He is very famous. My father made him sign an exclusive contract. There is one place in the mountains north of Kyoto that my father ordered him to build when I was a small child. A special office. This place had to be complicated, Japanese style outside, Western style inside, with many little rooms and offices, very different from open-room Japanese offices. Pieces of the building go under the ground."

"What was it for?"

"For private working. Keeping important things. Records. Papers."

Slowly I asked, "Why do you mention this place?"

"It's secret. Outside Kyoto, beyond Haradani." She paused. "A demon lives inside it."

"A demon?"

"A monster," she whispered.

"Some kind of guard? An electronic device, maybe? A burglar trap?"

She shook her head. "My father has told me."

"It sounds like some fairy tale."

She shook her head again slowly. But in the moment of revelation I didn't care. Now it was so obvious. What detail, what strand connected to his personal vendetta would he have stored to be found in that august corporate pile opposite the emperor's own garden? "That's where he keeps the contracts, isn't it?"

Her eyes gleamed in the half-light.

A TARNISHED SKY hung over the streets. Every few seconds we seemed to turn, slithering through lanes and courtyards narrower than a parking space. The patchwork of gardens and bonsai front entries, boulevards and dress shops, banks, and bakeries all looked exactly alike, knitted together by the tangled roads. A person could wander among these stones, bricks, power lines, and never find his way out.

"Meguro-ku," she said as we passed a two-story building forked by train tracks. "Here is Yutenji Station." She smoothed a stray lock behind her ear. At this hour people flowed by, office commuters and students on their way to the grind.

"Is his place close?"

"Yes, very close." Steering between a bicyclist and a plant nursery, she nudged the car down an alley. We passed a little restaurant with a round red paper lantern above the door. Then a smell teasing through a steel-grilled window woke me up. Bacon. Frying bacon.

"Here is his house." She swung the Mercedes into the tiny driveway.

Before us sat a small cement bunker. Red tiles covered the gable. Two palm trees bracketed the sides. A flight of pink granite steps ascended to a wood-paneled door, for all the world like something out of Spain.

An old man opened the door.

"Diego-san, *watashi desu.*"

"Ayako." He blinked at the sunlight beside her head. "Ayacita," fixing his gaze in that spot even as she bowed low. *"Ohayo goza-i-mas."*

"Buenos días." She reached out, affectionately laying her hand on his. He patted it without sending one single glance my way.

"Mi amada, como estás?"

"I am well, thank you. And you?"

"Quite well. It is still hot. I enjoy the heat." His smile flexed. "I have not seen you since the spring."

"Sumi ma sen, Diego-san."

"De nada." He shrugged without reproach, then once more tilted the one-ended smile. "Please come in." He gestured to the dark *genkan.*

"Diego-san, I wish to introduce to you a friend."

"Ah yes. The reason we are speaking English." His nose lifted. His face pivoted in a delicate quest. "This gentleman?"

"Yes, Diego-san. This is Taylor Deeds, from America."

He squinted in my direction against the sun. "How do you do?"

"Fine, thanks. I'm glad to meet you, sir." I held out my hand. His own hesitated. Then he proffered it but barely halfway, leaving it to me to come forward, grip the thin armature.

"You are from the Southern states, perhaps?"

"Yes. I am, in fact."

He nodded solemnly. "You may imagine it is your accent that tells me. I won't allow you to remain deceived. I lived in New Orleans—it is true, many years ago. But Ayako must have found you in Minamoto Mansions."

"That's true."

"Otherwise she wouldn't bring you to me." With finality he turned and walked back through the genkan. His dapper black jacket and waistcoat melted on the darkness, then struck some more distant illumination as he placed one hand against the wall to steady himself, the flesh lit from within like an El Greco grandee's. "Please come this way. I was about to eat breakfast."

"We don't want to interrupt," I said, but he merely waved dismissively.

"I digest only dishes from my native place." He led us through a damp hallway into a dining room with a long, high window. Below it in one corner stood a round table set with two placemats. "Latin confections. Manioca, which I must import. Tocino con pico de gallo y pappas fritas. It's an indulgence of sentiment which my stomach demands."

"I picked up the tocino down the street," I said.

"Please, I hope you will join me in tasting some. Ayako learned to enjoy Spanish cuisine with me while still in high school. Ignacio!" he called out. "Ayako-san esta aquí. Por favor, cocinar algo mas tocino por nuestra huesped."

"Sí, Papa," a boy's voice called from another room.

"Ignacio is a fervent cook, but he often burns breakfast," said the father. Groping around, he found the tallest chairback. His palm caressed it for a moment. "You have escaped from the vallado?"

"With Ayako's help."

"Of course. It would be the only way. When I designed it for her father I performed my work conscientiously." Maneuvering around the chair, he lowered himself down. For the first time I realized he wasn't quite as old as he'd seemed—maybe fifty-five. "Please, be seated."

"Thanks." I pulled out two of the other chairs.

"Before we discuss more I wish to request a favor. Mr.—Deeds, is your name? Did I apprehend correctly?"

"Yes, sir. Taylor Deeds."

"Ah." He nodded, propped elbows on the tabletop, folded his hands together, and rested his chin while perusing some invisible locus near the door. "Tell me, do you happen to observe that painting?"

I scanned the gray walls. "Which one?" Three paintings in gilded frames hung opposite the table in the room's other end. Two were portraits of a man and a woman in nineteenth-century clothes flanking the door; the third was sequestered on the far wall by itself, just beyond the sun's rays. Jewel colors burned from a forest darkness.

"Have you seen her?"

"Yes."

"Please. If you would not object. Describe what you find. Paint her for me. And her setting."

Ayako glanced at me.

I pushed back my chair. "Well. Hm."

He waited. The expression on his face was calm and empty, without expectation.

"From here I see a nude blond woman lying beside a pool in the woods."

"Ah." He sighed. "I see." He closed his eyes, sealed his lips.

"That's roughly." I stood up and walked closer, peering. "I can go into a little more detail."

His lips parted. "Yes?"

"A woman is lounging above some water. Her skin is pale pink. Translucent. She's lying there, round, smooth, like a seashell. Thin-walled. Glowing when you hold her up to the light." I paused.

"She's very—feminine. Her breasts are small but full. They look like the pointed end of a peach. She's kind of an armful. Solid. Early twenties, maybe. Very blue eyes, glass-clear. Thin gold eyebrows. Gold hair is stream-ing from around her forehead into curls and waves halfway down her side. It drapes her plump shoulders like a cape. Her lips are curving in a faint smile. Gold bangle bracelets with blue stones—sapphires, I guess—ring both arms above her elbows. They shine very rich and bright against her skin, stressing her nakedness, stressing the lemon yellow hair. Her skin is like camellia petals. The artist has dappled red shadows in the crevices of her body—underarms, navel, the little nook between her thighs"—now I was going for broke—"so, judging from that and the gloomy forest, the time must be evening, just on sunset. She's wearing a string of red beads. Coral. They drape across one nipple." Which was erect.

Diego sighed, eyes closed.

"No, uh, pubic hair. Just the mound, smooth. The pool reflects just a little pink stain. Beyond that it catches the forest, the greenish sky and black trees. You get the feeling there's something hiding deep inside that forest—like a jungle world of life no human has penetrated. Or hiding in the pool. She's completely at home. A mirror is lying on the moss next to her elbow. Carved black wood, ebony. It shows the side of her face, and—wait—" I bent forward, squinting closely in surprise "—another face, very tiny. Right beside hers. Peeking from behind her hair. But it's at just the wrong angle so that we only see its reflection, we can't see the original—person."

"Is it a person?" asked Diego quietly.

"No. It's a child's face, sort of pink and white and rosy, like a cupid's. But his expression isn't Cupid's."

"What is he then?"

"It's a devil." I straightened up.

"Ah!" Then, "Why do you say that?"

"It's cunning. Wicked. Grinning."

He nodded, eyes still closed. His features had relaxed their discipline. "And do you find her beautiful?"

"Oh, yes. She's beautiful."

"Thank you."

I returned to the table and sat down. "Who painted her?"

"A pupil of Titian's. A young Dutchman, strangely enough, who traveled far to study. He did not achieve fame. He didn't even produce many pictures. His name remains obscure. Only this one little image survives that I know of. This one little curious masterpiece. Venus. So pleasant and tranquilo, so ominous. Our treasure. For three hundred years she has been in my family, first in Barcelona, then to Argentina when we immigrated. Now here." He opened his eyes and waved toward the silent room. I realized all had fallen still, the faint clatter of pots and pans from the kitchen had died. "The one circumstance that has made my blindness most difficult to bear is not the fact that I can no longer work. Design buildings. Draw the blueprints for the office towers and department stores and suburb prisons of Minamoto. But that I can no longer see her clear blue eyes, like glass," he nodded. "The young woman lying by the secret pond. Except through the eyes of my rare visitors. My son's occasional friends, who for the most part cannot give me the singularity of their vision, the dark hearth flaring for one moment into light. Which makes me see her in an entirely new way. For the first time. The unexpected gift of this affliction."

After a pause I said, "I hope I helped."

"You paint a different painting. The shell. The jungle with secret life." He tapped his forehead above the blind eyes. "Now I add yours to my collection. Muchas gracias."

"De nada."

He smiled that solemn flexure. "Tell me. What are your intentions?"

"Desayuno, Papa," said the boy, coming in through the hallway door with a platter in each hand.

"Ignacio, muy bien."

Setting the steaming platters down in the middle of the table, Ignacio moved back. "I'll bring the *café*."

"Thank you. You heard the painting Mr. Deeds has made? The seashell glowing in the moss?"

"Sí." He looked about sixteen. He was wearing the uniform I'd seen children wearing outside the enclave, a white shirt, navy pants, and a navy sailor's jacket left unbuttoned. He glanced shyly at me, then at Ayako. *"Ohayo."*

"Ohayo goza-i-mas," she said.

"Uno momento." He rushed out. Returning with the coffeepot and some extra utensils, he arranged them quickly, eagerly, on the table, sliding the already-set second placemat in front of Ayako. Then he headed for the door.

"Won't you join us?" asked Diego.

"I don't have time. I will be late to school if I miss the next train." His accent was an odd mixture of Spanish vowels and an elided Japanese *r*. "Today is a test."

"In that case, go, go. Come first." He held out his arm. Ignacio ducked in, hugged his father, hastily pulled away. "Adiós," said Diego airily. "Estudio un poco."

"Hasta la noche. Adiós, Ayako-san. Good-bye, Mr. Deeds."

"Good-bye," I said. Mr. Deeds. Good grief.

"He wants to go to college in America," said Diego as we heard the front door slam. "New York." He shook his head, smiling.

"Sounds okay."

"It is not possible."

"Why not?"

"There are problems involved in our leaving Japan. Just at this moment," he said. The blue eyes gazed into their nighttime middle distance.

"You mean Minamoto won't let you."

"How do you say this, Mr. Deeds?" The platters on the table steamed fragrantly between us: the bacon, fried potatoes, the peppers and tomatoes and bread.

"Well, sir. Considering how much you know."

"Ayako has told you of—more than the vallado? Minamoto Mansions?"

"Yes."

He ruminated. Ayako reached for the pot and poured two cups of coffee. Her eyes remained primly down on the food.

"Has she mentioned locations to you of any kind?"

"Some mountains north of Kyoto. Haradani?" I said.

"Ah." Air expelled from him. He sat very erect, one hand fingering the cup Ayako placed before him.

"You asked my intentions. I'll tell you. I intend to liberate some pieces of paper from a stronghold in Haradani."

"Papers."

"Some documents I don't think are just."

"I comprehend." He blinked, then raised the cup to his lips and drank.

"Are you equipped for such a task, by chance?" he asked.

"I think so. Partly. I mean, you can figure out the reason we're here."

He nodded, took another sip, set the cup down.

"I can get so far. I have a few skills. But I need some directions. Advice," I said.

"Ayako, you are asking this of me?"

"Yes, Diego-san." Her voice was low.

"It is what you wish? To help this man. Taylor Deeds."

"Yes."

He sighed, carefully pushing his cup and saucer back. "Mi amada."

"Perhaps you yourself know of a document stored in the building I've mentioned that you'd like dealt with somehow," I suggested.

"Ah, Mr. Deeds." He picked up his fork, balancing it between his fingers. "We each have our tyrannies. Into which we have entered. With which we have agreed to comply at different times. Is that not so?" Reaching for the bacon platter, he drew it near.

"Depends on your motive for compliance."

"Ito Minamoto was once a good employer. He hired me to imagine his buildings and spared no expense in their execution. This is a rare pleasure for an architect anywhere in the world."

"I'm sure it must be."

"When I contracted glaucoma and went blind he assured that my son and I were properly cared for. For a price, of course. He is not nostalgic."

"Your silence." I sipped the coffee.

He made a moue of distaste. "That sounds quite melodramatic."

"Please, Diego-san—will you help us?" murmured Ayako.

"But what would you expect me to do?"

"Give me the directions," I replied. "Then, show me whatever codes there are, tricks, passages, to break into the stronghold and find what I need."

He smiled. "Is this all?"

"I guess."

"Are you taking him there, Ayako? Surely not."

"It's good for me to stay here in Tokyo," she said, which was the first I'd heard of it.

"He will go alone through Japan."

Neither of us answered.

"Of course you speak no words of the language."

"That's about right."

"Is there a plan you can explain to guide him to reach Kyoto and Haradani, Diego-san?" asked Ayako politely.

"If you mean, so that he may find his way through Tokyo, then yes. Naturally." He shrugged.

"What?" I asked.

"Buy a map."

"A—" I sat back.

"A copy of the *Tokyo Metropolitan Atlas*. It includes all the train and sub-way stations, their routes, the station for the *shinkansen,* the route to Kyoto. It is translated also into English. Ayako, mi muchacha preciosa, you have never ridden the subway in your life. It wouldn't have occurred to you. So privileged, always driven by car." He smiled fondly. "Even when she would come to visit me in early high school her driver would bring her."

"A map! Of course!" I said.

"I have one I will give you. You are young, no doubt your travel experience is limited. These maps are suppressed near the vallado, you may be sure. By the way, you must also acquire a schedule for the shinkansen—the bullet train. It departs every twenty minutes if memory serves. And Ayako, give him sufficient money. You have money, Mr. Deeds?"

"Only back at Minamoto Mansions. One hundred million yen sewn into the lining of my duffle bag."

"Perhaps no longer. You will need a great deal. For safety's sake."

"Money is okay," said Ayako, also sitting forward now.

"So—map, schedule, money. The particular room you seek lies deep under the ground. You should also take a lantern. Flashlight? Now I will show you the sole surviving blueprint to the redoubt beyond Haradani. Supposedly destroyed. No one knows it exists but you. Like the Dutch pupil of Titian's, mi obra maestra." He stood up. "My masterpiece."

AT NOON WE stood in the dusky genkan once more, climbing into our shoes. "What will you do once you have freed you both? Destroyed contracts?" he asked.

"Then I'll go back to Minamoto Mansions, get everybody out, fetch Ayako, and take her home."

"Ah." The blue eyes looked as glassy as Venus's in the painting. "Out of Japan."

I paused, savoring the heft on my tongue. "I'm going to marry her."

He declined his head gravely. "So I assumed. Which is of course one reason I am helping you."

Ayako stared. Her mouth parted. I reached out and took her arm.

"You know the risk? The full consequence of these actions?"

"I think so."

"And what is required to free her." His hand stole over hers, gripping it tightly. The knuckles whitened.

"Oh. One other thing. You haven't told me about the demon."

"The demon?" He frowned slightly. His eyebrows rose. "But I can tell you nothing about the demon. It is of course what you will face yourself."

"Well, I've promised. Whatever it is. Whatever it takes, I'll do it."

"I can believe that you will do so. But this is another culture. It would serve well not to forget."

"Listen. Once we're out of here, my father could do something for you. Or for Ignacio. Both. Or—whatever you want."

"I'm sure he could, Mr. Deeds. If you are successful." Smiling, he shook his blind head. "Thank you."

"You could get out. Start over." There was in the fatality about this cement house socketed tightly into its real estate an aura that made me feel paralytic, as if no occupant would ever again leave. Like the house of Ronnie Dean Jordan. "Would you like me to at least tear up your contract?"

"If you achieve your quest? Penetrate Haradani? And identify the ancient Japanese calligraphic inscriptions naming my name?"

"Yes."

His smile persisted. He turned toward Ayako. "Sayonara, mi preciosa. I remember your face." He lifted his hand to touch it.

"Good-bye, Diego-san." She was crying. Silent, stealthy tears spilled from her eyes. But her face showed no expression at all. His hand dropped without having discovered moisture.

Courtly, he turned back to me.

"Good luck, Mr. Deeds."

"I'll find it," I persisted. "I won't leave Haradani without it."

Gently he shook his head "no" once more. "We are all, at some time or other, the instruments of betrayal."

18

Her eyes stayed with me long after I caught the train at Naka-meguro Station.

No one could have told at just a glance that they were filled with tears. *Trust me,* I'd asked her. *Don't worry.* Her discretion was perfect until the last moment; outside the Mercedes no public touch passed between us, except one.

Opposite me an elderly woman in a neat voile blouse, pseudolinen trousers, and high heels sat sedately reading a pamphlet, her hair shining blue like an artificial carnation, sumptuous among the black heads all around. Beside her on the velvet bench, people jounced along stark upright with their eyes closed in sleep. Two schoolboys hung on to the ringed straps in the car's aisle, shirttails flapping, wisecracking over the panty-clad heroine of an obscene comic book. Two seats to my left a young pregnant woman in a pink dress with a lace collar, short white socks, and tennis shoes smiled lovingly down at a bucket of Kentucky Fried Chicken. The air smelled airless. Not one stroke of graffiti marred the train's enamel. Not a single candy wrapper littered the floor.

Poring over the arteries and ganglia veining the atlas's paper land, I tried to memorize each stop—Shibuya, Meiji-jingumae, Harajuku—tracking the ballpoint she'd used to stitch them together before she demonstrated how to buy tickets from the machine. Hidden in my rear pants pocket was the address of the inn where she'd told me to stay in Kyoto. The money lay wadded against my passport. Change jingled in the other pocket. The blueprint, folded small, I'd stuffed down my underwear, right above the tool kit on its thigh strap. Scrawled inside my wrist was the number I would phone when I'd finished. Telling her to meet me. Printed across that, her lipstick kiss.

I couldn't afford to be afraid.

At Shinjuku Station I straggled up steps and down rabbit holes, past glass sandwich counters and magazine stalls selling juice and beer and hankies and neckties, tracking the red circle of my line to the right platform just in time to feel the next train whoosh to a halt. The Marunouchi Line.

So far I hadn't even seen a policeman. Now the paranoia began to grow; I stood a foot taller than everyone else, swaying in the yellow-white light of the packed car. Who knew what eyes Minamoto had hired? Corporate cops? Yakuza? I wasn't in a gray Ford Escort any longer. These people all looked so genetically harmless, so kin to each other—reading, resting, dreaming stoically through the miles, wondering how such a gigantic beefy bumpkin had gotten here. Good question. Sweat broke out, cladding my skin with chill. *They must smell me,* I thought. No deodorant. The metal ring slipped in my hand. The train stopped too often, I couldn't keep up. My mouth dried. My teeth felt like cotton. By the time the roman letters TOKYO appeared through the window I was choking with anxiety and relief.

WE WERE LEAVING the deep city behind. Now factories bulked outside the windows, piles of concrete flung up against that late summer sky, interspersed with still more convoluted streets and warehouses and motorcycles sliding through the heavy industry. Somewhere out there lay Tokyo Bay, which Steve Shaver had said was mostly garbage. Seagulls swatted against the updrafts. I sagged back into the seat, so tired I could hardly think. The effort of crawling my way through the maze of Tokyo Station had been the most draining yet, collapsing me into this fast clean car so that I could sit and mindlessly relive what it had taken to get here: ticket, thirteen thousand yen; pay at the window; what window? machine—no, window; he doesn't understand English; "Shinkansen, Kyoto, please"; no reserved seat; two tickets; no, one ticket in two paper strips; tracks that way—no, downstairs; no, up steps and through double tunnels, then downstairs; hurry, that policeman's looking; wrong turn, wrong tunnel, run back past those shops selling wooden lunchboxes; he's watching, you stick out like a sore thumb, don't stop, no questions; he's still watching, go the other way, run, run past the beer vending machines, past the porno machines; the next tunnel to the gate; wrong platform, which is it? the woman selling shoe polish, does she know? grinning, grinning, jabbering, pointing—that way! Kyoto that way! *Hai, hai,* the other track, this platform, yes! Ticket? Christ, the two tickets? doors about to close, thirty seconds more, the clock, the clock says, here's the ticket. Get in.

The train started moving just like that. Easing out of the station, picking up speed, rushing faster, but so quietly you could barely tell.

A man in a business suit walked down the car. Lifting his bag above the rack to stow it, he paused, eyed the seat next to mine, refolded the bag into his arms, and walked on. The man one seat ahead lit a cigarette.

A female robot crooned through a loudspeaker, welcoming in Japanese. I caught the name Yokohama. Soon an apron of water appeared through the tinted window, a sea blue and silver-green, glittering. We passed docks. Factories. Houses. The woman across the aisle flipped down her tray table. Her little boy banged a toy. Air-conditioning cooled the car. I fell asleep.

When I woke up it was from a braid of dreams. Throughout them Ayako had spoken, sometimes explaining, sometimes begging a favor. One time I was in the black tunnel fumbling for the doorknob. Something was waiting on the other side. A horror lurked there, listening, holding its breath; it would gnaw and crunch my bones. "The demon," whispered

Ayako. "I'll demon you!" I roared. Every nerve sprang ready; he was coming from behind, slashing his teeth, I could feel his breath hot on my ankle, full of germs and disease. Rabid. The loudspeaker caroled softly. I woke up. We were in the country. Tilled gardens, terraced fields, slopes thick with forests spread outside, riverbanks cut sharp and shaded with bushes, mountains jagged-spined in the far distance of the blue air.

WHEN WE'D CLIMBED into the Mercedes outside Diego's house, I'd reached over and touched her cheek. "I want to take you home."

The car door chunked closed. She stared at the window. "To USA?"

"Yes."

"What would we do?"

"Get married."

My heart jumped, *blam,* as I said it again. This time to her alone, in private. On the one hand I could hardly believe I'd stated such a crazy thing out loud and on the other I felt absolutely sure. Looking at the black hair fanned on her neck, hearing her voice, feeling the sweet sipping consolation, the tact, the poultice to suck up all pain, end it forever, that certitude became the stillness in the crumbling, twirling world.

"You don't have to stay here any longer. I won't have you being a slave to this notion of your father's. The *giri.* This *on.*"

"Ah yes." Her eyes cast down.

"I love you."

At last she turned and looked. Her lips parted. Her eyes were shining. Seeing them I reached over and buoyed her across the seat over the console straight into my lap, crushed her into my arms because she was never going to leave them, I would never let her go, I planned to clasp her there, both of us locked in this perfect spin, this perfect spin at last, the clean spin I'd waited for through all my life of spinning and falling hard, the gravity's release that throws you high instead. I crushed our lips together. Her tongue darted.

She smelled like the Wise Men's gifts to Jesus.

"Marry me," I whispered.

"Yes, okay."

"Oh God." Her body fit against my chest.

"You will take me to Texas when you go?"

"How could I leave you? I'll never leave you. Anywhere," I whispered. "Never."

"Your father will welcome me?" Her eyes half closed. She tipped her face back, as if drugged, or falling asleep, or wary.

"Sure."

She sighed. I studied her features, tracing their soft planes. "The daughter of his enemy."

I rubbed my forehead against her upturned throat. "Are you kidding? He'll probably throw a party and name you queen. You'll have saved my life. Risked everything you have to get us out safe."

"Safe." She closed her eyes. Her lips pressed tight. I saw her throat convulse.

"Look—don't worry about the Texas end. I promise. I give you my word."

"Your promise?"

"Ayako, I'll do anything to make you happy."

FOR THE NEXT hour I watched as towns and rice paddies flew by. Houses clustered in the valley clefts. Sometimes they would compose a village. Long shaven rows of some crop shone in the sun like bolsters on a bed. The hills themselves rose up in smooth green loaves of earth, or picketed with woods. A girl pushed a sandwich cart; I bought a can of green tea. Sounds fell muffled, as if I wore earplugs or was going deaf. I watched the woman across the aisle probe a rice mound with chopsticks. She took the lid off a wooden lunchbox, fished out a tempura prawn, and presented it to her son. After the tea I scrounged the paper out of my rear pocket. Ayako had printed her roman letters carefully, stroke by stroke, inscribing below their Japanese kanji. Practicing over and over I mouthed the words she'd written: *"Shimogawaracho, Higashiyama deska."*

"Shimogawaracho, Higashiyama. Arigato."

He'll never think of looking in this place.

Why is that, Ayako? Why not?

Meticulously she'd narrowed her eyes, biting her lip, pressing the pen point neatly against the paper.

THE NEXT THING I knew we were pulling into a city.

LATE AFTERNOON LIGHT coated copper on the tall buildings and tiled roofs of the Kyoto skyline.

Underneath the station I wandered through a mall. Handcrafted silks, pottery, porcelain, paper, printed ties, filled the souvenir-counter shelves. When I emerged the parking lot was jammed with rush-hour vehicles. Taxis stood ranked, every cab identical to the next, each backseat shrouded in a starched white doily. The uniformed drivers sat clutching their steering wheels between white-gloved hands. You could have eaten off the trunk lids. Suddenly I thought: *Now this is a far cry from Mexico.*

The cab door swung open, the driver operating it by a lever under the dashboard. As I stooped to climb in, an English coffee shop sign caught my eye: *Quick Mother.* A pang like thirst in the desert struck my soul. The mirage vanished. The shop was closed.

"Shimogawaracho, Higashiyama deska," I pronounced.

The driver turned and looked inquiringly at me. He asked something short. I repeated myself. He frowned, perplexed. "Here." I handed him the paper.

"Ahhh." Studying the kanji for several seconds, he nodded and shifted into gear.

"WHY WON'T HE think of looking there, Ayako?"

"Because I know of this temple through my father. The—monks?" She'd raised her brows. "The monks accept guests."

"I see," I'd said, but of course I was lying.

"They will not ask papers for your name. It's a place of much history," she'd evaded. So finally I'd turned her around to face me, and asked her one more time.

THE STREETS OF Kyoto are laid out on a grid, nothing like Tokyo.

We drove through wide avenues with stores and houses built right out to the curb. Every block or two we passed a shrine or temple. Their gate doors stood open; inside I glimpsed gilded wood, orange-painted pillars, trimmed trees, gravel walks, stepping-stones, pagodas. Statues sat cross-legged within miniature open-faced thatched houses on stilts. In one, five rocks dressed in print aprons stood around posing as loaves of gray bread in costumes. Someone had arranged a bowl of oranges beside them, an offering, I presumed. The traffic seemed much easier here—fewer cars, the sidewalk crowds sparser and more relaxed. In the falling evening it looked like the kind of big town where neighbors stand around watering the door-sill plants, grandfathers walk the dog to buy a paper, kids play outside before supper or until mothers call them in to do homework. Every few yards a restaurant or café displayed a paper lantern, either red or white, floating on the dusk like small moons. Charcoal fires smoked the air, sizzling with fat. An old woman toddled past, guiding a cat on a leash.

A river we crossed lay between weedy banks. People lingered on the bridge looking down at the jade water. Lighted signs flickered on the stone department stores, the street signals flashed, the strolling crowds began to gather numbers. GION, said a corner sign beside a traffic light. I remembered what Red had told me: context was as important as reference point. *Gion* meant something, but not to me. Beyond the Western-style buildings I could see blocks of low wood-shuttered houses with sliding screens crowding the alleys, a Japan from old pictures. A geisha stepped through a doorway. She poised, waiting for a car to pass. Under her arm she carried a cherry silk bundle. Her wooden sandals towered six inches tall; her white face drifted against the twilight, bow-lipped in red. Orange, blue, and pink brocade flowed to her ankles, sashed by a wide butterfly knot. She might have just left a medieval inn. But she, I realized as the cab rolled on, was a truth located in this time, now.

We crossed an intersection facing a shrine with a bright orange-and-white gatehouse. Gold beam ends fretted the balcony. The inner precincts took up an entire block like another big park. *"Yasaka Jinja,"* the cab driver tossed over his shoulder.

"Arigato."

He steered up a small street edging the shrine grounds, turned right, and stopped. "Shimogawara!" He waved expansively toward the tree-lined avenue.

"This is it?"

"Hai. Shimogawaracho."

I looked up the cobbled slope. Plaster walls banked it, topped by a thatch awning or bamboo lattice. Leafy branches overhung the doors set in the walls. Some doors looked smooth as girls' arms, silvery yellow sticks lashed together with twine. Thin-slatted reed blinds covered second-story windows. The street wound gently up a curve. There were no signs at all. I checked the meter, dug into my pocket, and counted out the coins.

When he levered the door open I scrambled out, confronted with the blank housefronts and hidden gardens of a *National Geographic* world.

SHE'D WRITTEN THREE numbers on the slip. At first I couldn't find any gate door numbers. Soft air settled around the treetops. Cicadas sang. A couple passed me, dressed elegantly for dinner.

I crossed the street. A long black car pulled up beside a wall; the driver got out, opened the door, and three men in dark blue suits emerged. One of them murmured to the driver, who nodded and watched, arms folded, as the others passed through an open gate into a garden lighted by a stone lantern above a waterfall. A kimonoed woman came out to greet them, bowing deeply. After a few minutes another car arrived, parked on the curb, and disgorged five more businessmen, who entered the garden, talking agreeably, while the new chauffeur leaned against the hood and smoked a cigarette. The same woman bowed on the inner steps.

I felt very alone.

The first driver went over to join the second. They spoke a few words. The smoker turned and glanced somber-lidded at me.

Purposefully I stalked up the street. Beyond the curve I could still hear their voices. My beard itched. Stale reeks wafted up from my shirt, which was ringed with sweat. A hallucinatory buzzing locked with the insects. I stood resting a minute. No numbers anywhere. After searching from curb to curb, I fell short of breath and stopped again opposite a wooden building three stories high, its roofed fence gate sheltered by dark, glossy bushes. Splashing sounds came from over the garden wall. Where was I to find the numbers I needed? Where were numbers? Where was I to find, where was I? Where?

The gate squeaked as a man opened it. He wore red track shorts printed with cartoons of Betty Boop and a blue short-sleeved Kewpie-doll shirt. In one hand he carried a broom. His head gleamed bald as a baseball.

"Excuse me," I cleared my throat and crossed the paving stones. "I'm looking for a Rinzai-Zen temple. Number 692. Can you please help me?"

The ageless eyes shone green in the dusk. Wrinkles feathered their corners. He said a name, asking, hand on the broom.

"Yes. That's it!"

Stepping aside, he gestured to the gate he'd just opened. "Welcome to this temple. You desire to stay for the night?"

Cicadas shrilled in the garden. My nerveless hands fell to my sides. "Yes. I do. Domo arigato."

"One moment." Quickly he moved, muscular, competent, calves flexing. The broom swept over the front steps, whisking away leaves and dirt. I closed my eyes. In six seconds he'd finished. "Please come inside and I will show your room."

SOMETIME IN THE late evening, after I had gone out once more to the main street, eaten a tempura dinner, and then stopped in a little half-lit grocery store called Food Howdy to buy hardtack snacks of rice slabs, deep-fried peas, ragged wafers, and tiny seaweed fritters, I approached that gate once more.

"It's the safest place," she'd explained, "because of history. My father hates this temple."

"Why?"

"He dislikes the past connection with his name." Her hair brushed intimately against my wrist. I felt her shoulder, small, fragile under the silken knit. "In 1867 there was war in Kyoto between the shogun government and the emperor. The samurai patriot Ito fought for the shogun. He and his friends called their warrior group Escort Party for Emperor and at the gate to this temple they nailed up a sign."

"What did it say?"

"Imperial Mausoleum Guard Station."

"Huh!" I circled my arm around her. "What happened?"

"In the battle after, Ito's party lost. The emperor's men tore the sign down. Ito and his samurai fighters were killed."

"That's too bad."

"My father feels shame in the name Ito. Bearing that name reminds him of dishonor. Our first shogun family name should not confuse regarding my father's devotion to the emperor. He says Ito should have died for the emperor's sake, in the old style. To write such a sign was worse than shogun loyalty only. It was a shame act."

"So this temple is safe because of Ito's audacity?" It was not until this moment that I'd apprehended the bitter depth of her rebellion.

I stood in the darkness listening to the doves cooing mournfully in the trees, thinking of my own father biding time in his grandfather's fortress. He sat cradling the red lacquer telephone, trusting it would ring soon, hoping for my safety. Our bond bridged across miles, forged through the link of mind and blood. I stared at the wooden gate. To do this thing, to hide like a virus in the heart's chamber, filled me with a strange fear.

"You will never be found. He will not look for you there, of all the places in the world."

I opened the gate and walked through.

THE OLDER MONK was ready for bed when I nudged off my shoes in the genkan. I could see him through the lighted shoji doorway of his room, dressed in a dark robe, propped up on a futon watching television. Earlier when the younger one showed me to my room the old man had bustled to the kitchen in his house slippers, limping a little, sidling around the place where we stood blocking the passage, ignoring me.

Stripping down in the bathroom, I could feel the warm, sticky darkness through the window. Hot water jetted from the showerhead; I held the hose close until finally all that was left was a pure exhaustion like the afterglow of sex. Only purpose burned still. The soap bar smelled fresh; I was tempted by the cedar tub steaming in the corner, but considered what shape I'd be in when they fished me out like a boneless whale filet next morning. Plunging my shirt in the concrete sink, I scrubbed it with the soap and hung it on a hook to dry. Then I crept past a pair of bath slippers appliquéd with Mickey Mouse and back through the kitchen where the younger monk stored his collection of minimotorbikes. Twenty-seven at last count, he'd told me, showing them off before dinner: his hobby. The monks' lights had quenched. In the passage the floorboards chirped like nesting birds. Every footfall shivered through wooden walls. Crickets sang; otherwise all lay dead quiet. A full moon rose above the trees. I watched it for a few minutes, then slid the screen to climb the narrow stair to my third-floor room.

"PLEASE, YOU MUST stay inside the temple. Don't go into the streets all day."

"Will he be watching that close?"

"By then he will be home in Denenchōfu. Before he leaves Osaka he'll verify you have escaped."

"Will he know how?"

She'd looked down, studying her lap, her face a mask. "The paper I showed to the guard wore his *mon*. His—crest? Stamp?"

"Seal."

She nodded. "The guard didn't know me. He saw only the order."

"But who else could have gotten hold of the seal?"

She shook her head. "He will think for a long time about that question. He will ask Matsudo and other people in his companies. Then he will solve it." She looked up. "Perhaps he won't believe such an idea at the beginning."

"But sooner or later he'll have to. Because nobody else could have managed access to his private seal. Right?"

An imploring look of sad terror filled her eyes. She blinked at me, not speaking.

"Listen. By that time you'll be on a plane to Texas," I stroked her hair, bundling her into my arms. "Safe. Safe with all of us. With me."

She closed her eyes.

"Don't worry. He'll get over it. I guarantee. You're his older daughter. No matter how mad he feels at first, you'll both make up in the end."

"Please to promise. Don't go into the streets of Kyoto before time," she whispered.

THE MORNING DAWNED hot. A single grilled window aired the little room. A paper shoji formed the wall facing the passage. Four tatami mats padded the floor under the futon. At the other end shoji opened onto closet shelves. Otherwise the room was empty.

I lay listening to the scratch of sweeping in the courtyard. Two crows cawed a harsh conversation. My mind had rested throughout the night; now plans refined, crystallizing in that oppressive space until I could see at last the hard facets, cup them dense in my hand. I folded the sheet, emptied all pockets, and arranged their contents on the bare futon. Money, passport, blueprint. The temple scrap with her phone number copied on the back from my wrist, the lipstick token smudged. I kissed its pink jot. The train schedule. The bus map complete with routes from Kyoto Station. The tool case from my thigh. The small steel key inside.

I fingered the key a moment. Then, unfolding the notated blueprint, I started to prepare.

An hour later I went downstairs to the bathroom, pulled on the dry shirt, and washed for breakfast. The dining room lay just below my staircase. The younger green-eyed monk breezed in carrying a legged tray and briskly deposited its bowls of pickles, fried tofu swimming in broth, vegetables, soy, and wasabi. I sat alone on a floor cushion eating so fast I hardly tasted the food. The next time I saw him he was accompanying the old monk through the street gate, their Zen robes fluttering under wide straw hats.

I returned to my room to memorize Diego's floor plan for the twentieth time.

IN THE AFTERNOON the crows called. Doves moaned their replies. By now I knew how true prisoners must feel. Peering out the wooden window grill, pacing the tiny cell, I checked my watch and thought: in two hours, one hour, I'll leave to catch the bus.

A few minutes before five I went down to the monks' vacant room and placed twelve thousand-yen bills on the phone table next to the television, together with a note saying thank you and good-bye.

THE ADVANTAGE OF a bus, Diego had said, was that late in the day it would be packed with all kinds of people—tourists and foreign students as well as locals. The routes were simple. You could master their circuit at a map glance. Kyoto's grid placed bus stops at all major street corners. One lay nearby Yasaka Shrine. You paid a coin machine. A cabbie, on the other hand, would remember individual fares to anyone who might ask.

Only one bus went up to Haradani, the last stop on the line.

The rush-hour crowd stood crammed so closely that I couldn't bend to look out. All day a still, bleached-out sky had hung above, but now the breeze picked up; everyone was going home cheerful: schoolteachers, insurance actuaries, dye workers, and grocery-toting housewives reading their papers. At each stop people climbed off. Seats became available. Soon I could see 360 degrees out the windows. We headed north into a residential suburb all at once reminding me of Bernice; the houses had little front yards, stone façades, new plasterwork; civic plantings flourished on the corners. At the last of these neighborhood lanes the bus began to climb a narrowing grade. Woods bushed to either side. The odd villa perched alone on a stone table or miniature cliff. The bus ground up steepening hairpin turns, chuffing, doubling back. Long shadows quilted the roadbed. We passed the entrance to a parking lot; beyond it a tall mortuary chimney billowed smoke. Shrubs grew wild among the pines and cedars. Vines knit light into a golden geometry; ducking, I saw dark tunnels under the boughs. At road's end a bedroom village spilled across the hillside, with modern apartments, shops, two-story houses, toys in the windows—My Little Pony, Hello Kitty, Akira. Fathers parked their cars in driveways, children dawdled out to greet them. Neighbors stood chatting by the curb. The bus stopped.

The brown and blond heads had all got off long ago. There was nobody foreign up here except me.

UNDER THE BRANCHES cicadas whined. The mountains had turned violet during sunset across the valley of Kyoto; now they condensed to a solider dark. Thin clouds sheeted the sky, obscuring the moon.

Four hours ago I'd slipped down from the bus and headed toward the woods. One or two onlookers smiled. A woman had nodded politely; a man had stopped and asked a question, probably wondering if I needed directions. But only one direction was required: north. *Go deep into the forest. You will find it is possible to tread between the trees, although you must take a sharp knife. Keep pointing to the north at all times. If you do this you will not become lost. Perhaps difficulties will arise because there is no path; however, you must overcome them. You are strong, no?* Diego had designated by memory the real track that led from Haradani to the headquarters, but of course I couldn't take it. Since leaving the village I'd slogged at least three miles, clambering up ravines, thrashing through undergrowth, sinewy trunks, branches that whipped back in my eyes. The rosiny pine scent sharpened. A hot darkness gathered. I could barely see my own hands. I spun around in the layers of leaves to seek my lost way.

When the first dizziness struck I stopped still, waiting for its flood to drain. Rustles shook the ceiling as an animal jumped from a bough. A bird twittered. Black air wheeled through my skull; I was slipping, feeling the old tilt toward the decaying slush on the forest floor. North? Where was north? I grasped a bush. The currents cleared. I drew a deep breath and turned too quickly. When the next wave swept over I stumbled, pulse thumping, crashing to my knees. There was no path. No trail opened through the tumuli of leaves; no stones lay anchored, ready to follow. Groping around the matted twigs with flattened palms, I swore. Vines latticed walls. All directions poured down the vortex; direction no longer existed, in every hypotenuse lay only the dark pointed cavity: my failure, my death. Tar coated my tongue. I couldn't breathe. They would catch me. I began to drown. Then suddenly I thought: Wait. I know this place. I've been here before.

Or was I dreaming it?

I knelt beneath the cedars. Recognition floated slowly upward, surfacing like a thought. The jungle stripes of leaf and vine imposed their own limitations. But the sky could tear beyond them. I stood, braced against a pine trunk so panic couldn't knock me back over. Then, gingerly, I dared to twist my head and look up.

Against the blackness, off in one pocket, flared a weak glow.

Branch by branch I heaved myself up the tree. Soon my head broke clear; I could see the mountains' backbone, I could see, to the south and southeast, the blazing city. Turning around I faced opposite, straight into the dark.

You are strong, yes, I said to myself.

I slid down the pine trunk, patted it, and began to forge north once more. When at last I came to the clearing I knew I'd reached the place.

FROM UNDER THE darkness between the trees I watched a rabbit sprint across the mown lawn toward a grass tuft. In the clearing, its roof thatch evenly clipped, lay the evidence of the hand of man.

What kind of electric-eye system had he installed? I wondered. The house shell built like a seventeenth-century farm dwelling might count as superstitious security in Ito Minamoto's mind, but camouflage only goes so far. The whole place smelled contradictory. Stone walls met wood under the quaint peaked roof. The bamboo fence, rural, lashed in a crisscross pattern, spiked up at the top. The gate was bamboo also, opening onto a garden. Since much of the complex wound underground in corridors hundreds of yards long, it could be that Minamoto had forgone more technical precautions. Such was Diego's belief. Diego had no records of alarm circuit wiring. I surmised that, this being the late twentieth century, records would probably lie.

But where was the demon?

The house stood dark. Shutters sealed the lower windows. For one second I had a flash of intuition; I recalled the primitive system my father had relied on for his own headquarters before the night I'd skipped right through it. Enemies choose each other, I thought, they home in, knowing some unconscious mutuality. I recognize you, Ito Minamoto, because somehow, somewhere, we, too, are alike.

Could it be possible, I wondered, watching the rabbit skitter like a fat moth returning to cover, that there was actually no system at all?

The tool case weighed down my hand. I laid it in the pine needles, wiping my palm on my jeans. Something snagged against a crease. I looked down. At the knuckle base jutted the ring's shank. No gold glimmer caught the moonless sky. Without another moment's deliberation I picked up the case, stood, and walked around the clearing perimeter toward the front fence.

But demons, I thought, are alive.

Reaching into my jeans, I once more pulled out the knife Ayako had taken from Diego's kitchen and ceremonially presented to me. Unwrapping the handkerchief around the blade, I settled its black haft in my palm.

THE CLOUDS SLID back just when I reached the gate. I stood six foot four, peeled by full moonlight like an onion. Molten silver laced shadows through the garden, the maple boughs caging rocks on the moss.

I lifted the latch. The gate swung open.

I heard a splash.

For a second I froze. Then, dropping, I crouched in a fetal ball, knife gripped ready.

Nothing stirred.

After several minutes I rose once more and passed through the gate, every nerve alive to the alarm I might set off. Moonlight rinsed the stepping-stones. There, to the left of the stout farmhouse door, under a boulder's shadow, a pool lay bowled between the mossy backs of earth.

By accident I nearly stepped in. It lay black and still, its edges speared with tall iris, the surface stretching for several yards. I stared down. A shiver darted through my blood. The bottom was indiscernible. Fern fronds grew to one side. Water, lapless, like a tube of night, filled its depths, and it sucked the moonlight up in its dark eye, absorbing it under the boulder's cope so that the light vanished with no reflection.

Suddenly I understood where I was.

I backed away from the pool's edge. Moss felted my footsteps. It was as if I'd become a shadow, half ghost.

Then something moved just beneath the water's surface.

I couldn't wrench my gaze away. A pale fleshy foot reached diagonally across the pool under the fluid skin. I could see the dark spot where toes bunched, I could see its searching, groping progress. Any second now it would burst through and open like a lotus. A scream gathered in my throat. I clenched the knife tight.

Another shape, splotched and elongated, joined the first, browsing lily pads at the pool's lip. This time the head poked beyond the boulder's shadow, the blunt nose.

"Those fish you see in rock gardens and museum pools," I rattled in the long-past tropical sunlight to Granddaddy. "Bloodlines going back to ancient Japanese emperors. People name them like pets."

Unclenching the knife, hoisting it ready, I grinned savagely at the koi, dug two fingers into my pocket, and slipped out the key.

THE HEAVY FAÇADE timbers looked old. For an instant doubt assailed me: was this the right building? But the keyhole under a wooden bar gleamed with new steel. The key nicked in like butter. The door opened on fresh-oiled hinges. Inside, it was pitch-dark under a high, raftered ceiling.

For a long moment I stood there not breathing, listening.

Go left, Diego had said. Waste no time in the upper floors. *Under no circumstances.* The trapdoor will receive the same key. I know Ito Minamoto. His thrift and custom demand that he change no arrangement unless absolutely necessary.

Was upstairs the demon's lair?

At last I moved, feeling through the still, cool air to the far wall. On the dirt floor my burglar feet made no sound. Once I skirted past an object encased and rising like some immovable chaise: the earthen stove. But this time disorientation tripped me into clarity. Darkness, to the cat burglar, is like falling in love.

When I found the trapdoor under a seat cushion I paused. Whatever lived on the upper floor hadn't heard, or if so, was keeping silent. Where would he be? Of what was he capable? The feeling of empty rooms, dusty rafters, untouched hallways grew strong; the house seemed becalmed in neglect.

Unlocking the trap with the key, I raised it high and stared into the dungeon.

Dank air blew up from buried concrete walls. A mustiness filled my mouth. Thought failed before that endless vacancy. The shaft seemed to plunge through soil, the strata of gravel and clay, straight down to the core of the world.

I held the knife ready. Stepping carefully, I lowered myself into the well.

Shallow footholds carved its slope; the muffled scrape of soles grazed the eardrum, fell away. Retinal images burst and died, soaking up the blackness. Rafe's eyes appeared within my mind, closing like mica on infinite nothing; moving through that cold absence, I felt the subterranean tomb extend, the underworld realized. At the bottom I hit another door.

Additional keys were not entrusted to my possession, Diego had said. *The next lock you must pick.*

I fished the pick ring from the tool case together with the penlight I'd stolen from the monks' minibike storage and for which I'd left the extra money.

If it turned out to be an electronic coded pad I was done for. But by now I knew it wouldn't. At last I'd grasped what Diego had tried to tell me; I understood Minamoto's traditionalism. This farmhouse wasn't a fortress of high-tech elaborations—holographic traps, laser eyes, computer cameras. It was real. I'd broken in here to find contracts written and sealed in ancient Imperial court style on rice-paper scrolls, hidden the way a courtier would hide them. A lord of medieval Japan. His one big concession to modernity the recent steel lock on the front door.

My fingertips skated the wooden face, brushing a metal shield. Fondling it, I discovered the slot in the middle and switched on the penlight. It shed a thin copper glow, dimming already. The batteries. I hadn't double-checked the batteries.

The fifth try worked.

The darkest dark will swallow you, I thought, and still not be as dark as Rafe's eye. But this came close. The doorway yawned on blends of blackness, beyond gradation, below any cave.

Left, said Diego. *First go left.*

I tucked the knife under my arm, opened the tool case, and drew out the thin nylon rope. Tying one end to the pick ring, I clutched the remainder in my free hand, stuck the pick back in the lock, and twisted until it jammed tight. I gave it a tug just to check. At that moment the penlight died. I shook it. When it didn't rekindle I placed it silently on the floor, took the knife from under my arm, and set out.

When you reach a forking turn left once more, he'd said. Imagine the blueprint always before you. Playing the rope out, I reached the next corner.

At the end of some alleys are doors, at the end of others, nothing. Wall. The crust of the world. You cannot know what lies behind all the doors. Minamoto's secrets, perhaps his wealth. But the door you want, there is only one.

Now turn right.

I felt the corridor split and stopped, probing out with my knife hand into a middle passage. Turning right again, I scraped the rope against a concrete corner. The floor was hard moist dirt. I could smell it, the smell packed nose and ears and eyes and throat like wool. The next middle passage seemed correct. When my forehead bumped the door at its end I knew I'd better pause, think, reverse, and turn yet another right, the blueprint fixed in my mind's eye, the only thing I could see.

In a left-hand passage a few yards farther on I stopped. Something was breathing.

The breathing grated. As it gushed in and out I held my own breath. It loomed behind me in the dark, snuffling hot, and its bestial volume implied large lungs, a capacious skull, a well of air, a being gross and thirsting for oxygen. I jabbed the knife outward, gasped to let breath go. The panting ceased.

Warning prickled all over. My hair stood on end. The knife was slipping wet in my hand, I thought of that prick to Rafe's jugular, the blood spurting, sluicing my eyelids and arms; I knew what I'd done, how hard I'd pressed, relentless on his bubbling screams, how he'd screamed and the eyes had shuttered down on that infinite black—help me, love me, arrogant gringo bastard—how the lonely, isolated years reaching back into early childhood were as kinked as these very tunnels, as labyrinthine as life itself *bastard! bastard!* stumbling, falling, learning to jump like a trout aside from my own gravity had fashioned me and vomited me forth to this moment; I heard Ayako's words: *A demon lives inside, a monster.*

What could live in tunnels and never come out? What kind of mind would it have?

What had Minamoto created?

The rope nearly fell to the floor. I caught it. The breathing had stopped—now where? behind? to the right? Which tunnel, which way to go? The monster demon born not of horror but achieved by horror, stashed away, waiting to feed on what shunned it. Waiting. For prey. *I can tell you nothing,* said Diego. The vertigo backed up like sewage, threatening my mind's eye. Icy sweat trickled down ribs. My bladder felt too full. I forced my feet forward, one step, two groggy steps, not making a sound, hardly upright, turning, turning, turning.

The tunnels forked three ways.

Go left.

Again, at the Y, go left. Brain tumbling. Fight through the handicap, do it, listen with your spine, each distinct vertebra, each single dead cilium of your inner ear. There is no sound. Only the black tide behind which he's waiting.

One more turn. Right. Stand up, *focus!* Is there a door?

I groped out and patted the end wall. The end of the tunnel. Nearly the end of the rope. A door met my hands. Not wood. Steel.

His strongroom.

In desperation I slid my rope hand down to search for a lock, found a knob instead, and turned it.

LIGHT CRASHED AGAINST my eyes like a breaker. Someone shrieked. Lunging blindly I gashed toward them with the knife, stabbing to kill. Then the vertigo thundered down, slamming me to the floor, helpless, throat bared ready for the claws. Breath roiled into the spinning light. The room telescoped into a bare white room.

I blinked straight into the radiance of his smile.

The wheelchair that propped him up stood about two yards from the door. His huge lantern-shaped head canted at an angle. Joy charged the brown eyes rounding under their pouched lids.

Dizzily I struggled to my knees.

He watched me, lips parting. When I heaved the rest of the way up and the knife dropped to my side, he followed it, grin wide and gaping, his face a vista of wonder.

"Uh," I said, and cleared my throat.

"Hai! Hai!" he blurted.

At first I was so stupefied nothing came to my head. Against the far wall stood flat wooden drawers stacked narrowly into a recess. Below, a low table with two floor cushions. The drawers glowed with wax polish. Their guardian lurched a little in the wheelchair, flinging himself with excitement. "Holy God," I whispered.

"Ah?" he tried again.

I licked my lips. "What—who are—"

He beamed.

"Ah—look. My name is Ta—Taylor Deeds."

"Ahhh!" he said, and blinked as if imitating. Then he burst out laughing. His knob-ended arms banged happily on the chair tires like flippers.

The little feetless legs kicked against the footrests. The barrel body shook. His laugh barked merrily as a seal's.

Wind careened back through my lungs. I stepped into the room. "What are you doing here?"

He cocked his head, charming, mischievous.

"You come down here for the night, maybe?"

"Ee-yay." His eyes crinkled, meeting mine, inviting.

"Through the dark." I tipped my head toward the blot outside the door.

"Ahh." The wheelchair rocked gently as he bounced. His eyebrows waggled. His mouth, too large for his face, had dropped open like a steam shovel while he listened.

"Are you—are—don't tell me—"

"Desuka!"

Something constricted inside my chest. "Oh my God."

"Hai-ai-ai!" he cried again, this time his grin so broad it could have scythed hay.

A rage sparked. "Are you here all by yourself?"

He goggled.

"Look. I'm sorry! Oh, Lord. I could've—I nearly—hurt you." As I stepped the short lunge toward him my voice cracked.

Someone else spoke.

I wheeled, tightening to spring, knife gripped high. A woman scurried from inside a doorway on the right-hand wall where she'd been hiding. Both her arms pushed out to fend off attack; she ran to the wheelchair and squatted before it, jabbering, her face transfixed with fear.

I stared from her to the knife in my hand.

She flinched. The chair rolled. Quickly I scrabbled out the handkerchief, wrapped the blade, slid the knife down the jeans waistband, raising my hand once more to show her its emptiness. "No! No! See?" Turning to the boy, she patted his legs, murmuring rapidly, soothing with little motions. He chortled in pleasure. His face took the darkness from the corridors outside and transfigured it into blazing light.

"Ushi-oni?" I said.

The woman winced, eyes indignant. Then she rose, stepped behind the chair, and placed both hands on his shoulders. He looked up in trusting curiosity.

"I didn't know," I whispered.

Her gray hair was slicked tight in a bun. Her mouth drooped at the corners. The protective glance she gave revealed enough.

"Truly, I didn't know. I'm sorry. To disturb you. God—I had no idea. I've just come"—I glanced from her to his shining grin, rage beginning to coil and smoke inside—"to get some papers Mr. Minamoto keeps here."

"Minamoto Ito-san desuka," she breathed, her face unreadable.

"I'd guess probably in those drawers over there."

"Mina-moto desuka," he said, echoing.

"I never dreamed that I'd—that he—" In the room, I thought. That a human being would have actually sealed up and buried another human being alive. In a room twenty feet below ground.

No human mind, no right body. The human parts broken.

She asked me something. The only thing I understood in the question was the next-to-last word. "Ito-san . . . ?"

"Minamoto." Who locked you in here. Telling his daughter the most terrible, poisonous lies. I pulled a deep breath, let it out, and turned to the boy. "Your sister's father."

"Mina-moto," he crowed. The woman bowed twice to me. Then she bowed her head.

He looked nothing like Ayako. The gene code transcending all countries and racial pools had cast his features in its universal kinship; the wide mouth slit, flat-boned cheeks, slanting eyes of the Down's syndrome child made of him pan-human, brother instead to those others from the manifold countries of the globe. But his delight transcended theirs.

Demon monster. Animal.

But his mother had died. Mine had not.

"Jesus." I went to the floor cushion and knelt down. The nurse watched me, hands on his shoulders. She frowned and smoothed his hair with love.

"Well. I don't know what to say."

The boy observed me with eyes wide in anticipation.

"This is ridiculous—impossible." Cruelty beyond mind, the cruelty of a man to a worm. Look! said Ronnie Dean Jordan. Look! cried the girls he'd organized, whispering, calling while I writhed and twisted, Taylor, it's me!

I got up. "Excuse me," I whispered. Then I skirted the room's center, steadying myself against the wall, keeping as far from their vulnerability as possible. The door on the right stood open. Inside the next room I glimpsed two futons, a built-in stove, a steel sink, utensil shelves, stocks of food, toys. The nurse huddled back, wheeling the chair aside when I reached the drawers. "Please, excuse me," I mumbled again, and in a daze started opening them. Her breath hissed. Motionlessly she watched while with hesitant fingertips I lifted out sheaves of cloth, happi coats, a woman's cotton panties, pairs of boy's underwear, clean white T-shirts. You have no right, I thought. Disgust burned. My head drummed. My hands' violating touch made me sick. But isn't this what burglars really do? I thought. Isn't it? *The door you want, there is only one,* said Diego's voice. I opened empty drawers, closed them, found stacks of indigo cotton pants, a stack of worn, frayed diapers shoved back in a corner, a pile of flimsy papers with bright-colored children's pictures.

"Hah!" he cried, rolling his eye and smiling when he saw those.

"I'm sorry," I whispered, "sorry." I couldn't swallow. No scrolls.

Shutting the last drawer I went to the kitchen/bedroom. The only receptacles were the shelves. Searching the smooth plastered cement walls for a closet I found a tiny bathroom with a toilet, shower, and cedar tub. Set above the kitchen sink another latched trap opened like a wall safe, empty except for a wooden shelf attached to cables: a kind of dumbwaiter for supplies.

I came back to the main room. "We've got to get you out now."

The nurse patted him, saying nothing.

"Look. This is—I'm so sorry. But don't worry. I'm getting you out. Everything'll be okay."

He smiled. Leaning forward, he banged his little knobs eagerly on the tires.

Oh brave new world, I thought suddenly, looking at his face. Except for the nurse I was in all likelihood the only human being he'd seen in memory. I stared at the pure result of seventeen years spent away from the mind of man, and all at once I felt it knife around my soul, scalpeling the despicable acts and deceits and betrayals cankering since Texas and Mexico, cutting them away like dead flesh and tissue, trimming them off to leave only a heart pulsing with wonder and pain.

How was it possible that he existed?

The nurse asked a question.

"I'm sorry. I don't understand."

She asked it again.

"I don't speak Japanese. I—the best thing to do—we'll go upstairs and find somebody."

"Haiii!" he laughed.

"We'll go to his sister. Ayako."

She muttered, distressed.

"Is that all right with you? Do you know her? Ayako? Ayako Minamoto?"

In agitation she turned, fretting with her hands.

"See—she doesn't know! About this. She has no idea. That he's down here. Or that you're—she's got to see for herself." *Demon monster. Animal.* "We'll help you, we'll both take care of him. Don't worry."

"Hai!" he cried loudly.

"Look." I pointed to her, to him, to the chair, to the door. I made shushing motions. "Can you—you got it? You understand?"

She frowned and shrank back, bewildered. Suddenly the claustrophobia, their helpless years of loneliness, the sense of tons of dirt overhead, forced my rage to its crest. "Come on! Let's just go!"

I strode to the chair. As I grabbed the handles and began to push him toward the door his smile faded.

"Ahh?" he asked uncertainly.

"*Eee! Yamete!*" shrieked the nurse, seizing my elbow.

"No. Out! This way!" I rushed us to the door. His cry broke thin and clear, a wail of question, of loss. The nurse started screeching and whacking me while he kicked the chair in alarm. Stooping, I snatched the rope up in one hand without letting go of the chair handle. "It'll be all right once we get to the top," I yelled as she pulled my elbow and we shoved out into the dark.

The rope gnawed into my hand where I wrapped the coils, working my fingers up each inch, breasting forward through the great engulfing black to prevent the nurse from dragging us back. The lighted chamber glowed behind but only for a few feet before the corridor turned. The deeper we went the shriller Ushi-oni screamed, thumping his stunted arms against the metal, his terror echoing and ringing down tunnels, cul-de-sacs, soaking them like the blackness, corrupting their long silence.

"It's okay. Not far. We'll be out soon."

"*Yi-yieee!*" wailed Ushi-oni, throwing his head from side to side. Moisture flew onto my invisible rope-bound fist: saliva, snot, tears.

"Shh. Don't worry!"

"*Aiyyee!*"

"Please calm down, please!" His weeping sliced into my heart. Seventeen years they'd been underground with only each other. The nurse tending his every need, she whose life he'd usurped, who would obviously throw away her own for his sake, who loved him utterly. In all that time he'd never known fear.

The wheelchair caught on lumpy ground, tilting forward, nearly tipping him out. "Sorry!" I gasped. "I'm sorry!" The nurse clung to his arm, gibbering hysterically. "We'll be there soon." The rope skein fattened on my fingers as it erased the path behind us. Yard after yard, turn after turn, his fear mirrored my own journey to his door. Tires jogged against shinbone, elbows crashed into cement, bruising when I rounded corners. Pitch darkness flapped across our faces. Somewhere in the distance blew fresh air.

"*Yamete, yamete,*" panted the nurse. I felt her stumbling.

"Can't you smell it? We're almost there." I slowed down. She was hanging like a rag onto the chair.

"*Ya-me-te,*" she groaned.

"Look." At last I stopped the wheelchair. The rope came to an end and snubbed against the lock-pick ring. My knuckles knocked wood. Above our heads, at the top of the angled twenty-foot slope, was a square of pale yellow light. "Look," I said softly, bending over the almost invisible Ushioni and pointing upward. "See?"

He made no sound.

"We're here. We've made it! Safe," I coaxed. The nurse dropped and cowered against the footrest. Helping her up I tried fruitlessly, blindly, to dust off her trembling shoulders. "I'm sorry. But it's okay now. See the light?"

Why was there a light?

"Ahh," she moaned.

"It's not too steep. You can make it. Just start heading straight up. I'm right behind you with Ush—with him." I patted her in encouragement. The boy's eyes were closed. I could barely make them out, their pouchy phosphorous lids.

Why was there a light?

"I'll carry you." I picked him up. He weighed so little—not like Ramón, not like Teresa-Maria, not even like his sister. The barrel chest hardly rose and fell. His limbs clenched against his rib cage. The face that had shone with joy now lay quenched, a tight, stupid, pitiful mask. It couldn't be dawn yet, it was too early. I hadn't been gone long enough. He whimpered. Then stopped. Far back through the blackness, his weeping had dwindled and now, as he rode between my arms toward the light, the cries reverberated forever inside my brain.

Harm, harm.

Following the nurse up the slope I already knew. But there was nothing more to be done, no further deed to commit. The jungle pyramid stair climbed and climbed. The erosion begun in the dark tunnel would soon be complete; I would bear him captive out, lay him at the head of the flight bound ready for the instrument to rise and plunge. Grief rose in me then, harsh, harrowing, a pain such as I'd never imagined. The only evil that had ever existed in the white room, I thought, was what I'd brought in myself.

19

A man stood in the front door shadows.

Across the room from him under the lantern light Minamoto knelt beside the earthen stove, his hands on his knees. Opposite him sat Matsudo.

All three turned, their eyes glimmering.

"Wah!" Matsudo yipped in fear. The nurse's spectral stagger up through the floor stopped him at first. As I rose behind her, erupting from the underworld, he threw himself in front of Minamoto: *"Gomen nasai! Gomen nasai!"* His face was wild. The nurse shrieked, lurched, nearly tumbling back down the hole, and I sidestepped to block her. Minamoto's stare stayed rigid. The firelight played across his balding skull.

"Evening," I said.

Matsudo mumbled, sweat springing out like oil on his polished forehead. The dapper craftsmanship of his body looked absurd in that position.

"I said good evening to you."

Glacially Minamoto peered from my face to the boy in my arms.

"What's the matter? Didn't you ever learn manners?"

"Mr. Deeds!" Matsudo gasped. "How do you find yourself here?"

"I use a compass."

He cowered to Minamoto, gabbling frantically. *"Gomen nasai—moshi wake arimasen—Soushi—Daimyo—"*

"*Damare!*" cracked Minamoto.

Matsudo bowed his head, cringing. Minamoto grated another order. Matsudo's head yanked up. "Mr. Deeds, you must leave at once, you are present incorrectly, you must go back—go back to—"

"The Lascaux caves?"

"Who is this woman?" He turned, spitting out a question in Japanese. She quailed to her knees on the floor.

"She's in shock. She's been locked in a dungeon under the ground for seventeen years. Leave her alone!"

The shadowed man quickly looked toward the brown pottery teabowl and bamboo whisk arranged by the fire.

I glanced down at the boy. His eyes lay open. Their brown depths searched up to mine in a pained confiding. His lips worked, gulping, no longer the rictus but snatching air and releasing a high-pitched mewing from way back in his throat. I cradled him tight to my chest, I held him tight, close, trying to soothe his moan. His heart beat hard, rocking his frame, knocking against my own sternum, and I couldn't tell if it was my heart or his I was feeling or where one left off and the other now began.

"You are criminal," pronounced Matsudo.

"Shh, now." Drool strung across his chin. The nurse gave a little miserable cough.

"You arrive here with no right. We will arrest you, the police will—"

"I don't really give a damn." I'd seen now who the man was by the door. There was no hope. "Gentleman. Allow me to introduce to you Minamoto Ushi-oni-san, the adopted son of Minamoto Ito-san. That's the correct form, isn't it?" I stalked forward into the light.

Dead silence fell.

An iron teakettle hanging from a rod seethed over the flames. Tenderly I cradled him, gently. He whimpered. Our hearts were pounding together beat by beat. The little arms lay tucked between his thighs, he stared up at me so riven in desolation that my voice shook; I didn't know how to tell it, if I could go on. "Do you understand what I'm saying?"

"Mr. Deeds!" barked Matsudo.

"Yes, I understand," said the other man unexpectedly.

I looked toward him.

His calm eyes roved over the bundle. He took one step from the shadows. Only the ongoing spinning calculation behind his glasses revealed any thought or emotion, the changing sum of what he was watching.

"I'm glad to hear it. It's Kawai, right? Nagisa Kawai. Well. I sure hope your boss won't punish you for it."

"You have said this woman has been locked up. You have stated that this boy in your embrace is Mr. Minamoto's son."

"Nagisa-san!" cried Matsudo in outrage.

"Adopted son."

"Ah. For all purposes, his son. Perhaps in reality."

Minamoto stiffened inside his voluminous suit.

"*Omae wa kubi da!*" Matsudo roared.

"*Damare!*" cried Minamoto. His eyes sharpened on Kawai.

"Did you know about this?" I asked Kawai. Some essence had changed. He was not responding with the proper subservience. Suddenly I realized he was not simple; danger emanated from him, softening his tone.

"You make strong and direct statements. Having worked with Americans I understand that this manner is common."

"Did you know?" I persisted. If he made a move I would kill him. The knife was in my waistband.

But the boy occupied my arms.

"Your confrontation of Mr. Minamoto breaches acceptable limits."

"I asked you a question."

"Please, Mr. Deeds—sit down."

"Go to hell." He took another step toward me. "I'm warning you." He paused.

My arms were shaking. "This boy has been a prisoner trapped his entire lifetime in a room twenty feet under this house. Suffering deprivation of light, fresh air—his sisters, other people, more than—more *certainly*

than the Americans you've got imprisoned out in Saitama. And this boy"—
I held him close, safe, he stared only up at me, at my incomprehensible
twisting mouth and raging eyes—"happens to be the child of Ito Minamoto's dead wife. The brother of his daughters. His sacred ward, due to a
promise of *on*."

Minamoto grunted.

Matsudo peered in growing horror at Ushi-oni. All cultivation was
deranged now, his hair awry, his faultless suit askew in the jerky firelight;
the manicured nails looked torn, his very shoes had lost their sheen.

Kawai turned to Minamoto. "Daimyo," he murmured, bowing, and
added one word.

"*Mph*," came the answer.

Kawai bowed acknowledgment and turned back to me. "Mr. Deeds. How
do you know this? According to your résumé you are a neurobiologist."

"My father knows about Ito Minamoto."

He looked blank. "Your father."

Minamoto wheezed out a note of command. Kawai turned again,
bowed. "It seems you have left Kan Nai in order to make the discovery you
enjoy concerning Minamoto Ito-san's private family relationships."

"Enjoy?" His weight was warm in my arms. I felt the eyes, stunned and
imploring. "I came here for some contracts."

"Contracts? What kind, please?"

"What do you think?"

He considered while the teakettle simmered over the flames. Minamoto sat implacable, both hands like dried claws against gray trousers.

"Maybe it's a bad habit he's got left over from his prison camp days
during the war, locking people up."

Kawai held his head very still. Then he turned to Minamoto, whose
eyes struck the firelight. No word passed. Between them was traded only an
audible swallow, an infinitesimal breath.

"If you came for the contracts binding your compatriots to their hon-
orable agreements, you are stealing."

"You bet. So let's call the police." I stood straight and hoisted the boy conspicuously in my arms.

"Ah. Please, will you now sit?"

"You've got to be kidding."

He held up both hands. Then he meditated a moment. The air of danger gathered, reined into control. Bending his knees he lowered himself carefully to the tatami and folded his hands. "Please."

There was nowhere safer to sit than beside the crumpled nurse. As I lumbered down she reached out trembling to stroke Ushi-oni's shoulder. A stealthy crooning came from her chest, and his eyes rolled toward the sound, lungs heaving harshly in response. I held him tight, tight.

"Perhaps we may talk," said Kawai.

"What about? I'm here. And I know what you'll do for sure as soon as he gives the order."

"Yes?"

"Tell me. Just out of curiosity—are you aware that the Americans at Kan Nai are declared missing by their families? Were you there the day the U.S. Consulate sent the deputation out to Saitama to check up?"

"Ah yes."

"Good. Some people, including my father, are now ready to alert the federal government. So whatever you do to me here tonight, it won't matter. Any day now they'll bust you."

"Your father?"

"A. J. Deeds, of Deeds Multiple Holdings, Incorporated."

He drew a breath. "Ahh, really. Deeds Holdings." He paused. "Of—Dallas, Texas?"

"Yes." Then I remembered the detail that had been eluding me since I'd recognized him. "That's right. You weren't at the welcome banquet, were you?"

A judicious glint shone behind the gold-rimmed glasses. "I have only worked for Kan Nai seventeen weeks. Not long enough to be permitted to attend special banquets. But please—they will bust, you say?"

"Expose his little compound out there for what it is. Bring the world's attention to what he's been doing. You understand?" I cradled, my arms beginning now to give under the weight of his heavy head, his inert body.

"Ah yes. This possibility is lately noted."

"Personal vendettas are one thing. But with business—" Then I registered. "Noted by who?"

Minamoto's eyes glittered from the webwork of wrinkles.

"You are correct. The wisest and most disciplined person labors continually to keep these circles separate," Kawai agreed.

"Who?"

Kawai paused.

"Korose!" Minamoto croaked.

Kawai absorbed the command, eyes lowered, and instantly I knew it was what I'd been waiting for. I clenched, ready to slide the boy down, leap to my feet, pull the knife.

But Kawai didn't move.

"Korose!" Minamoto repeated it. For a moment Kawai remained bowing. Then quietly he spoke. He did not preface his remark with *daimyo*. I thought I heard the name Anjiro, but it could have been a phonetic trick.

Minamoto stared, eyes narrowing.

Kawai turned. "Mr. Deeds. Can you please tell me why you approached this problem using your personal discretion? Rather than enlisting the help of these networks you mention?"

I prickled at his sudden professorial chill. "Minamoto has been blackmailing my father."

"Ah yes?" he said after a pause.

"He's been threatening his companies. My father defended them by complying with Minamoto's legitimate offers to employees. But now he knows what really happens. His honor is at stake."

"Yes?" he asked again.

"I am his son." Clutching the boy against my chest, the son his father had rejected, disclaimed even as he kept his promise, the concept of *son* I'd hoped to redeem.

"The associative economics of this project it would seem are unfeasible," Kawai murmured as if contemplating some boardroom chart.

"You're not really with Kan Nai Incorporated, are you?"

"Ah, yes. I work as manager for Kan Nai. However, my first loyalties must belong to my original employer. This is a different firm in Minamoto Daimyo's same keiretsu—Kyushu Equipment." He bowed slightly.

I stared at him. Then: "They know."

"It concerns all businesspeoples that uncontrolled publicity be avoided. We wish only the best relations with our international associates."

"They planted you. You're a spy."

"I am a humble salaryman." He bowed. "Mr. Matsudo is the acting president of Kan Nai Incorporated. Is that not so, *Kaicho?*"

Matsudo cranked to stiff attention like a windup toy. The perspiration dripped down his face. *"Omae wa kubi da,"* he snapped.

"Hai. Of course. I understand," bowed Kawai without inflection. "But you are the person responsible for the Kan Nai Americans project?"

The silence expanded. A coal shifted ticking in the pit. The thin steam, the hissing metal, indicated the kettle had nearly boiled dry. Suddenly Matsudo cried out and bent his whole torso to his interlocutor.

The poor stooge bastard, I thought.

"Nagisa-san—" He began to rant in Japanese.

"We should perhaps both please speak English for Mr. Deeds?"

Matsudo's jaw dropped. "Of course they are my responsibility. The fault of any organization or planning is all mine," he blurted.

Kawai nodded. But the speech seemed too pat. Even the nod was a sop. "Mr. Deeds. Is it possible to ease our mutual concerns?"

"If I reclaim the contracts."

He looked down, pensively studying an imaginary picture limned against his trouser knees. When he looked up his glasses lenses winked.

"Perhaps you wish to ask the appropriate person?"

I sighed. "Mr. Matsudo. Mr. *President Hiro* Matsudo. Will you please give me the contracts binding all the Americans throughout the past nine years to Kan Nai Incorporated?"

Matsudo opened his mouth, shut it. Some faint seeping current, the subtlest lean of air, seemed to emanate from Ito Minamoto's effigy. Matsudo's mouth popped open. "The contracts are filed for safe permanence," he said hoarsely.

"Great. So, would you fetch them for me, please?" My surprise was draining. I no longer felt much. He lay, his breathing even now, the laboring finished, his infantile warmth and weight and smell nestled within my arms, and I only wanted him to go to sleep and wake up reversed into the place where he'd first started.

"Fetch them—"

"Bring them out," I barked. "Go get them out *now*."

A coal of wood fell in the firepit.

"Ah!" he whispered. Then he bowed to Minamoto, bowed to Kawai, whipped about, strode to the wall beside me, and I realized why no one had noticed the trapdoor flipped back: the wall's dark wood melded with the shadow, and although the lantern dangled above the stove its rays fell short of the open hole. Flush with the wood paneling above it were set drawers and small doors in old-style cabinetry work. Matsudo opened a recess and drew out a sheaf of scrolls.

"Your papers, I think," observed Kawai.

Matsudo turned and dumped them beside my feet.

"Fine. Thanks. Now untie one, would you?"

He balked. A tiny sound came from Minamoto. Matsudo stooped then and picked one up, his clammy hands leaving dark smudges on the gray brocade. Slipping the knot, he let the scroll drop open. When I saw the red-stamped crest I knew. Black characters marched up the page apexed by a bright red signature: Mark J. Fetzer, someone I'd never heard of.

"Another," I said.

He snorted and picked up a second scroll. The sheet fell like a banner unleashed, its paper flecked with gold: Rebecca Willis. Dallas, Texas. 2nd September. "Show me all of them."

Kawai nodded. Matsudo knelt, untying each cylinder.

"Thank you. Now would you please roll them back up?"

"Mr. Deeds, we have been curious about your departure from Minamoto Mansions. How did you find Mr. Minamoto's retreat here in Haradani tonight?" asked Kawai.

"It was an independent action. I'm here alone—on my own."

"Ah yes, you mentioned your compass."

Minamoto's eyes shone with a blistery light. He twisted his head one centimeter, lips tightening.

At last Matsudo finished. "Now, pick them up in a bundle and stick them two by two in the fire."

Matsudo turned to Minamoto, eyes wide. Minamoto stared silently. As Matsudo went to the earthen oven's firepit and began to feed the dark red coals, the flames licked up, brightening. Acrid paper smoke rose. The nurse coughed. "You might want to open the front door," I said.

"Now, Mr. Deeds. Those were the only copies, is that so? But their destruction does not legally dismiss the signatories. Unless of course Mr. Minamoto agrees to their release?" His deference to Minamoto, bowing low, was now only a polite formality.

"Oh, I think he does." I looked at Minamoto, the dead husk propped upright.

"Then I may assume there will be no retribution? On an official plane."

I shook my head. "So long as the follow-up occurs today. But I can't really answer for the others."

"Ah yes."

I looked down at Ushi-oni. Exhaustion had pulled his lids downward until only a gleam remained. "What about him?"

"My connection with the Minamoto family falls in the circle of business interests only," Kawai said smoothly, averting his eyes.

"Well," I said, "I'm sure as hell not going to leave him anywhere. If something can't get worked out this minute, he'll have to come with me."

"Daimyo." He bowed and turned away.

On the far side of the stove Matsudo was poking the last of the scrolls into the flames, pretending to be deaf and dumb. I looked at Minamoto. "It's not like I didn't warn you," I said.

His lips drew back. "You spoke of honor and service. You swore an oath," he grated.

"And this is how I've kept it."

For a moment the flames crackled and sputtered on the quiet. At last the bitter syllables of the hateful language had been shoved out; now they shattered again from between his lips like glass. "He will live in a hospital."

I held him, feeling the heart thud. "A good one. With a school. For people with his disability. Today. And she goes with him." I nodded toward the huddled woman. "And you won't hamper me in any way from leaving Japan."

His lips clamped on the final humility he didn't even yet know he was promising himself.

"That's it, then." I closed my eyes. I took a deep breath. Then I looked down at the sleeping boy. The skin pallor startled even in that dim light. Except for recent shadows under the lids he looked younger than a newborn baby. Tears prinked my throat. I could feel him growing heavier.

Slowly Minamoto straightened erect, coughed, rose to his knees, and stood. "Here." He pointed toward his vacated cushion.

Then I clambered up, bore him over, and laid him curled into this bed. His rough chop-cut hair fell across his sleeping eyes.

"My driver is outside the house," said Kawai, also rising. "Please allow me to offer his service. He will take you wherever you wish to go."

"Thank you," I said.

"Ah, Mr. Deeds. By the way. Does your father have other children?"

I looked into his face. "No."

"Ahh. How interesting." His head tilted, lenses flashing.

I turned. Minamoto stood peering at the sleeping boy. His eyes burned with the dying embers of his rage, and as I watched they began to gutter, hardening into an isolation so cold and stellar and infinite that there lay no possible route of return. The boy expelled a sigh. I looked down at the slack lips, eyelids thick as saucer edges, steeling to tear myself from his warmth, from his heart hammering, to free myself of the vision of phantom innocence. Then I went to the woman crouched on the floor, and bent to her ear.

"*Sumi ma sen,*" I whispered. "I'm sorry."

She blinked once, breathing down the well between her crooked knees. Without another glance I stepped through the open doorway into the dawn pearling the koi pool.

THE ROAD WOUND down the mountain, brief, forest-walled. The black Lexus skimmed through Haradani like a kestrel swooping toward water, rounding the houses where early morning lights burned over breakfast, blew backward, snuffed out amidst the trees. At that hour Kyoto's outskirts lay almost deserted. By the time we reached the blocks near the train station a few trucks were delivering vegetables to grocery stores, a taxi or two cruised the narrow paving-stone alleys. A shop rolled up its window blinds on handmade brooms and wooden rakes. We passed a shrine fence where a man stood unlocking the red gates; deep inside, a gong boomed. Two pagodas towered over the yard, gold fretwork glinting in the sun. Next door a bakery opened its doors and released the fragrance of steaming baked bread. One of those ephemeral signs in English floated across its window like a mirage: WHITE LOVER.

Outside the train station the parked yellow buses were already billowing exhaust. Several schoolboys in sailor jackets queued to board. The Lexus driver veered to another lane, pulled up against the curb underneath a steel roof, climbed out, and opened my door.

"Domo arigato," I said.

"No problem."

The words jolted me. His incomparably tailored black suit and cap looked pressed and brushed, his white gloves bridally clean. The accent sounded pure L.A. It was as though somebody had paused beside my seat at a heavy metal concert and dropped a Bible verse in my lap. He stood there waiting, the air of dispassion worn like part of the uniform.

"Please tell your boss I appreciate it."

"Sure." The face remained closed tight. Passing it was like coming up against the automatic turnstiles before the JR platforms. "Take it easy," he said.

"I will." I nodded good-bye and went into the station.

Already a short line of people stood buying tickets for the shinkansen. When the time came for me to count out money I suddenly felt as if my brain had numbed; fingers fumbled over the blue thousand-yen notes, fatigue roared up through my blood and sinkered thought. After the smiling clerk patiently made change and issued the ticket I wandered through the mall until I found a telephone booth. Retrieving the paper from my rear jeans pocket I dialed the mobile-phone number scribbled on the back.

It rang twice.

"*Moshi moshi,*" breathed a small, clear voice on the other end.

"It's me," I said. Then I leaned against the canopy and shuddered.

20

Narita Airport was mobbed with people setting out on ski trips. It took forty-five minutes to find her among the crowds of down parkas.

She stood beside the departure-tax vending machine. "God," I whispered, holding her against me, smelling her. The dizziness swarmed my head and I had to swim through it toward those fragile parts: limb, eyelid, cleft, floss and bisque, buffed ivory and sweet, sweet bone, each distinct yet mended integrally to the rest—the tendons, pearls, toes, the fingers finely turned and charged with their own volition. Her cheek lay against my chest. I buried my face in her hair. She was mine.

She was free.

"Are you all right?" she asked.

"Yes."

She swallowed. Her eyes were wet. She held still as a mannequin. "Did any bad things happen?"

"I'll tell you later."

"My father?"

"It's okay. It's done."

Families ambled by, glancing in our direction. Skiers laden with nylon equipment bags lined up to pay their departure tax, peering at us, disconcerted by passion. Reluctantly I let her go. "It's all handled," I murmured. "Don't worry."

"I did the things you told me." She'd begun now to tremble. Tears gathered and spilled. The polished surface—the well-cut hair, discreet face, delicate movements, couturier suit and expensive pumps, the black Hermés handbag and gold bracelet, the monied guarantee of the world's goodwill—seemed no longer integral to those closer parts but merely camouflage for this terrified, iron-willed girl who stood on the threshold of a new world, ready to step naked out of the old one and leave it behind.

"Good. That's great," I whispered.

"The tickets are here." She touched her purse. "But you must check at the airlines desk with your passport."

"Okay. How much time do we have?"

"The plane departs in fifteen minutes."

"Hell, we'd better move!"

"I bought quick tickets. Continental Air is holding the plane for us."

I started to reach out and grasp her hand. Then I paused. "Wait. Listen, Ayako. Are you truly sure?"

She looked up. Staring at my eyes, my face, my mouth, as if I were the one who could be changing his mind, poring over every atom the way she'd done the first time she'd ever spoken in the backseat of the limousine, she searched in desperation for safety. In her eyes I suddenly saw her brother's.

"Come on," I said, grabbing her urgently, pulling her close. "Come with me. Don't go back, don't stay here."

"Yes," she breathed.

"Let's go." I marched toward the airline counters with her cinched inside my arm, not giving a damn for all the eyes skipping off us affronted by such public love but cleaving her to my body like a regeneration of that long-surrendered legendary rib. She hurried to keep up, legs pumping, high heels clattering.

"Where's your luggage?"

"I checked it."

"How far? Where are we flying?"

"To Honolulu and Los Angeles."

"That should do it." We were racing now, the last trickling lines breaking apart to go board their flights even as we rushed up to the jaded boy clerk and I hauled out my passport and slapped it down on the countertop and she whisked the ticket from her purse and laid it onto the green passport cover.

The clerk picked up both documents. "Ah! Yes, this is in order. You're seated in first class. You need your boarding pass," he said. "Please fill out the departure form." He pushed it over for me to scrawl, and then seemed to take an hour to tap information into the computer, combing through numbers, abbreviations, waiting for the printer to zip out its response. For one panicked instant I thought that Minamoto had broken his word and alerted customs; but then the answer spewed onto the screen, the boarding pass slipped into my hand, seat assigned next to hers; we were running together through the airport, frisked through security, past X-ray check, down the concourse, toward the gate, just as the attendants bowed the last passengers into the boarding corridor and got ready to close the door. We shoved the passes into their hands. They smiled, tearing and returning: everything in order.

In twenty seconds the seat belts buckled across wide leather and we dropped into the deep cushioning rest of the forward compartment, having never once, except at the metal detector's very brink, let go of each other's hand.

ONGOING ENGINE HUM enclosed us in that usual jet-plane illusion that no one outside your seat row can hear you. Our forearms lay notched side by side, palm heel to palm heel, vein to vein, alive. The cabin's hush enveloped us inside its hollow roar. From fingertip to elbow, for a timeless limbo before dinner, and then during its service—while the flight attendant poured champagne and bourbon and smiled and spread the stiff white napkins on our knees and presented the steak sliced thin as Kleenex and

the sashimi, white beside its pale green wasabi cone, and the delicate shredded cucumber and chocolate mousse with strawberries—and after coffee
and green tea and then on through the first movie when the lights finally
clicked off, we sat eyes half closed in the delirious stupor, holding back,
barely keeping our hands off each other, unable to speak.

Eventually she let her head sink by degrees. It rested on my shoulder.

"Your father's okay," I bent and murmured in her ear.

"You have *seen* him?"

"Yes."

"He was there? In Haradani?"

"He may still be, so far as I know."

The shock in her tone fell muffled by our isolation. Across the aisle a
television flickered over the face of a sleeping executive, chasing grooves
around his mouth, puttying them with shadow.

"He wasn't alone."

"Who was with him, please?" Her voice turned tremulous. I pressed my
lips to her crown, sliding my hand up and down her shoulder.

"Matsudo. And Nagisa Kawai."

"Ah!" For a little while she sat silent, face hidden by the angle of her
head. "Were they—good-mannered?" she asked at last.

"Kawai was. In the way you mean. Actually," I said, "I found out he
works for somebody very high up elsewhere in your father's keiretsu. Like,
another large network of companies. Maybe next in line."

She let her fingers go limp.

"I think he reckons he'll be doing business with me—with us sooner
or later. At some future date," I said.

Her expression, concealed by gloom, might have stayed the same. She
made no sound. But after a moment I felt her gradually crunch down in
the seat against my chest, slowly shriveling, contracting into a rigor of
grief, until her shoulders jerked and she bent forward and balled up small
as a child, and I put both arms around her and grasped her and whispered

my love and stroked her hair while her body shook with the violent quaking of those dry, silent sobs.

WE WERE THREE-FOURTHS of the way to Honolulu when at last she raised her head.

"In the United States, do many people live who will recognize my name?" she asked.

"Your family name?"

"Yes."

"I don't know. Well, yeah, sure. They'd know the bank, and the electronics company and the cars. They don't necessarily have to know you're part of the real Minamoto crew."

"I am no longer." Her eyelids dropped.

"No. I guess not."

"I will need to find another one."

"Use mine."

She smiled wanly. "In the beginning?"

"Well—it doesn't take long. Just however long you want. I'll be telling my father who you are, of course, but anything else is up to you."

"Up to me." She said it, not questioning the meaning, but turning it over for the first time, tasting its fit against her teeth. "Perhaps I will stay Minamoto?"

"If you want to. Why not?"

"Why not."

"It's yours by right. You were born with it." Reflexively my thumb sought out the signet-ring shank inside my knuckle, massaging the gold. She chewed her lip, peering down at the leather seat and its sleek chrome appointments. "You're a free woman."

She looked back up to me, eyes bright. Slowly she smiled. "Yes," she said.

• • •

ONE HALF HOUR out of Honolulu, an apparition loped up the aisle toward the cockpit and rapped with command on the pilots' door. Instantly a blond flight attendant stepped forward, still in her apron. "Sir, may I help you?"

"I want to look at the instrument panels."

"I'm afraid we'd have to get permission from the captain for that."

"If you must insist." He stood waiting, wearily aiming his nose.

"Sir, I'm afraid the captain's very busy right at this moment. We've just been advised of heavy turbulence—"

"Precisely why I'll check the instruments."

"Are you a pilot, sir?"

"Not of 747s."

"Good grief," I muttered.

"Will you please return to your seat and fasten your seat belt? The captain is about to make that announcement."

"No. I'll stay here until I ascertain instrument functionality, including altitude and speed. Some idiot was playing with a laptop back in that sewer pipe you call economy. You did nothing. So after ordering him to turn it off I want confirmation that no control has been impaired."

"Oh, no," I groaned.

He turned. "Oh, it's you."

"Thomas, what are you doing here?"

"Presumably the same thing you are."

"I mean, how come you're on this plane? I can't believe it!"

He cocked his head upward and sniffed. "The entire Kan Nai personnel roster was released from employment this morning. With of course acceptable long-term severance compensation for the upper-tier specialists. The U.S.–Nippon collaboration has been dissolved. But perhaps they didn't consider it necessary to inform you."

"I've been gone."

"So I heard. There's been some talk as to whether you've actually breached your contract."

"Oh, I'm afraid I have, Thomas."

"I'm not surprised." His supercilious gaze surveyed me as someone who has dug his own grave, and then it swiveled toward the attendant who still hung suspended between assisting him back to the other cabin and calling for help. "Have you asked the captain?" he asked her.

"Sir, you must please return to your seat. Any minute we'll experience conditions—"

"Thomas, listen!—Sorry," I said to the attendant. "Are the others on board this flight?"

"Which others?"

"God Almighty. You are the most—Martha Franklin. Red Franklin, Steve, Becky Willis. All the others from Kan Nai, from the Minamoto Enclave."

He shrugged. The attendant was beginning to look stern. "Some of them, maybe. I haven't bothered to notice whom."

"Holy hell—"

"I'm assuming that I'll of course be restored to my former position when I get back to Dallas," he added. "Your father assured me it's probable. I told him they can hardly have expected to fill it in so short a time. Eleven days." He stretched his chin out and scratched his knuckled Adam's apple. We hit a bump.

"Sir—," warned the attendant, bracing both hands against the seats.

"Are you going to inquire? No." He opened the cockpit door and whipped through quick as a sidewinder.

"Sir! Wait!" Running after him, she bounced on tiptoes through the unsolid air.

"Who is he?" whispered Ayako. She looked down. Her face had gone still with embarrassment.

"Your father's greatest loss." The flight attendant emerged escorted by a second, trying to drag Thomas bodily behind them. He knocked them both away with a jab of his elbow. "Excuse me, please," I said to Ayako, jumping up.

"Here, let me give you a hand." I grabbed his arm, frogged it once hard in the bicep with my fist, yanked it into half-rotation against his spine, and goose-stepped his weedy length back down the aisle. "You are such a jerk. How is anybody ever going to get paid enough to put up with you?"

"What's his seat number?" gasped the second attendant.

"Put him in there!" cried the blond, and pointed me toward the empty right-hand bulkhead seat.

"My pleasure." I lowered him by the arm, jamming him as deeply into the upholstery as possible. Then I took the belt and buckled him up tight. The odd thing was he didn't even fight, but sneered as when he'd stood languishing over the prospect of raw fish on his way to Tokyo a few days before.

"Thank you," mouthed the flight attendant to me behind Thomas's back. "Sir, please remain seated now until we're clear of the turbulence," she smiled down, drifting almost weightless again as we hit a bad spot.

"Was that an air pocket or a trough?" Thomas asked coldly.

"I assume a gully." I squatted on the floor below him. "Tell me—what did you mean, my father assured you of a probable job?"

"Just that."

"You mean back in Dallas, before we left?"

"No. Over the telephone when Martha what's-her-name called him from Kan Nai in Tokyo. I removed the phone from her to inquire. She and her brother have taken a different plane, along with Becky Willis. This one was too full and I naturally insisted on the only spare seat."

"You talked to A.J.?"

"Yes."

I felt my head rock. "What did he say?"

"What I've repeated."

"What did Martha tell him?"

Thomas shrugged. "The general rough picture. A—His ex-employees have been handed their immediate tickets home. B—You have been missing for seventy-two hours and Matsudo claims no one has any idea where you are."

I rocked back on my heels, stunned.

"She phoned him once more from the airport while we were waiting to board our flights."

A paralysis set in. I stared up at the disdainful face wedged between Continental stripes. Slowly I said to myself, "He might think I've made some kind of trade."

Thomas pursed his long lips. Then suddenly he surprised me. "I believe that occurred to what's-her-name. She mentioned something of the kind quite clearly after I returned the phone to her. A trade."

There was a silence. Like hostages, I thought, feeling dizzy. Some martyr, showboat, foolhardy arrangement.

Thomas raised his nose.

She'd left him in the dark like that, I thought. Well, she'd had to. She'd had no choice. So he wasn't going to know until we'd landed.

Then once more I remembered his words to me: *All you have to do is phone. Just pick up the phone.*

The phones attached to our seats didn't work over ocean: I'd asked the flight attendant about this when we'd boarded. When we get to Honolulu, I thought, reassuring myself, I can reach him then. As soon as we're through customs. As soon as we're home.

The blond stewardess bent over me and said, "We'll be landing in about fifteen minutes now. Have you filled out your customs declaration?"

"I guess I need to do that." She smiled as I walked back to first class.

Ayako looked up as I sat back down. "Hey," I said, and wrapped my arm around her. "We have to fill out some forms for U.S. Customs. I'll help you with yours."

"Thank you."

"Did you bring much money with you? Cash, checks, credit cards?"

"Yes," she said. "Also American dollars, fifty thousand."

"I've got two credit cards on me that I can use to get us to DFW once we've landed in L.A. But the rest of my cash was left in the enclave and probably confiscated."

"Who was that man you walked with?"

"When? Oh! Thomas? Don't worry. I resettled him back in economy."

"You hit him?"

"Only a tap on the arm."

"You forced him to walk."

"Yeah, well. When guys like that behave like turkeys, you've got to herd them a little."

"You hit guys often?" She wore a look that I'd seen before.

"Not really. Why?"

"You cause a scene?" she whispered.

"A scene?"

"You enter the scene where there is a problem, and talk loudly and fight?"

At first I couldn't dredge up the memory of where or when I'd witnessed that expression. But then suddenly I did. I stood once more before a museum case displaying bronze implements, watching the rigid, shuttered stillness drop over her as I joked about the nature of a holy baby rattle and declared myself an ignorant fool.

"Is that what it seemed like to you? A fight?"

The look was worse than disapproval. I saw her mortified eyes.

"Ayako, I was helping those two women deal with a moron who got rough with them."

"In Japan you would have made them wear an *on* to you by helping."

"In America, we say, 'Think nothing of it.'"

"I need to learn American," she said.

"You will. I'll teach you what you have to know. What'll come in handy."

"I am dead to Japan," she murmured. She looked down at her hands folded against the black fabric of her skirt, and her sweetness wrenched my soul.

"No. Don't say that. Things might take time, but they'll work out. You'll see. You'll make it up with your father."

She shook her head.

"Yes you will. Because you don't have to wear that *on* anymore."

I had wanted to wait until we reached mainland America and a quiet place before going into the details of my revelations at Haradani; I'd wanted to save the news as my gift to her, my offering to our future life. But I knew now I'd tell her when we landed on Oahu, the inaugural patch of U.S. soil.

"Is it possible?" she asked. She turned her face to the window as if unwilling to reveal to anyone else the hope transfiguring it.

"It's already done. Remember? You're free."

She nodded jerkily at the windowpane. "Thank you, Taylor. I am free."

"To marry me," I assured, and swept her close as if the touch could eradicate all seismic tremors between us and heal the secret wound just beginning to suppurate.

Ten minutes later the captain announced that we were about to land; everyone must keep to their seats. Ayako pulled away to open her purse. Her passport lay on top. Across the front of it was gilded the big stylized chrysanthemum that I'd seen on the gateway doors to Yasukuni Jinja, many-petaled, perfectly symmetrical, the emperor's aegis and blessing on his subjects.

THE AIR WAS cool and damp. A tropical wind blew through the automatic glass doors. We stepped out into the night facing a double-lane street backed by a high retaining wall beyond which I could imagine palm trees, orchids in flower, high-rises, the whispering, crashing sea.

Customs had processed us long before the other passengers had reached the arrival gate. I needed to find a telephone. But this first moment, our first breath of local air, I wanted for Ayako alone.

"Welcome to America," I said.

"Ah yes." She glanced sideways up and down the length of asphalt. Fragrant gusts from invisible frangipani bushes drenched the wind. I pulled her close and kissed her.

"Is this what America is like? This climate?"

"Hardly. We're on an island in the South Seas, only halfway home. Just wait until you feel that hot Texas sun and the nip of a blue norther. We should be due for one soon, this time of year." I kissed her again. Desire tightened up through my chest, shortening breath.

"We may stay here—how long?" she asked.

It was around 10:00 P.M. A few cars were parked in the temporary spaces against the curb, releasing passengers, unloading luggage. A cab rank lined up about fifty yards to our left. The sidewalk lay nearly deserted. "We've got one hour before the plane takes off for L.A. Look, there's a bench. Do you want to sit down?"

She shook her head against my arm. "Please, I wish to stand."

"There's something I want to tell you."

She must have known. She didn't look up. Her face remained nestled against my chest, her body went still. She made no sound.

"Up there at Haradani I found something you need to know," I said. "I discovered it before your father got to the farmhouse and we had our confrontation."

"Please, don't speak of that now," she whispered.

"I have to. It's going to make a big difference to your life. It's a surpr— well, it's unexpected. Not what you could even dream. In its way, it's very good news."

She said nothing.

"Diego gave me the blueprint to the tunnel system below the house and told me that's where I'd find the contracts. Remember? He said only one room was the room I wanted. He was wrong. The contracts weren't down there. They were stored upstairs, in a built-in cabinet."

"Ah yes," she whispered.

I paused. "Something else was kept in that room."

I held her so close. She had shrunk within my arms. She made no sound at all.

"You'll never imagine what it was," I said. "You thought some kind of demon lived there, remember? But it wasn't a demon. Not at all."

She didn't move.

"Diego sent me to your brother. To Ushi-oni."

A big green Cadillac pulled up against the curb. The driver got out, closed the door, and slinked up the sidewalk through the automatic sliding doors without so much as checking for a police officer.

"He's not dead, Ayako."

She'd begun to quiver. Her head bent into my chest like somebody trying to burrow into a wall.

"He's very much alive."

Her head bucked, once, and then pressed, stiff-necked.

"Ayako, listen. Don't cry. It's all right. It's wonderful. Your brother's alive. He's a poor little retarded boy with a birth defect, but his human mind isn't broken at all. He's been locked up all alone with his nurse under the ground all these years. His arms and legs are—well, dwarfed. But there's no demon. No monster. Nothing like that, Ayako. Your father lied to you. He's—he's the purest human being I've ever seen. Do you understand? And he's been okay, he was happy until—" Something rose in my throat.

Her fists drew up involuntarily, spasming bony and white-knuckled on my chest. They thumped a soft tattoo of despair. "Ayako, you can meet him," I said. The joy and relief I was offering surged up, a great buoyancy that I wanted to hold for the rest of our lives. "Did you hear that? Don't be sad. He's out now. I got him free. He's going to be all right. You can meet him! We can bring him here."

Slowly, slowly her head tilted up to mine. Her eyes shone stunned and blank.

"You did not kill him?" she whispered.

"What? Kill him? No, of course not! He's completely safe—"

I stared at her face. The growing horror in it. The absolute ruthless conviction.

"Kill him?" I asked.

She licked her dry lips. She caught the lower one between her small white teeth, let it go. Her eyes grew round, ghostly.

"Kill him, Ayako?"

"You killed a man with a knife," she answered.

I stared.

"You are American, from Texas."

My arms went slack. They began to slip away from her shoulders, her body.

"You say you would do anything to keep me happy. You wish to save me."

"Ayako." The sickness rolled up from my gut, breaking as a black oily scurf coats over clear green water.

"You say I'm free. For this freedom I went against my father. I destroyed my father. Minamoto. Because of this Matsudo will assume responsibility, he will pay it for my father's sake. And this because of what I have done to get free from Ushi-oni." Her lips were moving but her words fell scarcely heard on the breezy tropic night, just loud enough. "He is alive. The damaged thing that killed my mother."

"He's your own brother."

"In Japan we lock such people away. They are sent far away. To islands. They are shame. Ushi-oni has taken my life, used up my life." Her eyes looked metallic now in the airport streetlamps. They gleamed.

"No. Your father did that."

She stared, implacable.

"You picked me," I whispered.

She nodded neither yes nor no.

"You thought I'd do it. You picked me right from the start." I swallowed. "A barbarian."

"I love you for all things," she whispered.

I shook my head. I couldn't speak. Gently I stepped away, looking down at that upturned face, sick from so deep inside that I found it impossible to look elsewhere soon enough, at some other thing, any other; I couldn't look at all.

"Taylor. When we marry in Texas, then perhaps I will be freed," she murmured. She reached down and fondled her handbag, standing alone on the sidewalk, stricken as her brother had been, but not like her brother. Not like her brother.

"I have to go."

"Go?"

"I have to get home."

"Home. To Dallas, yes?" she said.

"I'm sorry."

I took another step back.

"Taylor." Her face blanched; she stared into my eyes.

"I'm sorry," I said again. "I'm really, truly sorry." So sorry, I said silently, shaking my head, the old vertigo gone, erased, absorbed into the winding tunnels where his incandescence also lay doused by darkness. A trade. A foolhardy showboat exchange. Quality for quality, triumph for triumph. So sorry.

"Are you leaving me here?"

"You don't know me." You can't know me. I don't know you.

"On this island?"

"I'm sorry," I whispered, the echo reverberating down the empty tunnels through centuries, millennia, aeons. I turned on my heel. I walked away, step by step, moving inside the sliding glass doors with her still standing on the sidewalk under the streetlamp. I walked loosened and light-limbed in the trance to the Continental counter and handed them my ticket, lips moving, navigating through hollow time, through infinite space, ahead of where she still stood on the sidewalk alone; I asked if there was a flight that night from Honolulu to DFW nonstop and the woman said yes, yes, there was, a brand-new service in fact, newly scheduled for the upcoming winter season. And was it full? No; they would change my ticket, it was not full, five seats left, credit card or cash could make up the difference, I would fly straight out, the plane left in twenty minutes, I could just make it. Barely make it. I could just hop on.

Just.

NIGHT HELD THE world. Below it the air dropped thousands of feet into a roiling sea. Below the sea, life thronged, the further world, seething and cold, with forms moving like pale luminous word-shapes through the darkness, devouring a gobbet, darting into a cave, flicking a tail before vanishing once more into that endless expanse saccing the globe like the translucent membrane on a frog's egg. Endlessly round. You might trim yourself like an arrow, plunge linear through it, and keep pushing down — past water, through galleries of sand, plates, crust, strata, the geological debris from genesis — until the sea condensed to a mineral funnel pouring into the rock-sheathed nucleus and you at last faced that pure, flensing radiance which is the core. Which is both enlightenment and death. Or: you could keep paddling round and round the endless circuit which is of course life. Or you could soar. Above the world, chill stars.

The plane droned on for hours. Dinner and breakfast came on trays. Cardboard food on sawdust tongue. The flight attendants moved like spirits before my vision, bending, clearing away; I hadn't seen any legible body or face since I'd left her standing on the sidewalk, the sidewalk burning like a sheet of phosphorous on my memory, her small, stark figure marked against its glow in one black stroke.

Eventually it was dawn. The reddish pink rail cut across the blackness and turned gold, all to gold and silvery golden blue. The vaults of blue air filled the world, so rarified a color that it evaded its name the way a fish eludes through the murky darkness. I sat within it, watching, and thought suddenly of that Yucatán shark swimming somewhere below the green glazed waves, thought of how he'd missed eating me that spring day, having been battered off by a chance saving God-sent menace I hadn't expected and he hadn't seen. While we all paddled and swam the circuit together.

Then the plane reached land. We flew over the surface of black soil and mauve desert and green fields and pastures and mercurial lakes cupped under the brilliant autumn sun, the ridged mountain knees, spiked forest, across the continent, until Texas spread beneath us in a carpeted world and far below us the plane's shadow skittered over it like a blue moth. I began to develop sensation in my arms and legs. I began to wake up. I looked down at my home and found it good.

And all at once, at last, I remembered what I hadn't done.

The thought exploded. The telephone in the Honolulu airport. My father waiting beside the red lacquered box, wondering at the spaceless, timeless, messageless dark, the vacuum into which I'd disappeared. The simple procedure: Pick up the phone. Slip in the credit card, tuck the receiver beneath the chin like a violinist ready to play music. Dial.

Dallas wasn't far away. Now it lay so close. I would call him the minute we landed. Yet already the grief of missed connections began to throb inside me. *Too late,* whispered a voice. *You're too late. You should have called from Hawaii; if you'd remembered there would still be time.* I stared at the cloudscape, thinking of how he should be talking to my mother right now, hearing at last that long-anticipated sweet hello; I thought of what he'd said to me the night before I left; and in the full daylight flooding through the windowpane I could see him lying there, slumped on his sofa with the red lacquer box still in his hand, and I saw as if on an X ray the one image left scorched inside his skull after all the other lights had gone out: the tricycle in the glass case, the monument where my life started and his ending began. And I knew that he was dead.

EPILOGUE

It is possible that when Theseus, after slaying the Minotaur, emerged from the depths of the Labyrinth and took ship from Crete, he was filled so high with rejoicing that he had no thought of the grave promise his father had exacted from him. Doubtless the prospect of going home to Athens bearing in deliverance all the sacrificial victims until then lamented as dead would have occupied his mind. Certainly it prompted much feasting and wine-pouring amongst his companions. For days he stood above them, a hero under the blue Mediterranean sky. The love of Ariadne stole his waking moments. The monster's death roars echoed down his dreams. And shipboard is a forgetful place; in clear water and hot sun the movement of waves can dissolve time, lull the senses, and send the most urgent conscience to sleep.

Nor perhaps did the promise brush his memory when, halfway home, he landed at the island of Naxos.

There he escorted his betrothed to shore and then reboarded his ship. Ariadne had fallen seasick; they needed fresh water; there were many tasks to attend. And whether it is true that later, under cover of midnight, he weighed anchor and secretly slipped away, or that a storm rose up and threw the vessel too far out to sea to make harbor again, the gist remains that he left the island and never went back. Thus was the young princess—who had betrayed her own father to save his life—abandoned—some say to die of grief; others, to die bearing his child; still others, to be consoled by *a god. But whatever his excuses and her fate, surely these matters would have fixed Theseus's main attention, distracting him from details.*

Before many more days of voyage had passed, the scents on the breeze told him that he was approaching mainland.

No doubt these too suborned his thoughts—the crisp pine resin, the breath of wild narcissus, the acrid bite of smoke. Joy among the returning prisoners grew to fever. "We are home, we are home!" they cried. "Not eaten by the Minotaur with our bones lying in the dead-end corridors, or picked clean in a courtyard, but ready to greet our mothers and fathers, friends and sweethearts. Praise the gods, home to Attica. Praise Theseus our rescuer. Look, the hills! There sits Sounion Head and its beacon light. There waits Greece!"

Little wonder he forgot the word he'd pledged his father: that he would change the ship's black sail of mourning to white should he return alive.

So when the ship put safely in at Piraeus, and they brought the news to the Acropolis, it was too late for remembrance. Night and day King Ægeus had kept watch for the first glimpse of a sail in the distance. The way they told Theseus of his father's suicide was this: "In grief he has leaped from the cliff where he stood, his body spinning toward the water like a man returning to his daimon. The space he left bare on the rock must now be filled. Behold, my Lord; welcome home. You are our new High King."

OFTEN WHEN A *promise is the request of another, it does not weigh so heavy as the vow forged in the giver's own heart. Desire fires the blood; the longings of others are pale in comparison, distant flames. "I will bring you to Athens and make you queen," he'd said to Ariadne. "I will change the sail," he'd told his father. The promise wrested is an intention skewed: "I will come home in triumph, a destroyer," he'd told his father as well, and that was the promise he kept.*

HE RULED A *long time, surrounded by his mistake. During his reign he achieved greater things than any Hellenic king before him. He is said to have unified Attica, given laws to its three estates of landowner, craftsman, and farmer, and founded the first principles of democracy. He grew famous for his protection of ill-used slaves and* servants, and his shrine remained their sanctuary for centuries to come. Adventure and new ideas flowed from his mind. Great wars were won by his hand. But the site of his father's drowning took on the old king's name; the very means of death became the waters of the Aegean. He could never escape its fact. Even in late years, while held a prisoner in the Underworld and forced to sit in the Chair of Forgetfulness, groping for lost memories of that dead beloved son or the Amazon wife or battles fought, he would shake his head in puzzlement, sighing. Yet in the back of his eye would stay forever the black swan falling, the figure caught in midspiral, the clean drop into the empty sea.